Roma Tearne is a Sri Lankan-born, Oxford-based artist, filmmaker and writer. She trained as a painter, completing her MA at the Ruskin School of Drawing and Fine Art, Oxford. Her debut novel, *Mosquito*, was shortlisted for the 2007 Costa First Novel Prize and 2008 *LA Times* First Fiction Award. *Brixton Beach* was a TV Book Club Best Read and *The Swimmer* was longlisted for the Orange Prize in 2011 and Asian Man Booker in 2012.

Praise for Roma Tearne:

'Tearne . . . writes with cleareyed love for the country of her childhood and depicts its lush decay in painterly detail . . . Hope, love and history collide with an unsparing force that resonates into the contemporary world' *New York Times*

'Tearne captures the desperation, fear and hope of love during wartime' *Publishers Weekly*

'Tearne's layered novel is fresh and relevant' *Library Journal* (starred review)

'Moody, painterly . . . Tearne links her love story to national politics with a vengeance' NPR, All Things Considered

'Wholly satisfying' *Kirkus Reviews*

'Tearne charts the patterns of love and loss with beautiful prose' *Sunday Times*

'Tearne's training as a painter shows in the subtle descriptions that fill each page with lyrical power' *Independent on Sunday*

The
Road to
Urbino

By the same author:

Mosquito
Bone China
Brixton Beach
The Swimmer
The Last Pier
The White City

The Road to Urbino

ROMA TEARNE

Gallic Books
London

A Gallic Book

Copyright © Roma Tearne, 2012

Roma Tearne has asserted her moral right to be
identified as the author of this work

First published in Great Britain in 2012 by Abacus

This edition published in Great Britain in 2020
by Gallic Books, 59 Ebury Street, London, SW1W 0NZ

A CIP record for this book is available from the British Library

ISBN 9781910709481

Printed in the UK by CPI (CR0 4YY)

In memory of my father.
And for Barrie,
Oliver, Alistair and Mollie.

Contents

I

II

III

IV

V

We live, not as we wish to, but as we can

MENANDER
(GREEK DRAMATIST, 342–291 BC)

One had a lovely face,
And two or three had charm,
But charm and face were in vain
Because the mountain grass
Cannot but keep the form
Where the mountain hare has lain.

W. B. YEATS

I

1

Learning to paint a fresco

Last night I dreamt I was in Talaimannar again. With the ancient lighthouse casting yellow stripes across the water and the rock rising steeply against the sky. The sea was calm and Adam's Bridge was clearly visible in the dusk. In my dream Good triumphed over the demon Ravana and I saw once again the rutted lane that led, through a thicket of trees, to the old beloved place. Through the unlatched gate I went, followed by I know not whose footsteps, with the scent of lotus flowers all around me. Towards the lighted house I walked with steady gaze and saw again the rattan roof on which the rain had tattooed out a sweet, sad song of childhood memory. When I woke my face was wet.

'I want to find my daughter,' I cry.

In spite of all my efforts, my voice comes out in a whine. It is morning. Grey and dull. And we are sitting in a windowless room where neglect and cigarette smoke and lavatories stifle the air. Someone has repainted the walls. Beneath the mango green there are hints of a Venetian red. Away from nature, green holds no attractions. On one wall I notice a mark, dark and strangely shaped. I stare at it. Normally I would wait behind bullet-proof glass for my visitor. But you are no normal visitor. Glancing sideways at you, I see a thin, tall woman in a trouser suit. Someone

3

I would never have noticed in a crowd. I expect you could say the same thing of me. We have shaken hands briefly, a formality that does nothing to reassure me. My hands tremble. As I watch, you pick a small thread from the sleeve of your jacket. It is red like your bag. Red like the colour in the painting.

You are silent after my outburst; hands resting on the table, hardly moving. A door bangs and then another door bangs in some other part of the building. They bang as though there is a sea breeze somewhere. I hear faint footsteps fading into nothing. I must focus.

'Don't you see? I am her father,' I say. 'Please. You must help me.'

There is no hiding my desperation. After everything that has been said about me for months, the shocking nature of my crime, my supposedly inscrutable air, all that bravado begins to crumble. I search your face for a hint of pity. Please, I think, please. And then I am talking, talking. As if speech alone can save me.

'My name is Lynton Rasanagium,' I tell you. 'Don't bother with the Lynton. People call me Ras. I am fifty years old.'

Far away in some corner of my mind I hear the sea. Soft as a sung lullaby.

'I am here because of a series of unfortunate events for which I am only partly to blame.'

No, wait, that's not right.

'I am to blame for what I did, but understand this: every act has a past. Events don't materialise from nowhere.'

Maybe I will have to die before this becomes an acknowledged fact. Why are you shaking your head?

'Let me finish.'

You stare unblinkingly, without the slightest movement in the muscles on your face. I have to control myself as best I can in order to stop the feeling of dizziness that has been dogging

4

me for weeks. This takes effort and I'm weak through lack of sleep.

'Call me Elizabeth,' you say, in a clipped voice, cutting me short.

The edges of your mouth tighten.

'And let me give you these to sign, first.'

You hand me two pieces of paper and point to the crosses on them. I sign.

'Now,' you say. 'We don't have an awful lot of time. There are just four weeks before your hearing and this charge of theft is of a serious nature. So we need to concentrate quite hard.'

Once a thief always a thief, I think. Where have I heard that before? The papers are calling me a terrorist. I shake my head. Terrorism is another matter. I know the law has provided me with your service, but actually, the only thing I'm interested in is seeing my beloved daughter again.

'Can you get her to visit me?'

'I will try,' you say. 'But your case is a serious one, so let's not waste time.'

I am silenced, momentarily.

'All I need is for you to deliver this letter,' I say, pushing it towards you. 'And maybe you could send her an e-mail as well?'

Please.

'The truth is,' I continue, following my own train of thought, 'most people who commit crimes aren't bad in any clear way.'

After I was denied bail things changed and the media, who had hardly noticed me before, began their campaign of hate.

'One small mistake leads to a bigger mess. And then, before you know how it happened, you find yourself in big trouble.'

You frown.

'What you did was hardly a small mistake. It wasn't shoplifting,' you say sarcastically, your mouth tight.

'But can't you understand how it could happen?' I persist.

You say nothing. Then suddenly you make a small movement of impatience and instantly I am frightened again.

'Wait, wait, don't go. I'm sorry. I don't want to waste your time, I promise. I need your help. Just listen for a minute, please.'

See how quickly I start pleading, how easily I am derailed. You hesitate.

'Mr Rasanagium,' you say with some difficulty. 'Ras, I have some questions that need urgent answers. It is important you answer them as best you can. I understand your concerns about your daughter and I will pass your letter to her. I will also e-mail her. I will do all these things for you, but you must see, I'm not here to discuss your daughter.'

I am stunned.

'I need to know the reasons, in your own words, as to why you stole the painting,' you continue. 'Take your time. Begin with your childhood, if you like. It's always good to have a context. But we have to focus on my questions.'

You mean something else, of course. People seldom say what they mean.

'I am a stubborn person,' I say, slowly, refusing to be bullied, wanting to go back to the beginning in my own way. 'Both superstitious and occasionally religious.'

You shift your feet.

'Some might say I am unforgiving,' I add. 'That I bear grudges. Certainly, it is true, I cannot forget past injustice.'

You are looking at your hands. Then you raise your head and there is a sudden flash of colour. Your eyes are extraordinary. They look as if they have been ground from the pigment lazuli. I was told that in this joyless place you are one of the few people on my side.

'When I was a child I lived with my mother and my brother Sam. My uncles lived in a large house nearby with my grand-parents. I had four cousins. Three of them were boys.'

Instantly you start writing furiously, head bent. I gaze at you and remember our house. There was no glass in the windows. Only bars. This being the tropics, the air needed to circulate freely. Sometimes small birds would lose their way and fly in before disappearing swiftly out again with a soft confused flutter. Why do you sit so unnaturally still, Elizabeth?

'My father had died. The circumstances of his death were never talked about. I remember him only vaguely and any questions I asked were always met with silence. So that was the first puzzle in my life.'

'Yes,' you say, without looking up, indifferently. 'Go on.'

'Listen, people have heard all the stories about the Sri Lankan Jaffna Tamils. They are bored by them. So all I'm going to say is this: Sri Lanka is in a mess, but if you book the right package tour and are interested in cricket the place is fine for a holiday. Just don't delve too deeply.'

'I know something about Sri Lanka,' you tell me.

Ah, yes! My ex-wife Helen would have mentioned it. Distracted, I begin to imagine Helen's quiet, reasonable voice, painting me in the light that best suited her.

'Ras and his brother escaped long before the bloodbath,' she would have said. 'They were the lucky ones. Really, Ras had nothing to complain about.'

If only it were that simple.

'Eventually,' I say, struggling to stay calm, 'after my grandparents and the girl cousin died of dysentery in the government camps, the rest of us, my brother and my male cousins, escaped, one by one, bearing the label, Lucky Ones.'

You stop writing. Your expression is unreadable. I try to breathe more slowly, speak carefully, keeping all hysteria out of my voice. Despair creeps over me.

'I was the only one to marry an English girl, the only one to have a child.'

7

Far away in some distant corner of my mind I hear jazz being played jauntily on the piano. Lola, I think. My Lo La, do you ever think of me, now? I used to sing your name to make you fall asleep.

'When she was born,' I say, 'in those first five years of her life I used to tell her a story every night without fail. I called them my thousand and one tales from the Indian Ocean. It drove Helen crazy!'

Perhaps this was the beginning of our inevitable roll towards divorce. I stop speaking. The truth is, I have never seen a mixed marriage that works. But that's another story.

'To begin with, Helen and I loved Lola in equal parts, like besotted fools. Lola was utterly beautiful.'

I look at you but you say nothing. Again I notice your blue eyes. Like sharpened steel.

'But after some time, a year or two, Helen started to get jealous of my slave-like adoration of the child. She began to scold my Lola for almost nothing. This angered me. I had not yet started the affair that would cause me to leave Helen, but I'm sure her treatment of Lola didn't help our relationship.'

You look at your watch. It is time for you to leave.

Before your second visit I make a drawing of a black beetle. Across its back I draw a deep red line. Then I draw a knife. But someone steals the drawing.

'Why a painting?' you ask, as soon as you open your notebook. 'What on earth made you think you could get away with stealing it?'

I am struck by the abruptness of your voice. Actually, I want to ask you a question, too. Since your visit I've been feeling very suspicious of you.

'Did you really send her the e-mail you promised? And give her my letter?'

'I did,' you say. 'And her words were, "Tell him to go to hell."'

I slump in my chair. That's her, all right. We . . . her mother and I, brought her up to be forthright.

'Why a painting?' you repeat, the edge returning to your voice.

And you tap your pen on the table.

'Before my family was killed I wanted to be a painter,' I say, ignoring you.

Everyone was busy involved in the war. Either they were for it and wanted to fight, or they were against it and wanted to heal the sick. I was too young to have an opinion and in any case I had my eyes focused elsewhere.

'Where others saw blood and injustice, I saw things that were broken.'

'How do you mean?'

I hesitate, wanting to describe the feelings that used to envelop me whenever I watched the sunlight pouring onto the bullet holes in the walls.

'I used to notice light,' I say, finally. 'On the ground, slipping into cracks, spilling over destroyed buildings.'

There is a silence. You don't understand, of course. Eventually I say, 'I used to think a wall could look beautiful even with chipped and peeling paint, with holes in it.'

I smile, forgetting who you are and you look solemnly back at me. The mark on the wall glows, unexpectedly.

'There are holes in the brickwork of the Ducal Palace,' you volunteer suddenly, and I agree, surprised.

You are referring to the place from where I stole the painting. Neither of us can think of anything more to say after that.

'So, why did you steal it?' you ask, relentlessly.

I swallow. To make you understand, I have to go back to the beginning. To the day I stole some paints from my classroom. On that morning there had been no school and I sneaked into the bombed-out church nearby and painted a picture of a flock of red birds. I have always loved the colour red. I think perhaps because the earth in Jaffna is red.

When the teacher found out he came to find me.

'Why have you done this?' he asked. 'Why have you stolen from what little we have?'

I was silent, the truth being I didn't know why.

'Tell me,' the teacher said, shaking my arm, hard.

He was a man with a reputation for a temper.

'I don't know, sir. I just thought that if everyone died in the war people would still come and look at the painting.'

I said the first thing that came into my head. Really, I was more worried about saving my skin. But the teacher was looking at me in a very strange way. Suddenly he turned his back and stared out towards the sea.

'Sir, you're hurting my arm.'

'All right,' he agreed, letting go of me. 'But next time, don't just take the paints. Ask me, first. Don't be a thief.'

'Yes, sir,' I said, relieved. 'Can I go now?'

'In a minute,' he said. 'First let's take a look at your handiwork!'

We walked towards the rubble. The statue of Our Lady had no head or arms and some of her body had been destroyed, too. But you could still see who she was by her clothes. We stood looking at my painting.

'Not so bad,' the teacher said, eventually, adding softly, 'you have used the colours of Fra Angelico.'

I had no idea who Fra Angelico was. Overhead the sun had moved sharply through the leaves of a tamarind tree and a bird stirred in it. I grinned, for the danger seemed to have passed. The teacher pretended to hit me across the head.

'Don't do this again,' he said. 'Remember: once a thief, always a thief.'

But the heat had gone out of his voice.

'Now we're going to find your grandparents,' he said. 'Let's see what they will say when they hear about the things you've been getting up to! And I can see I'm going to have to give you a much needed lesson on how to paint on walls. It's called the art of fresco painting!'

I do another drawing today. It is of a hand. Like the hand of the angel in Fra Angelico's *Annunciation*. I wait all day, but towards the end of the morning when there is no sign of you I think, oh well, you've lost interest. Then, finally, you arrive. I notice you are breathless. And you give me a small, tight smile.

'Right,' you say. 'Where were we?'

'Long afterwards,' I tell you, 'after we lost everything, we fled, my brother Sam and I, like Jews from a camp, or bees from smoke.'

Running for our lives, grateful for that unmarked door out of Paradise. There was nothing – nothing, you understand – we believed we would miss. I look around this room we sit in and shake my head. Relativity is like the sun; sometimes it illuminates one place, sometimes another.

'You have to experience real horror to understand the manner of our leaving,' I say.

'I'd like to go to the East,' you say, and something in me snaps.

'There is no magic in a country that has been at war for as long as mine has,' I tell you.

My voice is harsh.

'Even the women are robbed of their mystery and shrivel in the blistering aftermath of conflict.'

I have silenced you.

'I dreamt of a flock of green, raucous birds, last night,' I continue. 'They were pecking the black seeds from rotting fruit. I dreamt of black magic and bright colours, and death. Before I woke.'

'I can't stay long today,' you tell me briskly. 'Obviously you've always loved looking at paintings. Is this why you wanted a job at the National Gallery?'

A love of painting has been my curse, I think.

'That was chance.'

'Tell me about this . . . chance.'

Do you really enjoy doing this all day, Elizabeth? What is it like to observe a man in a cage? Self-pity descends like a shroud over me as I speak. I must resist.

'I was just an attendant, you know,' I say. 'A floor-walker, a nobody who made sure the public behaved. I wasn't expected to *care* about the paintings. That was my luck, a bonus.'

'And you were there for almost twelve years.'

I nod. You start gathering up your things. Elizabeth, I want to say, life isn't easy to pin down. You pause. There is some uncertainty in your face.

'Well, we seem to have strayed away from the point, again,' you say, finally. 'I'm sorry, I'm going to have to go. But tomorrow we must get back to your childhood in Jaffna. And I want to hear about your mother.'

You have no idea how those words wrench at my skin, how they rip away at the wound. Raw flesh exposed as though it were yesterday. I open my mouth to speak, but you hold up your hand.

'Tomorrow,' you say.

And then you leave, before I can ask again about Lola.

2

A blinding light

You are late. I have been waiting. To wait is the fate of the
accused, I suppose. So I can't complain. This morning you wear
a dress instead of your usual severe trouser suit. I see it move
under your dark coat when you shift in your chair. A soft blue,
like your eyes today. I am struck by the loveliness of the colour.
Your eyes are your best feature, I want to say. Naturally, I don't.
Maybe I'm saving the compliment for a more needy moment. An
awkward silence comes to sit between us. The mark on the wall
seems to have changed colour. It has become a darker green, like
the underside of a leaf, washed by an invisible rain. For a moment
I am distracted, but then I return to my chief concern. Still no
word from Lola. I am compelled to ask the question once more.
Where is she? Why doesn't she reply to your message? Is she
upset? Just a little, even? Tell me.

'No,' you say, shaking your head. 'Sorry.'

Brutality. You deal in it; perhaps even enjoy it. One needs a
thick skin in these circumstances.

'Wasn't she even slightly curious?'

'No,' you say, again.

Your voice sounds kind enough, but I know how quickly
patience runs out.

'Let's focus on your childhood, again,' you say. 'Let's start with your mother.'

But focusing has never been easy, I think. And most of my childhood passed in a dream. I move my eyes away from the corner of the room where a small pile of dust seems to have gathered since I was last here. Then I look you full in the face. I want you to understand the effort this takes. Ah! Lola, I think. Lo La. Wasn't it only yesterday that she was four years old? I used to carry her in my arms, wrapped in a towel after her bath, giggling and wriggling, a slippery mermaid returning to her green bedroom. I remember she chose green.

'Is this the colour of the mango tree in your Jaffna garden, Daddy?' she asked, and although I could no longer remember that particular tree, I nodded.

'Yes, darling,' I said.

In spite of her mother's wishes, we painted it the tender green she wanted.

'She'll hate it in a few days,' Helen warned, but it was worth the risk. Lola. Lola, flesh of my flesh.

'The need to dream saved me from what was going on,' I say, eventually, staring at the wall.

We sit for what seems like ages, encased in an unbroken silence, and I tell you, 'Ma used to laugh and say, "Look, he's dreaming, again!"'

You look steadily at me. And take a deep breath as if you too feel the lack of oxygen in here.

'I have a clear memory of my mother.'

With no warning, I am back in Jaffna, age five, sitting on the step while she prepares our food. Three red chillies strung against an uncut lime dangle from the door handle; she had hung them there to ward off evil.

'Ma,' I say, 'you look pretty.'

It has been raining on and off all day, but now it has

stopped. There are puddles of plummeting sunlight on the ground.

I suppose the humidity must have shot up, because she has opened the back door to let some air in.

I have come in from the back yard, where I was playing with Sam.

'Go and wash your hands,' she says, giving me a funny look.

When I come back, I see she is crying, but I have got used to her crying like this, suddenly, and for no reason. It no longer alarms me.

'What's for dinner?' I ask.

All over the world, children ask the same, simple question. The poignancy of it does not strike you until the day the question stops. For by then, either the giver of food has vanished, or the child no longer exists.

'Sit down and you'll see,' Ma says.

I stop talking, gripped in a vice of memories, cramped by them.

'Go on,' you say, your voice nudging me. 'I'm listening.'

Trying not to be angered by your flat English voice, avoiding your eyes, I tell you. Ma was a small woman. The saris she wore were bright once but too much washing and hanging out in the scorching sun had made them fade.

'The East can make everything fade,' I say.

You make no comment, simply move your foot, restlessly. We return to our earlier silence. Then I force the years apart, once more.

'Every morning Ma washed the sari from the day before and hung it on the line.'

The sun shot an arrow of light through the damp, threadbare fabric, falling in a rainbow on the ground. I liked to stand in that pool of colour and watch my hands and legs change as though I was a chameleon. It would be many years before I heard the word chiaroscuro.

We ate the same food every day. Rice with stones in it, if we were lucky, and some dhal and chillies. Ma warned us to eat slowly and carefully so as not to break our teeth.

'There are no dentists I can take you to,' she told us.

By five I knew already we did not belong to God's chosen people. Dentists were for the children God wanted to keep smiling.

There is one night that stands out clearer than all the rest. A night full of stars and a heart full of childhood happiness.

'What happened?' you ask, and I laugh.

'Nothing. Nothingness happened!' I say.

Ma stroked my hair as I ate. She kissed the top of my head. She did the same to my brother even though he shrugged her off, irritated.

I knew he wasn't really angry but showing her that he cared was too difficult for him.

'I was made in a different way to Sam,' I tell you, quietly.

Touch was what I craved, so when she kissed me I grinned and swung my legs.

'My love for Ma was simpler and I didn't mind who saw it.'

I pause, unable to go on. Pictures from that night travel towards me from a million miles, like stardust from some other universe. Ma washing plates, wiping her hands on a spotless cloth. Taking us by the hand and walking along the lighted lane, hoping against hope that Father might return.

'When I met Helen,' I tell you, 'I foolishly thought that at last I could give up the ghost of Ma.'

Covering my feelings from myself for so long had become a burden and Helen, I hoped, would release me from this burden. That was another of my big mistakes.

'On that night, I sat at the yellow Formica table in my short-sleeved shirt, eating from my favourite plate. All I felt was an intense, unaccountable happiness.'

I know now it was simply the contentment of a healthy child. Ma was with us and I was eating. There was no more to it than that. The light bulb made the blue of the walls as brilliant as a kingfisher's wing. A black spider crawled like a shadow up to the rafters. We helped ourselves to more food. No one could cook like Ma. Somehow she managed to make the dhal taste different each day. Before he disappeared, our father grew onions and there were still some plants left in the ground that came up each year. Ma would dig them up and fry them until they were brown and crisp and almost burnt. Then she would sprinkle a little oil and salt over them. She would slice a few chillies and, now and then, there might be dried Maldive fish, or some coconut. She was planning to make our onion plants last a long time. She didn't say how long a 'long time' was.

Ma liked watching us eat. She used to say it made all her hard work worthwhile. Looking back, I see that cooking for us and cleaning the house were the only creative things left to her. Everything else had been taken away. Father, the large garden we used to have, the piano. We were nobody now. Ma's brothers and our grandparents wanted us to move in with them, but Ma refused every time. She wanted to stay where we were in case Father came home. I remember there were lots of arguments on the subject.

'I want the boys to have as normal a time as they can,' she told our uncles, who told her she was crazy.

Normal didn't exist, they said. What on earth did she mean? Sometimes Sam would laugh too, as if he was on the side of the uncles. Then Ma would look as if she were going to cry and I would feel a piece of my heart tearing. I would stand as close to her as I could in order to offer her what comfort I could.

'I am cursed with a photographic memory,' I tell you, now. 'On the night I told Ma how pretty she looked, she had been arguing with her brothers again. Our grandfather was worrying about the three of us and had sent them to plead with Ma to bring us to Chichin Road. But Ma remained adamant. She would wait for our father to return.'

That day there had been no school, so I was at home. I heard every word of the conversation.

'Chitra, you are being unbelievably selfish,' Uncle Harold said.

'Can't you see how vulnerable the boys are here? They could be snatched at any moment,' Uncle Rubin said.

There was a pain in my chest.

'He's not coming back, Chitra. Why can't you accept it?'

Ma shook her head. Her face had become closed. Immediately I went and stood beside her. Showing solidarity. Shut up, I wanted to shout. And then Uncle Percy, seeing my face, said quietly, 'Let her be. Leave them alone. Who knows when the vans might come for any of us? Who knows if it is safer in our house? These might be their last days all together. So leave them, leave them.'

After they had gone, their cups of tea undrunk, Ma turned to me and smiled a wobbly smile. She had won another small victory. Her freedom remained hers for a few more days.

'Come on,' she said. 'Let's go and dig up an onion.'

I understood she wanted to make our evening meal a special one. To make up for all the upset.

In the yard I drew a line in the earth with a stick while she fetched water from the well.

'What are you doing?' Sam asked, coming out.

He had been re-reading the comics our father had given him on his last birthday. Sam read fast and well in three languages. He was clever and hated not being able to go to school. Bored and unhappy, he used to fight with me simply for something to do. Whenever this happened, Ma would take him aside and talk to him. She never raised her voice like the other women in our street. She used to say there were enough angry Tamils in the world. She wouldn't join them. But when she was out of sight, Sam could do what he wanted.

'Why are you making a mess with the dust?' he asked, trying to take the stick from me.

All the time our uncles had been in the house Sam had stayed out of the way. I sensed he was angry about something, but I knew it was no use asking him.

'It's a drawing,' I said. 'I'm going to draw the chittadowa.'

'What for? What's the use of drawing it on the earth? The rain will wash it away.'

I looked at him, puzzled, not knowing how to tell him it didn't matter. That simply drawing the bird was enough and the memory of what I was doing was all I would ever have anyway. But I hardly had the thoughts, let alone the words. Sam was laughing at me.

'Idiot Ras! Idiot Ras!'

And he smudged the line. I watched his bare foot. My bird had been broken before I could finish it. Ma, coming back with the water, saw our faces and knew something wasn't right.

'What are you doing, Sam?' she asked in English.

She always spoke in English when she was angry.

'Why do you look upset, Ras?'

We were both silent. I did not want to betray my brother. Ma looked from one to the other and sighed.

'Sam, son, leave him alone. Go and water the vegetables for me, will you?'

She gave him the bucket and smiled down at me. She was wearing her pale green sari. Her other one had been drying in the sun all day and she would iron it later. She was wearing the earrings that Father had given her at her last birthday when she had turned twenty-three. I thought she looked beautiful, just like Our Lady. Sometimes when she made us say the rosary at night or if we were able to go to church, I would close my eyes and dream that Ma was God and could make everything better again.

'Were you doing a drawing, Ras?' she asked.

I nodded and she nodded back. Satisfied.

'Good,' she said. 'Then finish it.'

I watched her back as she went into the kitchen. She walked as gracefully as the young girls in our school. The thought flashed across my mind that Father would have loved to see her as she was just now. Then I bent my head and drew the chitta-dowa. Quickly, before Sam returned to torment me.

'I have no idea when this happened,' I tell you, Elizabeth. 'What time of year, how long it was since our father was taken away in the night. All I know is that later that evening it rained and Ma rushed out to bring the washing in, calling both my brother and me to help. I remember burying my face in the dry clothes and smelling the scent of bone-dry sunlight caught in its web of cotton. I remember the hiss of Ma's iron as she folded and smoothened the cloth. I remember her hands moving swiftly and the light catching the sovereign gold of the wedding ring she still wore. I remember the chittadowa singing. If each of us is defined by a single moment in our lives, then this was that moment for me.'

'Ras,' I imagine her saying now, kindly, firmly, 'did you do something bad? Oh, Ras, tell me, quickly.'

And I would tell her, twisting my fingers together, so that she would bend down and untangle them and hold them in hers. And the touch of her hand would calm me and make me brave once more.

I stop speaking, overwhelmed by a rush of memory. You are staring at me, Elizabeth. I stare back at you. You look away. What game are we playing, I wonder. I continue.

'Ras,' Ma used to say. 'You don't have to do *everything* your brother tells you to. He can be wrong, you know.'

She would turn her dark eyes on me and force me to look at her. And I would hear her bangles jangle and move as if they were dancing in the air around her head. And then she would say what she always said, even on the anniversary of Father's disappearance with her face swollen with crying:

'Ras, Ras, you mustn't join in with the others. You must be different. There is too much anger amongst the Tamils. The world has forgotten us because of our anger.'

And she would cry a little, but she would hug me, too. Ma, I think, on this ruined day, so many, many years later. So many, many thousand miles in another direction, in a place where I no longer have the ability to know if it might be raining or not . . . Ma, I am thinking of you.

The bell rings. The hour is over. I climb up through the crater you made me conjure up, leaving the smouldering past. Now that I have started, I want to continue.

'Write it down,' you say, nodding.

I suppose you mean to be encouraging, but desolation lies across me like a knife.

'I can't come tomorrow. But write it down and you can give it to me at our next meeting,' you say again.

I stare at you, unable to think who the devil you are. A woman with scraps of a Titian sky in her eyes. I watch as you walk away, back to whatever your life is. We are nothing to each other, Elizabeth, I think. But I will write it down.

F for foxgloves, G for geraniums, H for hollyhocks, I write. That was how I learnt the English alphabet at school. Luckily there were pictures of these flowers, or else I wouldn't have known what they looked like. There are no foxgloves or geraniums or hollyhocks in Jaffna. I said the words over and over again out loud, and then fixed them in my mind with other words that made more sense. F for Frangipani, G for Gecko and H for Hoppers . . .

I hand my homework to you at our next meeting. Then, even before you can ask, I continue where I left off.

'Because the school was often closed, Ma decided to teach me to read, herself.' She would stand beside me, pointing out the words with a thin *ecekl* stick, the pleats of her sari moving gently as she talked to me.

'Write it for me, Ras,' she used to say. 'Join the dots. No, not like that. Yes, that's better. Good boy!'

Her words are fixed for ever. Love, once given, I suppose, can never be erased.

'Come, darling, let's do it again. Until you are perfect.'

I stop speaking and there it is once more. The faded sari billowing out on the washing line in a glimmering arc and the gust of cool air passing over my face.

'Then, when I stopped the daily practice of thinking about her, when years had passed, when other horrors had overlaid that of her death, I came to believe that forgetting was easiest,' I say.

Only now do I know there is no such thing as forgetting. One simply has a lull; a small void, before the past rises like waves from the ocean bed.

After the night which I describe, there was a pause. I have no way of saying how many days or weeks passed. It was the monsoon season once more. That much I remember. The smell of a patch of red earth soaked with dusty rain was a joy to everyone. Because of the shelling, the school was again closed and Sam was bored.

'How am I going to learn anything?' he complained.

I didn't care. I loved hanging around Ma.

'My shadow!' she smiled at me.

The house was always spotless, I remember.

'We must keep it tidy,' she told us.

The implication, never spoken but always present, was that Father might return at any moment.

'Uncle Percy thinks she's mad,' Sam scoffed, when we were alone at night in our shared room. 'He's never coming back.'

I refused to rise to the bait. Secretly I prayed he would return.

'People who get taken in the white van never return,' Sam told me.

'What if they come for us?'

It was a question I thought about on and off. The terror and the morbid fascination lived with me constantly.

'They won't get me,' Sam said, grinding his teeth. 'I'll bite them.'

'I'll bite them too,' I said.

There was a pause. I heard Sam turning over in his bed. The light in the hall had been switched off. Ma was going to bed, her footsteps, the soft swish of her sari, that small boy's symbol of safety, drew nearer. As she approached our room she paused and listened. Then she came in quietly and leaned over each of us in turn. And kissed us.

'Go to sleep,' she murmured. 'Stop talking and sleep, my little birds.'

Although we pretended sleep, there was no fooling her. She laughed softly and pulled shut the curtain that acted as our door, and went out. Sam waited until she was out of earshot.

'You won't be able to bite,' he whispered. 'You've still only got baby teeth.'

But then when I said nothing, he added uneasily, 'I suppose I'll have to bite for you.'

You are smiling, Elizabeth, but your presence is irrelevant, for now my memories are unstoppable.

Listen. It was an ordinary night of tropical splendour with starlight falling on the edge of the sea. Night clip-clopping through our shanty town with her awful magic in tow, intent on leaving some in sleep and taking others to places of no return.

Silent, black-bandaged night, with its army boots treading carelessly across our lives, kicking a random dog that barked at the seaweed tossed on the beach. When my wind-ruffled eyelids fluttered into wakefulness and I called out, Ma appeared instantly by my side.

After such a night as this we awoke as noisy as birds. It was not for us to know we had finished our last refreshing sleep. That day, like all the others, cracked open under a sky so blue that, at the army checkpoint, an off-duty boy soldier flew a kite and was court-martialled for disobedience. Excited, we noticed everything with only half an eye, for on this particular morning we were at last able to go to school.

'Good! Good!' Sam said, satisfied.

'Eat your curd, Ras,' Ma said. 'And then I'll comb your hair.'

'Hurry up,' Sam ordered, frowning. 'I want to be early.'

Ma kissed us good-bye. We each had a tin box with our lunch in it. Green, red and scratched gold.

'Look after your brother,' Ma told Sam.

Then she went in.

That morning was a basketful of noises. Motorbikes and cycle bells jingled against each other. We passed the railway station. Skeletal plants grew in the cracks on the platform, grateful for the chance of a neglected life. There had been no trains since the army bombed the railway line two years previously. We passed the marketplace, where the shops were opening up their shutters. An army man was checking IDs. Another soldier pointed his gun at the people being checked. Sam walked determinedly past, looking neither right nor left.

'Come on,' he said quietly. 'Keep up.'

'I can't,' I said.

He glared at me.

'Yes, you can. Hurry.'

There was suppressed panic in his voice. It slid off his face in

24

drops. We were in this together. I walked a little faster although I didn't want to do everything he told me. He was so nearly the boss and the trick was judging which of his orders were important and which were not.

'Ras,' Sam warned.

He sounded a bit like Ma, and this alarmed me. We hurried on, our satchels heavy against our shoulders.

School was not as we had left it. After the shelling, part of the roof had caved in.

'Never mind, children,' the teacher said, as we stared open-mouthed at the rafters. 'Let's get on with our studies. That is the thing that matters.'

The morning wore itself like a beautiful piece of cloth and, before we knew it, it was lunchtime. I sat under the shade of a murunga tree and ate the patties Ma had made the night before. They were delicious. If only she had given me one more, I wished. Tonight I would remember to tell her that, because I was bigger now, I needed more to eat. I drank some water from my bottle and then decided to go in search of Sam. After lunch the whole school was to have PE drill and then the day would be over. I had traded one of my tin trucks for a tank with another boy and I wanted to show it to Sam. I could see him sitting with a group of older boys. They were playing marbles.

'Sam,' I called, 'look. See what I've got.'

I had got the tank knowing he would want it, hoping he would give me one of his comics in exchange. But I knew I must not seem too eager.

'Sam,' I called again, hurrying across the compound.

I saw one of the other boys nudge him and say something. Sam looked up and in that fraction of an instant, a blinding light streaked across the sky. I saw my brother's mouth move as if in song, but I never heard what he said. The noise of the plane, flying so low, the afternoon sun cutting through the shade, drowned all else. Everyone was screaming and running in all directions.

'Sam,' I screamed. 'Sam, Sam, Sam ...'

I went on screaming for a very long time and then when all noise had stopped and Sam had found me, things went into such slow motion that I had to struggle to adjust. Sam had turned blue, his mouth was grotesque and his eyes were full of light. When I could understand him at last I learnt that the bomb the army had dropped had fallen on our house. Killing Ma.

What was left there, inside our home, was so horrible that the people who came to clear up, the ambulance men, the neighbours, were sick at the sight and wanted to get rid of the thing as quickly as possible. Someone, our grandfather, perhaps, went to identify Ma. But they couldn't do that, either. There wasn't anything left to fit together into any kind of face. Shadows swarmed through the wreckage, bringing their own peculiar, vibrating darkness. For Ma had been chosen, picked out by her Karma, to pay the price for the existence of the Tamil Tigers.

A young boy with an old man's eyes

'Where have you been, Elizabeth? It's been nearly a week.'

Every day at visiting time, no matter what, I can't help waiting for my name to be called, to be taken from my cell and led downstairs. One constant visitor is all I need. It means that someone outside cares about me. And this gets me through the night and into the next day.

You tell me you've had a cold, but I think this was just an excuse for staying away. You look flustered. Have you been walking very fast? I ask because your hair quivers, as though it is a kind of liquid. I wait while you settle yourself, your red bag placed hastily on the table. Files, reading glasses, pen. I watch as you take out a small handkerchief and blow your nose. Your fingers are slender like a young girl's. Then I search your face for news of Lola.

'Has she contacted you yet?' I ask.

'No.'

'Will you e-mail her, again?'

'No. Let her take her time. Pestering is pointless.'

Pestering my own daughter? Is that what it has come to?

'Don't be touchy,' you say. 'What I meant was, let her think about the e-mail I sent. Let her think about your letter, too. Let her come because she wants to, not because she's forced. There's a lot of stuff about you in the papers at the moment. Give her time.'

Stuff? I don't care about the newspapers. There is more than one way of reporting the truth. Lo-la, Lo-la, I want to cry, like a man playing a musical scale. Lola, my child. Have you forgotten your father?

'Continue,' you say.

I look at you with a flash of loathing. The blue eyes are no compensation this morning. You take out your notebook, obsessed with recording my every word. What good will it do? Our interrogation room is quiet today and the small pile of dirt in the corner has been swept away. But there are traces of cigarettes, little flicks of ash, on this table. The cleaning has been done with an inefficient hand and I notice the walls are not really mango green after all. How could I have got that so wrong?

'What happened next?' you ask, softly.

'I see this story is to your liking,' I say.

A misery memoir that can be read like *A Book at Bedtime*, in a cultured voice. Something you can tell your friends about afterwards. I imagine you filing your report, adding statistical details, dates, times. Isn't that right? The walls are in fact grey.

'No,' you say, very quietly, so quietly that I am forced to lean forward in order to catch your words.

And it is at that moment, caught off guard, that I find myself disturbed by the scent of your perfume. It's been a long time since I thought about such things. What's that you say? Let me answer your question in another way.

'Of course it was terrible. I was only five. Losing your mother is one of life's inevitable sorrows, but if she is old and ill, if she is suffering, if she has had some happiness ... well then, you accept this as her fate. You know that all she has given you will guide you through the rest of your days. And somehow, because of this, you can go on to create the life she wanted you to have. But my mother did not have such luxury.'

I am looking at my hands as I speak. I feel the heat of a long-forgotten anguish burn my palms and, all of a sudden, I sense rather than see your sympathy. This, coupled with your scent, confuses me. Someone is rearranging the furniture in my head. The mark on the wall has shrunk. It has taken the shape of an insect in flight.

'Ma walked with the step of a young girl,' I tell you, slowly. There was so much life in her still, so much longing. How could one single bomb, randomly dropped, have wiped out so much, so instantly?'

The voices of the dead are like a wing beat in my head. The sky had been waiting, unbeknown to any of us, I think, ready for her star.

'It was like killing sunlight,' I say, shaking my head, engulfed by unutterable sadness.

Vivid and embalmed, it reaches me, still, across the years.

In answer to your question, do I remember how I felt, let me tell you: no.

I cannot remember crying.

'Someone told me I wet the bed for years after.'

But even that I do not recall.

'Helen once said, soon after we met, she felt as though I was constantly looking at the world the wrong way round. As if I saw it only in reflection.'

And although she kept saying it was impossible for her to get close to me, I never understood, never questioned her. I was too busy listening to the dead whispering to me.

'To have lived is never enough for the dead,' I tell you.

They need to talk about their lives. It is the eternal duty of the living to listen.

But Helen kept asking me, What happened next?

'Tell me, tell me,' Helen used to ask.

Then she would accuse me of hiding things from her.

'For years, I confess this was exactly what I did.'

The truth was, the pain was such that I needed to put it high up on a shelf. In a place out of reach.

You digest all of this in silence while I sit and stare at the wall, waiting. In the days when I looked at paintings all the time, I used to want to study the colour grey. It helped me make sense of things I would otherwise not understand. Now I no longer have any interest in any of this.

Sam and I drifted apart. The best way of dealing with our smashed lives was to fill them with pretence and we could only do this if we cast ourselves adrift from each other. School continued spasmodically but, apart from the pictures I still drew, I stopped being interested in my studies.

'We lived with our grandparents for a few more years before we were rounded up during another lengthy killing spree. I was ten by this time. Then, some time later, after the grandparents died, we were moved somewhere else.'

'Where did you go? How long for?'

I am silent for so long that you look up from your notebook.

'A camp?'

I nod.

'What was it like there?' you ask.

Still I am silent and you repeat the question.

'People in camps become totally depraved,' I say, finally.

'Meaning?'

'A man there told me that I was a young boy with an old man's eyes.'

'What did he mean by that?'

I sigh. You know, I think, wearily. You look at your notes and try a different approach.

'Tell me about your journey to Britain,' you ask. 'How did you get here?'

I shift in my seat. I don't have to tell you everything.

'Somebody found the money,' I say, not looking at you. 'After we were allowed out of the last camp.'

'Who?'

I shrug.

'Just someone.'

'Are you going to tell me who?'

'The father of a girl I knew.'

You give me a hard look. The blues of your eyes are chips of ice, but thankfully you leave it at that.

'We came to Britain on a flight via Malaysia,' I volunteer.

'Do you remember leaving?'

'Yes.'

'What was that like?'

Again I shrug. Why do you need to ask these useless questions? I am aware of my breathing. The air seems even staler today.

'How did you feel?'

'A speck of dust blown by the wind across land and seas can't tell you how it feels.'

One should not have to consider every breath in this way, I think. Breathing should be a human right. How did I feel? Is this what women ask in order to make sense of their environment?

'Nothing,' I say. 'I felt nothing.'

Loneliness is the immigrant's sleeping partner, I tell you, without bitterness. It arrives softly, like a lover appearing through evening shadow. Once again I am struggling with this stale air in my lungs. Closing the gate on our life, Sam and I walked away from all we knew. I was nineteen.

'It was fairly simple,' I tell you. 'I don't think we exchanged more than half a dozen sentences during the whole journey.'

31

'Why was that, d'you think?'

Questions, questions. I cannot bear this room a moment longer.

'Look,' I cry, 'find me Lola. Bring her to me. If I can see her, just once ... I know everything will be all right.'

'Lola comes later in the story,' you tell me.

'My God!' I say, before I can stop myself. 'You are a woman who likes to control *everything*, aren't you? Do you care nothing for my feelings?'

That shuts you up. You glare at me, biting your lower lip, and your hands move as if to gather up your notes. So you are leaving, are you? Like the others. Well, go then, I shan't stop you, Elizabeth. And at least it would be more honest than pretending an interest in my life.

There is a pause and you change your mind.

'Don't be stubborn,' you say, instead.

And now your voice is uncertain. There is an unnatural brightness in your eyes. The corners of the room pick themselves up and the floor moves in closer. As if it, too, is listening now.

'What's this? Pity? Keep it. I have no use for your pity,' I mutter.

'No,' you interrupt. 'Not pity. But perhaps your self-absorption stops you understanding.'

We glare at each other. Our spat has left a confusion. You take a deep breath and, being the professional, recover first.

'Continue, please.'

'I arrived by aeroplane,' I say, reluctantly.

The cousins hadn't got together their fare at this point.

'I travelled carrying the image of the sea with me.'

And even as I speak, I remember it. The soft, satisfied sighs it gave out; the waves surging towards the shore, hissing and foaming and receding. The ships below, like shrouded corpses resting on the water.

'I travelled with the sun towards its point of setting, not realising I would never have such quantities of light ever again.'

Only now, more than thirty years later, forced into this position of inactivity, do I fully understand what I have lost and what being an immigrant really means.

'I have been in this place for almost two months and not one member of my family has bothered to visit me,' I burst out. 'I am therefore forced to consider what it means to be alone.'

You appear to be listening intently, at last.

I wonder what you are really thinking as you sit in this bleak room. Our entire relationship is taking place here. I want to tell you that grey is a colour we all have to endure at some time or other in life. I am enduring it most intensely at this moment.

'No, I am not exactly depressed,' I say in answer to another of your useless questions.

A depressed person does not crave company. This loneliness is a different thing. Closer to melancholy, the lonely see the place where they once belonged as from a distant shore. After your last visit, I sat on my bed and thought about my home.

'Is it possible to be homesick after thirty years?'

'Perhaps,' you murmur. 'Perhaps you had simply masked it.'

Your voice is gentler. And yes, your eyes are definitely moist. I should feel triumphant. Instead I feel exhausted.

'The only way of reliving the past is through imagination,' I tell you. 'And then, only in certain circumstances.'

You nod.

'I would not be able to do what you do,' you tell me.

I open my mouth to speak, but you spoil what I was about to say by writing in your wretched notebook and the moment passes. We are back where we were before, with you trying to do your job.

'Tell me about Helen. When did you meet her?'

'Almost immediately!'

In spite of my mood, I laugh at the memory.

'Sam and I arrived in London,' I say. 'The father of the girl I told you about had a contact waiting.'

'Wait a minute, you haven't told me about this girl.'

'It's not important.'

'Let me be the judge of that.'

'The details are too tedious,' I say loudly, waving my hand. The contact introduced me to a Tamil family. I was sent to work in their petrol station. Sam went to a construction site.'

I avoid your eye.

'All our papers had been organised and were in order. The Tamil family had agreed to sponsor me. Sam was to be looked after elsewhere.'

You open your mouth to question me further, but I'm not having this.

'It was a deeper humiliation for Sam,' I say smoothly. 'As soon as he could, he moved from this situation. And he enrolled in night classes.'

'And you?'

'Oh, I didn't care. I quite liked the petrol station. There was always something going on. It was a lively place. I used to work late, but even that didn't bother me. I drew the people I saw coming and going, filling up. Red cars, blue cars, the bunches of flowers we sold . . .'

I pause.

I remember I bought a box of watercolour paints with my first pay packet. And painted the crimson tulips in the bucket outside. A man bought it from me. A total stranger!

You are no longer writing in your notebook. Are you going to start questioning me again about who paid for our ticket?

'The family I worked for weren't bad to me,' I say. 'They weren't good to me, either. Their indifference was typical, but it was also welcome.'

34

'Did you and Sam live together?'

'No, no. I told you, I lived over the petrol station. He lived elsewhere in London.'

'Are you telling me the truth?'

'Of course.'

'It isn't any good, lying to me, you know.'

'Who said I was lying?'

You let it go but the tension is there at the edges of your mouth.

'Unsurprisingly, Sam and I were already far apart,' I say. 'The surprise would have been had we drawn closer.'

This seems to satisfy you.

'One afternoon,' I tell you, 'a girl walked in to buy petrol and couldn't start her car up again.'

I was alone at the till, but she wanted me to help her.

'Why don't you ring for the breakdown people?' I asked.

'I don't have insurance cover,' she said.

She was a pretty girl, with wavy hair. When she smiled I noticed a dimple in her cheek.

'What's your name?' she asked me.

I was taken aback by her boldness.

'Look at you!' she laughed. 'Don't be so shocked, I only asked your name, not for your credit-card number!'

'It's Ras,' I said, feeling an unaccountable tightness in my chest.

'I'm Helen,' she said instantly. 'Since you're so curious.'

That was how I met her. I pushed her car to the side of the forecourt and called the boss, who took a look at it. Then we rang a garage who sent a tow-truck, and off she went. I didn't expect to see her again.

That night I dreamed about Helen. In my dream we were biting into a mango, together.

'She was your first girlfriend?'

'But when I woke I didn't know what I could do. We hadn't exchanged addresses and I had no idea how I could find her again.'

I told myself she looked too well-off for me.

'But she was your first girlfriend?'

'She wasn't my girlfriend.'

I waited four days, thinking about her. I didn't expect anything to come of it.

'On the evening of the fourth day I met Sam.'

We hadn't met for a few weeks. The silence begun when we were children had grown so large in our heads that it was stifling any affection there might be. After Ma died, people told me I looked like her. I have always been intensely proud of this fact, but I also had the feeling the likeness angered Sam.

Seeing each other only reminded us of what had happened and, as we both knew, it was better to forget. The pub we met in that night was Sam's local. The bar girl knew him.

'Is he your brother?' she asked, pointing to me. Several people turned and stared at me.

Sam nodded. We ordered our drinks.

'He doesn't look like you,' the girl said.

I could see she was merely trying to be friendly. But Sam scowled.

'I can't help that,' he muttered.

The girl laughed.

'Are you as quiet as him?' she asked me.

'No! He's the quiet one.'

'Clever too,' she said, leaning forward.

I stared. Her T-shirt was very low cut. She laughed again.

'He's always reading a book. Studying, aren't you, Sam?'

Sam nodded and drew me away to a corner of the room.

'Why did you talk to her?' he hissed.

'She knew your name,' I said.

'Why did you talk to her?' he asked again. 'Have you forgotten Rani?'

'Rani? What's Rani got to do with anything?' I asked angrily.

'You know. Have you forgotten your promise, then?'

'She likes you,' I said, pointing to the girl at the bar.

'I'm not interested.'

The old sneer had crept back into his voice. I was tired; I didn't want to think of him. I just wanted a drink and then I wanted to get back to my room.

'I've joined three A-level classes,' Sam said in a different voice a bit later on. 'Physics, Maths, German.'

'What for?'

'Why d'you think? I want to go to university.'

'I mean, why German?'

He shrugged. 'It's a useful language.'

Ten minutes had barely passed and we had run out of conversation. I needed a reason to leave, but I wanted to stay, too. He was my brother. We were all that was left of Ma. I didn't want to lose him completely. Besides, I felt sorry for him. He looked tired, and older than his age. I sensed that he was even more out of his depth than I was. The determination was still there, but the journey had stolen his youthfulness.

'Just a minute, who was Rani?' you ask suddenly, interrupting my thoughts. 'And what happened to your cousins?'

Startled, for I had forgotten your presence, I feel the floor creeping upwards. The mark on the wall is shaped like a cockroach now.

'My cousins had arrived in London,' I say. 'Sam was seeing them.'

'And you?'

'I was too busy.'

'Too busy?'

'Yes.'

But that evening Helen walked into the pub. I couldn't believe my eyes. There she was, with her cheesecloth shirt, her flared jeans and her friends. Making a great noise.

'She knew everyone, you see.'

I can tell from the intensity of your gaze that I've caught your attention.

'Was she pretty?' you ask, and I want to laugh, the question is so unexpected.

'Yes.'

We saw each other at almost the same moment.

'Helen!' I cried.

Perhaps all that dreaming I had done had given me confidence.

'Ras,' she shouted.

And she came over to me.

'Hey! Fancy meeting you. I was going to come in and thank you!'

'How's the car?'

'It's great. Fixed now, thanks to you. Come and meet my friends.'

'Can I get you a drink?'

'No, let me!'

We were talking as though we'd known each other for years. I was aware of Sam sitting beside me, shrinking into himself. Suddenly I felt like the older one.

'Perhaps,' I say, 'that was when the change in him began to take place. When he started to turn his back on reality, look inwards into the past. And misinterpret it.'

I pause. You are looking at me, one eyebrow raised. I'm not putting this properly.

'We were witnesses,' I say, slowly. 'War affects witnesses differently.'

There is a very long silence now. You seem to be working something out.

'We saw too much, too early,' I add. 'We interpreted it in our own way. Because of our youth. Perhaps our interpretation was wrong. Who can say?'

You write and I am silent, thinking about Sam.

'So what happened with Helen?'

'That evening? Oh, nothing much. I introduced her to Sam. We exchanged addresses. The other girls joined us for a drink and the bar girl came over, too.'

Sam did not stay long. He finished his beer and left, saying he had homework to do before the next morning. I saw he could not bear to be with us a moment longer, and the truth was I, too, wanted him to leave.

'I let him go without a word and we never met in that pub again.'

I had forgotten about the incident. Suddenly I see Sam's face, shuttered and helpless, looking as he did the day Ma died. Why could we not be kinder to each other? I become aware that you, Elizabeth, are looking at me in a way I don't like.

'You regret it?'

'Yes.'

It is just one of a thousand things I regret. I could have gone outside after him, had a word in private, explained about Helen. But I did none of those things and instead, with a wave of my hand, I forgot all about him.

'He was fragile,' I tell you now, with great reluctance. 'As a child he was the stronger, but his job was manual and it was wearing him out.'

Meanwhile, Helen and I began a relationship that consumed us for two years.

'Everyone thought we were perfect together,' I say.

'Everyone?'

'Helen's friends.'

She had a lot of friends in those days and they all liked me.

'With Helen's encouragement, I left the Tamil family and the petrol station.'

I got a series of jobs, first, selling cars and then, through some-one she knew, as a clerk at the local council offices. This in turn led to other jobs.

'They were all temporary at this point,' I say.

Helen and I went around with a group of her friends, laugh-ing together, making a great noise about nothing. She took me home and her mother flirted openly with me. Her older sister felt sorry for me because I had been orphaned. The story about Ma ran and ran. Everyone was outraged. But what was more interesting to them was they thought me very handsome.

'We made a good-looking couple,' I say with some pride.

'And Helen?' you insist. 'What did she do?'

'She was still at university, studying English. She wanted to be a journalist.'

I remember how, in our early days together, lying huddled in bed in my room, she would tell me how she hated all wars but most especially civil wars. One day, she said, she would become a journalist on *The Times* and write big articles about the waste of life. I believed her.

'You sound bitter.'

Do I? Maybe. But they were not grey days, I think.

'Only where Lola is concerned,' I tell you, and you hold up your hand.

'Wait. I don't want you to get on to Lola just yet. I want to know more about you and Helen.'

Lola is the only person I want to talk about, though. Can't you see what this absence is doing to me? I take another breath and the mark on the wall expands and becomes a cockroach filled with blood.

'Helen tried to love me,' I say, rearranging the thoughts in my head with difficulty. 'As I did her.'

And then it happened. She fell pregnant and everything changed.

'Deliberately?'

'No. It was an accident.'

'What happened, then?'

'Oh, she took it very badly. There was talk of an abortion.'

'You didn't want to be saddled with a baby, quite understandably.'

I stare at you.

'*Me?* Of course not! There was no doubt in my mind. Of course we were going to have it.'

By this time she had graduated and had got a job on the local paper. I, too, had been given a promotion at the county council.

'I persuaded her that we should get married. Her parents weren't pleased, of course, but what could they say? They wanted their grandchild.'

We married in June, when the roses were out. It was a small wedding, nothing grand. Helen wore a big white hat.

'And Sam?'

'Yes, Sam came. He wanted the cousins to come too. He was very thick with them by now. It was all a bit awkward, but we managed.'

Afterwards Sam gave me a lecture about Helen's family.

'Why was that?'

I frown.

'He was acting strangely and I thought it was because he disliked Helen's family. They were too wealthy for his liking ... he'd always been a bit of a socialist.'

I remember how he had angered me by asking Helen's parents for a donation for the Sri Lanka Tamil cause. Helen merely laughed when they told us, but I had been livid. Thankfully her parents simply told him they supported causes of their own choosing.

'Was that the beginning of his involvement with the Tamil Tigers?' you ask.

I nod.

Sam left the construction business and got a job at a firm that made electronic parts. I think he was making quite a bit of money. Having given up his idea of university, for reasons that were a mystery to me, he spent all his spare time with the cousins. Actually, I think there must have been a fair amount of Tamil activity going on behind the scenes. The cause was at its height, money was being sent regularly to fund the offensive in the war. I wasn't interested in any of it. In fact, I was scared. Peace between both sides was all I wanted. Not a game of blame.

'Besides . . .'

'What?' you ask, instantly, and I hesitate.

'Other things were more important to me than funding acts of aggression,' I say.

Somewhere, lingering along the very edges of my childhood, lay that shadowy figure of my mother. An all-but-vanished memory.

'But then,' I say, rousing myself, 'on a morning of dazzling beauty Helen went into labour, and love, as I had once known it, returned into my life.'

Lola, we called her. I chose her name. Helen went along with it. Lola, Lola, my small, perfect daughter. The light of my life, the second dawn, my journey's beginning on the road to Damascus.

4

Still-life studies

We are back in our concrete space together, under the sea. Someone has moved the furniture, so today I sit with my back to the cockroach on the wall. You must face it instead, Elizabeth. You are wearing a brooch on the lapel of your black jacket. It looks old and the colour is my favourite: a fresco red. Seeing my glance you take the jacket off but say nothing. I look away. You wait for me to start, pen poised. Like a stingray.

'We never had a honeymoon,' I say. 'But the baby moon lasted for a couple of years.'

You smile, faintly. Encouraged, I continue.

I unearthed my toy truck from long ago. The one I was holding when Ma was killed. How shabby it looked, here. I placed it on the shelf in my new daughter's bedroom.

Helen and I lived through this time roped together, rising nervously at dawn to the sound of Lola's cries; meeting her demands bleary-eyed, sharing the shift work.

'I behaved perfectly. Helen was the envy of all her friends.'

Her swarthy prince was better than any Englishman. The world turned into an orb of life-affirming blueness, the trees were filled with birds the colours of marzipan sweets. I began to draw the apples Helen placed in the bowl on the kitchen table.

Then, in odd moments at weekends, I started to paint a few still-life studies.

'The paintings were small,' I say. 'And somehow, although they started out as apples, they always ended up mangoes.'

Helen found this funny at first.

'You'll be painting coconut trees next!' she laughed. 'Your daddy's gone bananas,' she told Lola. 'Look what you've done to him! He's seeing things!'

I was. Everywhere I went I felt I was surrounded by the richness of home. Gone were the oppressive skies, the emptiness inside me. But underneath the ground something lay buried like an amputated limb. Dormant like certain kinds of black magic, frighteningly shapeless, moving like a headless worm. Under grass, carelessly covered over by coconut shells. Under twenty-three years of monsoon rain.

Outwardly, things changed so slowly that we hardly noticed. Outwardly, the past appeared an outgrown plaything, a metal toy, scratched by use. I did not know what I know now, that when a person lives in a camp for years he ceases to be part of any society.

'The truth was, I was still living in a camp.'

Maybe I still am.

Helen and I argued on and off. Like dance music we started and stopped, making up after each incident. History and life waltzed hand in hand. With only a slight tremor.

'I thought it was because we were so tired,' I tell you, shaking my head, saddened by such naivety.

'So what happened? When did it come to a head?'

'Not for a while,' I tell you.

Helen went back to work part-time.

'She wrote a piece about the hospital where Lola was born.'

The place had been filthy. After the birth the bloodstained sheets were not replaced for days.

44

'In the end I brought in clean linen from home.'

Helen wrote that the hospital was like an institution in a Third World country.

'That really did make me laugh. I told her she had no idea what medical care was like in a Third World country.'

But she was passionately interested in the health service in Britain. Her article was published locally and then picked up by a national newspaper. Then came a flurry of useless activity. Radio Four asked to interview her.

'She wrote a follow-up piece and for a short while she became a local celebrity. People, mothers in particular, stopped her in the street and thanked her for pointing out the state of things.'

I shrug.

'This gave her confidence.'

She began to write about other social issues.

'But even as her name began appearing here and there, our arguments were getting worse and I started to find her demanding in ways I had never noticed before.'

'What d'you mean?'

I glare at you, mouth open. Why do you keep interrupting me, Elizabeth? Your voice brings me back into this hated room again. I notice that some previous occupant has dropped a scrunched-up paper tissue. For a moment I can't take my eyes off it. To my amazement it has taken the shape of a different insect. Blinking, I turn to you, but all you do is repeat your question. Trying to find the words to describe what I felt in those early days isn't easy.

'Trapped, was how I felt,' I snap, before I can stop myself.

I have spoken with heavy irony, but you don't seem to notice.

'She said I didn't talk to her enough.'

'And? Did you?'

I turn my palms upwards.

'I thought I did. But she kept saying it was never the right kind of talk. I didn't know what she meant. I couldn't keep telling her I loved her, could I?'

'I don't know. Perhaps you never said it?'

But I did love her. Certainly, I loved the idea of her.

I feel despair twist in me in a hurricane of emotions. What if the paper tissue isn't what it seems? What if it really *is* an insect? Am I going mad? There is only so much of this behaviour you will take. My hands begin to itch. I force them to be still.

'She wanted a different kind of person to the one I was,' I say slowly, making a huge effort. 'She hated me being quiet. She didn't like it when I painted, either. She said it took me away.'

But when I talked to her, when I told her things about my home, she no longer listened.

'So what did she want? I don't know.'

I stop speaking and look at you. It's clear I shall get no response from you, either.

'I used to shout at her. "For Christ's sake, what the hell do you want from me?"'

She couldn't tell me. And there was another problem, looming.

'What?' you pounce.

'Sam,' I say, heavily. 'He was back.'

'Go on.'

Ostensibly, Sam came to see his niece, but in reality to pester me time and time again about the Tamil cause.

'News had come to him that a mutual friend of ours had been killed and he was very upset.'

'Who was the friend?'

'No one that would interest you. But Sam was distraught.'

I pause. Of course I too had been upset, but Sri Lanka was somewhere off the edge of my horizon. 'That person was no longer part of my life.'

'A woman, I take it?'

God, how cynical you sound. I don't answer and you look back at your notes.

'Rani,' you say, your voice neutral.

I'm not going to rise to your bait.

'Sam was getting on my nerves. His anger had turned to aggression. All he was interested in was weaponry: how to acquire it, how much it cost, the latest models . . . I hated such talk. It seemed to me he simply wanted to perpetuate the violence with aggression.'

'Have you forgotten what happened to Ma?' he would whisper, eroding my defences, angry, angry; we were both very angry.

Then he started on the old stories.

'You won't remember the way they came to take Father away,' he said. 'You were too young. But I remember. They tied both his hands. They blindfolded him. And they took him away, for ever. Someone told Ma that an army man kicked him in the head before shooting him. They told Ma the last sound Father heard before he died was the soldiers laughing. Ma had to live with that information.'

I was shocked by his talk but pretended indifference. Why was he choosing to tell me all this now, when my life had taken a turn for the better?

'You were too young, then.' he repeated. 'So what are you going to do about it, now?'

I tried to talk to Helen, but she was busy with Lola, busy with her articles on injustice in Britain. She had no time for my stories.

'There's injustice everywhere,' she told me, closing her ears.

On one occasion she threw a plate across the room shouting, 'What happened to your mother isn't *my* bloody fault!'

But every time she mentioned Ma, a kind of raw grief escaped from within me as if I was being boiled in a pressure cooker. I

47

bitterly regretted being so open with her. A certain hardness crept into our relationship. Ma's voice, too, began intercepting my thoughts, at that time.

'Don't fight, darling,' her voice cried.

Startled, I reminded Helen how, not so long ago, she used to say she would tell the world what had happened to me. But this was a hopeless tactic. It only made her angrier and so, in the long, sleepless nights that were the substance of early father-hood, I took to dreaming of Ma, instead. I saw her clearly. Young and lithe, she was, in that lime-green sari, with sunlight on her face. And there again was the faint jangle, coming back to me from long ago, of her sovereign gold bangles.

'Ma!' I called out in my semi-exhausted state, halfway between wakefulness and dreaming. 'Ma, I need you!'

Of course, I woke Lola with my shouting and an angry Helen banished me to the spare room.

'For God's sake, Ras, shut up!' she scolded. 'I've had enough of you. Get a grip of yourself. I'm sick of hearing about Sri Lanka. I can't even escape in my sleep. This has got to stop.'

I stop talking abruptly and find I am sweating.

'And all the time, unnoticed by me, Sam was working with a group of militant Tamils, plotting vengeance.'

'In what way? What sort of vengeance? Terrorist activities?'

Your questions come at me with machine-like speed. I swear the room we are sitting in is alive with bugs. The paper-tissue insect lies on its side, drowning. Unformed thoughts swirl around my head.

'Yes.'

'Bombs?'

'Yes.'

You make a gesture with your hands. Your face is watchful. Am I about to betray my brother?

'Was he making them?'

I shake my head. Everything is rotting in my mind. Insects or thoughts, what's the difference? You have a blank look on your face, Elizabeth, that frightens me. I see you look at the mark behind my head and wonder what you see.

'If he wasn't making them, then who was?'

Your voice is icy.

'They were, in Jaffna. He ... others too ... they supplied money.'

'I see. And are you telling me you weren't involved?'

'Yes.'

Your shoulders relax very slightly.

'Are you bored?'

'What?' you ask, startled. 'No,' you say. 'I'm not bored.'

Slightly reassured, uneasily, I continue.

'By Lola's third birthday the unravelling process was well advanced. I slept in the spare bedroom sometimes, but elsewhere too. Love, it seemed, took many forms and the disembowelling of a marriage has different stages. Fish scales and insect wings were invading our lives.

'The first affair is the one you remember,' I say.

Quietly, unnoticed by either of us, Helen's carefully composed still life had gone on ripening in that bowl on the kitchen table.

'I threw the first stone.'

I wait for your reaction, but you refuse to be drawn. The room is becoming a watery grave, encroaching, rising on top of me.

'She was a Spanish girl who worked with me. It wasn't serious. She was too young. I don't even remember her face, now.'

What I do remember was the sweetness of revenge and the reality of the guilt that followed.

'Sleeping in the same bed as Helen was impossible after that. So I picked another row with her.'

'In order to be banished to the spare room?'

I look sharply at you, but your head is bent in a gesture that I cannot read. There is a stain on the thin carpet. I search it for recognisable insect life.

'I'm not being sarcastic,' you say, looking up in the pause that follows.

Partially satisfied I continue. But now I worry that you think me paranoid. What the hell. None of this matters.

'It didn't last long,' I tell you. 'The Spanish affair.'

I couldn't bear waking up in the mornings in the spare room, pretending to Lola that I had been ill in the night, yet again. Lola was no fool.

'You have been fighting with Mummy,' she accused me, piercing my heart.

The look on her face was too much to bear.

Helen bought fresh fruit for the bowl. I taught Lola to draw them. Helen sliced ham off the bone and made Lola her favourite sandwiches. I began another affair and then drifted into one more. We were fighting less. Things were slowly going into cold storage, preserved for a later date.

I stop talking. Once more I find myself gasping for breath.

'Must I go on?'

'Yes,' you say, and I look at you properly for the first time today.

You have been coming to see me for nearly three weeks now.

'Am I supposed to be getting something from these visits? And if so, what?' I'm sorry if that sounds aggressive, ungrateful. I am neither of these things. All I want from you is help, to be reunited with my daughter.

'Can't you see how this is destroying me?'

'I know,' you say, and now you are leaning towards me and once again your perfume catches me unaware. Vague, long-forgotten longings open up in me like flowers after rain. I have a sudden memory of Ma standing under the shade of a mango tree. There are coins of sunshine dancing on her body, filling me with shot after shot of happiness.

'I want you to tell me everything,' you say. 'So I can defend you properly, so you might be able to leave this place for good.'

Your eyes remind me of light as it falls on water. I am struck by a new gentleness in your voice. Has it always been there? Or am I imagining it? The constriction in my chest confuses me.

'The facts are important, but so are the feelings that led up to them,' you are saying.

You have an old-fashioned and serious air today; one that I thought vanished decades ago. I nod. I am tired of fighting for every breath. Suddenly everything seems to connect: the sounds in the corridor outside this room, your voice, your silhouette . . . It is as if we have become a picture, trapped in time. As if the movement of your hand as you write mingles with the sorrow of what I am about to say.

'I threw the first stone,' I say again. 'And Lola's childhood fled.'

We split up when Lola was six. Our mutual dislike had grown so great it was impossible to do otherwise. The day is etched for ever in my mind. I met Lola after school on an afternoon of exceptional beauty, under a sky filled with the vapour trails of aeroplanes. I remember wishing I was a passenger on one of those planes, instead of walking down the tree-lined street feeling as though I was about to commit a murder. No one stopped me; not the lollipop lady waving the traffic to a halt at the zebra crossing, not the other mothers who chatted at the gate, nor the fathers who sat waiting in their cars. I paused by the railing, trying to hide, shaking. An executioner listening out for his cue; a king about to cut a ribbon. The gnawing pain in my stomach increased. It was worse than anything I had felt before. Then it started to rain. I stood under a tree, huddled, smoking, shivering. I had spent the morning drinking coffee and now I felt weak. I hadn't slept for days. The woman I was leaving Helen for was waiting for me to return.

'Don't be long,' she had said. 'Be strong. Remember, I love you!'

Oh, how we love to brandish that word.

'We'll start again,' she (her name was Adele) said. 'I'm young enough to have a baby, if that's what you want.'

I recalled her words in the steady fall of the rain, my face awash with water, while in the distance a bell sounded a clear and certain knell as the children began to swarm out of school. And, there, amongst the buttoned and hooded crowd, was the beloved face of Lola. She searched the group standing by the railings, her eyes full of an urgent preoccupation of her own.

She was looking no doubt for her mother, but it was me she got and instantly she smiled a beaming, wide smile that fatally pierced my heart. In that instant I saw my daughter as others would see her one day. With eyebrows that took wing on either side of her face, and hair, cut in a basin of black, framing those same, enormous eyes. But I didn't see how the small, delicate, mouth would one day be capable of uttering the harshest of words.

'Daddy!'

'Hello, darling,' I said.

'*Hello*, Dad! What are you doing here? Where's Mum?'

'I had a day off work today. So she said I could pick you up.'

Lola accepted this without a murmur.

'I thought we'd go somewhere for a treat?' I said, tentatively.

'Yes, *yes*, where?'

'Well ... the park isn't any good because of the rain. How about the museum?'

She pulled a face.

'How about the museum shop and café? For a cream tea?'

'The café upstairs? In the big place?'

'With the paintings?'

She nodded. Why was she so beautiful today, of all days? Her black eyes shone like polished glass under water. Her skin was astonishingly supple. Was this how Ma had felt about me? My whole body was tense as the day began disintegrating. I mustn't let it, I thought, in a panic.

'Okay,' I said, with the false cheerfulness I would soon cultivate as though my life depended on it, taking her hand.

So trusting, so soft, so small. I wanted to weep.

'Be strong,' Adele had said. 'Remember, she's not losing you. It isn't going to affect her.'

But hailstones of doubt assailed me. I thought of how I watched her eat her breakfast, before school. I thought of bedtime stories, her hair after it had been washed, the smell of baby talcum powder on a pillow not half as soft as the cheek that lay on it. My heart would surely stop before the day was out, I thought. Far in the recesses of my mind I saw the figure of Ma standing at the door waving us good-bye on that last morning.

'Look after your brother,' Ma had called.

But Lola had no brother.

She continued to chatter, unaware of the corner we were turning.

'I told Gemmy she could have it if she gave me something back. But she didn't have anything except her hedgehog.'

'Really?'

'It's her favourite hedgehog. I said if she wanted the doll then she would have to give it to me.'

'Of course.'

'She wouldn't. So I said no doll. She's just a baby, Daddy. Isn't she?'

'Yes.'

'Can I have jam?'

'When?'

'When we have tea.'

On and on she went, carrying me along with her. We took a number 3 bus into the centre of Trafalgar Square.

'Can we sit upstairs?'

'Yes, of course.'

'Oh, goody! Mum doesn't like sitting upstairs.'

I was falling apart. The top of a branch caught in the open windows and Lola laughed. The bus lurched from stop to stop. Lola's small hand slid in and out of mine, her voice running like a stream through my life. I was drowning in it.

'You *must* be strong,' Adele had said. 'Try to stay detached. Remember, Ras, this is the worst bit. It will soon be over and then we can start the recovery together.'

Yes, yes.

'That little girl will have a happier father and it will make her a happier person because of it.'

I know.

'Be strong, darling. Remember, I love you!'

'Dad, I like having tea with you. Can you pick me up every day?'

'What?'

'You're not listening!'

I stared down at her face, scowling now. Sweet Jesus, what was I doing? No, I thought, it's impossible. I can't. Then I remembered Helen's parting words:

'I want everything out by the end of the week.'

She wouldn't let me change my mind, of that I was sure. Tomorrow had already arrived. There was no going back to yesterday.

We went to look at Lola's two favourite paintings at the National Gallery. Daphne with her arms turned into trees and Martha and Mary's eggs. Then we went to the shop and I let her choose anything she wanted. She was a bit surprised, but quickly, with amusing cunning, she gathered up as much as she could.

'These,' she said looking anxious, handing me a variety of rubbers and pencils.

And then I saw she had pushed her luck and picked up two books as well.

'Hmm,' I said, trying to look stern. 'This is rather a lot, isn't it?'

She hesitated.

'Shall I put them back?' she asked in her five-more-minutes voice, the whites of her eyes round saucers of milky trust.

I almost turned away, but instead I hugged her to me, laughing, blinking, descending the steps of hell, my legs turning to jelly. Unable even to pray for help.

'No, darling, I'm only teasing. You can have them!'

The afternoon dragged on. We had tea. As if she sensed something was up, Lola was misbehaving. She loaded her scones with jam and dunked them in her juice. Then she wiped her hands on the table.

'Lola, stop it,' I said helplessly. 'Don't be naughty.'

It was a quarter to five. I should have told her by now.

'Lola,' I said.

Then I stopped. She looked at me and grinned. Far away in the distance I heard the beginnings of an explosion. In my hand was a stick of dynamite.

'There's something I want to tell you. Mummy and I are separating.'

Like an egg, I thought. Separating, not breaking, my lover had said. Remember.

'We're going to live in different houses from now on. You'll live some of the time with Mummy and some with me.'

'Fifty-fifty,' Adele had said. 'I'm looking forward to getting to know her.'

The ground was rushing towards me. With a great effort I sent it back to where it belonged. My hands were shaking badly. Lola had stopped swinging her legs. Chunks of scone and jam bobbed in her undrunk orange juice, untidy floating islands. A waiter came over, his face misshapen by my thoughts. His voice coming to me with the slowed-down sound of a distorted merry-go-round, asking if we needed anything else. There is nothing, I thought, anyone can give me now. I shook my head, aware that Lola had fixed me with her molten bright eyes. My darling, I thought, as I detonated the grenade.

'When?'

'From next week,' I said quietly. 'You can help me pack my things.'

As soon as the words were out of my mouth, I cursed silently.

'Where will you live?'

'Oh, not far. I'll still be able to pick you up from school. Just like today. Nothing will change. I still love you. I'll always love you, darling.'

'Where is your house?' she demanded.

I quaked before her gaze. Small though she was, she towered over me. I heard Ma's voice.

'Son,' her voice asked, 'what have you done?'

'Ma,' I replied, 'it wasn't working with Helen.'

'Did you talk to her about it?'

'No, Ma,' I said unhappily. 'You don't understand. It was different in your day.'

'What d'you mean, I don't understand? Do you think life was perfect for me with your father? D'you think we didn't have our fights before he disappeared?'

I shook my head.

'Now is not the time or place, Ma. Please!'

'*Where* is your house?' Lola asked, again.

'Do you think love comes without effort?' Ma asked.

I had never heard her use such a tone of voice with me. Her

face was obscured by the years of absence. There were too many questions firing at me.

'Dad!' Lola said shrilly.

'Answer your daughter,' Ma said sternly.

'New Cross,' I said faintly. 'It's . . .' I waved my hand vaguely towards the window '. . . it isn't far. I'll still be able to see you, I promise. I'll be living with someone else. She's longing to see you. She's heard so much about you.'

I could no longer hear my own voice.

Lola lifted her hand. Then she brought it crashing down against the table so that the islands of floating scones, the jam and the glass were thrown into the air and the teapot with its still-hot tea flew upwards like a white dove. Before beginning its downwards spiral of spilt and splintered mess. Amidst the commotion, the hurried feet of the waiter, the hooded gazes of the other people in the room, I heard my mother's voice close in my ear:

'Look what you've done,' she said.

I looked. On the floor were two painted eggs, smashed amongst the tea things.

5

Portrait of the artist cast adrift

The cleaner has aired the room. The moment I walk in, I smell the difference. He has washed the floor and the cigarette stub has gone. I know the cleaner is a man because I see him sometimes with his long-handled dustpan and brush, shuffling along, eyes down in the dirt. He is black, of course. Perhaps he has lived on the edges of things longer than I have. Today I am back in my usual seat, facing the door. Facing the mark on the wall. Old friend, it looks less like a cockroach this morning; more like a child's drawing of a teardrop. I stare intently at it while I wait for you, Elizabeth.

'Years later,' I tell you, after you've settled down, taken your coat off, got your notebook out, 'when I returned to the spot where I had murdered her innocence, the place greeted me with a ghastly smile.'

I shake my head, trying to dislodge the image of the corpse that rises up even now whenever I think of what I did to Lola. This, I tell you, was my real crime.

'I could not go into that café for years. It became a place where even the furniture screamed at me.'

'But,' you frown, puzzled, 'aren't you making too much of this? Surely thousands of people get divorced each year and they don't consider it murder! Lola was a clever little girl. She had a father who loved her: that hadn't changed. Why the fuss?'

I glance wearily at you. I hear your words. Are you talking about the thousands of people from stable backgrounds, the thousands of children who have grandparents, uncles, aunts, brothers, sisters? All living a bus ride away. I did not have any of that, can't you understand?

'Elizabeth,' I begin.

There, I have uttered your name. Something passes between us. There is an electric fence surrounding me and your eyes are searchlights on my face.

'Tell me what happened after you told Lola you were leaving,' you ask, too quickly.

But I cannot leave the scene of the crime, yet. Body parts were scattered everywhere, amongst the paintings, in the shape of angels' wings. Ma's voice, too, echoes from room to room in the gallery.

'There was no escape.'

There is no point in telling you the things Helen said; things I agreed with, incidentally.

'At least,' she had said, 'your mother couldn't help abandoning you.'

In the early days of the separation, Adele was fully sympathetic. She was in love with me. Enough love for both of us, was how she put it. Which was just as well because Lola, having run home taking my heart with her, was now playing hide-and-seek with it.

'Adele wanted me to recover. She suggested I took up painting again.'

My voice sounds unpleasantly loud, even to me. I stop speaking, thinking of that now insignificant affair for the first time in years. She was kind, I suppose. She wanted it to work between us.

'It was a last chance, you understand.'

'For you or her?'

'For her . . . for us both. But the first mistake I made was to tell her . . .'

'Yes?'

'I told her about Rani.'

I swallow. In the silence I hear the ticking of a wristwatch. Yours.

'That's something I didn't tell you.'

'Yes.'

'In Jaffna, in the last camp we were moved to, there was a young girl. Rani. She was pretty, intelligent. She liked me. Her brother had been killed in a skirmish with the army and her father desperately wanted her to get out. Once, he had been a wealthy man; he still had some savings. Actually, I'm certain he was part of the insurgency. Rani persuaded him to pay our fare to the UK. Being boys, we were in more danger than Rani. Her father agreed, but he wanted me to promise I would send for her as soon as I was settled. He wanted me to marry her. Well, of course I promised. I liked her well enough and we were desperate to get out.'

'But you didn't send for her.'

I shake my head. I do not want to think of Rani.

'And?'

'Nothing. I met Helen and forgot about Rani – something Sam never forgave me for. When things started to go wrong with Helen, I thought about Rani again. And when I first moved in with Adele, I told her the story. That was when I saw her capacity for jealousy.'

'I see. What happened to Rani? She got out of the camp?'

'She was gang-raped and murdered. Because of her father's involvement with the Tigers.'

We sit without speaking or moving.

'Why didn't you tell me this before, Ras?' you ask, finally.

Dimly I am aware of you using my name. But I have no answer. I know the whole truth can never be learnt. Not because I lie, but because it is impossible for me to tell it all.

'After my confession to Adele, we tried to get over it.'

I realised that things could get tricky over Lola, so I became watchful. I tried to hide my affection for Lola. Adele, too, made an effort. She gave up a room in her flat for me to paint in, uncaring of the mess I would make. So, with her encouragement, when I got home every evening, I started where I had left off. Only this time it was a self-portrait I began painting.

'I joined an evening class.'

That too had been Adele's idea.

'But it didn't work out.'

You raise an eyebrow.

'Well, I was spending all my time desperately engineering access to Lola. Often this could only be after school. Just for a few hours.'

'You didn't take her to your new home?'

I shake my head.

'Not much. The first visit had been a disaster. Adele made a cake, and to start with Lola behaved well enough. She was very quiet. It should have alerted me to possible trouble, but I was too nervous on my own account. Anyway, Lola answered all the questions, she said please and thank you, but when it was time to leave she gave an enormous and audible sigh of relief.'

'It would have been a great strain on her, of course.'

'Of course! But Adele took it personally. And later on she realised that Lola had stolen the cake, stuffed it in her school bag or something!'

I wanted to laugh. I couldn't think what the fuss was about. The cake had been made for Lola, after all.

'But Adele went on and on about it, saying Lola was a

common little thief. Saying Helen had put her up to it. Oh God! In the end, I couldn't stand it any longer. So I asked Helen.'

'What did *she* say?'

'She told me Lola had brought it home, unasked. She suspected it was an act of loyalty. Lola didn't want her mother to feel left out of anything.'

'Did you believe that?'

'I didn't know what to think. Helen refused to talk to Lola about it and Adele was waiting for an apology. What could I do? When I next saw Lola, she simply glared at me and wouldn't answer.'

I look at my hands, remembering. All that summer I tried to make it work between the three of us. I took Lola back to the house, telling Adele not to go to too much trouble, telling her Lola needed time.

'But it was a complete waste of time. Whenever she could, Lola stole something, usually food. And if I took her into my studio space to keep her away from Adele, then Adele got jealous.'

'So it became easier to take her out somewhere else?'

'Yes. I just picked her up straight from school and we'd go out for tea. Not that that worked either!'

'Bad behaviour even when you were out?'

'Oh God, yes! She was difficult about almost everything, demanding sweets, presents, refusing to speak if she didn't get what she wanted.'

My life seemed to have run aground. Adele couldn't get pregnant and started having tests. Helen was barely speaking to me and, naturally enough, I blamed her for Lola's behaviour.

'I think I was unfair to Helen,' I say slowly. 'And then I lost my job.'

All the time I had taken off to pick Lola up from school had been noticed. She was seven, nearly eight, by now. The whole country was swept up in New Labour fever. Optimism was in the air, but the ground remained as muddy as ever for those of us close to it. With no income from me and no child on the way, I was less of an attractive proposition for Adele.

'I had finished the portrait of myself. It was, I felt, accurate. But there was no one to tell me what to do next.'

I was thirty-five years old. This should have been the prime of my life. I was aware that women still looked at me with a certain interest; I was tall, fit, attractive even, to some. Yet all energy had drained out of me. The world was reduced once more to a small area of darkness.

'Most of life, in any case, consists of vast tracts of time spent in forgettable monotony,' I tell you.

Unexpectedly, you nod. The ceiling light seems to have a surge of power and the insect on the wall moves slightly. I feel dizzy.

'Only occasionally,' you say quietly, 'is it punctuated by events worth remembering.'

Taken aback, I blink and am lost for words. The walls glow a softer shade of green. I tell you the next three years that followed were simply a void for me. I had become skilled at forgetting, devious with my own thoughts, clever at tricking myself. Lola's withdrawal did not happen overnight, you understand, but bit by hostile bit.

'In the end, all the years of her early attachment to me might just as well never have existed.'

Helen contributed to the exercise almost without knowing. She was glad to see the back of me, glad to have me out of her bed. It was much simpler for her. She got to keep Lola and the house. The pain was entirely self-inflicted, but I was getting into deeper and deeper waters, fighting with Adele, unable to find a job. A kept man.

Then one day, pretending to go out looking for work, I found myself drifting towards the National Gallery. I had not been back since that terrible day. Once inside, the sombre Rembrandt gloom suited my mood. Hardly aware of what I was doing, my feet took on a will of their own and I found myself in front of Lola's favourite painting. Staring at the two-egg whiteness, without warning, my eyes filled with tears. What had I broken? And, in a slow, sad refrain, I heard Ma's voice once more:

'Son, you cannot go on this way. What's done is done. Find some direction, now. Please.'

I continued to stare at the painting, paralysed.

'I don't know how long I stood there,' I tell you.

Severed torsos floated before my eyes, carried on the river of my imagination. Mine was a born-at-the-wrong-time life, I remember thinking. So engrossed was I in self-pity, I did not notice the man who approached me until he was touching my arm.

'You okay, sir?' he asked.

The room swam under the curious stares of people to-ing and fro-ing. The man was elderly, one of the attendants.

'I found out later he was the most senior,' I tell you.

'What happened, then?'

I remember he didn't look English.

'I muttered something or other, I forget what. To my shame, tears were spilling on my face.'

I don't remember what happened next. He must have asked me a question, I suppose. Maybe we talked for a moment. I shrug.

'I think he suggested we have a cup of tea together. He was just about to go for his break. Not sure. Perhaps it was chance? Boredom on his part. Who knows?'

Wasn't life like that sometimes? Anyway, I tell you, I must have registered the kindness in his voice because I agreed to go with him. The strangest things are thrown up in the middle of a river, Elizabeth.

We went outside. I felt gravity cease to exist. People moved through their mysterious lives. The man took me across the road to a deli where the food was piled high against a glass window and the fritters and the falafel and the couscous salads waited to be consumed.

'He was called Hector.'

'Where is he now? Can we contact him?'

I shake my head.

'He died,' I tell you, shortly.

I refrain from self-pity. The truth is, I am glad he's no longer alive. I would not have wanted shame heaped on him by my actions.

'He found you the job?'

'Not straight away. First he gave me his friendship.'

That was almost all I wanted. We talked for so long that I remember the sun went down and a light summer rain began to fall. It was a sound that made me feel like crying again. For it spoke to me directly, telling me nothing could ever be the same.

'I no longer have a home,' I told Hector. 'The truth is, I haven't had a home for years, not since the day I lost Ma.'

I did not want Lola to be like me, I told him.

'She won't be,' Hector said. 'For a start, you aren't dead!'

I was numb, adrift from all connections.

'Perhaps it would have been better to have remained in Sri Lanka?'

'Nonsense,' Hector said. 'I'm a Turkish Cypriot. I left my home forty years ago. I was married to a Portuguese woman. We made a life together. Then suddenly she took off and left me. I have two sons. Oh, they're grown up now. So you see, it isn't uncommon. Now, pull yourself together. Remember you have what I would love to have!'

'What?'

'You have your youth.'

He laughed, unexpectedly. It was a good sound, the laughter of the happy underdog.

'First things first,' he said. 'You need a job.'

And that was how, staring at Lola's two white eggs, I got work at the National Gallery.

'The same day?' you ask.

'No, no. It took a few weeks.'

Meanwhile, other things were happening. Job or no job, Adele knew, as I did, that things were over between us.

'In the end, there was an event between the two of them that brought things to a head.'

'Adele and Lola? I thought you stopped taking Lola back to your place?'

'Well, I had tried to, but the problem was that Adele hated us meeting out of the house, too. So for Lola's tenth birthday we all went out for a meal, together.'

Things would be safer out of the house, I thought.

'We went for a pizza. Adele booked a table. Pizza was Lola's favourite food.'

I had secretly bought a cake and given it to the waiter to bring out after the meal with ten lighted candles.

'Lola seemed excited when I met her. I had bought her a new bicycle. And some books.'

In spite of Adele's protests, I took the presents to the school so she could open them straight away. Everything was fine. We went to the park and then on to the restaurant. Adele had taken time off work so we could eat early. But the trouble started as soon as Lola saw Adele.

'Daddy, why does Adele look so ugly today?' she asked.

I remember I wasn't angry to start with, just surprised at this uncalled-for rudeness. Of course I told her to apologise, instantly, and of course she wouldn't. Then Adele started:

'Doesn't your mother teach you any manners?'

Well, that did it.

'Yes, she does,' Lola said. 'And she teaches me to be honest, doesn't she, Dad?'

Oh God, then I got cross. Our pizzas arrived, but no one was eating. Lola still wouldn't apologise, Adele was close to tears and actually I felt sorry for her, for a change. I didn't know what to do. I kept uttering ultimatums, while Lola just sat there looking out of the window.

'In the end I smacked her.'

'You smacked her?'

'Yes, Elizabeth. I did.'

'And what happened after that? Chaos, I imagine?'

I look at you grimly and you shake your head.

'You're right. Adele instantly looked pleased and Lola instantly started screaming. Everyone was watching and this made her scream all the more. She just raised the roof. The waiter came over. I told him to forget about the cake. He tried to make us take it with us, but it was no use. We paid. And left, with me dragging Lola by the arm.'

I stop talking. A shudder runs through me. Lola was screaming abuse at Adele, shouting at me, telling me how she hated me.

'I took her home and when Helen opened the door she simply fled into the house. Then I went back to face the music with Adele.'

The next day Helen telephoned me and said Lola was never to meet Adele again.

'You can imagine what that did to my relationship!'

When I next saw my daughter, I told her that if she ever behaved so badly again I would never see her.

'You said *what*?'

'I was at the end of my tether.'

'But you were still seeing Lola?'

'Yes, yes. The visits were briefer, but they were still regular.'

Adele was the problem now, with her infertility. Listening to her sobs from the darkness of our shared bed, I counted the many beds I had lain on, beside people for whom I felt nothing. It was time to go. So I left.

'I got myself a small room and soon after began working at the National Gallery.'

The pay wasn't good, the shifts were long, but I didn't mind.

'I could meet Lola on my days off. I didn't mind the late closings. In fact, those were the best times of all. The later it got, the more the rooms emptied of visitors. That was the moment when the pictures came into their own.'

'Tell me about the Pieros,' you say, very quietly, but I shake my head.

Not yet.

'You went to Italy, didn't you?'

'Yes,' I say impatiently.

'Was that because of Charles Boyar?'

You know it was, I think. So why are you asking? Resentment resurfaces.

'Tell me about him,' you insist. 'How you met him, what happened . . . Tell me.'

I am breathless. It was bound to happen. We were bound to get to this point.

'I was introduced to him by someone called Alex Benson.'

I see you tense up. The lawyer in you is alert to possibilities.

'Alex used to visit the National Gallery,' I say.

Haunt it, was more the word that sprang to mind. He was nearly always the first visitor to arrive at the gallery. Hector introduced me to him.

That day we were on the same shift.

'By now, Hector had become my protector. A mentor of a kind, the father I would have liked to have had.

'Hector's own sons, living in Gozo, no longer needed him and I filled the space.'

'Tell me about Alex.'

'What d'you want to know?'

'Did you like him?'

You are alert, watching me. I choose my words carefully.

'Not a man I could relate to,' I say.

'How so?'

I am silent, not wanting to say too much.

'You don't like him?'

'It isn't that, exactly.'

I must be careful, I think. This man might help my case. But then I think, why do I care about my useless case?

'He's a hard man,' I tell you. 'Unlike Charles Boyar.'

'Interesting,' you say.

Alex was writing a novel based on Rembrandt's life. On that particular day, when I met him, I happened to see him in room 23 where the Rembrandts are hung.

'I recognised him and decided to ask him about the Pieros.'

'He does remember you vaguely,' you tell me, and I almost smile. The lawyer has been doing her homework, I think. Well, they did say you were the best barrister I could hope to have.

'Yes,' I say smoothly. 'That first conversation was brief. Although I did meet him again after that, in Italy.'

I don't want to talk about Alex Benson, so instead I tell you how I asked him about the Piero della Francescas that I had become interested in. Alex said there was very little information on Piero.

'You should talk to Charles Boyar,' he told me, with half-hearted interest.

I was just a gallery attendant, after all.

'Charles Boyar is the expert,' Benson said.

I told him I only knew the curators by sight. We were the

front-of-house men and women who guarded the paintings. Invisible people, unnoticed, unimportant. He didn't seem interested.

'Just a minute,' you say, raising your hand, looking through your notes.

I wait.

'You haven't told me why you were so keen on the Piero della Francesca paintings in the first place,' you say, finally. 'You need to tell me that first.'

All right. I will tell you.

'One morning I was moved to a different part of the gallery.'

I remember gazing without much interest at the gilded altar-paintings of saints.

There were room after room of these two-dimensional figures in static prayer. I found them depressing. I was on the early shift and was seeing Lola after her piano lesson that afternoon. I could not afford to be late. Things were tricky between us. I didn't want to rock any boats.'

I was to collect her and take her to the park near her home. She would have her bicycle with her, so there was no point in bringing her back into town. However much I told her to leave her bicycle at home, on the days I picked her up, she ignored me.

'I was staring at a painting, thinking about Lola, when a voice interrupted me.

'"Have you looked in on Room 65, Ras?"'

It was another attendant, a woman, someone who made a point of always talking to me in the staff room.

'I had a vague sense she hunted me out when our breaks co-incided.'

'Take a look at *The Baptism of Christ*,' she said. 'Piero della Francesca.'

I had never heard of him.

Windowless and small, empty of visitors, the room was entirely mine. I stared. The painting that caught my eye first was almost square in shape. There was so little paint in the foreground and it had a curiously unfinished look. Or perhaps someone had cleaned it too vigorously, I thought. And removed some of the pigment. There was a sense of dust and abandonment that reminded me of some other place, as yet unidentifiable. The child lying naked on the ground lifted his trembling arms towards his mother. Vulnerable, exposed, newly born. While above him, perched in unusual stillness on the roof of a ruined shed, was a solitary magpie.

'In Sri Lanka,' I tell you, 'they say a lone magpie heralds sorrow.'

Already, I felt, in this painted nativity was a forewarning, but no one was heeding it.

'And only then did I see the look on the young mother's face, the blue and the red of her dress, her lovely serenity. And in that moment I realised these were the exact colours that I had used in that bombed-out, dusty church from long ago.'

Far away in the distance, in the painted landscape of winding river and laurel trees, was a place that seemed puzzlingly familiar. Was this Italy? I asked myself.

I had no idea how long I stood gazing at the painting, astonished by those curiously secret, beautiful faces. Finally the supervisor came and moved me on. But the image stayed imprinted on my mind for days, its dust-filled air haunting my dreams. I knew I needed to find out more about the painter.

'So when did you actually meet Charles?'

'A day or so later. He came into the room where the Pieros were. I saw his badge and boldly introduced myself.'

'And Alex Benson?'

I shake my head.

'Nothing more until Italy.'

71

'Are you certain?'

'Of course. Why shouldn't I be?'

'How did Charles get you on the trip to Italy in the first place?' you ask, writing furiously.

I swallow my irritation. You are not really interested in Piero's art, I think. You just want to know what happened next.

'If you only knew how weary I am of this story. I have repeated it over and over again. I believe it has been plastered across every broadsheet around the world. Why ask me again?'

'No, no,' you say firmly. 'You misunderstand. I'm interested in your *first* trip to Italy. Not the second one, not yet, anyway.'

'I told you, I went there when Lola was seventeen,' I say.

You look at me encouragingly. Your obvious curiosity fills me with resentment.

'Because you had by now fallen in love with the Pieros?' you ask sharply.

I can just imagine you in the courtroom. I can see the cut and lash of your tongue, wig on head, liquid glint of two blue eyes, the forward sweep of long lashes. Your face is suddenly alert, the cheekbones pronounced in the shadows that fall in this desolate room. Surprised, I find myself wondering if you are what is called beautiful. Perhaps it is only a trick of the light.

'Go on,' you say.

I notice you are wearing a jacket of some soft blue material, matched almost exactly by your eyes. Did you hold it up against your face in a mirror this morning, comparing its colour with your eyes? How lovely your eyes are. You are looking at me, lips parted, no doubt wondering what this old coloured man is thinking. The room expands slightly. I notice that the tops of the skirting boards are covered by a thin line of darker grey paint.

'I had asked Charles why there was hardly any information on Piero della Francesca and he told me there had been a few interesting papers written for a conference on him recently.

'It was clear I was interested, so he talked to me about *The Baptism of Christ*.'

I was fascinated, not having known until then what an art historian could do with a picture. How he could collect a story from it, like a hummingbird siphoning nectar from a single rose. I found this magical.

'D'you see the straight road?' he asked me, pointing. 'See, it runs to the city gate. It was the road that identified the town of Sansepolcro and the valley of the volcanic crater in which it nestles. It was from those hills that the water from the Tiber spilt into the valley below.'

I told him I loved the name Sansepolcro, already. But I had no idea where it was.

'It's in Tuscany,' he said solemnly.

Then, seeing my face, he added, 'In Italy, in a place of enormous perfection.'

There was nothing superior about him, nothing present except his enthusiasm for the painting. I could not decide his age, but I was instantly drawn to the man.

'Look,' he said, 'see how light penetrates all the way to the bottom of the riverbed? People called it the Miracle of Jordan.'

I was puzzled by his words, for I had heard something similar before but couldn't think where.

'It was an ancient tradition,' Charles said. 'At the moment of baptism the river, seeming to recognise Christ, reversed its flow.'

And then, in a flash I remembered. Ma had told me this story.

That was when I decided I would bring Lola here on our next access day. To tell her what her grandmother had told me.'

I joined the National Gallery library after that and began to spend as much time as I could in their reading room. I looked for everything I could find on the early Renaissance in Italy. There were many things I didn't understand.

'And did you?' you ask me, unexpectedly. 'Did you take Lola there?'

I shake my head.

'No. She wouldn't come.'

I am silent.

'Sometimes when I went to the library Charles was there, too,' I continue. Whenever he saw me he made a point of speaking to me and once he gave me a photocopied essay that he thought would be of interest. He was a genuinely kind man. I told him I was curious about the ways in which the Christian story was represented in the paintings.

'I was brought up a Catholic,' I remember saying, 'but we never saw the pictures you have here.'

Western art and the images such as those I saw every day in the gallery had never reached our country, I told him. I don't know what made me tell him this, but I could see the idea interested him.

'No reason why they should have,' he said. 'Christianity and its reach was merely another part of the misguided story of Empire.'

I was struck by his honesty. No one, except that long-ago school teacher in Jaffna, talked in such a way.

That autumn, on my days off, I would often go back to the gallery as a visitor. At last I seemed to have found a small oasis of peace. It was my only solace, for now Lola and I had begun to move rapidly and irrecoverably apart.

'It wasn't entirely her fault, Elizabeth. I was to blame here, too.'

Briefly, I began a relationship with a gallery attendant, the one who had urged me to visit the Pieros. You are looking at me strangely, Elizabeth. Is the truth working against me, yet again?

'I missed picking Lola up from school three times.'

'How on earth did you manage that?' you ask.

74

You sound outraged and I bow my head.

'I see,' you say.

'I forgot, yes. They rang Helen at work. It took her ages to get to the school. The class teacher took Lola home for tea . . . Oh, it was a mess!'

'So you alienated your former wife, too.'

'Yes.'

The after-school visits tapered out for a while.

'I went round to see Helen. Took her flowers, bought Lola presents.'

Eventually, after much persuading, Lola came out with me to the gallery and I talked to her about the paintings.

'But it was clear she was only doing her duty.'

'How old was she now?'

'Oh, twelve . . . no, perhaps not quite. She was bored anyway, often sulky, wanting to be with her friends instead of me.'

'Well, that *is* understandable, isn't it?'

Yes, Elizabeth, yes. I know it is. But I still felt terrible about it.

Then one afternoon, when I was at another low point and the September air was masquerading as August, I bumped into Charles. I had not seen him for ages but the moment he saw me, he smiled. Was his friendliness fake? I didn't think so. Without hesitation, he invited me into his office.

'The room was high above the rooftops of central London,' I tell you, and you appear to write down my words.

I could see swallows and hear the sound of traffic as a faint smudge in the distance. Somewhere out of my sightline was Nelson. Bookshelves and posters covered the walls. On his desk were objects of beauty, pieces of history, from Africa, from Egypt, from India. Evidence of a cultured life lay scattered all around.

'You like the view?' Charles asked, peering at me.

'It's much more than the view,' I said.

And I told him about the Jaffna school teacher's house that I had once seen as a boy.

'Nothing as grand as this,' I said, pointing to the book-lined walls, 'but it, too, was a room from a different kind of life.'

Charles looked curiously at me.

'Do sit down,' he said, pulling out a chair.

Outside, birds wheeled in large circles around a cloudless sky as I told him about the northernmost tip of land that had once been my home. I did not want to tell him the country was Sri Lanka. I had noticed people were impatient with the place. So I let him think it was somewhere in India.

'A land full of sorrow,' I told him, and I was struck by his face as he listened. Here was a man who might, in a different sort of life, have been my friend.

I told him about the fresco I had painted on the ruined church and the toy truck I had been holding at the time Ma had been killed. I had carried it halfway across the world, turning it into a symbol of beauty, a piece of my own history that sat somewhere on a shelf in my daughter's room.

'I didn't know that,' Ma's voice interrupted me, coming from a long distance of sea and sky.

You have missed so much of my life, Ma, I thought. Charles smiled at me and offered me tea. The afternoon wore on while we talked and thoughts of Lola faded slightly. I told him about the railway station that no longer had trains connecting to the rest of the country and how this had made us feel so awfully cut off from the world. Then, picking up the wooden figures on his bookshelf, I told him about the army looters who stole our ancient artefacts to sell in other parts of the world.

'This is the kind of place I come from,' I said.

Still he did not ask me where it was but listened gravely, not saying much, giving me space to speak. Even Hector, for all his kindness, would not have understood.

'So you see,' I told him, finally, smiling apologetically, 'this is why Western art has passed me by. I have been too busy longing for some kind of art of my own.'

I fell silent, abruptly. I wasn't sure how interested Charles was and suddenly I was embarrassed. What a fool I was to talk in this way, I thought. But then he spoke.

'You are a fresco painter,' he said, shaking his head, smiling, 'who has never been to the land of frescoes! We must see what we can do about that.'

'Ah! So that was when you went?' you say, interrupting this long monologue.

I hold up my hand. Elizabeth, please, don't simplify the events of my life. I stop. And wait for you to finish what you are writing.

'No, that came later. I'll tell you about that another time.'

You continue writing, furiously. What can you have to write so much about?

'All in all, in the five years that followed,' I say, 'I hardly saw Lola. A dozen times, perhaps? Birthdays, after the event, so she could collect her present. Christmas, if I was lucky. And when I did see her, she was rude to me and we fought. I suppose I was jealous of her relationship with Helen. Besides, adolescence was beginning to change her. I couldn't fight that, could I?'

I think for a moment.

'Actually, she wasn't pleasant company, you know. So what was the point?'

Suddenly exhausted, I am unable to go on.

'You never tried to talk to her? About what had gone wrong?' you ask.

I shake my head.

'What was there to talk about? She disapproved of my life, clearly, and she wanted to take charge of her own decision-making, I'm guessing.'

'I see,' you say. 'So she had suddenly become the one in charge?'

I cannot look at you. I'm not sure you understand or can even sympathise, but I tell you how I limped on from day to day. Hardly aware of how I felt, catching only brief glimpses of my daughter. The change, begun on the day she floated islands of scones in her orange juice, was now almost complete.

'At fourteen Lola was tall for her age. Her figure could no longer be mistaken for that of a child.'

Lola, my Lolita, child of my loins, flesh of my flesh, what had I done to you?

By the time she was seventeen, I was on the move again. I rented a room close to where my brother lived and contacted Helen. I wanted to try once more to patch things up.

'She doesn't want to see you,' Helen said, before I could explain. 'I'm not being difficult. She's bored with your life.'

That night, after many years of silence, I rang Sam. Then I went over to his place and wept. I cried for the longest time.

'Well?' Sam said, finally.

His face was set in the same expressionless mask I remembered. He shrugged. What can you expect? his shrug said.

'I don't know what to do, Brother,' I told him.

I spoke in Tamil. Grief for me is always best expressed in Tamil.

'Help me,' I begged.

'You want to forget?' he asked. 'Or start a new life? Which?'

I felt a new harshness beneath his words. I noticed he had new gold fillings. My brother, I saw without envy, was richer than I was. He had passed me by.

'Both.'

He looked satisfied.

'Well, then,' he said, 'first I must tell you that I am involved in a new and daring venture. We have bought a plane. And we are organising an attack on some Government headquarters in Colombo. The time has come to kill a few of those bastards. But in order for me to help you, you must come to the meetings. Get involved, give money, care about those less fortunate than yourself.'

He is wrong, I thought. His barely hidden aggression was not to my taste. But then again, I thought, maybe this way I would forget my own mistakes.

'How old is Lola now?' he asked.

'Seventeen.'

'Tell her, the next time you speak to her, I would like to see her.'

I nodded.

I went back to see Helen after that, determined and ready to blame her.

'You must try to persuade her to see me,' I said. 'She needs both parents in order to develop normally.'

'Pity you didn't think of that earlier!'

'Helen, I have never stopped loving her,' I pleaded. 'What I feel about Lola gets in the way of everything else I try to do, every new start I try to make. You know this is true!'

'I don't want to hear about your problems,' she said quickly.

But just for a minute, her voice had softened very slightly.

'Don't you know, Elizabeth?' I ask, forgetting, for a moment, who I am talking to, 'We never truly forget the nuances that exist in a discarded relationship. How strange this is. How does such knowledge remain long after love itself has fled?'

You look at me with an expression I cannot identify.

I was aware that in some corner of her heart Helen was sorry for me. But I knew, too, that she would do nothing for me.

'She had found a new life, you see,' I tell you. 'With someone else.'

It gave her the excuse to pretend I had no part in Lola's life.

6

Blue is a colour with infinite depth

What's this, Elizabeth? Today, you come with a present for me.
I am silenced by the unexpectedness of it. A recording from an
opera on an old portable cassette player?

'For me?' I ask, surprised.

'It's only the second act,' you say, as if this makes some sort of
difference. 'When Rigoletto is betrayed and loses his daughter.
Do you ever listen to opera?'

I shake my head, unable to speak. Your blue eyes appear to be
mocking me. Thin light seeps in from the corridor; soft, grey-
green in colour. No, no, don't turn the light on. I want to bathe
in natural light, however distant, however faint. There are shadows where none were a moment ago. Today the mark on the
wall looks like a dragonfly in flight. I feel less tense without the
strip lighting; but then the warden comes in and says we must
have the light on. As if this green twilight is dangerous; as if I
might escape through it.

I spent last night reminding myself you are doing only slightly
more than your job requires. Alone, in the darkened cell, with
only a pale moon as company, I made a drawing of your hands.
From memory. Staring at it, I felt beyond the inhabited world,
isolated from all of life. The window was a weightless, barred

eye. A straight line led from the moon to my eye. Other heavenly bodies twinkled with cosmic joy. They were laughing, I thought, at the smallness of a being that possessed only a talent for suffering. I blink, remembering.

We continue to sit in silence. You are the first to break it.

'I felt I pushed you too hard,' you say.

You sound embarrassed.

'On yesterday's visit, I mean. I was trying to get you to be as accurate as possible.'

You wave your hands in circles. I watch them and once again a rogue thought circles my head. What lovely long fingers, I think. What would you say if I gave you my drawing?

'What's the weather like outside?' I ask, instead.

'The bluebells are out. Miles and miles of them.'

In the woods behind your house, you tell me. I try to picture your house and fail. Your life is shrouded in mystery, Elizabeth, I think. I might as well try to imagine travelling to last night's moon. Almost as though you read my mind, you tell me something about yourself. Not much; just enough to give me a glimpse. A door opens a fraction, and I catch sight of another life.

'It isn't a grand house,' you say, sounding diffident. 'But in summer there are dark, almost black, roses, growing all over the door.'

You tell me you have lived there for years. The way you say it makes me wonder what those years have been like. I have a moment's certainty: you haven't always been happy.

'It was my father's house,' you say, and then you close the door.

Why is it so rare for human life to connect? I was told you were one of the best barristers in this field and that I was lucky to have you, for free. The most humane. I can't remember who said that, but I promise to listen to your opera.

'Today you don't have to talk about the past,' you tell me.

You feel I need a rest from it, you laugh. You have a lovely laugh, Elizabeth. I wonder how many people have told you this. With an aching feeling, I understand some of the things I missed in my life. Conversations such as the ones we've been having, for a start. The room begins to close in on me.

'Nonsense,' you say briskly, in answer to something I must have said. 'This isn't the end.'

And although you can promise me nothing, not if my daughter will ever reply to your e-mails, nor if my sentence will be long, still, you feel there are some good things in store.

'I want to tell you about Italy, now,' I say, making up my mind.

You nod. If that's what you want, your nod seems to mean.

'Now is as good as any other time.'

'Lola was seventeen,' I begin, and then I stop speaking.

I see a picture so clear that it brings me to my knees. Her hair falling over her face, the look of concentration as she bites her bottom lip. Of what is she thinking? What is she grappling with? Her eyes are angry. They have been angry since she was six. But she is tall, like a Jaffna Tamil girl. When she walks towards me, she moves her hips unconsciously in a way that reminds me of Ma.

'I will never love anyone as much as I love Lola. Except Ma.'

There is a tiny pause. I swallow.

'Do you think that was why all your relationships haven't worked?'

'Probably.'

Nothing has ever been resolved in my life, I tell you. I see from your eyes that you agree.

'That's what all these talks have been about,' you say. 'Getting a clearer picture.'

And then you tell me that Lola looks like me, and for the

second time today you leave me beyond speech. What are you doing to my heart, Elizabeth? In this room of such little light?

'The first time I saw her, when I delivered your letter, that's what I thought,' you insist.

Lo, Lo-La, my girl with the dark eyes. My dearest daughter. Memories come back to me in shreds, like the long wisps of smoke trailing from the burning homes in Jaffna.

'Some time later Charles Boyar came looking for me,' I say.

You have begun scribbling in your notebook. I breathe deeply. I hadn't seen him for a while, I tell you. I believe he had been away in Italy working on his book.

'Ah!' he said, when he saw me. 'Hello, Ras. How are you?'

He remembered my name. I was delighted.

'I've been thinking about you and your love of the Pieros. I'm taking a party to Urbino in the spring. To see *The Flagellation*. Would you be interested in coming?'

Taken aback, I stammered. How could I tell him I would never be able to afford it? My new flat had two rooms. It was more expensive than the last. He hesitated.

'Don't worry about the cost,' he said. 'We always carry one subsidised place for staff. You only need a small deposit. The main thing is, would you like to join us?'

He looked encouragingly at me.

'What about Hector?' I asked.

Hector was about to retire; perhaps he would like a holiday.

'Hector's been to Italy many times. And he'll be going back to Cyprus in the summer, anyway. But you'll enjoy this trip. It's only for four days. Do – if you feel you want to.'

I blinked.

'By now I was no longer painting, Elizabeth.'

There was no real space in the place I had moved into. The landlord made spot inspections and the smell of oils would have given it away. I didn't want to get thrown out.

But I was reading a lot. I had been reading about landscape painting after the Renaissance. So the thought of a trip to Italy was hard to resist.

'Good. That's settled then,' Charles said. 'I'll send you details. We've got your address, haven't we?'

And with a wave of his hand he was off down the corridor at tremendous speed, to some meeting or other.

That night I allowed myself to be excited. All week I had been unhappy because Lola had cancelled another meeting with me. It was the third cancellation in a row. But now I had something else to think about. And later on I dreamed I was back home, walking along the beach with Ma and Sam. In my dream the blueness of the sea was a colour of infinite depth. It burnt down into the very centre of my body. It was so pure that it brought tears to my eyes.

'Why are you crying?' Ma asked in my dream.

Even in my dream she sounded sad. But Sam had walked ahead of us and didn't want to look at the sea. I woke then, and remembered the trip to Italy. Getting out of bed, I went to make myself a cup of tea. It was five in the morning. I felt like a person who had suffered a long illness. Everything had been erased, every feeling, all memories. Only an endless blankness remained. Italy might help me, I thought.

'Are you okay to go on?' you ask, breaking the spell.

'Yes, Elizabeth,' I say.

We flew into Pisa with its wedding-cake tower. The Alps were still snow-capped. The air was clear and when we landed there were strange smells of coffee and cigarettes. It was the first time I had been out of Britain since I left Sri Lanka. The shock of arriving at a destination that had nothing to do with my past lifted my spirits in a most extraordinary way. And almost immediately the thing that hit me was the unfamiliar sounds of the language. The lilt and hurried cascade of words, the unfamiliar gestures, fingers drawing imaginary lines in the air, laughter that was loud, all of it, left me speechless with wonder. How had such a place existed without my knowledge? With no warning at all I felt my heart rise at the sounds around me.

'A coach took us to a hotel somewhere in the interior,' I say.

It was dark by the time we got there. There were no mountains to be seen but we knew they were there, obscured by the night, visible from beneath the stars. I had my own room with a shower.

'The floors were covered with simple terracotta tiles, the sort that suggested this was a place normally hot in summer.'

Although that night it was freezing.

'We ate a simple meal of pasta and pesto and drank a delicious local wine. I was tired and so, excusing myself from the rest of the party, I went to bed.'

Everyone had been quite friendly but there was no sign of Charles. Later I lay in my narrow bed, piled up with blankets, listening to the utter silence all around.

'And in that moment I realised there had never been a time in my life without noise. Peace such as this was something alien to me.'

I lay for a long time thinking of Lola, wishing I could have brought her here when she was small. Towards midnight, the church clock chimed the hour faintly in the distance and some time after I must have fallen into a dreamless sleep.

The next morning we were up for an early start. In daylight the whole valley was quite a different place. The sun was out and now we had a sense of how hot the summer would eventually be.

'Our first stop was Monterchi,' I tell you. 'To see the *Madonna del Parto*. Then after lunch we planned to move on to Arezzo to see the *Legend of the True Cross*.'

'So it was a proper trail of the Piero paintings,' you say, sounding surprised.

'Oh yes! Absolutely. A day later we were to go to Urbino before flying back to London.'

Charles met us at Monterchi.

'He had come by car and joined us in the little museum.'

I stop talking, wondering how on earth I can describe what I saw there.

'The fresco of the Madonna is very beautiful,' I say lamely. 'Have you seen it?'

You shake your head.

'Ah, then you should,' I tell you. 'The face of the pregnant Virgin is very, very still. This is a painting about peace. She wears a dress of deepest blue.'

Charles gave us a brief talk about the history of the fresco. How it had been painted for a chapel in the cemetery at Monterchi.

'In the Second World War,' he said, 'the locals bricked it in for fear of the Germans damaging it.'

Afterwards we went to the café that's just next door, where a small crowd of local people were having a heated argument. Not understanding, we stood, listening, while Charles translated for us in an amused way. The owner of the bar was in the middle of a heated argument with the priest, who refused to commit himself until the bishop gave his verdict. Fascinated, we watched as the mayor himself arrived. The fuss was apparently over a young pregnant woman from the area. Only two days previously she was thought to be carrying a handicapped baby, but this morning she had given birth to a perfectly healthy child. Some of the women in our group began to clap, and at this, the owner of the bar grinned and handed round shots of grappa, pointing out the proud father. The woman, he told Charles, had come regularly to the museum to pray before the fresco of the Madonna del Parto. She had wanted a miracle. And now, he said, she had got one.

'What do you expect?' an English voice cried. 'This is Italy, after all!'

After a leisurely lunch we moved on to Arezzo and the much anticipated visit to see the *Legend of the True Cross*. It was blisteringly hot by now, but the church was wonderfully cool. And there it was, stretching above us in an endless canopy of scenes. With the distant, frescoed hills, burnt to the ashen colour that the real hills would soon become. A horseman rode a lonely road, past white trees, towards a castle. Above him a few clouds floated in the pink-painted dawn. And everywhere were the Piero figures: aloof people, engaged in some obscure drama spanning centuries and continents. There were virgins and emperors, dying warriors and men in tall hats with the faces of remorseless judges, all with the same impenetrable stillness. Mesmerised, I noticed how the paint had faded in places, leaving naked stretches of wall, blotting out half a battle, the legs of a torturer or the face of a young woman. An incredible array of wounded and fallen men lay across that vaulted ceiling, their unsmiling handsome faces and eyelids as heavy as stone, looking down at us with a perpetual detachment and even, I felt, a kind of contempt. Spellbound, I could not take my eyes away. Like that day in the National Gallery, the moment became fixed. And then, once again, like the scent of perfume returning, came the memories from over thirty years ago. I saw myself choosing, without understanding, the burnt umbers, the ochres, the cadmium reds; colours that had not yet, in those early troubled days, acquired a meaning but already held me in their grip.

Outside, in the sleepy half-shuttered town, the barometer continued to rise and after a while, when we had sat and contemplated the frescoes, or wandered about in the cool apse, we broke into smaller groups, some going in search of shade and an ice cream, others to take photographs. I went off on my own, walking through the narrow deserted streets. I had forgotten the sense of freedom that comes with warm weather. The sun fell on my back. I kept looking at the marvellously blue sky as I thought of the woman to whom a miracle had been granted today.

At dinner that night I felt disadvantaged by more or less everything. The other guests were dressed for the occasion. I looked around for Charles but he seemed to have disappeared, once again. There was nothing for it but to join everyone at the long table.

'He's gone to meet his wife,' the woman next to me told me. 'I'm dying to see her. Apparently she's much younger. He was a bachelor for years, you know, and then he fell madly in love with her. Romantic, isn't it!'

She laughed.

'I'm Pam, by the way,' she said. 'You know we're to be invited to his house on the last night? I'm looking forward to it. Charles is an interesting man, don't you think?'

I was served a bowl of pasta.

'Do you know him well?' I asked, for something to say.

'Oh yes, I was on the course he ran last year on the Renaissance. His courses are the most popular, they get filled up the moment they're advertised. What about you? How d'you know him?'

'I work at the National Gallery.'

'Oh, really! Are you one of the curators? Should I know you?'

Shame, like spilt wine, spread over me. I avoided her eyes.

'No.'

'What do you do then? Oh, sorry, I didn't catch your name.'

'I am Ras.'

'So, what do you do at the National, Ras?' she insisted.

I could see a piece of basil stuck between her teeth. She took another sip of wine and the basil disappeared.

'I'm an attendant,' I said heavily.

It had been a long day. The wine was giving me a headache.

'Oh!'

We ate our lamb in silence. Then:

'Where are you from?' she asked.

'Sri Lanka.'

'*Really?*'

She brightened up.

'That's funny! I've recently come back from a holiday in Sri Lanka. We went all over the island, Sid and I. The expat life is pretty wonderful, really.'

I told her I had no idea.

'No, I suppose not.'

She laughed.

'Well, I can tell you it is. Wow! On our last night we went to the American Embassy for a garden party. My goodness, they know how to entertain. Their parties are much more lavish than the British.'

I stopped eating. Pam's face was close to mine, she smelt of fat from the lamb.

'Forty years ago I did voluntary work in Sri Lanka. That's how I know. Nothing's changed. That's Sid over there, by the way,' she said, pausing for breath. 'He's my husband.'

She reached for the bottle and poured more wine into her glass. Then she took another mouthful of food.

'There were lots of roadblocks on this visit. And the people were more on edge than on our previous visit. The President is nicknamed "Mugabe"! Did you know that? Anyway, thankfully, Westerners are not targeted.'

'Good God, Ras!' you interrupt me, loudly, dropping your pen. 'What did you say?'

I look up, mildly surprised by your tone, and I see your face has become flushed. Why, Elizabeth? You are angry? The mark on the wall has doubled in size. I can't make out its shape today.

'What a bitch!'

I am startled by how sweet your unexpected anger in my defence feels. Shaking my head, I ask you, What was there to say? The woman went on and on talking about her trip.

'There were some bea-u-tiful outdoor pools,' she told me, closing her eyes. 'You could watch the hawks circling overhead while you swam. Hard life, eh! We did loads of shopping, picking up bits and pieces, a birthday present for my daughter, Jo, things for the house. We went to Ethagama and Kosgoda and later in that week we went on to Batti, which, as you probably know, is *still* a war zone. We had to be very careful of course.'

I watched, mesmerised, as she pursed her lips to form a perfect 'O'. Crows' feet clambered across her sunburnt face.

'Batti?' I asked.

'Batticaloa. Sid called it Batti because the idea of a war in such a place seemed so batty!'

She laughed at her own joke. The meal wound down, coffee was being served. I pleaded tiredness and headed for my room. As I left, I heard her speaking to her neighbour.

'What a serious young man!' she said, not bothering to lower her voice. 'Too good looking to be on his own, eh?'

I did not sleep well that night. Several times I woke, frightened and perspiring. The pillow under my head was wet and twisted like wrung-out washing. Pam's descriptions of Sri Lanka were not anything I recognised. A phantom, other, heart throbbed within me. We Jaffna Tamils are not seen as people who struggle. We are told that time heals, I thought. But it is the opposite. The further away the trauma, the more the wound festers.

We left early the next morning after a hasty breakfast. I searched the dining room for Pam but thankfully she was busy talking to someone else and didn't notice me. Then on the coach I managed to get a seat on my own, for lack of sleep had left me tired and dispirited. I couldn't face the thought of talking to anyone. The drive to Urbino was partly along the autostrada and partly through the mountains. It took most of the day. Through the coach window I watched a Tuscan landscape of pines and cypresses. The roads were empty, the sun was already up, but all I saw in my depressed state was death everywhere, hiding in the trees, waiting.

I looked at my own reflection in the window and saw instead the discarded faces of dead relatives. The light was no longer soft. It burned my eyes and was filled with a silent violence, and in the gentle hum of voices I felt only fear. Memory caught me by the throat on that long drive through the Apennines and began to play its tricks. I imagined I could see Ma through the window. Hugging me, laughing as I ran off, in that last moment of plenty. Never knowing I would be a child for just a few more hours. Leaving the image of that grave face, those eyes that would later ask for forgiveness through all eternity. I could not shake off such miserable thoughts.

The bus was slowing down. We had arrived. Before us was the fortification of the Palazzo Ducale, its walls filled with holes in which birds nested. There was a cheer from the front of the bus.

'Here we are!'

I felt feverish and could no longer bear to be part of this group. What on earth had possessed me to come on this trip, anyway? Panic gripped me. All for a few paintings done by a long-dead artist. The bus stopped. People began climbing down. I could see Pam ahead of me, still talking incessantly. I'm in no state for this, I thought, desperately. And then through the window of the coach I saw Charles Boyar waiting. Catching sight of me, he waved, and something lifted in my heart at the sight of his friendly face.

'Hello,' he greeted me as I stepped down. 'I'm sorry I didn't have a chance to speak to you last night. How did you enjoy the *True Cross*?'

I told him it had all been wonderful and he peered sharply at me and I fancied he caught something of my mood.

'I had to meet my wife at the airport,' he said. 'Her family were flying back to the States after a holiday and I had to say goodbye.'

He pulled a face and laughed.

'Is your wife American?' I ventured.

'Yes,' he said. 'She is. You'll meet her tomorrow. I'm taking everyone back to our house for dinner.'

I wondered what his wife felt about that. Helen would have gone insane at the thought of so many people she didn't know arriving unannounced. But perhaps this American was different.

'She loves entertaining,' Charles said. 'Now then, you have a treat in store for you. Ready, everyone?'

As always, his enthusiasm was infectious. Our group was clustered by the wall, noisily taking pictures of the rooftop view.

'I'm afraid no photographs when you are in the palace,' Charles told us.

There was a chorus of disappointed grumbles.

'Oh, how mean!' said Pam.

She was standing quite close to me. I could smell her perfume and her wine-soaked breath. Filled with a violent loathing, I pretended not to see her as we followed Charles into the palace.

'I must tell you, Elizabeth, I have never seen a building like it, before or since.'

You stop writing and look at me intently as I describe the marble stairs, stained in the softest of pinks, sweeping up towards the wide hall, the chandeliers that glowed from high ceilings and the old windowpanes, made that way in order to filter out the harshest sunlight. Rooms where centuries of use had made the handrail as frail and worn as a beloved's hand. I shake my head and stop speaking, unable to convey the magnificence of the place.

'Oh, but you have,' you reassure me softly, without taking your eyes off my face.

Momentarily, your expression distracts me.

Then I tell you how our group simply hurried past all of this, glancing only in a perfunctory way at the religious paintings, while I, on the other hand, held back, walked more slowly, drinking it in. I was flabbergasted by the airiness and the light in this extraordinary building.

'Ah! To have come from that to this!' I murmur.

Here and there were inscriptions in English: the Room of the Wedding of Federico and Battista with its fragments of frescoes which neither age nor wars had diminished in loveliness. But how had it survived? History moved before my eyes. In sharp comparison with my homeland. I thought again of the teacher who had first talked to me about art. In Sri Lanka, I thought bitterly, so few cared for our national treasures, our libraries, our precious buildings.

'Centuries from now, when tourists come to visit, what artefact, what iridescent fresco will they find?'

I laugh. Only bullet holes, Elizabeth, only ruins.

Crumbling temples, broken carvings, destroyed statues, dust. That's what I thought.

Anger, hard and invincible, took hold of me, so that quickly, in order to dispel it, I walked past those rooms in search of the others.

'And it was then, Elizabeth, that I saw with sudden clarity how it would *always* be for me. How everything in the world would connect in some awful and mysterious way with my early loss.'

The group seemed to have disappeared. I wandered on into different rooms, tombs that had no names. Charles had told us to look out for Raphael's *La Muta*, and now I stumbled across it stopping for a moment to gaze at the woman's inscrutable face. Here and there, in shaded corridors, were paintings of saints, pictures of the Virgin, the sleeping Christ. And always, everywhere I went, that final, terrible image of the figure on his gilded cross. But of the Piero there was no sign. Standing beside one of the high windows I gazed across the tops of the trees at the patchwork of terracotta rooftops that was the town of Urbino. From somewhere came the faint strains of organ music drawn out in one continuous note; rich and sorrowful. It seemed impossible that I should be here.

All of a sudden I heard Charles Boyar's voice and knew the painting could not be far off as, hastily, turning a corner, without fanfare or noise, I came upon it. Silenced, I could only stare. For with one hand on his hip, almost in the same attitude as the pregnant Madonna in Monterchi, the young lord of Urbino stood, barefoot and serene, between two expressionless men. Swallowing, I moved closer. What were these men plotting? Or perhaps they were arguing? What terrible irrevocable decision had they come to? Moving closer, I examined the rest of the painting, the part of it these men could not see themselves. Involved in their own concerns, they seemed not to have noticed the act of cruelty taking place with such elegance inside the building. Christ stood, an impassive figure, white-clad against a white column from which a light shone. The arms of the flagellators were raised languidly; Pontius Pilate watched with only a marginal interest. Suddenly, I was struck forcefully by this group of people, so preoccupied in their own concerns that they had no idea of the act of unimaginable awfulness taking place in a room close by. In a flash I connected it with my own life.

I stop speaking, for you are still staring at me, Elizabeth. You have written almost nothing in the last few minutes. Uneasily, for I cannot imagine what you might be thinking, I say the first thing that comes into my head.

'Do you know what Christ died of?' I ask you.

You move your head very slightly.

'Suffocation,' I say. 'Eventually, the position on the cross makes it impossible to go on inflating the lungs.'

You say nothing and I tell you.

'A slow, terrible death.'

The storm which had been threatening burst over Tuscany in the afternoon, washing dusty terraces, clearing the air. It stopped us going straight off for lunch. In any case, I wasn't hungry. I knew I would never see this painting again in my life and I wanted to look at it for as long as I could. People came and went silently as I stood stubbornly, rooted to the spot, gazing at it. In the end it was Charles who found me.

'Ah! So you found *The Flagellation!*' he said. 'I hope you aren't disappointed?'

I told him I was surprised at how small it was. I had expected something larger. I was finding it difficult to speak.

'And I didn't expect the sky to be so blue,' I added.

'A Tuscan sky,' Charles agreed, pointing towards the window, where the rain beat heavily down. 'But I'm afraid today is the exception.'

'The man in the middle,' I said, pointing, not knowing how to express my feelings.

We stood in silence, gazing at it.

'The greatest small painting in the world, in my opinion,' Charles murmured, finally. 'Yet no one knows what it means. It's an enigma.'

'The man in the middle . . .' I said, again.

'He's a ghost,' Charles said, adding quickly, 'I mean, *current* thinking is that he's dead, and that's why he stares straight ahead, ignoring the other two. The man on his right is possibly his father. In real life the Duke had just lost his only son. We think that is who the boy is meant to be.'

'Look,' I said, 'the Duke's got a thin piece of red cloth on his shoulder. I didn't see it at first.'

'Yes, well spotted!' Charles cried. 'It is generally thought he's about to appoint the man in the hat as a Cardinal and that the red scarf is an indication of this. It's all speculation, of course. Which is, in a way, part of the fun. We'll never know. So you can make your own interpretation, if you like.'

I told him I already had.

'The man with the tree behind him . . .'

'That's a laurel tree, see? A symbol of accolade,' Charles said. 'Or a triumph over adversity, if you like.'

'The man in front of it stands the same way as the figure of Christ,' I said. 'Look, his entire weight is resting on his left leg.'

'Bravo! We'll make an art historian of you.'

I smiled. The blackness of my earlier mood had lifted, slightly.

'How are you enjoying the trip so far?'

'Very much. I'll never forget it! Thank you!'

'Pleasure. And it's not over yet. Don't forget to look at the other pictures too. *The Madonna di Senigallia*, for instance. That's very beautiful too.'

But I could not take my eyes off *The Flagellation*. The more I looked, I told Charles, the more it spoke to me.

'I can see you're really bitten by the Piero bug,' Charles said, amused. 'Right, well, I'm going to the café where the others are. Take your time, no rush. We're leaving at about four. You'll find the shop on the other side of the courtyard, if you want to buy any postcards. Join us when you're ready.'

After he left I stood a moment longer. Time rolled away and I was transported to a sunlit place of my own. Where the deafening sounds of insects and the smell of wild fenugreek and my mother's voice calling to me had once been my entire world. I would paint it, I thought. I would paint my home. Outside, as is the way of all hot countries, the rain had swiftly cleared and the purple hills appeared to spread once more across a sky of infinite blue. Turning, I hurried towards the bookshop, wanting to buy Lola a postcard of the painting. I needed suddenly to reach out to her and repair the damage between us. For, having seen this painting, with the shock of the experience still glowing within me, I wanted to tell her what I had discovered. How it was that suffering always went hand in hand with indifference.

7

An altered perspective

'Don't you know, Elizabeth,' I ask, 'that the past, no matter how remote, simply lays the foundation for the present?'

You give me a look that suggests you think I'm straying off the point, again. But, surely you must see, stone after stone, all history is a foreshadowing of our existence.

I have no idea why I said this. I notice with new astonishment how fine your skin is. Quickly, but perhaps not quickly enough, I look away. We both fall silent. After a while I continue.

The sunlight had begun to bleed slowly from behind the mountains as we drove along the autostrada. The sky took on an appearance of marbled pink. I could see the evening would be long, for the sun was not ready to fade. Everyone was quiet in the bus as it sped towards the hotel where we were spending the night. I sat at the back, my head filled with the colour and images of saints and martyrs, of serene young women under laurel trees. The day's brilliance spun before my eyes. Charles Boyar had left separately to go to his house in the foothills of the Apennines. We would be dining there later.

We were travelling east following squadrons of starlings. It was still only five o'clock, still hot. In the last part of the afternoon, sitting in the walled garden, drinking tea, it had seemed as if summer had finally broken through and the air was filled with the scent of orange blossom. And although my sadness stayed like smoked glass between me and the light, it was less desperate now. In England, I thought, there was never enough warmth, never enough sun to give me a real sense of satisfaction. I could live here, I told myself. And then, with a clutch of pain, I remembered that, in England, Lola would be leaving school, walking home through the streets of Streatham, her long hair gleaming, her fingernails painted. Trying not to look like the schoolgirl she still was. At home I would be finishing my shift for the day. Maybe I would take one last look at a painting I was currently interested in, maybe, as this was Friday, I would rush back for my life class. Whatever it was, I would do it alone.

'Piero della Francesca was one of the first artists to paint emptiness,' Charles had said. 'There is no room in Piero's world for human feeling. He makes no attempt to get the observer to identify with the emotions of the actors in history, simply presenting it to us.'

Perhaps that was the reason his work had moved me so much. Muteness was something I understood.

Alongside us, through the window, I saw the hills of Tuscany once more, pale and waterless, dissolving into a higher mountain range. But still, here and there, dotted beside distant castles were trees that looked as though they had been painted by an Italian hand. I knew when I got back I would look at the paintings in the National Gallery in a completely different way because of this trip. I knew, too, I would not pass this way again. Eyes, look your last, I thought, there are ghosts everywhere.

The coach turned in the direction of Parma and we headed towards Pontremoli, our final stop for the night.

A few hours later, a different driver picked us up and took us to the Boyars' house. By now the sun had moved further down the valley and was just above the mountaintops, giving them an appearance of ever-deepening purple. The driver parked in a lay-by and we walked the rest of the way. Some of the women began to pick wild flowers to give Mrs Boyar as a present. Everyone was in a mood to party. Everyone, except me. The mantle of depression, having shifted, now descended with even greater weight. I could only put it down to the fact that we were leaving for England in the morning. We walked slowly up the steep road in single file, pausing to admire the spectacular view of the mountains covered in a cascade of greenery. Long ago I remember being told there were places in the hill country of Sri Lanka that were this way. Kandy, where the tea was grown; Nuwara Eliya, too. But I had never been to the hill country. I had never been anywhere in my own country, I thought.

Charles was waiting for us halfway along the dirt track. In the distance behind him we glimpsed the corner of a strawberry-pink villa. It looked just like a child's drawing of a house.

'Nearly there!' he called.

He had changed into a light pair of linen trousers and a white shirt, and seemed to have stepped straight out of the tropics. His wife, I forget her name, was waiting on the terrace. I pause.

'She was a very beautiful woman,' I tell you.

The sort of wife I would have expected a man like Charles to have. There was a son, too. Eight years old, I think.

'Delia!' I say suddenly and I see your jaw tighten. 'That was her name. I remember she said she *loved* laurel trees.'

'She's crazy about them,' Charles told me, looking at her.

I felt they were having a private joke. I felt their perfect ease with each other.

'It must be the mythology that hangs around them.'

We were standing on his terrace, sipping a glass of some fizzy wine in tall expensive glasses. The view was breathtaking.

'I want to plant them across that strip of our land,' Delia explained.

I heard the faintest trace of an American accent in her voice.

'Look! Do you see the ones already there? Right up to the little farmhouse on the other side?'

I looked to where she was pointing.

'There used to be a whole grove of blue laurels growing across this hillside,' she said. 'I would like there to be one again.'

Restorers, I thought. That was what these people were. The other side of the Imperialist's coin. Looking up, I was about to speak to her, but she had turned slightly and was listening to Alex Benson. I remember thinking, so he's here, too. I did not like that man.

'You'll have to wear a long white dress like a Greek goddess,' he was saying.

I remember thinking his voice was troubled, unhappy. I wondered what was the matter with him. She's lovely enough as she is, I thought.

'Blue laurels?' I said tentatively, and she turned to me immediately and nodded. 'Yes, I think it's the variety you find here.'

'They appear in the painting of *The Flagellation*,' Charles said, coming up and filling my glass.

And then he said, teasingly, 'I'm very jealous of Ras. Today he saw the painting in the flesh for the first time. What a marvellous thing that is!'

'Oh yes!' cried Delia. 'The first time *is* magical. Although,' and she smiled broadly at her husband, 'there are other pleasures in familiarity.'

The wine was cold and very delicate. I had never drunk anything like it in my life. I guessed it must have been expensive. The whole house, with its terraces and its views, its smooth terrazza floors, spelled understated wealth.

'There is a kind of laurel tree in Southern Asia,' I said hesitantly. 'They strip the bark from it and use it for medicinal purposes. It's what we call cinnamon.'

Several people turned and looked at me with interest.

'He's from Jaffna,' Pam said, loudly.

I stiffened, but she went on to talk about her holiday, instead.

'Ras used to paint frescoes when he was a child,' Charles told his wife quietly. 'And now he works at the Gallery. And loves the Pieros best of all.'

She turned her dazzling smile on me, but then something altogether different caught her attention so that, looking over my shoulder, her eyes widened with a different kind of pleasure.

'Oh, here's Matt,' she said, as a small, sturdy, fair-haired boy came hurrying into the garden.

'Mum, Giovanni's here. Can he stay the night?'

'Matt, darling, say hello to Ras first. And then you must wash and change your shirt!'

'Yes, Mummy, but can he?'

'Say hello, darling.'

'Hello,' Matt said hurriedly, before turning towards his mother. He had the same charm of any small child. Lola used to have it, too. This boy was using his mother for the rehearsal, I thought. An event of which he as yet knows nothing, an event where he will break someone's heart for the first time. I watched the two of them, puzzled by something familiar about her face.

'Would you like to go for a walk around the garden?' she asked, after the boy had gone indoors to wash and change.

I smiled.

'How old is he?'

'Eight, nearly nine. Determined to have his own way!' she said, pulling a face, laughing, unable to hide her pride. I liked her.

'Yes,' I said.

'You have children?'

'One. A girl. But she's older . . .'

I hesitated. This woman had a sympathetic face. The sort of face on which no shadow had fallen. Karma, I thought. That was what good Karma brought. And for no reason at all I thought of Ma.

Perhaps it was the woman's loveliness, perhaps it was the wine or the purple light that raked across the garden, but I found myself telling her certain things about my life.

'What sort of things?' you ask, instantly.

There is the smallest of pauses. I notice your face has become flushed. You look a little agitated. What has disturbed you, Elizabeth?

'I told her how beautiful Lola was,' I say. 'How distant we had become, and then I told her about the war that had brought me to Europe. And how it had ravaged our lives.'

'What did she say?' you ask.

Again I have the feeling something is annoying you.

'She listened,' I say simply.

Without interrupting.

'I had the feeling her attention was genuine,' I tell you. 'Like yours,' I add.

We are both taken aback by this addition. It slipped out. Neither of us knows what to do with its presence in the room. So, tactfully, we ignore it.

'She wasn't thinking about the next guest or the cooking or whether her son had obeyed her,' I continue. 'No, she listened, in the way true listeners do.'

I remember I said something or other about one's past never going away, and she nodded, agreeing that yes, the past had long tentacles. Remembered pain was the worst, she said. I recall being struck by the remark.

You are looking solemn, Elizabeth. I would like to ask you,

What you are thinking? And tell you that your eyes are like scraps of sea. Of course, I say nothing.

'We had moved away from the house, by now, Delia and I. And were walking down the slope of the garden.

'Look,' she told me, pausing by the statue of a nymph, 'here's my laurel tree! We bought the house because of it. See, it has blue flowers. Imagine a whole grove of them, turning this slope blue. That's what I want.'

I looked up towards the mountains opposite and asked her about them.

'Oh, it's beautiful, up there, in spring,' she said. 'The wild flowers come out all over the prati, the meadows. Round about now. Pity you are leaving tomorrow or Charles might have taken you up there.'

We had dinner on the terrace as darkness began to fall. Alex Benson brought out great bowls of citronella against the mosquitoes. I saw that he was perfectly at home with the Boyars. Our hostess lit some candles and a few fireflies flickered in the trees. I had no idea they had them here in Europe. Seeing them made me think of Sam. I hadn't been in touch with him for months.

'It's like the tropics,' I told the person next to me, a retired teacher of art.

The conversation moved around the paintings we had seen. Someone was talking about the *Madonna del Parto* in Monterchi.

'It is alleged Piero's mother had just died when he painted her,' Charles said from the other end of the table.

Overhead, the evening star was out.

'It is the most human of the Madonnas I have seen.'

'Did you like it?' Alex asked me.

In the silence that followed, I felt he wanted to trick me into saying something foolish. But almost instantly he caught sight of our hostess and, hurrying over to her, missed my answer.

'There was some desperation to him, Elizabeth, something entirely on the outside of things.'

I shrug.

'No, Elizabeth, I don't really know what I mean,' I say lamely.

Then Charles came over to see if I was all right, and I remember thinking how I preferred him to that Benson fellow.

'Have some more wine, Ras,' Charles said.

There was shouting coming from somewhere deep in the garden. Charles laughed and looked over his shoulder.

'Matt,' he called, 'can you make slightly less noise!'

Children wheeled around on bicycles in the shadows. There seemed many more than the two I had seen earlier. Delia gave a wry smile.

'I think we've got the whole village here tonight,' Alex said.

They had toyed with the idea of buying a house for years, Delia told us, but they hadn't found one until now. It had needed to be perfect, she said, laughing at herself. This one was.

I watched her face in the flickering light, wondering how old she was. She had what one might have called a classical face. I would have liked to attempt a painting of her. And then I thought, yes, of course, that was it; she reminded me of the Madonna we had seen in Monterchi. And as I watched them both in the circles of light, I asked myself again: what did it take to acquire such a life, lived in this gentle way? Day after day?

'Oh, look!' cried Pam. 'I just saw a shooting star.'

'We get plenty of them later on in the summer,' Charles told her. 'On Saint Lorenzo's day in August the sky is filled with hundreds of them.'

'Look, there goes another one!'

Soon we were leaning back in our chairs, watching the Milky Way moving imperceptibly across the sky. Staring into space, it seemed to me as though all the lost years of my youth were floating by.

'You must come back,' Delia said as we left.

She shook hands with me and I agreed, yes, knowing I would not.

We walked up the hill towards the minibus and the last I saw of Charles was the silhouette of him waving as we drove back to our hotel.

'And that was it,' I tell you now. 'Visit over.'

The next day we left on the early morning flight from Pisa. The mist followed us most of the way to the airport, but when our plane was airborne it rolled away. We turned out towards the sea and I caught a glimpse of searing blue with the sun beginning to ripple on it, turning the water to silk. It would be another hot day, but I would not be there to see it. A long and narrow strip of empty sand appeared below us and a moment later we turned back towards the land and flew over the mountains. I peered down, searching its green-furred folds as the aircraft sped north towards the Alps. Somewhere down there below me was the road to Urbino. Somewhere too was the house where we had dined last night. And I thought once more of the family with their charmed lives, living in those hills; and also of how the perspective of the land was altered when seen from this height.

II

II

8

In which Alex Benson begins
his narrative

Of course, come in.

'Did you say your name was Elizabeth *Saunders*?'

Well, naturally the evidence, when I come to give it, will be the Truth, the Whole Truth and nothing but the Truth! What else would I do? Lie? Mind you, I'm not saying I'll be any *use* to you, but do sit down and I'll try to be entertaining, at least. Here, let me take your coat.

'I met him twice. That's all.'

Don't look so disappointed, Ms Saunders. Did he say I was his best friend or something? No, I'm not being facetious.

'Would you like a glass of my latest discovery, Elizabeth? May I call you Elizabeth? An exquisite Pinot Grigio from the Veneto? Or would you like some Lapsang tea?'

Could you give me some idea of what angle you are looking for, exactly? How well I know the other two? It's a long story. Have an olive? They come from my own trees. Try one.

When I was a teenager, my mother used to tell me I had no morals.

'"Spineless," she used to say. "No sense of right and wrong." Here, put the stones here.'

She led me to believe I disappointed her. I must say, the feeling was mutual. I lost interest in her from the moment she returned, overwrought and belligerent, from Rwanda, having discovered injustice in a big way. Don't look at me like that, Elizabeth Saunders! It's true!

'I was fourteen when I first became articulate about my dislikes.'

When I was younger we took our holidays in strange foreign parts. Other parents took their children to the beach in Cornwall, to the French Riviera or to examine the ruins of ancient civilisations. My parents were more interested in examining recent history, heading straight for areas of human conflict. My father was part of an organisation that studied the mess made by wars. My mother advised the Red Cross. They had a particular nauseating slogan they used to trot out, exclusively for my benefit:

'Better a clearer-upper, Alex, instead of a starter-upper.'

Oh God, what a couple of bloody bores they were!

'See these children, Alex,' my father used to say when we were in Guatemala, or Peru, or Bogotá, or Rio; and later on, in parts of India, and tsunami-wracked Sri Lanka, 'these youngsters would give their eye teeth for what you take for granted. For clean water and a better way of life.'

Honestly, what was the use of having clean water if you *couldn't* just take it for granted! I grew up in this way, observing humanity, first trying to kill each other, and then trying to exercise justice. Rather pointless, wouldn't you say? Anyway, back to the day my mother returned from her field trip to Rwanda.

'She was tired and snappy from doing so much good so far away. No doubt seeing me lolling around the house irritated her too. I can understand that now, of course. Having had a similar experience with you-know-who.'

I was actually reading a play about the Holocaust and wanted to talk to my mother about it. I thought she of all people would understand, but not a bit of it.

'I started to read a powerful bit out to her. She listened, without comment. And then she went to fetch a blackcurrant tart from the freezer.'

I seem to recall the two actions followed each other seamlessly. It seemed to me she had no interest in real suffering and this, being adolescent with high moral standards, made me furious. Hypocrite, I thought; do-gooding, liar. By now I was sixteen, almost seventeen.

'From then on I decided I would model myself on my namesake, Alex, in *A Clockwork Orange*.'

You are looking a little peaky, Elizabeth. Have another glass of wine.

'No, no, don't misunderstand. What I mean is, the moral dilemma in *A Clockwork Orange* suited me, at that moment in my life. It is better for a man to choose to be bad than to be conditioned to be good. That was the message I took from the book. Unfortunately, it was during this crisis of inner struggle that I met Delia. The timing was bad, I agree.

'Oh, goodness, yes, I knew Delia long before her marriage. We were teenage sweethearts for nearly two years.'

Interesting that Charles didn't tell you that!

Her parents came to Oxford after her father got a Chair at the university. Naturally, my parents got to know them.

Delia was a few months older than me. I had never met anyone quite like her.

'Within weeks we became inseparable and a month later, inevitably, we were sleeping together.'

You may notice me hesitate, Elizabeth. I have not spoken of that distant summer for years.

'Together we formed a unit against the world. Rather conveniently, Delia did not like her parents either.'

Looking at your bent head as you write furiously in a note-book. I can't help thinking what a funny, serious person you are, Elizabeth. But to continue ...

'Delia was born in New Jersey.'

Her maternal grandmother, now dead, was Jewish, and after a time Delia told me her story. She was called Anna. In 1940, when she was twenty, she was sent to New York on one of the last boats that were prepared to carry Jewish immigrants.

'Anna was pregnant with my mother, at that time,' Delia began.

I can't say I was terribly interested, Elizabeth. I was at the height of my *Clockwork Orange* mania. A posturing youth with simple preoccupations. Of course I wasn't the most sympathetic of listeners. So anyway, out it came: the big story! Delia was obviously paying me a compliment by sharing it with me.

On the afternoon she first told me the story we'd had some fabulous sex.

'Oh, for goodness sake, Elizabeth. Lighten up!'

Surely you were a teenager once? I laugh only because your face is comical in disapproval. But, to continue.

'We were lying naked in my parents' bed at the time. In spite of Delia's protests.'

They were away on a trip, you see, so I knew it was perfectly safe, but it worried Delia. Am I embarrassing you, Lizzie?

'Well, as far as I was concerned, this was an added bonus. Dee's worry, I mean.'

I remember the wild satisfaction I got from making love to my girl in their bedroom. Oh, how my defiance stretched itself across the luxury of that double bed. How I would have loved to have seen their faces had they caught me at it. Come, come, Elizabeth, don't be so shocked, so early on. I've only just begun! Anyway, it was here that Delia began her story.

'My biological grandfather was Austrian,' she said seriously, pausing, biting her nails.

'Jewish?' I asked, not understanding the significant look she gave me, wishing I could have a cigarette.

'No. *Austrian*, Alex. Anna met him long before the war, when they were in their teens. There must have been others with similar experiences. It must have been isolating.'

Their relationship, Delia told me earnestly, stretching her long naked legs under mine, would eventually cause problems. Anna's father, suspecting the way things were going and what lay ahead, refused to let the friendship continue. In a panic, he decided to force Anna to leave for the United States. As far as he could see there was no other choice.

'She never saw her family again,' Delia said, looking at me with the air of someone wanting a reaction.

'Hmm,' I said.

'Her parents made repeated attempts to get their younger children and themselves out, but by then it was too late. All of them were to perish in the camps.'

I looked suitably disgusted.

'And your Austrian grandfather?'

Delia's eyes widened. In the bright, white, afternoon light that slipped in through the branches of the mulberry tree outside, they were almost transparent, the pupils closed down. I rolled over and put my tongue in her mouth, trying to distract her, bored with this old story about dead people I'd never met. But she pushed me away, frowning.

'Stop it, Alex!' she said. 'Anna never heard from him again, you know.'

'I wouldn't have let you go so easily,' I said, nibbling her ear.

Delia ignored me. Which naturally had the effect of increasing my interest.

'Yes, Elizabeth, I agree, I wasn't the most sensitive of characters.'

According to Dee, Anna had had only one opportunity of seeing her young man before she left. And on that evening, she told him she was pregnant.

'She was a bit of a goer, then,' I said, laughing, hardly caring, more interested in exploring the places between Delia's legs.

'Shut *up*, Alex,' she cried.

I could see she was getting really worked up and I thought this funny.

'Let me finish. Anna told me he was inconsolable. He wept, you know.'

Ah! I thought. Then, seeing how much this impressed Dee, I thought I'd do something of my own to impress her. But when I rolled on top of her she screamed with annoyance. So then I had to hear all sorts of boring stuff about her grandfather not being such a bad man. Just someone born in the wrong place at the wrong time. I sighed. Why did girls, even the pretty ones, always try to complicate life, I remember thinking. Unfortunately, Delia wasn't ready to give up yet, so there was nothing for it but to allow her to finish.

'My grandmother Anna believed he died somewhere on the Russian front,' she said, sounding as if she had learnt the story off by heart.

I yawned, my interest in sex decreasing rapidly. For heaven's sake, Elizabeth, don't give me such a look, I'm just being honest. I was a hot-blooded youth. Didn't you ... oh, never mind! And, don't worry, I certainly paid a price for my carelessness, later on.

'The night before she left,' Delia continued, 'a premonition of sorts had sent Anna into her parents' bedroom when they were asleep. The photograph album she wanted was in her mother's wardrobe. After she had stolen it, she stood for a moment in the darkened room listening to their breathing in an agony of suppressed grief. It was the last time she would gaze at their faces, the last fragment of their life she would witness.'

When the war ended, a desperate Anna tried to find the father of her child. She tried to find her family, too, and eventually she did.

'That at least had been straightforward,' Dee told me. 'Her mother's name and her sisters' too, were recorded in Auschwitz. Her father had lost his life in Dachau. There was even a photograph of him in the records. He had survived the longest, only to be gassed in the last hours of the war.'

Just before liberation.

'But of her lover, there was no trace,' Delia said.

I groaned, inwardly, full of resentment. Delia seemed to have forgotten my presence, altogether. It seemed it was my fate never to escape being told stories of unspeakable horror. What was I supposed to say? I looked sideways at her. If only she could look as she did without having such a complicated brain. But it wasn't over yet. Oh God, no! There was more to come.

'Everyone was telling Anna to think of those Jews who were not as lucky as she was. At least now she would have a spot where she could lay flowers.

'So, seeing the mood in her adopted country, understanding perfectly, filled also with a monumental guilt, Anna kept silent.' I nodded, wishing I could have that cigarette. Hurry up, I thought, so we can get on with something altogether more interesting.

It was years before Delia's own mother, Sophia, found out the truth. One day while Sophia was playing the piano, Anna told her that, before the war turned him in another direction, the father she had never seen had wanted to become a concert pianist. It was a stupid, fatal admission, for bit by bit the truth came out and Sophia learned her father had in all probability become a Nazi officer. There followed an almighty row between Anna and Sophia.

'They didn't meet or speak again until I was born,' Delia said dreamily. 'And by then everything connected with the past had been destroyed.'

Sophia never played the piano again, but – and this was the worst part of it – Delia was forbidden from doing so, either.

'They were the weirdest family, Elizabeth,' I tell you, now. 'I never took to Sophia.'

You scribble something furiously and I wait. My frivolity has annoyed you, I see.

'Meanwhile,' I continue, 'Delia was growing into a little blonde girl with Aryan features.'

One day, when she was about ten, she heard Anna's version of the story.

'You look exactly like your grandfather, darling,' Anna had said casually. 'You have his eyes, his hands, his face. You even walk like him.'

If the wind had shaken her grandmother's face, Delia felt, tears would have fallen.

'What happened was terrible. There was no excuse,' Anna told her granddaughter. 'I have read the accounts and, of course, I understand this was a planned, deliberate destruction of a people, but . . . I can't deny my love for him, either. And here you are today, so young, so strong and so beautiful. All because of him.'

Ten-year-old Delia had been deeply moved by all of this.

'War destroys everything,' Anna told her. 'It goes on destroying everything for years and years afterwards. Like poison it seeps into people's hearts. No good can ever come of war. Why don't people see this?'

And worst of all, Anna told the young Delia, is the fate of those who take up the memory of the fallen:

'Memory can destroy. Those who cannot forget live in a twilight place, for remembered pain is the worst of all.'

Soon after this conversation took place, Anna gave Delia the only letter her grandfather had written. He had slipped it into her bag on that last evening. After Anna died, Sophia, knowing of its existence, tried to find it. Eventually, however, Sophia realised there could only be one other person who might have the letter. So she asked Delia.

'Of course I wouldn't let her have it!' Dee told me.

At that, Sophia, a high-ranking member of the Jewish community, began screaming at her daughter, calling her a Nazi sympathiser.

'Go to Auschwitz,' she told her. 'See for yourself what was done to six million of us.'

But Delia is capable of being supremely stubborn, too, Elizabeth. She retreated into silence and it was then that her mother delivered her chilling parting shot. The thing that was still, five months later, eating away at poor old Dee.

'Destroy the letter!' Sophia had warned. 'Or his evil sins will return to punish you.'

'Yes, I know, Elizabeth. It was the most terrible thing to say to a young, impressionable girl. Dee's mother was a real bitch.'

I stop speaking and think of that long forgotten day. In the excessive light and the uncertainty of our receding schooldays, I had told Dee she should forget about it. All parents, I had said, with an authority I did not feel, were fools. Forget the rubbish.

Easier said than done. Of course, she couldn't forget it. The story kept turning in her head and I began to dread the moment, usually after making love, when she would return to the subject.

'D'you think Anna *wanted* me to look for him, Alex?' she asked over and over again.

What was I meant to say? Who cared, I thought. He was a Nazi criminal, I wanted to shout. Don't fool yourself. But I kept my mouth shut, knowing we would fall out if I did. On and on she went, until I despaired of ever changing the subject. My desire for sex with her receded. Only joking, Elizabeth!

You have stopped writing. Why do you stare at me in this hostile way, Elizabeth? Yes, I know, I was very confused in those days. I'm not going to pretend otherwise. This is what I was. Do you want me to continue or not?

'No, no, *I'm* not annoyed. Relax.'

The following summer we took our exams. Delia was going back to America, to art school. I was going on to university in England. Our affair, though still passionate, was beginning to show signs of strain. The fact was, I was obsessed with sex, Delia less so. She wanted to talk, to travel, to paint, to discover new things. I just wanted to stay in bed. I imagined we would get married one day in the distant future when I was more interested in the kinds of things she was. We were still only eighteen, after all. There was plenty of time for all of that.

After our exams, we decided to go travelling. To find ourselves; I believe that was the catchphrase. My father had grudgingly agreed to support me for a year if I promised to settle down to some work on my return. Likewise Delia's parents, who seemed to have called an uneasy truce with her. I pause, savouring the memory of that moment. Then I turn to you.

'Let's stop for lunch?' I say. 'I need a break. Would you like a little risotto from last night? And some tea?'

I get a tight smile in return.

Now, when I think of that time it is always the landscape I think of first, I tell you, after we've eaten.

There is a photograph I still have of Dee. 'Look, here it is.'

I point to the figure of Delia standing beside a tall scotch pine.

We sit in silence staring at the picture taken on her nineteenth birthday. We had just quarrelled, I tell you. I stare at the photograph but what I really see is the ebb and flow of the events that followed. And today, I tell you, more than twenty years later, I can still say, through everything that I did wrong, and everything she has had to endure, my feelings have remained intact.

'That should count for something, shouldn't it, Elizabeth?'

'Yes,' you say, in your colourless voice.

Ah, Elizabeth! I think. Others have come and gone, other passing fancies, girls who have been part of my faceless past, women who have distracted me for a moment. But really, none have left a mark on those grassy banks of my youth as Delia did. She was the yardstick by which I sectioned off my life. Then as now, she remains everything to me; the person who has kept me in Italy for all these years.

We sip our tea while outside the sky has lost its lustre. Sighing, for my mood has changed, I continue:

'But that day, and in all the days that followed on that trip after our exams, I was unaware of her power over me . . .'

That day I was still Alex, slavish poseur, admirer of *A Clockwork Orange*, pathetic rebel-hero with no cause, show-off and fool. We went to Florence to visit the Uffizi and I strutted and pontificated on art.

'What I said was of no importance,' I tell you, quickly before you can ask.

I told Delia I had decided to write a novel, which impressed her.

'The other day, Elizabeth, in preparation for your visit, I came across it again and was struck by the longing suppressed in its pages.'

It was a book about, and for, Delia, really.

'I read the opening lines and there she was: her almond-scented skin, her surprisingly deep laugh, her cornflower blue eyes, breaking my heart, all over again.'

Silence. There is no reaction from you.

'And Charles Boyar?' you ask, eventually. 'Was that when you met him?'

I frown. I don't like your impatience, by the way, Elizabeth. Listen! I will tell you in my own good time.

Yes, we met him that summer. He was sixteen years older than both of us. I hesitate. Then I tell you.

We met him after the biggest quarrel we had ever had. Although for the life of me I can't remember what it was about. All I know is I had made Delia cry, again. I was always making her cry. It was part of my bolshy, yarblockos way.

'I'm sorry?'

'I'm quoting,' I tell you tersely. God, you're irritating! 'From *A Clockwork Orange*. I told you, that book was another one of my obsessions. I thought I *was* the book.'

So I made her cry again and paved the way for her eventual departure.

'And Charles Boyar?'

'Yes. We met him in a bar in Pontremoli where we were staying.'

Delia was in a bad mood, fed up with sleeping in cheap hotels with showers that didn't work.

'Hearing our conversation, Charles spoke to us. He was very friendly, offered us some temporary lodgings.'

I am aware I sound bitter. What the hell are you writing, now? You're seriously getting on my nerves, Elizabeth. Have you thought of becoming a therapist? Sorry, joke, joke; bad taste.

'Charles lived in one of the villages in the hills nearby, in a house he had rented for a year,' I say.

He told us we would be more than welcome to stay with him in exchange for some money for groceries.

'And I have the only bath in the whole valley,' he boasted, looking at Delia.

I have to say, we both liked him, instantly. Maybe it was because his life seemed much more purposeful than ours, maybe it was his air of seriousness and his gentle humour. He had trained as an archaeologist, he told us, but somewhere along the line had strayed into art history.

'I used to work on vestiges of the past and the clues they leave behind,' he said. 'But now I work with the clues within paintings.'

I remember we were both fascinated, drawn to him like a magnet, like the kids we were. So, accepting his invitation without a moment's hesitation, fearlessly, we loaded our rucksacks into his car.

'You'd never find the place, if you didn't know it existed,' Charles told us.

And he drove us along the tortuous mountain road up towards the village of Cargalla, with its cluster of red-roofed houses nestling in a dip in the hillside. Ah! Cargalla! It was the very first time I heard the name. The sun that had been beating down remorselessly on us a moment before went suddenly behind a cloud. It looked like rain.

'A small thunderstorm,' Charles remarked. 'It'll pass quickly enough. Let's go inside.'

I picked up my rucksack and followed him into the house. Delia was close behind.

'Oh my goodness!' she exclaimed.

Over the door frame was a small bas-relief of a crocodile eating a man. The date was 1836.

'How strange,' she said, unable to take her eyes off it. 'Poor man!'

In the kitchen, Charles opened several bottles of beer that steamed cold vapour. There was a streak of lightning.

'Look at the sky!' Delia cried.

She appeared to absorb the last of the light. I gulped the cold liquid down, avoiding her eyes. I was still annoyed by our quarrel. But when Charles told us he had two separate single rooms with rather small beds in them I remember I became a bit desperate. Why hadn't he mentioned this before we agreed to move in?

'No, no, really, Elizabeth, you misunderstand. He was a very unworldly man. I honestly don't think he realised we were lovers.'

But in view of our recent row, I saw that Delia was quite happy about the new sleeping arrangements. A few days apart, she hissed, pushing me away firmly, would do us both good.

'I felt she was being unbelievably nasty and decided to punish her with a show of indifference.'

Besides, there wasn't very much I could do; our money was running low and Charles wasn't charging us much. That night over supper he told us that he worked part-time at the National Gallery in London. We told him rather grandly that we had been studying Italian art and had just been to visit the Uffizi.

There was clearly no woman in his life. It was also obvious, from that very first moment, that Delia was consumed with curiosity about him. And much later, when we parted somewhat drunkenly in the passageway outside her room, I had the distinct impression she was enjoying herself. She did not let me into her bed that night, or the next, and I lay awake, burning with rage, listening resentfully to Charles moving around in his study.

During the weeks that followed he went to the university in Pisa and Delia and I were left alone in the house. But instead of going to bed, as I had hoped, we continued to bicker. Suddenly, the rows had begun to take on a more serious aspect. On the third morning of Charles's absence, as we ate our breakfast of brioche and coffee, things came to a head. At first we talked, half amused, half fascinated by Charles's solitary life. But we couldn't spin it out and fell back into silence. I remember thinking how desirable she was looking. I badly wanted to sleep with her, and to this end was even prepared to go along with her endless talk about her past. But for once she didn't want to talk about her grandmother.

'There are a lot of things that we don't agree on,' she said instead.

'I suppose so,' I agreed, thinking how much I wanted to kiss her.

It had been almost a week since we had made love.

'I wish,' she said, 'we had met a bit later on in our lives.'

Suddenly, with no warning at all, I was angry. I told her I was fed up with her whingeing.

'No, I won't listen,' I said. 'We met when we did and this is the only time together we will have before you go back to the States.'

'We might have been more . . .'

'No, Dee,' I said harshly. 'You're always trying to slip out of the present moment, and I won't take it any more.'

Delia bit her lip. Then she picked up her coffee and went out onto the terrazza where the heat was beginning to rise. I watched her go and made a decision. We seemed incapable of showing each other the kindness we would have shown strangers. Years later, I wondered what might have happened if she had come back in and said to me, It doesn't matter, leave it, we are still very young, one day we'll start again. Or if I could have said to her, I will try to give you all you want, marry me and somehow we will come through. But we were only nineteen with no ability to speak in this way. It was as though someone had sewn up our lips.

Eventually, as I sat in silent rage I heard a small sound and saw her standing in the doorway with her back to the light. I could not see if she was crying. I doubt that I would have let myself care had she been. The day was at its brilliant best, the sun highest in the sky. Cicadas buzzed noisily.

'It looks as if we've come to a dead end?' she said.

I did not want to hear the question in her voice.

'I'm going away for a bit,' I said instead, a hard knot in my stomach and in my voice. 'Coming?'

'No.' She shook her head. 'Where are you going?'

'Naples,' I said, full of bravado.

'We can't fly back for another month.'

I nodded, my chest tightening.

'I'll come back before that. If you are still here, we'll go to the airport together.'

'Fine,' she said, indifferently. 'What shall I tell Charles?'

'Anything you wish,' I replied nastily.

Even then, I believe, we wanted to hear in each other's voice the sound of hope.

'You went?' you ask me.

I nod, closing my eyes. To this day, sadness descends at the thought of my foolishness.

'Yes, Elizabeth. I went. Without a backward glance.'

I too had a great capacity for stubbornness.

By the time I returned, almost a month later, it was all over between us. The dynamics had changed. Not obviously so, you understand; she wasn't in his bed or anything, but even a fool could see something had broken between us. I think for a moment.

'For a start, she looked different,' I tell you.

I remember walking down the cobbled lane that led to the house and hearing their voices through the open door. I could hear Delia laughing; and then I heard Charles's voice. I found her sitting on her favourite cane chair on the terrazza. It was evening again. A lone bird sang in the olmo tree near the house. She was looking up at Charles, shading her eyes against the sun. He handed her a drink. The moment is fixed firmly in my mind, for it was at that moment I knew with the clearest certainty that I loved her and wanted her back.

'Alex!' she cried when she saw me.

I thought she sounded guilty, but a moment later she was kissing me on both cheeks. I must have looked startled, because she burst out laughing again; light, careless laughter. Cruel laughter. I had done nothing but think of her for weeks.

They both looked the picture of health.

'Did you get much work done?' Charles asked, and I guessed this must have been the story she told him.

I took my bag into the bedroom I had used before. Delia was emptying some shopping into the fridge. When I returned to the kitchen, I could see what a cosy scene of domesticity it was. But even then I ignored my unease, telling myself he was too old for her. I went out onto the terrazza and I heard them laughing together and I overheard Charles say:

'You have invaded my space like a noisy cat!'

'God I'm *so* hot,' she cried, kicking off her shoes, avoiding my eyes as I came back in. Her toenails were painted a strawberry pink; her long legs were beautifully brown.

'Have you had good weather in Naples?' Charles asked.

'He's very brown,' Delia said quickly.

'Yes, thank you. I've almost finished my first draft,' I lied.

We were both talking fast.

Outside, the peregrines that hovered high above the mountaintops were nose-diving into the long grass in search of voles, and the heat rose with the noise of the cicadas. I gazed into the distance. Delia and I would be going back to England in a few days and then she would leave for America. I desperately needed to talk to her.

'Let's spend your last week touring the countryside,' Charles suggested. He was pouring some cold wine and Delia was making a salad.

'We've been to some wonderful places,' she said. 'We must take you, Alex. Can we, Charles?'

He was smiling at her and talking to me. All the signs of an intimacy were present in little suppressed gestures but, again, I chose to ignore them.

'Of course,' he said, smiling some more.

I said nothing. I told myself there would be plenty of time on the plane and when we were back in England for Delia and me to talk properly.

'I had come to a decision, you see, Elizabeth, while I had been in Naples. I had decided I would go to America with Dee. And I was planning to tell her this on the journey home.'

Looking back, I see clearly how things stood, but none of us wanted to address it. And so, for what was left of that last, blisteringly hot week, we roamed the hills of Lunigiana, free-wheeling through empty villages. All around us there appeared abandoned houses in need of renovation, and stupidly we fell into a game of pretending we would buy one together. Then, on our last day, we found the hill town of Lusuolo and went in search of a restaurant. The place was almost deserted apart from a couple of toothless old men leaning against a wall. I was aware of their curious stare. Here we were, two men, one older than the other, and a girl with long golden hair. Which one of us had got the girl? I fancied they were thinking. By the time we had finished looking inside the Romanesque church that Charles had wanted to see, it was almost the siesta hour. We found the local trattoria. A dog sat panting on the gravel driveway. Charles went in and spoke to the owner.

'It's okay,' he shouted to us, 'they'll serve us.'

The kitchens were almost shut but they agreed to make us some pasta. We were given a carafe of cold local wine. The grapes used to make it, Charles informed us, grew all along the railway line.

'Did your girlfriend enjoy the meal?' the waiter asked me afterwards as I paid the bill.

'*Purtroppo*, no!' Delia cried, laughing up at the man, striking a pose of mock-despair. 'I belong to no one!'

At that a shadow seemed to fall on the afternoon. It was an

ineffaceable moment, a cameo carved out of our collective consciousness. I wanted to hit her.

That night the weather turned cooler. As I closed my window, it struck me that I had been away from England for only a single summer but it felt much longer.

'What will you do?' I asked Charles curiously. 'After we've gone, I mean? What do you do in winter?'

'Believe it or not, I have a job, you know!' he smiled. 'Normally I'm in London.'

'I'm trying to get him to visit me the next time he's in New York,' Delia piped up, 'but he refuses to mix business with pleasure. So I shall have to keep coming back here.'

She sounded unhappy. Charles sipped his wine, saying nothing. I sensed another imperceptible shift in tension.

'Next year,' Charles said lightly, 'I have to courier a painting to Washington.'

'And?'

'I shall visit the US,' he said self-consciously.

He stood up to close the shutters and we all moved indoors as the first drops of rain began to fall.

'I don't have to be back in the US until the beginning of October, you know,' Delia said, hesitantly. 'I want to take a trip to Vienna.'

I said nothing. I was still smarting over her comment at lunch.

'Why don't you come with me, Alex?' she asked, unexpectedly.

Still I could not speak. The feeling that something had gone irretrievably sour settled in my stomach. I was suddenly certain Charles wanted me to leave.

And later, lying in my chaste, Delia-less bed, I told myself it was indeed time to move on. The slight shower had cleared as quickly as it had begun and now Venus was high in the sky.

Outside, an owl hooted sweetly and was answered by another. And then the clouds rolled away, and the moon came out, and the Milky Way flung itself across the wide, dark sky, while I lay thinking angrily of Delia and how much I had come to loathe this place. I did not think I would return to Italy for some years.

9

In which Alex is given
some blue glass

'Maybe it isn't actually a person you fall in love with, Elizabeth, but words ...'

I pause, making you look at me. But you don't give much away, do you?

Why *are* you so interested in this story, Elizabeth Saunders? How can any of this possibly be of use to your client? You say you want a complete picture, but how will this story help you?

I hear you sigh. 'I trust my instincts,' you say.

Sighing, too, I continue.

'It was meeting Delia again, speaking to her after so long, that brought home the strength of my feelings for her. Until then, if I remember correctly, I had managed to convince myself I had forgotten all about that summer.'

'When did you see her next?'

I realise I am reluctant to elaborate on the intervening years. They were years of pointless struggle on my part. I had gone to Europe dissatisfied and stubborn, in search of inspiration, and I had returned home empty-handed, depressed in a manner I couldn't understand. I went to university in a half-hearted way, achieved a mediocre degree and began working as a hack on a newspaper.

'I had a small stipend, a private income of my own, left to me by a great-aunt, so with this and the money from my journalism I made a living of sorts.'

My parents were openly disappointed. All the high hopes they secretly nurtured had come to very little. Our mutual antipathy had dampened down somewhat and, although I no longer hated them with my old clockwork violence, we were not close either. In any case, they spent most of their time abroad, doing good, and this gave me the perfect excuse for not seeing so much of them. Then one bleak winter day I received news that they had both been killed in a car crash in Bogotá. It was my first brush with mortality. When the dust settled, when the mess of death was cleared up and ordered into a pretence of normality, when the house in Oxford was sold, I felt, not surprisingly, completely alone.

'It wasn't something I had ever felt before, you see,' I tell you. 'Yes, I had a girlfriend, but you know ... she wasn't anything special.'

I wave my hand in the air. This conversation is doing strange things to me, Elizabeth.

'It is difficult to explain the deadness I had been living with for years,' I say.

Difficult, partly because I didn't realise it myself.

An idea came to me for another novel, but I did nothing about it. Then a vacancy for an arts editor came up on the newspaper. I applied for it without hesitation. I began a new relationship. I was always beginning new relationships, you understand, ever hopefully. The girl this time was called Elena. From a distance she reminded me of Delia.

'We saw each other after work. I took her to a few of the plays I needed to review. We seemed to share the same taste.'

Her mother, she told me, was half Jewish. For a moment I was tempted to tell her Delia's story but then decided against it, not wanting to resurrect past emotions.

All that winter Elena and I lived in each other's pockets. Having a girlfriend anchored me. When we were together we had a reasonable time.

'It snowed heavily after Christmas. The roads were treacherous, there was never enough grit on them, so Elena and I abandoned the car and walked in Epping Forest, instead.'

The woods, white and encrusted with ice, resembled a black-and-white negative. I felt content for the first time in months.

'Elena and I stayed in bed, making love and laughing, feeding each other when we were hungry. Yes, I felt normal.'

Whatever normal was.

She admitted to wanting children. I took this to mean she meant with me. I confess the idea was alarming, but it was cold outside and the future seemed shrouded in a distant mist. In January temperatures fell further and uninterrupted blasts of winds from the north glazed the air with a lacquer so blue it was virtually black. On such days, when the light itself was in short supply, the sun produced a peculiar kind of radiance in the few hours it shone, reminding me of my schooldays.

'Elena and I went to look at the Rembrandts at the National Gallery. Unconsciously, I suppose I was hoping to bump into Charles Boyar ...'

I pause and stare at my hands. I am surprised at the depths of my self-pity. I feel, rather than see your eyes on me.

'I felt as if I was marking time,' I say finally.

Occasionally, at night, I dreamt of my time in Italy, but mostly I lived in the moment.

Spring broke through with a slow, sparkling thaw. With its arrival came a message that electrified me. Delia was coming to London. She had, with some difficulty, traced me through the newspaper. The strength of my reaction astonished me. In an absolute fever of excitement I realised I wanted to clear my flat of Elena's presence, I wanted to buy fresh flowers of my choosing, I wanted to play the music I had not played for years.

'As luck would have it, Elena's parents were going to Spain for Easter and asked her to accompany them.'

'Will you miss me?' she asked.

'Of course,' I lied, waving her off.

Within a few hours I had removed all trace of her from the flat. The sun shone with a hesitant joy. My pleasure at opening the door to Delia is hard to describe. I had not seen her since we had been nineteen. We were both twenty-four now. Youth had delivered its promise. Suffice to say she was changed and yet not so changed, glowing with a new happiness very different from anything I had seen before. But then came the first disappointment.

'I can only stay a few hours,' she said. 'I'm flying to New York, this evening.'

And that was when she told me. Hardly waiting until I had made the coffee, breathless, like a child who had carried a secret for too long, trusting me implicitly, she told me.

'What could I do but listen?'

No, they had *not* made love, she said, laughing a little, flushed with the champagne I was plying her with. No, not then. Not until late the following year, and even then Charles had been reluctant to become involved because of the difference in their ages. It had been she, Delia, who had pleaded with him, she told me, blushing.

'Can you believe it, Alex!' she said.

No, I thought. I can't. Jealousy hadn't begun working in me.

'It was worth the wait,' she continued, sighing, 'simply because it made it so special.'

I swallowed. Their lovemaking, she told me, was slow, languorous and without the least trace of precipitation.

'I remember those were her exact words.'

They'd move for hours, cradled by a rhythm that seemed to be part of the earth itself.

'She said that?' you ask, incredulously.

'Yes. Why not?'

Silence. What are you writing now?

'No, of course not, Elizabeth. Of *course* she wasn't trying to make me jealous. She didn't want an affair with me.'

Stupid woman! It isn't what you think.

'I was her oldest friend,' I say, trying to keep my patience. 'Delia was just happy and wanted to share her happiness with me.'

I stop speaking and shake my head. Perhaps I'm making things appear more complicated than they really were.

'All she was doing was sorting out her feelings for Charles by talking out loud,' I say. 'Actually, I think she hardly noticed me.'

I laugh, uncertain.

'Really?' you ask.

'Yes, really, Elizabeth. You must understand, she trusted me. She had no idea of the curious erotic madness that would take root in me. Why should she?'

I am silent, remembering my own crazy imaginings in the days and nights that followed. Desire, once kindled, does not go out so easily. The idea of their pulsating bodies, that unabated throbbing . . . it had never occurred to me to question why she might have told me any of this.

'What else did you talk about?'

Oh, Elizabeth, you fill me with despair. You sound so disapproving!

'I was curious about the future. What they planned to do, next, that sort of thing.'

She sighed with pleasure. She was calmer, I noticed, quieter, too, as with great deliberation, she began telling me their plans.

'She wanted children. Charles, perhaps less so. They hadn't discussed the matter really, but she was certain he would want whatever she wanted.'

I asked her about her search for her grandfather. Had she given up on the idea?

'Of course not!' she said.

The trip to Vienna, in abeyance for years, was now less important in the urgency of this new love.

'She left me, that night, after a light supper, kissing me goodbye, telling me that Charles wanted to meet up with me. Yes, I told her. I would meet him. I agreed to everything. I wanted to go to the airport with her, but she insisted she would be better off alone. I suspected she would be having a long conversation with Charles on the way there and didn't want me around.'

After she left, I walked out into the damp night and I remember brushing against some white lilac overhanging a garden wall. The scent smote me like a bereavement. Loneliness pierced my heart.

'Elena returned and I tried to pick up where we'd left off. Making love to her, I pretended she was another. I dreamt of Delia. I dreamt of her in pieces: a shoulder, a lustrous eye, the shaft of her thigh like some shattered piece of statuary. Try as I might, I could not get her out of my mind.'

I shake my head.

'What then?' you ask.

'Then ... nothing.'

That spring was a mockery of emptiness. I was desolate. I've no idea if Elena realised how I was feeling. All I remember was her unexpected tenderness towards me, which I accepted as my due and without question.

'Charles contacted me. He would be arriving in London to deliver a book that would eventually make his name.'

'*The Frescoed Past?*'

I nod. You've heard of it? Or just done your homework properly?

'He'd been working on it for years. No one had ever connected medieval archaeology with Renaissance colour quite as he did. It was a brilliant book.'

It was an obsession of his. What he called the blue tears of the Virgin Mary.

'He'd found a site,' I tell you. 'It must have been a place of worship once. Scattered all over were dozens of blue glass beads: tear-shaped droplets. Later, he discovered they were the debris of an early medieval glassworks. And later still, he started connecting the glass with the ultramarine used to colour medieval paintings. It was a brilliant piece of detective work!

'You picked up your friendship again?'

Again I nod. Yes, yes, of course.

'Elizabeth, what you must understand is how strangely innocent Charles is. Honestly. You'll see this when you meet him. I'm not even sure how much he knew about what had gone on between Delia and myself. Anyway, he definitely wanted to be friends with me.'

He brought me some of the blue glass and talked with great enthusiasm about his work. I listened, knowing he was too private a man to talk about Delia. But, really, I had no interest in what he was saying; all I wanted to talk about was her.

'He was in London for a few days, flat-hunting. So I saw quite a bit of him.'

It was only on his last night that he told me anything about himself. I was struck more by what he left out than what he said.

'How do you mean?'

I pause.

'Well . . .'

I'm not putting this very well.

'He's an opaque man,' I say. 'Innocent and inscrutable at the same time. It was clear he was very much in love with Dee, but . . . well . . . it was odd that he had never married before. He was not an unattractive man.'

I hesitate, aware of your eyes on me.

'He was intrinsically timid,' I say at last, not sure if this is the right word to describe him. 'And I think he found it difficult to trust anyone.'

But he clearly trusted Delia, in spite of the doubts.

'Doubts?'

Because of the age gap between them.

'Do you think there was a pattern, then?' you ask.

'No, no. Definitely not,' I say, shortly. 'Not at all, in fact. Delia was a very different person to . . . *her.*'

I cannot bring myself to say more.

'I mean, in their age difference?'

I am silent, not wishing to be drawn.

'So what happened?'

Annoyed, I remain silent. I am not obliged to say more. Really, this business of the stolen painting is nothing to do with me.

'Charles went back to Italy,' I tell you, finally, reluctantly. 'I continued with my lacklustre relationship with Elena, ignoring what was staring me in the face.'

'It wasn't satisfactory any more, with Elena?'

I think about this. Am I being truthful?

'No,' I say. 'It wasn't any good at all.'

Having re-established contact with me, Delia now began telephoning me. She was working as a curator in a large New York gallery, organising international sculpture exhibitions. Big contemporary names, you know? It all sounded excessively glamorous compared to my life. We talked about the ways our lives had unfolded, as though the conclusion had already been reached. She talked about starting to paint again. We talked as people who know how things will be: with certainty. At least she did. I just pretended. Luckily for me, these conversations always took place when Elena was out of the house.

I pumped up my affair with Elena into something interesting, even though it was very clear that her relationship with Charles was the thing that absorbed Delia. All I got in return for my lies was a preoccupied expression of pleasure that I seemed happy.

That autumn, I took a short break from the newspaper I was working on and went to Spain with Elena. When we got back, Delia had moved into their new London flat and was busy organising a party to launch Charles's book.

'It was meant as a surprise.'

Elena helped her. Strangely, the two had become friends. I say strangely, but really, why was I so surprised? Anyway, they planned the party, together.

'Charles had no inkling of what was going on until the moment we all filed in from the garden, holding our glasses of champagne.'

Needless to say, he was delighted. I remember we opened the back door and lit a line of garden flares that drew the scent from the honeysuckle bush.

'Towards midnight someone brought out a guitar, but then, as we perched around the garden talking and laughing, there was the sound of an almighty crash. It sounded as if it came from inside the house.'

It stopped the music and we all rushed in, only to find a shelf with a heap of lovely old crockery on it had collapsed. Maybe the shelf wasn't fixed properly, maybe some recent building work had loosened the screws in the wall. Dismayed, we surveyed the mess.

'All my most precious things are gone,' Delia said into the silence that followed.

It was months before she could speak of the incident. The crockery had belonged to her grandmother Anna, shipped out during the war; irreplaceable stuff that survived that journey from Dresden only to be broken in London, in the last years of the twentieth century.

'That's history for you,' I remember saying, trying to comfort her. 'Random from start to finish.'

Some of Charles's blue medieval glass had broken too.

'Nothing lasts for ever,' he said, as he swept up the bits that night.

He had seemed curiously unruffled. Sorry for Dee, of course, but unperturbed, otherwise. I am silent, thinking.

'I think . . .' I say, 'nothing upset Charles as long as Delia was safe. That was all that mattered to him.'

But it ended the party.

'A few months later they announced their marriage. None of us were surprised. They were already considered a couple.'

There followed a smallish wedding down in Suffolk at Charles's mother's house. Nothing grand, just a few of their closest friends and some relatives.

'Oh yes, Delia's family was there. They really were a curious lot, Elizabeth. With none of Delia's charm.'

I watch you scribble furiously in your notebook and refrain from comment.

'After the wedding the Boyars left for the States,' I say.

Delia went back to her gallery and Charles was working with the Museum of Modern Art in New York. He was organising a huge exhibition to take place at the National sometime in the future and was in the process of deciding which paintings he wanted to borrow.

'They invited me to visit, but I too was busy – and who wants to be in the company of the newly wed?'

'No,' I say coldly, in answer to your insinuating look. 'Nor would I have wanted it.'

I hope I've made my point, Elizabeth.

'I can't remember how long they stayed in America,' I continue, annoyed.

I seem to remember Charles writing to me from California about something, but I was determinedly busy with my own affairs.

'What do you mean?' you ask. 'You lost touch?'

Again, the sharpness of your tone grates on me. If you don't let me tell this in my own way, I'll stop.

'Whatever my unconscious reason, we did not meet up for a year or more,' I say smoothly.

As summer turned to autumn again, I toyed with the idea of marrying Elena. She was the best on offer, as far as I could see, and I didn't want to lose her.

But how very strange life is; how it contrives to make events collide in order to cause the maximum havoc.

Then one day I ran into Delia!

She appeared out of the blue, plunging me into blackness. Any idea I might have had about clinching matters with Elena evaporated.

Ah! Elizabeth. Do not talk to me of obsession, for there is nothing I do not know about its nature. Othello could not have felt as terrible as I did, nor Hamlet either.

'I was blinded once more. It was much worse this time.'

'Really?'

I don't know what you mean, but I think I'll ignore the tone in your voice.

'She was like a ripe yellow Russian plum,' I say. '*Tkamali*, they are called. You find them in Georgia in the interlude after winter.'

Light flowed transparently through her; she seemed thinner, more lovely than I remembered, her eyes a deeper blue. I observed, without understanding or caring, the dark rings, the hollows that lay around her lids. That too enchanted me.

'Alex,' she cried, and I thought how pleased she was to see me.

I suggested we have a coffee, lunch – anything to delay her. Instantaneously, the day was infused with a deeply beautiful light. As though strained through glass.

'We had lunch. I had met her coming out of a doorway in Paddington and hadn't taken much notice. Now, over lunch with which she simply toyed, she told me it had been the Praed Street Clinic.'

The name meant nothing to me.

'There's something wrong with me,' she said. 'I don't think I can have children.'

Still I paid no attention. I was distracted by her face.

'Charles is a lucky man!' I said, without thinking.

She burst into tears and instantly there was a waiter hovering at her elbow. People were looking at me.

'Well, after that we left the restaurant, obviously. And went back to my place.'

And talked. Even though I couldn't stop thinking how beautiful her eyes were when she cried.

'At first,' she told me, 'everything was fine.'

They were content with each other, constantly being invited to parties. The gallery she worked for got written about in one of the glossy magazines and there was a small piece about Delia and her new husband with the headline, 'The New York Generation'. A famous photographer took a picture of her and it appeared on the cover of the magazine. People started recognising her on the street. It would have been everything they could possibly have hoped for, had it not been for Delia's growing desire to become pregnant. From what I gathered, Charles didn't much mind either way.

Summer in New York was hot so they went to Cape Cod to swim and sunbathe and make love. Delia began to paint. Charles was happy simply pottering about on the beach, reading, sleeping.

'He did most of the cooking,' Delia told me.

The beach was secluded; the two of them took to swimming naked and making love on the sand dunes before going back into the sea. It was hot, utterly blissful. They couldn't get enough of each other. With the arrival of friends in the neighbourhood, things became more lively. There followed invitations, for drinks, a day's sailing, a barbecue. Then Delia threw one of her parties, she couldn't resist it, and suddenly they had netted a whole new bunch of friends. It was the usual stuff; how they were. Always, though, they were glad to slip away together, sighing, knowing the night would be long and sweet.

It wasn't until later, in the autumn, back in New York when her best friend fell pregnant, that Delia began to worry. Then within days the thought had taken up residence in her mind, refusing to go away. What if she could not have children? Nothing Charles could say made any difference. She calculated that she had been off the pill for almost two years. Why then wasn't she pregnant yet?

There began a round of tests and the word infertility was mentioned. Naturally, once she had a name to her anxiety it became progressively worse. Soon Charles was wondering if it was because of his age. So off he went to be tested, but passed the first hurdle with flying colours. Plenty of sperm, the doctor had said, adding another blow to Delia's rising panic. She began to see herself as something outside the great human cycle. Wherever she looked, all she saw were women with babies. It mattered not a jot that her name as a curator was beginning to be associated with the arts in a serious way, or that her face was photographed at every private viewing; all she saw was barrenness.

A month passed and another. In November, Delia decided she didn't want to be in the US full-time. She would return to England and see an old friend, a specialist in infertility. That was where she had been when I bumped into her.

They were to live in this state of limbo for another two years. Delia kept her job, commuting between London and New York. Charles published another book during that time. I was still with Elena . . . just. The momentum had gone out of our relationship and, by mutual consent, all talk of an engagement had been dropped.

Soon Delia's parties started up again. Perhaps they were a little less frequent, a little more desperate. I sometimes wondered if they drank more than they should, but no one except me knew the scale of the problem. Most people thought they were still childless by choice.

'Once or twice, I remember, there was talk about buying a house in Italy, but it never came to anything.'

I think for a moment. Had my obsession with Delia reached breaking point by then? I cannot be sure. Sometimes, during the day, when both Charles and Elena were at work, I would find an excuse to ring her. Sometimes she would ring me. We would talk for hours. The specialist could find nothing wrong with her. She was still young enough to conceive, so why was this happening? Usually the conversations would end in tears. Sometimes I would take a cab and collect her from their flat. And we would go towards the river. I don't think she ever told Charles about those afternoons. I certainly never spoke of them to Elena, although once I remember her sniffing the air on her return from work.

'You smell of perfume,' she had accused me.

'What did I do? Laugh, I suppose, Elizabeth. What does a man say when he stands accused? I couldn't very well tell her that although I was meeting Delia all we talked about were temperature charts and conception graphs.'

While all I could think of was my own unbearable desire to turn the clock back.

'It was laughable,' I tell you. 'So I laughed.'

In this way, very slowly, the tip of winter passed into a lightless New Year. Elena and I had been together for exactly four years.

10

In which he discovers those things desire throws up

History is full of obsession. You know what I mean, don't you, Elizabeth? My own history had its fair share of them. When I was very small, four or five, I used to watch as my father cleared our garden of birds. For years I watched as he stoned the trees into silence. His compassion did not extend to birds. He was at war with them for eating his seedlings. I used to look at the cat-apult on the hook behind the back door and hate both him and his obsessions. My mother too, when not travelling, indulged her own strange desires. Her mania was for sponsoring children from other countries. She never brought them back to Britain, thank God, but still it was a particular passion of hers: to do good. Now Delia, or rather her absence in my life, was fast becoming my particular obsession. Thoughts of her ate into me like acid and like my parents before me, I imagined no one would notice.

Of course it wasn't so. The first to breathe in its destructive scent was the person closest to this insanity. Elena, the woman who, foolishly, still wanted my children. I had reckoned without her sharp eyes. Subjected to my madness on a daily basis, she was silent at first. But – and I'm sure you'll agree, Elizabeth –

desire, like radiation, cannot be contained. It seeps and spreads and saturates everything so that even the coffee I made each morning began to be flavoured by my desperation. To want must surely be the world's saddest verb. I want, I wanted. Yes, it was everywhere I looked, in every wintry sky, in the wrought-iron starkness of the leafless trees, in the frost that broke my garden pots, in the dead roll of leaves on paving stones, in all that I ate, or drank, or spoke … Everything became infused with my desire. How could Elena not notice?

She noticed it in the clothes I wore.

'Why do you keep wearing that same jacket?' she said, first.

It was the jacket on which Delia had wept briefly. I had found a long strand of hair on it. And used it to mark a page in a book. *Her* DNA pulsated from that book. Everything in me ached at the late-night sight of it. Realising the oddness of my behaviour, I tried to rationalise my feelings.

'You need some new clothes,' Elena said. 'Let me buy you some.'

I wanted nothing from her, but accepted the inevitable only to go back to wearing the same old jacket. I was making an elegy for myself.

And then, one wintry night Charles rang and invited us both over.

'A quiet dinner,' he suggested, as though the parties they had been having had wearied him. When she opened the door to us, I saw in the cold dusk that Delia's lips looked pale, vulnerable. She wore hardly any lipstick, her hair escaped softly from its pleat. All evening I watched her. At one point she shook her head and her hair tumbled down. I watched her scoop it back up in great handfuls. My hand shook with the longing to touch her, so instead I went outside for a cigarette. Please God, I thought, don't let Elena join me. When I returned it was clear they had been talking about me. What did I care?

Covertly, I continued watching Delia. Would they make love after we left?

On our return home I locked myself in the bathroom, saying I wanted a long soak in the bath. For some days I had been suffering from insomnia and Elena had repeatedly told me to have a hot bath before I went to bed.

'I didn't mean tonight!' she said, surprised. 'It's nearly one o'clock.'

I could see she was upset about something, but all I wanted was for her to go to bed. I needed to be alone.

'Don't worry,' she said, as though reading my mind, 'I'll be asleep by the time you're out.'

I grunted. It was the furthest we were both prepared to go. In the bath I went over the evening, like a miser counting his gold. Delia had gone into the kitchen to dish up the food. Soft light poured out from the lamps dotted around the flat. I had followed her out unnoticed. Watched as she took off her rings before beginning to bone the fish, head bent in complete concentration. She wore an expensive wristwatch, her best shoes. Beneath her apron she was dressed for the evening. The scent of perfume was on her shoulders. I imagined leaning over and placing my lips on them. She was completely absorbed, unaware of me standing in the doorway.

'Can I help?' I asked eventually, and she turned and flashed me a smile.

Her mouth was wide and generous; I stared. Dark smudges under her armpits, the fragrance of a full bouquet of white wine on her breath. I saw her underlying concerns, the things that mattered in her life, reflected beneath the expression in her eyes. Meals, I thought. Bed linen, clothing. She wanted there to be children somewhere beyond the hum of voices, the crackle of the fire, the warmth of cushions and rugs. I saw that, for tonight at least, her dreams, though still clinging to her, were in abeyance. And I thought for all that she had wept on my shoulder in the past, tonight her feelings were concealed.

'Alex, thank you,' she said, her smile widening.

Was it my imagination or was her look tonight specially for me? Outside, through an open window, we heard the creak of bats' wings.

'I don't know what Charles is up to. Could you give him a shout?'

'I think he's pouring drinks,' I said.

We heard piano music. Delia took a pan off the stove hastily and washed her hands. Her air of distraction continued and she frowned, biting her lip, unaware of her hair loosening again.

'Do you like salmon?' she asked.

'I don't know which I like more, catching or eating them.'

'Of course, a fisherman. I'd forgotten. My father used to fish, too, remember?'

Her neck was like those saints in the paintings Charles admired so much. Submerging myself in the bath water, closing my eyes in ecstasy, I recalled the moment, wondering what she was doing now. With her guests all gone, not bothering to draw the curtains, I imagined glimpses of her undressing; lean arms, lean legs, bikini underpants. Lying in the cooling bath, I went over all of this, bit by bit. Charles was altogether out of the frame.

Elena was still awake when I went into the bedroom. She was sitting up in bed. I saw with mild surprise that she had been crying. I glanced briefly at her, taking off my watch. The image of Delia's narrow wrist flickered before me.

'Are you having an affair?' Elena asked.

I felt a chill wind draw across my nakedness, like a sword. And then I remembered Delia's rich, unguarded laugh, amongst the flowers and the glasses and the end-of-dinner smoke of Charles's pipe, and I was calm again. I tried to concentrate on what might be going on in their flat, but was hindered by Delia's laughter, once again. And Elena's voice.

'Don't be silly,' I said, getting into bed.

Delia had drunk freely that night, holding out her glass to have it filled by Charles. At one point I had caught him looking at her, his eyes crinkling at the corners, holding the empty wine bottles up to the light before opening another one.

'Is that all you're going to say?'

Delia put a CD on. I had stared at her hands.

'Listen to this,' she said.

The music was Italian jazz.

'It's the next one,' she said.

We had waited until the slightly husky voice had begun singing. *'Andiamo'*. Delia smiled. Slipping off her shoes, she sat with her bare legs drawn up beneath her. The bottle of wine discarded by the lamp glowed, its emptiness the colour of a cathedral nave.

'What's this, then?' Elena shouted, breaking into my thoughts.

She was holding a small handkerchief, edged with lace.

'It was in your jacket pocket.'

My face tightened. So she was going through my pockets now in the old clichéd way.

'Did you steal it, then?'

Via con me.

'Listen,' Delia had said, 'just, listen to the cello!'

Her arms had been bare, her hair long, undone. She had moved her head in two quick movements in time to the cello. The thought had come to me; they wanted to go to bed but were too polite to say anything. I sighed. The night ahead was long, Elena was preparing her roadblocks, her boulders. There would never be enough salt to rub in our wounds. Our misery could not end without a showdown.

'Of course I didn't steal it,' I said. 'I've no idea where it's come from or whose it is.'

'It's Delia's.'

'Oh, really?'

In spite of myself, I felt a hot flush of excitement. Here was an unexpected trophy coming to me, unasked. And I remembered in a flash a handkerchief in Delia's clenched fist.

'Why would I take Delia's handkerchief, for God's sake?'

There was an absolute silence. The clock on my bedside table moved in time to my heartbeat.

'You like her rather a lot, don't you?' Elena ventured.

Her voice had thickened. I saw the fine hairs on her upper lip. I knew we were doomed.

'Don't think I'm stupid,' Elena said, exposing the bone with a flash of insight.

We are neither creatures of air or water, I thought, sadly. We have no element. Nothing sustains us when we fall.

We got through the night. But we were not to be let off so lightly. After the first lot of treatment, Delia fell pregnant only to miscarry a few weeks later. Then, a few months later the same thing happened again.

'For Delia, the miscarriages were a kind of absence made tangible, you understand, Elizabeth. She was inconsolable,' I tell you, watching you write.

Then I continue with my story.

By now our phone conversations had tailed off, we had stopped meeting.

'Why? Well, partly because I suspect she was too disturbed by events and had become disinclined to speak.'

I, too, had become reluctant to disturb her by too much intimacy. I had decided I should make one last effort to save my relationship with Elena.

'I had convinced her, with some truth, that I had no idea

149

where the handkerchief had come from. Perhaps I had picked it up absent-mindedly.'

I went further and offered to return it to Delia myself, but the thought had horrified Elena so much that the subject had been dropped.

'What happened to it?'

'To tell you the truth, I have no idea.'

After a time, that evening receded. Day-to-day life took over, dreariness settled in again. And although Delia was never far from my thoughts, I avoided the Boyars. Elena, too, was trying hard with me, although the question of our own future, whether we would start a family ourselves, was not brought up again. Guiltily, I convinced myself that Delia's difficulties had put Elena off.

'The business of procreation had never interested me, but now I saw it as something rather more ghastly. No wonder men shy away from the thought. Sex tricks you into it and then pushes you out into the cold. No, of course I didn't say that to Elena!'

Then, one night in the following spring, Charles came to see us. It was late and he was alone. Delia, he told us, was out with a girlfriend. It had been raining heavily and he was soaked. Elena took his coat off and fussed over him. We hadn't seen him for ages. I thought he looked nervous, Elena thought they had had a row. We conferred in hasty whispers in the kitchen, animated for once, brought together by our curiosity. In fact, we were both wrong. Charles was almost swooning with a mixture of delight and relief and had wanted to shout his news to someone.

'Delia is thirteen weeks pregnant!' he said.

They had passed the dangerous period and she had had a scan. Now at last they felt safe enough to speak of it.

Other people's news tangled up with our silted lives.

'It's never easy, is it? No matter even if you don't want what they have, you mind.'

The self is all.

'I can see you don't agree, Elizabeth. But I'm being honest, remember. Do you really believe the people who say they are happy for you? Can you trust their words, Elizabeth?'

Our lives are always in someone else's hands, I tell you, watching as you scribble in that notebook of yours.

'I may not paint a pleasant picture of myself, but at least it is a true picture I paint. This is the kind of man I am,' I say.

On that night, after Charles left, we were both silent, sitting among the empty glasses, listening to the rain outside, the footsteps of others on wet pavements. Elena mumbled under her breath.

'These are the moments in their marriage,' Elena observed later, 'that they should treasure. They are moments that cannot be dismissed.'

I knew she wanted me to talk about us. She wanted permanence. She waited. I said nothing. After a while, she sighed deeply.

'Some relationships are like tattoos,' she said. 'You want it at the time, you try to have it implanted in your skin, and then you can't get rid of it. It remains and you become unhappy about it.'

I shifted restlessly. What do you want of me? I wanted to say.

'What do you mean?' I asked, eventually.

Elena shook her head. 'I mean, some couples are part of each other: he thinks what she thinks. It's automatic. But not every marriage is like that.'

I nodded. No, this was not us, I wanted to shout. And then I thought: We both hate them, for different reasons, but we both do.

We sat like the Macbeths, staring at the pictures in the fire.

'I'm being honest when I say, if we could have killed that baby and their contentment, then and there, we would have. It would have died, like a small animal, very quietly. We both had our different reasons.'

I knew that night I wasn't anybody's friend. Not Elena's, not Charles's, not Delia's. Love was what I wanted, not friendship.

'In spite of everything, I am a conventional person,' I tell you.

The Boyars went to Italy. To Monterchi, to see the Madonna again. Elena and I carried on regardless.

I stop speaking because you raise an eyebrow. Do you have to write down everything, I say, Elizabeth?

'Yes,' you say. 'At this stage, I can't say what might help to create a rounded picture.'

I shrug. Really, I don't care. I am no longer interested in your client. The telling of my story is enough.

'What I mean by that,' I continue, 'is that there wasn't anything dramatic going on in our lives. All that was going on was completely hidden in our heads.'

Charles and Delia weren't our only friends. In the months that followed, I had two brief affairs that rid me, for a time, of my desperate hunger for Delia. In any case, I told myself, she would soon be as swollen as the *Madonna del Parto*. Elena loved me enough to drop the subject of children altogether. That summer, I took two weeks off work and went to Italy alone. I was planning a series of articles on art galleries around Europe and had decided to start with the Uffizi. Elena would spend her annual holiday with her parents in Spain, once more. We told ourselves the break was what we needed.

'Yes, of course it crossed my mind that I might bump into the Boyars. It would have crossed Elena's mind, too, I'm sure. But we said nothing, using silence as a camouflage.'

Somewhat to our surprise, a small amount of trust had entered the back door of our relationship. She left for Spain, and after she had gone, while I was packing, I discovered Delia's handkerchief, washed and ironed. Elena had placed it neatly amongst her clothes. For the first time I noticed a white strawberry embroidered on one corner with the letter 'D' beside it.

'The sight of it, so carefully folded, touched me. I'm not sure who I was sorriest for, Elena, or me.'

The trip to Italy was my first in years. Inevitably, I made comparisons. On the last visit I had stayed in a small apartment near the centre of Florence. Now I was better off and could afford a luxury hotel room. On that first visit everything had been fresh and exciting. I had thought I would one day be a writer; life had been full of endless possibilities. Now I was that writer, but where was the excitement?

'I finished my work at the Uffizi and on an impulse took a train to Pontremoli.'

The landscape changes dramatically from Parma as it enters the mountains with their soaring rapids, waterfalls and chestnut forests.

'The closer I got to Pontremoli the more agitated I became. It was only now that I began to see the extent to which Delia had colonised my mind.'

I arrived at five. After the frenzy of Florence, the air was wonderfully cool. The town was only just waking up from its siesta and in the little medieval square where we had once passed many idle hours the cafés were opening their shutters. There was an open-air opera in preparation for later that evening and I wondered whether to buy a ticket for it. I was staying in a hotel close to the town, but in the morning I had decided I would hire a car and drive deep into the mountains. I wanted to see if I could find the house Charles had rented ten years ago.

'I admit, I was rather hoping to bump into them. No, no, they hadn't said anything about being in the area.'

A melancholy mood descended on me. Perhaps it was the sweet and insistent sadness of a bird calling invisibly from a nearby tree. I sat out on the balcony of my hotel room and sipped a cold beer and watched as the blue Tuscan dusk began to gather. It transformed and clarified the mountains while all around me the trees began to shed their dark shadows into the air. I should be ringing Elena, I thought, but weariness stopped me from doing so.

'I felt as though I had been carrying around a great weight that would never go away, Elizabeth,' I tell you.

I suppose it was the first time in months that I was properly acknowledging how I felt.

'I'm being as honest as I can. At that moment I saw no future for me. Not with Elena, not with Delia, not with anyone.'

As I sat contemplating the view, I heard snatches of music drifting up from the square. The opera was in full swing. A few locals were standing on their balconies, listening, and for a moment I wished I had bought a ticket. I might be in Bar Bellotti, now, sipping a Campari, I thought. A moment later the phone rang shrilly. It was Elena, checking on me, knowing no doubt I wasn't going to call her. Soon I would go down for my solitary dinner.

'I didn't find the house until a week later and, no, I didn't see the Boyars. I believe they had travelled further south on that occasion.'

Eventually it was chance that led me to the village of Cargalla. It wasn't on any map, you see, and the people I asked had no idea what I was talking about. What, in any case, was there to say? That three people from England had stayed there for a whole summer years ago? Had loved and quarrelled and left?

'I drove all over the valley in that week and then I crossed over into the next one, returning every night to dine in solitude in the almost-empty hotel. One hairpin bend is the same as another.'

Towards the end of that first week, admitting defeat, I decided to drive towards Parma, on the old Paso della Cisa instead. It was almost the end of August. Roses spread across sun-warmed walls;

September would soon be fattening on the vines, and in the distance I heard once again the lovely sound of goat bells. Mesmerised, I almost missed it. But something made me turn right and there, suddenly, was the village nestling in a slope on the hillside. I couldn't believe my luck.

'I have often wondered since, what would have happened if I hadn't found the place? How would all our lives have turned out?'

I shake my head. Events seldom happen out of the blue, Elizabeth, mostly they unfold from other smaller events. You stare at me, palely.

'Yes,' you say, and I see with surprise that you are trembling. Are you cold, Elizabeth?

'No, no, carry on.'

But I can't. Something about you is bothering me. What is it? Can I get you something to eat? A drink, perhaps?

'Let's have a small Campari?' I say.

This is only the second session we have done together.

'I feel as though you are my ghost writer, Elizabeth,' I say, smiling.

I am only half joking. You laugh and then you stretch, I watch you from the corner of my eye; you are beginning to relax. Suddenly I am interested in you. Not that you're my type. But there is something attractive about you. I could imagine a man loving you, perhaps, even having some kind of obsession. Yes, it is possible for me to imagine it, I think. I carry in glasses filled with rosy liquid, plates, olives, thin slices of salami. Some crisps.

'*Salute!*' I say, raising my glass.

Yes, I think, you have a certain quiet charm. Does your client, this man who you are trying so painstakingly (so hopelessly, I might say) to help, appreciate this, I wonder?

'The house was waiting there for me,' I tell you. 'Like a sleepy animal waiting for love to wake it.'

You sip your drink, slowly, and a little colour comes back into your face.

'I remember, I parked the car and stared with open-mouthed astonishment. Yes, I thought, with delight, this was it.'

Once more I was running down the slope towards the hamlet of lost content. It must have rained here earlier, for the rough grass I trod released a wonderful cool scent of wild thyme and mint.

'I had found the house, but it was shuttered.'

The garden had been allowed to grow wild and as I walked around it the grass hummed and crackled with the secret life of a thousand insects. The sound rose and fell under the hot sun. An old woman was gathering pink speckled beans from a patch of cultivated land nearby. Her bright red headscarf fluttered against the magnificent backdrop of mountains. On an impulse, I went over to her. A grass snake, disturbed by my feet, slithered politely out of the way. I was excited.

'Is it possible to rent this house?' I asked the woman, in my rusty Italian.

I wasn't prepared for her response.

'Alessandro!' she said, grinning at me. *'Sei Alessandro? Di dove sei arrivato?'*

'You remember me? You are Emma?'

'Yes, yes. Of course! You stayed with the *signor inglese*, yes? And the beautiful girl who sometimes painted?'

I had forgotten that Delia used to paint. But I nodded and smiled at Emma, delighted. Over an espresso she asked me:

'So what happened to her, the girl? Does she still paint?'

I saw how their curiosity must have been fired, how their imagination would have worked.

'No. She doesn't paint. And she got married.'

'You?'

I shook my head, ruefully.

'Ah! The other one?'

Yes, the other one.

'But she was fond of you too. Maybe it was difficult for her to choose?'

Maybe. We drank our coffee in silence. Emma told me how hard the winter had been. She talked to me as though we were old friends. The last time I had been here, I had hardly spoken any Italian.

'You look well,' she said.

And then she told me about her husband's farming accident and how he had lost an arm. She spoke calmly, shrugging. I frowned, following her with difficulty.

'If you live and work with the land,' Emma said, 'you run risks. There is always a struggle with what you expect and what you get.'

I couldn't work out how the accident had happened, but it seemed her sentiment was a good one to apply to life, generally. She laughed.

'Yes, I suppose so,' she agreed.

As it was now lunchtime, Emma insisted I eat with her. Of her husband there was no sign and I didn't like to ask.

'You want to look round the house afterwards?'

'Who owns it?'

'I do. It has always been in my family.'

She fixed me with a pair of bright, dark eyes. Her face was tanned and weathered. I wondered how old she was.

'You are interested in it?'

I laughed. My interest was academic, I said in bad Italian.

'Allora!' she said, amused, pouring me a glass of clear pale liquid from a green glass bottle. 'Last year's,' she said. 'Bevi! Bevi!'

We paused and drank the wine.

'It's lovely,' I said.

'Last year was a good year.'

She brought out some goat's cheese and a small *torta dell'erba*. And there was a hunk of bread softened with olive oil. We sat out on her terrace and surveyed the view.

'If you are interested in the house, I can give you a good price,' she said.

I told her it had been a whim that had brought me here. Then I found myself telling her what an impression that holiday had made on me.

'Also the girl,' Emma said.

Her eyes had closed sleepily in the bright light. Also the girl, I agreed, before I could stop myself.

'And you? You have someone?'

I told her briefly about Elena.

'But your heart is not completely there, is it?' she said, touching her breastbone.

'No, no,' I protested. 'That's not the case.'

She said no more and when we had finished our meal she took a key off the hook on the wall.

'Let's go.'

The house was exactly as I remembered it. The desk, where I had tried and failed to work on my book, faced the mountains, still. The stove that had acted both as cooker and heater had a little soot on it and Emma immediately apologised and began to clean it up. Otherwise all was as before.

'How much do you want for it?' I asked, just as she knew I would.

She laughed, her eyes soft.

'You like it?'

I nodded. This was it, I thought. I could see myself living here. Perhaps this was where my life would really begin. It had been on hold for years. Too long. Emma was right, I had everything, a woman who loved me, enough money, I was young. So why did I act so defeated? On an impulse I turned to my elderly companion.

'Yes,' I said. 'Very much! I want it.'

That night, returning to my hotel, I surprised Elena with my news. Then I sat out on the balcony looking at the stars. And much later I dreamt I was back once more in the house, with the sound of running water in the bathroom with the enamel tub that stood on four cast-iron lion's paws. I dreamt that Delia was lathering her legs, covering them in a glistening film of soap. And as I watched her in my dream, she stood up, letting the water stream over her as she examined her face in the steamed-up, old-fashioned mirror.

11

The blue Madonna

'I found some builders.'

The plan was, I would spend six months of the year in my new house, doing it up while working there. When she realised this, Elena became upset all over again. The hopelessness of our crippled relationship was surfacing once more.

'And us?' she asked in dismay. 'And your work? I can't leave England for so long. Can you?'

I told her I had negotiated a different contract with my editor. I told her that I planned to start working on my long-forgotten book. And then I told her something that I knew would leave her speechless.

'Let's get married,' I said. 'Let's make up our minds once and for all.'

There, I thought, I had decided. The time had come to cast aside my pointless longings. Perhaps the house was giving me another chance. As far as I knew, Charles and Delia were still somewhere in southern Italy. It amused me to imagine their reaction when they found out I had bought the old house.

'They won't be able to travel for much longer,' Elena had said.

I ignored her. I did not want to think of Delia's child.

Having accepted my offer, Elena enjoyed her new status as

my fiancée. She became rather sweetly happy while I watched uneasily. There was still no sign of the Boyars, for which I was profoundly grateful.

'We planned our wedding. It would not be big.'

Elena was in a hurry. Perhaps she was worried I might change my mind.

'How did I know this? I didn't for certain, although my own ambiguity was so obvious to me I assumed she had picked up on it.'

I didn't want anyone to know what I was about to do.

'Just the Boyars,' Elena said, firmly, and that was that.

But the Boyars, suntanned and preoccupied with their own affairs, returned home subtly different. Alert as ever to the nuances in their marriage, I noticed instantly a new gentle deference in Charles. He treated her as if she was a kind of visiting dignitary, leading her to an armchair, making sure she was comfortable, relieving her of whatever she was carrying. A slower, clumsier Delia, less inclined to nervousness, accepted his tenderness without a murmur. I could not bear any of it; her changed shape, her air of preoccupation; their obvious closeness.

'I tell you, Elizabeth, I don't know if you have ever suffered from unrequited love, but things were much worse than I had expected.'

You say nothing but I notice that your eyes are very bright.

Delia's baby was due in a matter of weeks.

Of course there was no escape. We accepted their invitation to dinner at their flat. Anything else was unthinkable and Elena, triumphant now, told them our news almost as soon as we arrived. Her haste irritated me, I must admit.

'When?' they asked in chorus, shaken out of their own private involvements, delighted for us in the way insular couples do occasionally raise their heads to notice those around them.

'Oh, well done, Elena,' Charles congratulated her. 'You managed to do what no one else could. You've shifted him from stale bachelordom!'

I laughed along with them, but inside, I felt as though I was dying.

'We ought to look for a place in Italy ourselves, Dee,' he said vaguely. 'Fresh, unpolluted air is just the thing for young lungs.'

Delia smiled gently.

'He's decided to take his parental duties very seriously,' she said.

We might just as well be elsewhere, I thought, bitterly. Somewhere in a distant part of London a police siren sounded, faint but urgent. Charles poured me another beer. Their happiness was a wall over which we could not climb.

'Come out and see ours, first,' I said.

The evening, like all the evenings I had ever spent with Delia, was a disturbing confusion of proximity and distance that depressed me. The road ahead was unknown. Elena sat a foot away from me with schoolgirl precision, feet together, sipping wine. I barely noticed her for a ringing silence was going on inside my head. A silence that could not be penetrated, though I spoke through it, nodded, made conversation. I looked around the flat. It had begun to fill up with baby paraphernalia. Everything I had known, had ever had access to, was falling apart and fading. And a terrifying, gaping abyss was opening up. Elena, wearing the ring bought on impulse and given to her in desperation, continued to chat quietly. I broke into a sweat. Even her laugh irritated me.

'If it's a girl, we're going to call her Anna, after my grandmother,' Delia was saying.

She smiled at me. Her hair looked extraordinarily silky and unbearably golden in the candlelight. She drank no wine; her fingernails were bare of polish. I loved her.

162

'Alex is going out to the house in a few weeks,' Elena said. 'To check on the building work.'

I felt as though I was taking part in a bizarre parlour game.

'Oh, I would so like to see it again,' Delia murmured.

The emphasis of her words, her voice, the flutter of her hands, echoed unbearably in my head. It would go on repeating all night. She was wearing a blue dress, shapeless and long. Flax, I thought, vaguely. Was that the fabric? Charles smiled admiringly at her. Soon you will be a mother, his look implied. Listening to their voices from a long way off, I was aware of many things. Of Elena, who had still not seen the house in Italy; Elena who no longer complained, but who, on some level, sensed my desperation and could not bear it.

'Don't you think?' Charles repeated.

Delia was laughing. I must have missed something. I was conscious of the bones of her wrist as she moved her hand.

'Just like Piero's *Madonna del Parto!*' Charles said. 'Don't you think, Alex? She looks like her?'

I could not look at her. The conversation rose and fell away and I was there, but, like a fugitive, no longer part of any of it. My head ached, I wanted to go away.

'You should come to stay,' I said instead. 'Afterwards, I mean. When the house is done.'

But before I could leave for Italy, Delia went into labour and twenty-six hours later, her baby, a son, was born. They called him Matthew and their life was never the same again.

We sit in complete silence. You and I, Elizabeth.

'I understand,' you say, with unexpected sympathy in your voice.

'Do you? Really?'

You have stopped writing and you give me a piercing look. I feel an odd sort of empathy with you today.

'Being on the outside of things, I mean,' you mumble.

I wait.

'In my working life, that's often a good thing,' you laugh.

Your laugh is girlish, but at the same time, I feel, under-used.

You look as if you might say more, and I wait. But you don't.

'I was the first person to visit the child – after his father, that is.'

Delia held him close with a matter-of-fact gentleness, as if she had been doing this for ever. She smiled at me over the head of her son and I saw immediately that she was unable to conceal her passion for him. I had not seen her more tender. I approached her with a glass of champagne in hand, ice clinking, sun shining, a deep chill within me. The radio was playing Mozart. I remember it all distinctly, Elena's gushing enthusiasm, my stiff smile. And I was stopped cold in my tracks, for I saw how far outside the circle of attention I really was. Delia, her face and arms lit by a gilded beam of sunlight and Charles, sitting quietly at his wife's side. It was a picture of exclusion and containment, I thought.

She went back to gazing at the child with unflickering eyes. She wore blue again. Did she only have blue dresses, now, I wondered? My hand trembled, I wanted to cut the heart out of that bright dress. The baby had been sleeping but now he woke and made a small sound and Delia smiled. After a moment she began to sing. No one spoke. I had not once heard her singing voice, which was unexpectedly low and deep. The child did not take his eyes off her and the sound filled the room. Charles continued to watch them both and the sickness in me increased. The beam of light moved, fell on their feet, as though they were at the centre of a stage and the spotlight could not follow them well enough. She finished singing and after a moment raised her head and I felt, rather than saw, for I had looked away, that her glance had moved from the child to me. I turned towards her, then. Her eyes did not fall but her face went suddenly sad. It was only for a second. then she looked again at the boy and touched his head.

'Will you be his godfather?' she asked me.

In the hot room, noisy now with the infant's cries, I felt not premonition, nor the guilt that would have seemed ineluctable if I had seen someone else in my place, but an absolute exaltation as though in one swift moment my life had become miraculously simple. I did not recognise any fear mixed in with this happiness. I just was happy.

Elena was making baby noises and I saw how hopeless it was for her. But Elena I knew would accept this as she accepted everything that hurt her, with no outward sign of disturbance. I remember thinking with a kind of defiance that she understood much more about my present state of mind than she did about my past.

We were married a month later.

In the end, the building work on the villa took almost a year. But after it was over, after I had added another bathroom ('Don't get rid of our famous bathroom!' Charles had said), cleared the land, repointed and cleaned up the cantinas and turned one of them into another bedroom, the following summer, the Boyars visited. Bringing the baby.

'Elena's mother was dying, Elena had gone back to Spain.'

Yes, Elizabeth, I know it was convenient, and I was sorry, not just for her but for us both. It wasn't working, this marriage of ours. Barely a year, and we continued to grow only in unhappiness.

'Perhaps Elena had reached a kind of saturation point, perhaps I had become worse. Whatever it was, we were drifting apart with greater speed.'

In spite of all this, it was a good summer. Not perfect, because of the baby, but almost as it once was.

'I was re-writing my new novel, and that too was going well.'

My obsession over Delia contracted, became more manageable and vanished from my waking hours, though not from my life.

Outwardly, then, I was a man simply careless with his marriage. Inwardly, I was like the hull of a rotting ship.

The following year my book came out and in the brief flurry that ensued I started another. At last it seemed as if I had found a purpose. A few months later, in that winter, I gave up my job on the newspaper and took to writing full-time, going out to Italy as soon as the warm weather started. Elena joined me when she could.

'The Boyars began visiting every summer and by the time Matt was four we had become close enough to each other to constitute an extended family. As far as Charles was concerned, I had slipped into the role of his younger brother.'

Coveting his brother's wife. I pause, take a deep breath and continue:

'I longed to talk to Delia. But, for all her friendliness, there was a blankness between us that was unmistakable. Once, there had been arguments, struggle, resentment; later, support of a kind; now there was only a preoccupation with her own life.'

I had to be honest with myself. She did not need me. The question was, how was I going to be rid of my need of her?

'Year after year, like the swallows, they returned to Italy, renting a house in a nearby village, making friends of their own. While the child grew. For some reason, he was crazy about me.'

Delia began taking lessons in Italian. She was very serious about it, wanting to learn the grammar. Elena went with her for a bit, but soon stopped. Her heart wasn't in it.

'Matt started school in England and made friends in Cargalla in the holidays. He picked up local idioms unknown to any of

us, so that very soon he was better than all of us put together.'
But for his distinctive Anglo-Saxon looks, anyone hearing him
speak would have thought him Italian.

'He used to phone up and play little tricks on me.' I laugh.
'Pretending to be a local kid, he told me the tyre on my car had
a puncture!'

He had grown into a happy child. Loved by all, me included.

Yes, Elizabeth, don't look so surprised. Even I loved the boy.

Life was bearable, I suppose. I was neither happy nor sad.
Perhaps I had simply accepted the way things had gone. By now
it was clear to Elena I never wanted a family of my own and this
too helped her move away from me.

'Don't look so sad, Elizabeth. I was only doing what was best.'

It was gradual, I tell you. She had been fighting off her sus-
picions, but then one day, while in Italy, an innocent gesture on
my part, a smile from a local woman, nothing definite, made it
clear. For a while the mornings brought forgetfulness; the mornings saw us playing at normality. But in the end she could not
deny my unfaithfulness.

The years that followed were endless; not everything could be
remembered. Then came the year the Boyars bought a house of
their own. Yes, it was the one your client visited, Elizabeth. Matt
was nine. Until then, they had always rented a place close to
mine.

'The day they found it was clear; an iridescent day.'

The light was silvery.

'Elena and I had gone with them to see the place and I remember all the time this feeling of suppressed excitement on Delia's
part.'

The agent lived in the village below and on that hot afternoon, while the whole world was resting, he arrived with a key
to admit them, with some difficulty, through the huge front
door. Lizards basked in the sun on the wide veranda beside a

garden overgrown with wild fennel and thyme. A gust of wind broke against the trees with a slow, majestic sound. We stood looking about us. Light poured on the spaces where once furniture had stood. Here and there we saw tell-tale signs of another life: a damp patch on a wall, a black smudge of soot from an ancient flue. We sniffed the air and breathed in olive woodsmoke.

'Like incense,' Charles said.

He sounded excited, in the same suppressed way as Delia. As always, I felt invisible.

'Look, there must have been a sort of shrine here!'

'Dad!' shouted Matt. 'Come here, quickly.'

He had uncovered a small fresco under plaster.

'Don't touch anything, Matt,' Delia cautioned him. 'It isn't ours, yet!'

The estate agent shrugged. These kinds of frescoes were common at the end of the nineteenth century. They were nice, but . . . again a shrug, not significant.

'They're not Pieros,' he said.

Delia laughed. Such a conversation could only take place in Italy, she remarked, turning to me, delighted. Just for a moment, I stood with her. The others had wandered off and we could hear their voices echoing through the hollow spaces. I closed my eyes. Within the warm glow of the walls, I went into a daydream, imagining it was Delia and I who were buying this house together. Suddenly she linked arms with me.

'What d'you think?' she asked. 'You're looking solemn, Alex. Don't you approve?'

'I've decided which is my room,' Matt announced, coming in before I could answer.

'And my study,' echoed Charles. 'And Mummy can have this as her studio. It has that perfect northern light you painters want!'

I hadn't realised that Delia was planning to start painting again.

'And if Mummy has another baby,' Matt said, settling it satisfactorily for himself, 'it can have the room with the altar! It's a good room for a baby.'

Startled, I saw Elena's face and the expression on it, hastily wiped out. Delia still had her arm linked to mine. She and Charles were laughing.

'Matt's won again and got himself the best room.'

'Matt's fantasies,' Delia said, in answer to Elena's unspoken question. 'I can't go through all that again!'

Suddenly I shivered. How many children did they want? Each one would take her further away from me. All around the cicadas were drilling the garden with a dry buzz. A huge yellow lizard darted across the unswept tiles. Delia yawned. She was not that young, she sighed.

'Let's go,' Charles told her.

Outside, the air had an anything-might-happen feel to it.

'Are we going to buy it?' Matt asked excitedly.

'Shall we?' said Charles, half teasing.

The estate agent looked hopefully at Delia, but she was staring up at a fig tree, smiling, indulgent. The tree was heavy with fruit. I remember her fingers hesitating, touching one, almost picking it and then withdrawing. The sunlight had put everything in shade. There were some grapes on the vine and neglected roses growing against the front wall. The fig tree stood facing the room they had said would be her studio.

'I could draw it from the window,' she said, clinching the deal.

'They are wonderful fruit,' the estate agent agreed, adding shame-facedly, 'My son, he picks them.'

Abundance blocked the view, wasps swarmed on the fallen peaches. There was a blue laurel tree on the slope. I stared at

Dee, silhouetted against the purple hills. She was a woman out of a Piero painting.

'Yes, the view is really magnificent,' Charles agreed.

A series of images moved slowly in my mind. Charles talking to the agent, Matt running in the sunlight. In the dry, insect-filled heat I imagined Delia in a room darkened by drawn blinds. Delia, ready for sleep. Everything danced before my eyes, like stars held invisibly in a daylight sky. Elena was watching me watching Delia. Everything was poised as though on a pinhead.

'I'd say it was love at first sight,' Delia said.

'Can I bring Giovanni to stay for a sleepover?' Matt asked.

At that, the summer seemed to sigh and settle solidly on the hillside.

'We have to buy it first, Matt.'

'And do it up,' I reminded him. 'That could take some time.'

When it was finished, its success was largely due to Delia's planning; her tireless attention to detail. She stopped her work at the gallery altogether and came out to Italy regularly. I was out there myself; alone, writing steadily. Whenever she came, she stayed with me. Charles, busy with his work at the National Gallery, took it in turn with the nanny on the school run while Delia attended to the building work. For nearly a year she came out once a month. I tried not to rely on those visits, knowing they would soon stop, but it was easier said than done. I used to listen to the silence outside her tightly closed bedroom door, imagining her asleep. Wanting to go in, to run my finger along the meridians of her body.

In the mornings, hair hastily tied, dressed for a building site, she would drink her coffee absent-mindedly. She wore no rings; her hands were naked, her glance brief, inconsequential.

'What has happened to you and Elena?' she asked on one of her visits.

It was still winter, the weather bitter. I was feeding wood onto the fire. Then I washed my hands and poured us both a glass of wine before I answered her.

'It isn't working,' I said.

'Yes, I see. But why?'

I looked at her.

'You know I met this woman,' I said. 'She was the ex-wife of the Mayor of Parma. We fell in love and decided to have babies.'

'Alex, be serious!'

'I am. She had beautiful tits,' I said.

'Charles and I thought you were both so well suited.'

'Did you?'

'Yes, we did, actually.'

What was I to say? I sat down heavily.

'We have no patience with each other,' I said at last. 'We have different fantasies.'

Delia shook her head sadly.

'I always thought,' she said slowly, 'that one should love as my grandmother did. Or not at all.'

I said nothing. She had not mentioned her grandmother to me in years. Had she known how much I used to detest those conversations?

'I must search for my grandfather,' she murmured.

I did not remind her she had been saying this for years but had done nothing about it. She was looking at me and shaking her head again.

'Oh, Alex! What are we going to do with you? You have the look of a marvellous derelict about you.'

'Like a holy failure?'

'No, you're no failure. That's just a pose.'

Was she happy, I wondered. Had Charles really given her all she wanted?

'You know, I often think of them,' she said, referring to her

171

grandparents again. 'I think of them a lot when I'm here. You know the Germans were here, just behind the Gothic Line.'

I nodded.

'La linea gotica,' I said.

'I keep thinking, what if he had been here? Sitting out in some house in a hamlet. Just as we are? Playing cards, drinking wine?'

'You could check the records at Massa.'

'No. It's finished, done.'

Suddenly, she told me, she felt it all pass through her like an omen.

'I feel exposed.'

I told her not to be so superstitious.

The Boyars moved in and during that first spring the parties started up again. Matt was truly his mother's child, gathering willing slaves to him. Delia kept open house for what seemed all the children of a certain age from the surrounding villages.

On reflection, it was a good year. My second novel was optioned for a film, I was writing my third. Elena, coming over for a few days from London, was in good spirits. She told me she was going on a trip to South America.

'Alone?' I asked, surprised.

'No. With a group of friends.'

Intrigued, I wondered who they were, but felt I could hardly protest. I too had several friends who had been visiting me when I was alone. It was as if we were aboard ship; an old vaporetto, clean but slightly uncomfortable; the doors leading into the cabins were thin. We were the only passengers. I wondered why I always felt discouraged when Elena was present.

At her thirty-ninth birthday party, that Delia shared with Matt who was eleven, she announced she was once again pregnant.

12

In which history reveals
its many colours

'Yes,' I say impatiently. 'I think I met him. No, I can't be completely sure.'

There were other events that smothered that particular memory.

'In the Rembrandt room? I have no idea if it was there.'

How odd you are, Elizabeth. Such a contradiction, part professional, part ... what? This is your fourth visit, isn't it? Sorry I've lost track. And I confess I'm still confused by your interest in my story. I understand you want to help your client, but it isn't any use pushing me in this way. I tell you, I don't remember him that clearly.

'There had been a party.'

'There were parties all the time, for heaven's sake! I've told you what Dee was like. It was difficult to distinguish one from another. I believe the one you refer to was slightly different.

'How? Well, I think it wasn't an event with friends. I think it was a collection of his students ... '

An odd bunch, the sort that go on art tours.

'Charles ran them periodically for the National. He was very good with the clients.' Old ladies liked him. I was always amazed he bothered so much.

He was very enthusiastic about the Pieros.

'Anyway, there was a party on the last day of the trip.'

And of course Delia entertained them all. It must have been before they planted the laurels. So that tells you how long ago it was.

'I can't remember his name. Yes, maybe it was Ras. *Please* understand, I can't be certain, you can't quote me. Let me see the photo. Yes, yes, that's him. Goodness!'

The resemblance to Lola is staggering. Well! Goodness me! I feel winded. I *did* exchange a few words with him, you're right. But that's all I did. To be honest, the man didn't make much of an impression on me. I think he talked more with Delia, if I remember rightly.

'Well, because he was shy, I expect. Delia was very good at finding anyone who was overlooked. I've told you how she was when it came to entertaining.'

There was nothing untoward about the evening. Nothing to give you any clues, if that's what you mean.

We dined outside. The conversation was about art, naturally enough. I think there was a crowd of kids playing in the garden with Matt.

'I remember the guy said something naive; about Italy being beautiful.'

It might have been his first visit.

'I asked him what he thought of the Pieros. I seem to remember his response was a bit effusive. But . . . well, Renaissance art gets to some people that way.'

There had been tears in his eyes when he spoke of *The Flagellation*, I seem to remember. Or am I imagining this?

'What I mean is, he appeared to have fallen in love with the story. I think he had got it into his head the painting represented the indifference in life ... or some such thing ... Honestly, I wasn't paying much notice. It was amateur stuff.'

It isn't any good, I can't remember. Not with any accuracy. You're wasting your time, you know.

'One thing I did was ask him where he was from.'

No, sorry. I don't think he told me he was from Sri Lanka. No, of course I didn't connect him with Lola!

'By the time I met her, I had forgotten all about this ... Ras.'

I doubt Charles remembered, either, to be honest. If he even knew in the first place.

'No, Elizabeth, I can't say more. It was a very long time ago.'

Yes, I think I do remember the group staying for dinner then leaving soon after. They had to catch a flight back to London.

He was a gallery assistant. Would that be right?

'Possibly. I was surprised by his enthusiasm. Asians don't show much interest in Western art.'

Yes, okay, put like that, this chap was different. Wait a minute, let me think ...

'He did say he was a painter. Apparently, his first love was frescoes. Or did I get that from Lola? I think he read a lot. I remember a vague thought that Charles had taken the guy under his wing, in a Charles sort of way. He'd given him several books to read, pointed him in the right direction, suggested he joined in on the trip.'

I was more interested in Delia, to tell you the truth.

'More than that I can't say.'

Look, Elizabeth, I understand your disappointment. But let me continue with my story.

I had been supervising the whitewashing of the back of the house. It was a hot day. Even for April, even for Cargalla. Charles, Delia and Matt had arrived three days earlier than expected, by car. They had driven across Europe and arrived, laden with Matt's paraphernalia, Delia's antiques, Charles's books . . . oh, all sorts of things. I drove up the hill to meet them. They were noisy, excited at the thought of the summer ahead, their first long vacation in the new house. Delia was almost four months pregnant, no longer feeling sick, beginning to bloom. I stared greedily at her. It had been three months since we had been all together. The top part of the house was finished, the workmen would be back in a few weeks, once planning permission for the new studio came through. In the meantime there were windows to be found, and door handles, and tiles. Delia was a stickler for details and she wanted everything to be in keeping with the style and date of the house. Charles, too, was full of plans. For the first time he was to have a large study, with a mezzanine floor.

They had brought Matt's bicycle with them from London.

'I'm going to cycle on the mountain paths now,' were Matt's first words to me.

He flashed his mother a grin.

'And they won't be able to moan about main roads and mad drivers!'

'Matt,' Delia said warningly.

Even though she was laughing, I could see she was still anxious about this newly acquired freedom.

'Oh but they were so pleased to be back. The winter had been long and mostly spent in negotiation with builders.'

It was going to be a fabulous summer.

I had been charged with the task of getting Emma, our shared help, to cross to the next valley to air the house and put clean sheets on the beds. There was a hamper on the table with a few necessities.

'Coffee!' cried Delia. 'I'm dying for one now I've stopped throwing up.'

'I'll make it,' I said.

Charles was already unloading the car.

'God! I'd forgotten how beautiful it is here,' Delia said, gazing at the view.

'Isn't it! Now, I thought I'd leave you alone for your first night, but how about dinner at my place tomorrow?'

'You've no idea how much I've longed to be back here, Alex,' she sighed. 'More and more, London has begun to tire us.'

I finished making the coffee and we sat on the terrazza sipping it, waiting for Charles. Matt had already changed his phone card over to his Italian mobile and was ringing a friend. We could hear his voice in the background.

'*Ciao, Giovanni, sono Matteo. Arrivo! Arrivo! Si, si . . .*'

Delia smiled.

'Did Charles tell you he wants to live out here permanently?'

I shook my head. Excitement flamed in my heart.

'That would be wonderful. I'm out here more and more, too, you know. As you see!'

She gave me a sharp look but said nothing.

'You could send Matt to the International School in Parma. His Italian would be amazing.'

Delia nodded. She was wearing some sweet, rose-like perfume, unlike anything I had smelt on her before. It drifted towards me as she waved her arm in the air.

'We could rent out the place in London and then, after this one is born . . .' she paused, patting her stomach, not finishing her sentence.

She wanted to spend more time with her children, she told me earnestly. She wanted to paint, she wanted to cook meals, plant a garden . . .

And Charles?

'He could commute to London. His work is changing, too. There's another book in the offing, more research.'

She shrugged and leaned her head back in the chair, staring

up at the mountains that stood darkly against the sun. A lone peregrine sailed lazily past.

'Matt could go through the school system here, as you say. Take the IB, lead an outdoor life. Instead of being permanently driven everywhere in London.'

'You don't have to drive him around in London, Dee. He could walk. Or use public transport.'

She shook her head.

'I'd be worried,' she said. 'Did I tell you a friend of his has been mugged four times on his way home from school?'

'No. But that's an exception, surely?'

'I don't know ... I don't care, I'm finding it hard not to be anxious. You know ... everything seems fine, life is going on as normal and, bang, a day comes ... he's minding his own business, coming home and someone, some dysfunctional individual has a go at him.'

She shuddered.

'You're being over-sensitive,' I said. 'Must be your condition. Think of all the children who don't have anything happen to them.'

'No, Alex, it's not my condition. You know I've always been like this. I used to think of my grandfather ... my German one ... and what my mother said ...'

'Oh, Dee,' I said, before I could stop myself.

She gave me a reluctant, sheepish smile.

'Well, don't you remember? I told you: all that stuff about collective guilt, it goes round and round in my head.'

Still? I thought, surprised.

'Dee, you know that's superstitious crap. *You* aren't responsible for the collective sins of the German people, for God's sake! You're surely not thinking about that, still?'

She said nothing.

'Did you ever try to find your grandfather in the end?'

She shook her head.

'Let's not talk about it,' she said.

'Mum,' Matt called. 'Gio's mother is coming over to say hello to you. Can I go back with them? Can I? Can I stay the night over there?'

'We've only just got here, Matt. Can't it wait?'

'Oh, let him go,' Charles said, coming in. 'He's been patient for so long. He's helped get most of the stuff out and, anyway, Chiara's dying to say hello to you. Now that Matt's spilled the beans!'

They both laughed at the expression on Matt's face.

'What?' he asked. 'Wasn't I supposed to say?'

'It doesn't matter, darling. Everyone'll know soon enough.'

'You should have heard him,' Charles said teasingly. '*Ciao, Gio. Mia mamma è incinta con mia sorella!*'

'Matt, you didn't! What if it's a boy?' Delia asked, laughing.

Matt just grinned.

'But I don't want a boy!' he said.

I smiled at him. He was a good kid. I admit to struggling with some moments of jealousy when he was born, but Matt won me over almost immediately. There was nothing in him to dislike.

'They had been there for three days when Matt finally got Delia to agree to let him ride up to the other side of the mountain. To stay the night at Giovanni's place in Toplecca.'

That night Charles and Delia came to supper, as planned, and met up with all the neighbours.

'You know the Italians, Elizabeth. They love a pregnant woman.'

At the end of the week, Charles was flying back to London to see a producer. He had been commissioned to make a television series on the Piero paintings. He planned to be away for a week. In fact, he was longer than a week. Someone, a millionaire entrepreneur, wanted him to look at a painting at Christie's and give his opinion on it. Was it perhaps an unknown Piero! Delia was fine in Cargalla, Matt mostly absent at Giovanni's, and Charles couldn't resist taking a look at the painting. He would be back by the following Tuesday, he told Delia.

'I remember this clearly, because Delia promptly invited me to supper.'

Elena and I had started another round of long-distance arguments. In the end, she had decided to spend a few days in Venice with a girlfriend and I went to see Dee on my own.

It was a wonderful evening. Delia was extremely content with this pregnancy. She was calmer, surer of herself, happier and, with a painful insight, I saw at last the thing that had been staring me in the face for years. Her life had moved irreversibly elsewhere, she had consolidated it with Charles. I would never come between them.

We talked as old friends, peacefully, sitting out on the terrazza while night fell, unregarded. She brought out citronella candles, but as the ripe moon rose in the vast star-studded sky we blew them out and counted the fireflies flickering across the valley instead. An owl hooted. If this was happiness, I thought, then I had captured it, briefly. Would it have been any better had she married me? Would my happiness be any greater than it was at that moment? In the darkness a few fireflies came over towards us and I tried to catch hold of one.

'They always make me feel sad,' Delia said, stretching out her hand.

'You don't see them in Britain any more.'

'I know. And even here the season is short. In two months they will be gone.'

'They'll be back,' I said, and she nodded.

Overhead, a plane crossed the crowded sky on its way down the coast to Rome.

'Look,' I said, 'there's one going towards the Middle East.'

'Oh! Did you see that?' Delia cried. 'Did you see that shooting star?'

I shook my head and then we both saw one together and laughed. She put her hand companionably on my arm and bent towards me. Sadness of a different kind pierced my heart. What was done was done, I thought.

'Would you like a grappa, Alex?'

'What about you?'

'No, but I'll make myself a cup of tea.'

I didn't want to leave her. The ease we fell into when we were together was something I had never achieved with anyone else. So we continued to sit under the stars, drinking and talking quietly.

'Tell me about Elena,' she demanded. 'Oh, Alex, when are you going to settle down? Have children, even?'

She was half laughing, half serious.

'Never,' I told her. 'Never, now you belong to someone else!'

'I wish you would,' was all she said.

I had the feeling that she too was reluctant for this evening to end. It was the beginning of a big change for her. By Christmas her family would be larger, things would have to be organised differently, they would no longer have as much time alone. The madly-in-love couple would be gone, I thought. But how beautiful she looked that night, with her long hair tied loosely and her earrings catching the light from the window. Like a firefly, herself. At midnight we heard the church clock echo across the valley. Delia yawned and I stood up.

'Will you be all right on your own?'

'Of course. I feel completely safe here, you know.'

It was funny how she still didn't feel safe in London, I thought, whereas here in the darkness with hardly a neighbour in sight she was content. The owls began to call out to each other across the valley. Matt, who might have answered them, was somewhere else, preoccupied with other things, no doubt.

'In bed, I hope,' Delia said wryly. 'Although somehow I doubt it!'

We talked for a moment about how he had grown, how much happier he was when in Italy. Finally, when I saw she was becoming sleepy, I kissed her goodnight – a chaste, loving kiss – and left.

'Call me if you need anything,' I said.

She didn't call me and I heard nothing until almost five the following afternoon.

In fact it was Mirella's husband Giorgio who rang me. Giorgio had been strimming the grass verge near the road, a self-imposed public service of his, when his brother had rung him. The others, all our English friends, were at a big antique fair in Sarzana which had just opened. Later, I discovered it had been the farmer who lived at the top of the Prati who had actually rung Giorgio and not his brother. But in the confusion of that moment all I heard was there had been an accident in the meadow where a group of boys regularly gathered to have cycle races. The English boy was involved.

My first thought was to ring Dee, but there was no answer. Confused, I tried ringing a few others in Cargalla, but again no answer. So I dressed hastily and went out to the car. I thought I'd go straight to the Prati to save time.

The Prati di Lorgaghena is a meadow high up on the mountain; a national park of great scenic beauty. At the top there was a patch of bumpy ground where two herds of black goats grazed on the short grass. But there isn't anything dangerous and groups of boys have always played there, so I was puzzled. I knew the farmer who owned most of the land, even though I had only actually been up to the meadow once, long ago on that first trip to Lunigiana. As I drove down the valley and across towards the next one I saw Giorgio following behind. We both stopped at the first lay-by we came to. Giorgio jumped out of his car. He looked white.

'What happened?' I asked, alarmed.

He shook his head.

'Rapello didn't say. But it must be bad.'

I stared at him. How did he know?

'Rapello was crying,' Giorgio said shortly. 'Let's go.'

We got back into our cars and continued up the mountain. I couldn't understand why Delia's phone wasn't working. Surely she would have rung me if something serious had happened? I swallowed. It was hot. The afternoon sun was very strong as we drove across one ravine and up the next valley. Birdsong filled the air. This part of the mountain was sheltered and never got as much sun as our side. Consequently the vegetation was lush, the trees taller. The air smelt of crushed berries and fungi and dark wood. Light flickered on the windscreen as I drove. The shadow of a bird escaped and flitted through the deep lagoon of blue sky. Here and there I passed small clusters of iridescent flowers growing in hollowed-out shade. We passed a lorry loaded with logs and a group of older cyclists toiling up the hill. Sweat poured off their faces. Otherwise the long road up to the Prati was completely empty. As we reached the village of Toplecca, I hesitated, slowing down. Could it be possible that Delia was talking to the man who made marble work surfaces? I knew she was fitting out her studio. Pulling up, I flagged Giorgio down.

'I'm just going to check Delia isn't here,' I said.

Giorgio stared at me.

'No, no, Alex. She will not be there. She will be at the top.'

'Well, I'll just check, quickly. You go on. I'll catch you up.'

How did he know where Delia was? I turned and hurried towards the marble workshop. He called me back, but I was already in through the gate and I waved and walked on. But there wasn't a soul there either. I stood at the back, staring out towards the valley below, and Pontremoli, and in the distance La Spezia, with the sea shimmering in the heat. A lizard moved heavily through the long grass at my feet. There was a fig tree. I remember thinking its branches were so heavy with fruit they would surely break. I began to perspire gently. I called out a couple of times and tried the main door. It was locked. Delia was nowhere in sight.

My unease increased a notch as I went back to the car. If there had been a serious accident, oughtn't I to get to the top a little more quickly? As I got in the car I heard a faint but distinct sound, growing louder and louder. It was the oboe tones of an ambulance. In a moment it passed me swiftly, first one, then another two and then one more slowly some way away. Two police cars followed. Far away in the distance, I heard the whirl of a helicopter. I slowed down, staring open-mouthed into my rear mirror. Hesitating again, I wasted more time wondering if I ought to follow them or continue up the mountain. There was still no sign of Delia's car. I reached the point where the *strada bianca*, the untarred road, began. The houses had thinned out; there was only one at the edge of the path surrounded by pine trees. All its windows were shuttered; whoever lived there must clearly be elsewhere. At the end of this road I stopped. I wondered why Matt would have been allowed this far alone.

Getting out of the car, I looked around. Silence. Although I could hear faint goat bells somewhere in the distance there were none to be seen. A dog barked. I followed the sound on foot a little further up the incline of the mountain. The farm buildings came into view, then a clump of tall pines, and I saw a man in white overalls fixing blue-and-white police tape to cordon off the area. Suddenly I realised the place was crawling with cara-binieri. Men in overalls walked slowly around a spot slightly out of my sightline, heads bent, eyes scanning the ground. A blue-and-white-clad policeman with a clipboard and a mobile phone was walking towards me, waving his hand and shouting. I stood, still frozen to the spot, as from nowhere the sound of another helicopter came towards me. The noise was instantly deafening and I saw its doors open and a cameraman began filming.

'Get back,' shouted the policeman.

'What's happened?'

'There's been an explosion. An accident.'

'What? Tell me, please? What kind of explosion?'

'A bomb.'

'A *what*? Are you serious? My friend's son was playing, I . . .'

'Yes, yes, there were some children. I can't say more. The wounded have been taken to the hospital in Pontremoli. One has been airlifted to Carrara. But . . .' he shrugged. 'I don't know more,' he said in English.

Still no sign of Delia, none whatsoever of Giorgio. I didn't know what to do.

'Who was airlifted?' I shouted after the policeman.

He stopped and turned to me. Then he scribbled something on a piece of paper and handed it to me. I saw it was the telephone numbers for two hospitals. I went back to the car and clumsily began to search for my mobile phone. I was feeling very, very cold by now.

The hospital in Pontremoli could not answer my question. Neither Giorgio nor Delia were responding to their mobiles, so I had no choice but to drive back down the mountain into the town. The police were now busy setting up a roadblock at the top. Numbly I watched, grappling with the scant information I had been given. A bomb? Terrorists, obviously. But who? al-Qaeda? Why? Or was it a Mafia job? And if so, why, for God's sake? I could hear another helicopter as several more police cars sped past me on the other side of the narrow mountain road. There were no more ambulances. Whatever had happened, although clearly huge, was over.

At the hospital all was controlled chaos. Doctors moved quickly about while police and reporters milled around at the admissions desk. Still no sign of Delia or of Giorgio. Suddenly I caught a glimpse of Giovanni's mother disappearing along a corridor. I tried to reach her, but an armed guard stopped me.

'Look,' I said, 'my friend's son was playing on that mountain. I just saw one of the mothers . . .'

'Ask at information, please,' he said, shepherding me away.

But at the information desk, after an agonising wait, there was no news. Matt's name wasn't on the admissions list. Try Carrara, I was told, and they gave me another number. Delia was still not answering her phone. I tried talking to one of the journalists, but he shrugged his shoulders and turned away to answer his cell phone while picking his teeth. There was nothing for it but to drive to Carrara.

Traffic was heavy and it took me nearly forty minutes to get to the hospital. All the way, I kept checking my phone. There was plenty of signal but no message from Delia and with each kilometre the certainty that something terrible had happened grew. Eventually I was off the autostrada and heading towards the town centre, following the signs for *Ospedale*.

The town of Carrara has an oppressive air at the best of times, due largely to the massive vertical presence of the marble moun-tain range behind it. Even in high summer the huge dirty-white peaks give it a feel of curious abandonment. It is, after all, simply a mining town and has been so for centuries. Perhaps because of this, the life of an ordinary town eludes it and it remains seedy, no matter what. There are shops, there are bars, but most of Carrara's living goes on at the outskirts in large high-rise euro flats flanked by hypermarkets. All covered in a fine film of greyish marble dust. But the hospital here, also on the out-skirts, had a reputation for excellence. I pulled into the car park and almost instantly thought I saw Delia's car. Of Giorgio

I could see no sign. Hurrying into the A&E entrance, it did not take long before I found out more. Bad news seldom takes time. Matt was here. He was in the emergency room. Yes, he had been injured by a bomb blast. A chill passed over me. I demanded to see him, but was refused. His mother, I was told, was in the waiting room nearby. Yes, I could go to her. Was I the father?

I found her, crouched on a chair, alone. She did not see me at first and I hovered for a fraction of a second, my heart pounding. She was wearing a thin white summer dress I had once seen her wearing when she had been pregnant with Matt. There were marks all over the front of it. I thought it looked like dirt.

'Alex,' she whispered, raising her head. 'Alex, make them let me see him.'

I knew then it was bad. Even as I ran to find another nurse, even as I shouted at them for denying the child his mother, I knew, if they were keeping her away, it could not be good.

A doctor approached me while the nurse talked to Delia.

'You are the father?'

'No, a very close friend. The father is abroad. Why can't she see her son?'

'Mr . . . ?'

'Benson, I'm Alex Benson.'

'Mr Benson, the child is very badly hurt. We did not want to shock the mother, we were trying . . . he has been screaming and we wanted to wait for the morphine to work before . . . before she saw him, but . . .' She licked her lips and stared at me through her glasses.

'Can we see him, now!' I demanded. 'Now. The mother is pregnant. I don't want her distressed.'

'I know, Mr Benson,' the doctor said gravely.

Then she seemed to make up her mind.

'Come –' She took my arm and spoke to the nurse sharply in Italian.

'Dee,' I said, putting my arm around her, almost propping her up. 'Come, they're letting you see him.'

We went in through the double doors. Delia wasn't making a sound. There was a lot of activity going on in the room. There were very bright lights and green coats crowded around the bed. Someone was holding a drip up high. I saw a glint of metal. Italian voices, urgent and no longer comprehensible, fired rapid instructions. Unfamiliar vocabulary, words running into each other. I heard Delia whimper beside me and I tightened my grip on her shoulders. And then I froze.

Through the clearing beside the bed we could see Matt; or what was left of him. Something was moving amongst the bloodstained clothes, there was flesh of sorts. An eye – was that an eye? I thought, wildly, feeling bile rise in my throat. Something was wrong in the way his face was put together. The doctors pushed against me, urgently. Orders were being issued. The terrible noise continued. What was an animal doing in the room?

'Matt,' Delia said.

She took a step forward.

'Matt,' she said again.

The noise expanded into a scream, the thing on the bed moved frantically. Almost, I understood a word. Delia was struggling to reach the bed, but a doctor was holding her back. Everyone was speaking at once and the noise, that terrible noise, kept going on and on and on. A moment later we were hustled out, Delia almost dragged along by me, and then we were outside the door and that unearthly noise had grown faint. She was crying, clinging on to me, weeping hysterically.

'What have they done to him?' she asked over and over in a voice I did not recognise. 'Let me see him!'

'Signora,' a voice said soothingly, 'we need to stabilise him first, we want to get the dosage of the painkillers right first. If you see him, he will just scream. Wait a moment. Please, trust us. Go. Sit down. I will come back in a short time. I promise.'

The woman looked at me warningly.

'Come, Dee,' I said again. 'Come. Think of the baby. Come, I'm going to get you something to drink. You must do as they say. He's in good hands.'

I hadn't a clue what I was talking about. All I knew was I had to get her to a chair before she collapsed. Someone brought her a glass of water and I held the cup while she drank. Her face was streaked with tears. I could see that at any moment she would start screaming herself, and in order to ward this off I asked her what had happened.

'There were five of them,' she said, and now she was crying really hard. 'They were playing on the top and one of them, Valentino, someone . . . I don't know . . . found a buried object and called the others over. It was a shell, a cylindrical Second World War bomb. Unexploded. He pulled it, trying to get it out.'

'What? *What? The Second World War?*'

I buried my head in my hands.

'Oh my God, oh my God, my God, my *God*, no, no, no, oh my God . . . No!'

I stared at Delia. Her face was distorted, unrecognisable.

'Alex, please, get them to let me see him. I don't care if . . . I don't care how bad he looks . . .'

Her voice had thickened, she was getting frantic again. I watched for a moment longer as she twisted her hands together, scrunching up her dress. Her hair was all over her face. In all the years I have known her, I had never seen her in anything but an immaculate state before. Somehow this frightened me more than anything else in this surreal scene.

'Charles . . . ?' I asked.

At that she started howling so loudly that another nurse came over.

'Look,' I said angrily, 'this is the boy's mother. It's outrageous that she can't be beside him.'

The nurse stared at me, uncomprehending. I realised I was talking in English.

'Wait, I will check,' she said.

'I can't get hold of him,' Delia said. 'I've left messages everywhere, but he hasn't called.'

'Your phone is switched off.'

'No, I think it's the signal. But I've left the hospital number and he's still not phoned.'

'Probably he's somewhere in the library. Or on the underground.'

'You can come in for a moment,' the nurse said, appearing suddenly.

We went in. Again there was that unearthly crying coming from the bed.

'Matt, Matt,' Delia cried. 'Matt, darling, oh, Matt, Matt . . . '

'We don't yet have the correct sedative to give him,' the doctor said. 'As soon as we get the correct one, it will be easier for him.'

Easier! I thought. Half his face blown off, both legs too, and they could make it easier? I wanted to throw up. I wanted to run from the room, away from the terrible howling. To my ever-lasting shame, I wanted to drag Delia with me, but she had made it to the bed.

'Don't touch him,' a voice shouted. '*Aspetta! Aspetta!* Wait a moment!'

And then, as we stood there, horror-struck, witnessing the same terror a million people had experienced in this same land sixty years before, the noise stopped. And only the long continuous sound of a monitor cutting out indicated the strain had been too much for his young heart, and Matt had died.

*

We sit in silence. Darkness has fallen but the curtains aren't drawn. I notice you are gripping your chair, Elizabeth. Your face is pale, shocked. You are speechless. But I haven't finished, yet.

'When he died,' I tell you, 'there wasn't anyone, all the way down the valley to Pontremoli, who didn't know him.'

At the memorial service, the little church on the hillside was filled to capacity. People stood outside in the rain, there were cars parked all the way down the hill, I remember. I was the only one representing his family. Delia was in England with Charles, down in Suffolk. She had said she never wanted to hear a word of Italian spoken, ever again.

III

13

The black blindfold

A sharp intake of breath. Yours.

'What happened?' you ask.

I am touched by your concern. Do you really care?

'Of course.'

Are you restraining yourself? Other people's feelings are always interesting. Then I see there is nothing in your hand. Nothing from Lola. You've drawn a blank again. She will not visit me.

'Never mind her. Tell me what happened?'

No. I'm only interested in Lola. The insect on this wall beside me has grown eight long spindly legs. Don't dismiss my question. All else is denied me. I have a right to question you. You sigh; yes, I see you understand my helplessness. Why are your eyes so unnaturally bright? I have one other question for you, Elizabeth. I want to ask if your concern for me is genuine? But first, tell me, what news of my daughter?

'She's been silent. I don't expect to hear from her just yet. I've been talking to someone who knows her. Did you know of her affair with Charles Boyar?'

I shake my head. You have caught my attention.

'Charles? The man who took me to Italy?'

'That's correct.'

This is a new turn of events. I digest this in silence.

'What has Lola got to do with him?'

'She met him when she went on holiday with a mutual friend. They had an affair.'

'But he's a married man.'

I frown. My head is throbbing from the last two nights.

'Won't you tell me how you got the black eye?'

Still I puzzle over Lola.

'Ras?'

You look at me quizzically. The morning is dark, a murkiness hangs over the day. But your face: looking at you in this flat, unnatural light I think how beautiful you look today. This discovery, the certainty of it, shocks me and leaves me momentarily speechless. The air is heavy between us in a way that acts as a camouflage to tenderness.

'Who did this to you?'

Then your eyes take in my leg.

'Oh my God!' you say. 'Have you reported it?'

I shake my head and your face is comical in its horror. I'm sure I look grotesque when I smile. It's because they think I'm a terrorist, I tell you. My theory is the human species is getting worse not better. I believe in evolution in reverse. But you aren't listening.

'Wait! I'm going to tell someone.'

Your anger knows no bounds. You are shouting at the staff, asking them why they never saw how the other prisoner set fire to my leg. You are screaming at them, saying you will notify the press. I am moved into the sickbay until my leg is looked at properly. I get painkillers.

'And Lola?' I ask again, patient as an ox.

You have saved a little news till last.

'I don't know,' you say. 'But when you are better, you will have another visitor. Sam wants to visit you.'

I faint then.

The next time I see you, it is beside my bed. There is no Lola and no Sam.

'You lied,' I say.

It is not the most fortunate of remarks. The strain is getting to you, too.

'You can't,' you say, 'push people. They have to do things in their own time.'

I stare straight ahead with a gauze of unhappiness in front of my eyes. The sickbay is lax with the rules for visitors and, in any case, you are no ordinary visitor. If I reach out I could touch your hand, not that I would dream of being so impertinent. There is a delicate perfume around you again that reminds me of some place, long ago. I don't remember where.

'We need to continue,' you say. 'It is important that you don't lose your thread. Tell me.'

I close my eyes. The painkillers are working; my leg is almost bearable, considering I have third-degree burns. I have been putting off this moment but can do so no longer.

'You want to know why I stole the painting? Is that it?'

You have your notebook ready. I want to say that ever since the morning when I noticed your face looked different you have been growing more beautiful. Is it my sight or your face, I want to ask. But of course I don't.

'Why I stole the Piero?' I say, as though it is the heading for a lecture.

The sort I used to attend at the National Gallery but will never do again.

'Why?'

For a split second I cannot speak.

'Why? Why, Ras?'

A pause. You stare angrily at me.

'I was sacked. I had had three warnings for being late for work. Then they sacked me.'

'Why were you late for work?'

I say nothing.

'Couldn't you get up in the morning?'

'No.'

'Were you depressed?'

I am silent. You are silent. The room we are in is screened. Somewhere there are cars moving on roads, planes flying through blue skies, babies are being born and people dying. But I am back again at the Dispatch Club, watching the blurred film smuggled in by a journalist.

'Sam set up an event,' I say. 'He wanted me to come to it. There were several foreign journalists present, including the one who had brought the film.'

The room was packed. The film itself was only a few minutes long.

'Six men, blindfolded in black cloth. Naked, handcuffed.'

You are writing furiously.

'Their last human contact was a kick in the head before they were shot at point-blank range.'

'I saw that documentary, too,' you say, without looking up from your notebook.

I lick my parched lips and I can feel heat rise from me. I feel my whole body getting agitated. I can't bear to show emotion, I can't bear it. I must not break. The film itself was nothing new, I tell you.

'It was the reaction of the people in the room that I couldn't stand. There was a representative from the government who said it was all nonsense and one British businessman said he found Sri Lanka a great place to visit since the war was over.'

'So?'

'Nothing. Sam invited me to stay for dinner afterwards, but I couldn't stomach eating with those people. The businessman reminded me of the woman I had met on the trip to Italy. I knew most people meant well. The journalist who smuggled in the tapes had risked his life. But it was just a drop in the ocean. Nothing was really changing, and I was greedy for change, Elizabeth.'

I went back to my room. I had work in the morning; I wanted an early night. I wanted to be alone. I had tried to call Lola earlier that day but when I got no reply I had foolishly gone to see Helen.

'She's out,' Helen said, standing at the door.

I caught a glimpse of some movement inside. Was it Lola? Was Helen lying? Then I thought, no, Helen has a man in there.

'Have you met someone?' I asked.

'What's it to you, if I have?'

'I want to know if Lola has to live in a house with a stranger. It's my right to know.'

Helen laughed. She carried on laughing for longer than she needed to. Then she just stood there, above me, holding the front door, staring at me. She made me think of a stale loaf of bread put into a hot oven to be freshened up. I noticed something I had entirely forgotten: a crease at the corner of her mouth that had always been there and that gave her an expression of contempt. She is no longer young, I thought.

My life had come to a standstill and I wanted to end it. Abruptly I turned and left.

'I had been to the doctor the week before. He gave me some tablets. I wondered if I should simply take the lot.'

Self-pity is a crop that grows easily on defeated soil. It was a lovely evening. I crossed the river and walked down the embankment. There were young people laughing everywhere;

holding hands, living. There were people rushing about, busy, preoccupied with their busy lives. And there was me.

'I tell you all this so you can understand the kind of hopeless state I was in.' Really the central core of my life was ... and remains, Lola. Without her, I knew I would be lost.

'The next morning at work I heard about the Pieros that were coming to Britain.'

I had forgotten about the forthcoming exhibition.

'They were coming from Italy in a few weeks. It was a security nightmare. I asked some of the security guys if I could see the schedule.'

Then I saw *The Flagellation* wasn't on the list. Obviously, it wasn't coming. I had made a mistake. Bitterly disappointed, on an impulse, I made up my mind. I would spend some of my savings on a trip to Italy to see it there instead.

'On an impulse! You mean you planned to steal *The Flagellation?*'

I shake my head.

'No, no. I just wanted to see it again. I wanted to relive that first, wonderful trip. Look, I was depressed, confused. Charles Boyar seemed to have vanished. I hadn't seen him for over a year. Longer, actually ...'

'You didn't know what had happened to him?'

'What happened to him? I assumed he'd lost interest in talking to me. I never saw him at the Gallery again.'

'You didn't know about his son, then?'

'No.'

I shake my head.

'I seem to remember his wife was expecting another child. Was it a boy, too?'

'Ras,' you say solemnly, and you stop. 'Charles Boyar's son was killed,' you say.

I stare at you.

'Who killed him?'

You are silent for such a long time that I wonder if you heard my question.

'Not one person,' you say at last.

I see you are quietly close to tears. Your ringless hands rub one another. Something strange moves in my useless heart. I remember another pair of hands that made this same gesture. I remember unshed tears on a different face. I remember being loved.

'A whole generation of people, now dead, killed him,' you say.

The wound on my leg is weeping.

With great deliberation I lie staring at the sky. Thoughts come slowly. I can lie here in this hospital bed and no one forces me to get up, to stand in line, to queue. I can piece together the scraps of conversation that escaped me until now. What had you said? Lola and Charles Boyar? How? Why? My leg is throbbing again. Charles Boyar was married, wasn't he? But when you come in, I lose my questions. They bury themselves in the violet-blue of your summer dress. Startled, I remember it is Saturday. You don't normally visit me on a Saturday. Is this how you dress on your days off? The question lands unasked like a butterfly on my lips. Now your face is full of suppressed feelings.

'Yes,' you say, offhand.

But there is a dimple that flashes on and off like a switch. I wonder if you might be just a little pleased by the question. Once again I wonder, but dare not ask, how old you are. There is something so compact and private about you; or perhaps what I really mean is, I feel safe with you.

'Well,' you say, 'you'd better get on with the story if I'm to help you.'

But the tone of your voice, Elizabeth, forgive me . . . it's saying something else to me.

'Tell me what you do in your weekends,' I ask boldly.

Such courage can only be the result of so many painkillers. I think you think this too, because, after the smallest of hesitations, you nod, suppressing a smile.

'I garden,' you say gravely.

'H is for hollyhocks.'

'Yes. I have a lot of them. Mainly pink, but some very dark, almost black.'

I try to imagine you in your gardening hat. You laugh and I know I've guessed right.

'I used to have a cat,' you tell me. 'After my marriage ended.'

But the cat had run away. Like the husband.

'The garden is more constant.'

Loss is loss, I suppose. I am tall for a Tamil. But you are as tall as I am.

'Just answer me one question,' you say. 'It's been puzzling me for a long time.'

It dawns on me that I am not capable of refusing you much.

'Why a painting? Why not diamonds? Or money? And why *that* painting?'

I sigh. It is clear we cannot leave the subject alone for even a day.

'The judge . . . your sentence might be shorter, if I know your reasons. Don't you care?'

I don't have the heart to say no. Especially after you have made so much of an effort. So I answer you.

'I told you,' I say patiently. 'I didn't set out to steal it, but when the opportunity came my way . . .'

You open your mouth to speak, but I hold my hand up.

'Wait,' I say harshly. 'If you really want to know, let me

explain. When I had the chance, I took it. I didn't plan anything. You must believe this.'

I struggle to make myself understood.

'Go on,' you say encouragingly, but still I hesitate. Then I make up my mind.

'You mustn't forget I had been working for years in a gallery full of Western art. I saw just what these paintings mean to you British. How precious they are. Even if you never go into a gallery from one year to the next, still, they are part of your possessions, your sacred history.'

I swallow.

'Whenever we heard of a painting that had been stolen somewhere in the world, everyone in the Gallery talked about it as if it was a death. Do you remember the Cézanne that was taken from that museum in Oxford?'

You say nothing, concentrating.

'It was stolen on Millennium night. Well, the whole country noticed, people cared, the newspapers were full of it. Do you understand?'

I am frowning, desperate to explain this correctly.

'You mean, you took it for notoriety's sake?'

I shake my head violently. No! It was something else.

'Yes,' you say calmly.

And then your eyes burn through mine. Third-degree burns.

'I need to know.'

Don't you see? I did more for the plight of my people than if I'd taken a gun to the public?

Things, Elizabeth, things, I tell you. They matter more than lives.

'But didn't you know how your actions would be interpreted? That your motives would not be understood, that you would not get a shred of sympathy? According to the government in your country, the war and its effects are over. So the world will say this is just an excuse.'

You are speaking cautiously. I think you are frightened of my reaction. I shake my head at the idea. The effects of war do not pass to order.

'And why not diamonds or money?'

I pause. Then I laugh at the look on your face. I feel light-hearted. Reckless. Your hair springs upwards from your forehead like an unruly child. I've never noticed that before. What would you do if I reached out and touched it, I wonder. Hit me, I suppose; call the guard, never see me again. Ah! It was just a whim, Elizabeth; don't worry.

'History,' I tell you. 'The painting was a bit of history. I stole a bit of Western history. I knew it would cause a stir.'

I'm only half serious, but I see you believe me. Don't you know diamonds are much harder to steal, you silly girl?

The Flagellation is like no other painting in the world. Have you seen it?'

'Well, I've certainly seen all the pictures in the papers.'

We are both silent. I see I've offended you. Then I see that we are both angry, but we are also both on the same side. Something tells me I shouldn't say any of this to you. You need to discover it for yourself. And besides, there remains the ache in my leg every time I move it. And my other, separate need to see Lola.

'They will tell you that you achieved nothing,' you say quietly.

I close my eyes. I am too tired to talk any more. I want you to describe your garden to me. I want you to understand that I don't have your stamina, that I don't much care about my sentence, or my life. That freedom is a relative thing, and without Lola's love I might as well be dead.

On the night I speak of, after watching that video, I dreamed a dream of such horror that I woke up screaming. God had

spoken to me and my pillow was wet with tears. I am not a terrorist, I am not a murderer, I do not wish to destroy others. But
something needed to be done. There is a process going on in my
home; a process that is stopping the Tamil people from lament-
ing their loss. Memory is a basic right, denied us by a
government intent on whitewashing the past. It was four in the
morning, dawn was still an hour away as I lay thinking of these
things. All the old arguments were pointless. Put a group of
Tamils in the room and they will fight with each other, I
thought, wearily. What could I, as a lone person, do?

'We are so many,' I remember Sam saying bitterly. 'Intelligent
people, all of us. Professionals. Why can't we think of a plan of
action?'

I had looked at my brother and acknowledged what had happened to him since Ma died. Lying in bed in my cold, useless
room, in the early hours of that morning, knowing I would soon
have to get up and prepare for work, I felt my heart tip over.

That was the beginning. I had no thought of stealing a painting. But this is how the human heart is finally broken, I suppose.
Bit by slow bit. I am making no excuse, but despair comes in
many guises. The following day, after I heard *The Flagellation* was
not coming to London, I took my savings out and booked a
flight to Italy. There, that is my story.

'No drama, no sudden vision. Just a giving up.'

You look at me with an expression I cannot read, Elizabeth.
Forgive me for getting upset.

'Thank you,' I say as you pass me a handkerchief.

It is the end of this visit. I am exhausted beyond words.

The next morning Sam comes to see me. It is you who brings
him. A slower, older Sam, coming to terms with the fact there's
now a criminal in the family. As soon as you leave, he has to rub
this in.

'I always knew you would bring disgrace to our family name. I used to tell Ma as much.'

But he speaks humorously, for Sam. And he looks more frail than me.

'I've had to give up the cause,' he says. 'My angina is too bad.'

I nod. It is years since we sat together in this way.

'No good comes from meeting violence with violence,' he says.

Still I am silent.

'Desperation made me join the Tigers. What was the option? To stand by and watch the government slaughter civilians? Well ... there are too many of them, too many swept up with a desire for power ...'

His voice trails off.

'One day the tide will turn. But not in our lifetime.'

Sam is a man of few words. It is the longest speech I have ever heard him make.

'Those who break one of the Ten Commandments break them all,' he says.

I don't fully understand him, but I am so amazed by his presence here that I say nothing.

'We're not a family that has long life,' he says.

Mortality sits listening beside us. I agree. Already we have lived longer than either of our parents did.

'It was a foolish thing to do,' he says, finally.

And again I nod.

'But you know, the whole bloody world knows about us now.'

He glances nervously at the guard and back at me. Then he chuckles.

'They don't understand why I did it,' I say. 'Not really.'

He bows his head in agreement. We both know, what has happened is not over. Memory is a landfill in the ground; the grass at home has radiation sickness in each blade. The echoes of falling sparrows will not simply go away and those who try to forget will be cursed by their indifference. All memory is sacred, I think.

'They have stolen our lives,' Sam says sadly. 'Government after dynastic government; while the world looked elsewhere.'

I look at him. And I think: when I began to walk for the first time it was to his waiting hands that I went. How do you forget this kind of love? It is a moment of great sweetness, this remembering. We smile at each other as though we are kids again. Until now, neither of us had had time for the niceties of life.

'This government will get away with their crimes,' I say.

'I've brought you something,' Sam says, slipping an envelope through to me.

'What is it?'

He inclines his head and I open the envelope. Inside is a postcard of *The Flagellation*.

'In case you want to be reminded,' he tells me.

He is smiling faintly. Nothing will be resolved in our lifetime, I think. It pains me to see the look on Sam's face. It is Ma he remembers after all this time, I think sadly. Just like me. Oh, my brother, I think.

'We . . .' he hesitates ' . . . have been branded by the name of "terrorist". It hardly matters any more whether we are or not. You have done your bit. Now it's someone else's turn.'

Sam visits me twice more. A fourth visit is planned but he does not appear. He promised to bring me a Tamil newspaper and some bitter gourd sambals someone has sent from Jaffna.

'I'll see if I can get you a mango, too,' he promises.

But he does not come and I suppose something has delayed him. Much later on that evening, after the visiting hour, it is you who comes, Elizabeth, looking pale and out of breath. I notice you are still in your work clothes.

'Ras . . .' you say.

I am flooded with gladness at the sight of you.

'I have some bad news for you.'

'What sort of bad news?' I say, smiling.

You do not smile back, Elizabeth.

'It's Sam.'

He died that morning, you tell me. He had a massive heart attack in the night, but managed to call an ambulance. They came, they rushed him to the hospital, but then, in the early hours of the morning, he had another attack, so big it killed him instantly. The hospital rang his landlady, who found your phone number amongst his things. You then tried to contact Lola, with no success. After that you went to see the body, to collect his things. When you went back to his flat, you tell me, you found a jar of sambals and a single, ripe Jaffna mango on the kitchen table. You have brought them to me.

I am allowed out for the funeral and although I dread the event there is the faintest hope in my heart that Lola will appear. She does not. I, alone, standing between two police officers, represent the family. You are there, of course, Elizabeth, as are many from the North London Tamil community, glancing sideways at me. That night, when I am back in my cell, I dream of Ma once more.

'I am all that's left, Ma,' I tell her, in my dream.

'No you're not,' she says.

In my dream she sounds firm.

'You've forgotten Lola.'

'But, Ma,' I say, despair invading my dream, 'I haven't seen Lola for years. She's as good as lost to me.'

Ma shakes her head.

'Foolish boy,' she says. 'Sometimes things remain hidden for a long time. It doesn't mean they are lost. I've had a dream that news of her will come to you soon!'

But, Ma, I think, waking, startled, you are dead. How do the dead dream?

The next day I take the overdose of painkillers I have been collecting, secretly. I want to join Ma and Sam. But when I wake it's your face I see, Elizabeth.

'I was lonely,' I tell your accusing eyes.

You come every day after that, until I recover. I am surprised at how upset you are. But what shocks me most of all is the look of helplessness on your face, Elizabeth. You sit silently for hours by my bed while I lie with my face to the wall. Then, when I finally turn and look at you, you take hold of my hand.

'It's your life,' you say. 'You must do with it what you want.'

I see your sorrow and only then do I notice you are crying. It is my complete and utter undoing. For haven't I lived on the margins of life, powerless, neglected? I know about helplessness. The helpless are God's forgotten people. No one champions their cause. Or if they do, you can be certain it will always be those on the edges themselves who do so.

'I'm sorry, Elizabeth,' I say finally.

Not since Lola was six have I felt I mattered to anyone in any real sense. You nod, forgiving me. In that moment I pass by the bend in the river. You bring me yogurt to eat. And honey.

'I've been reading about Jaffna,' you say. 'And how they make a wonderful yogurt and honey from the Palmyra palm.'

Your unexpected shyness penetrates the thick fog in my head. I see that, even in this wasteland that constitutes my life, there are still things to learn.

'We call it curd,' I say. 'They used to make it in big clay pots.'

It is a long time since I have talked about the ordinary things of my home.

'You must go back, one day,' you tell me. 'Bring closure.'

I say nothing, touched by your sweetness. I do not want to think of the implications. Not now, maybe not ever.

'To love wisely is not always possible,' you say, as though reading my mind again.

Now, both of us know what we cannot say. So instead you tell me that seeing me in civilian clothes at Sam's funeral was not easy. Ah, Elizabeth, I think. Why do you trouble yourself with such a broken man? Even on rough ground, it would seem, roses bloom. We sit in silence, thinking our own thoughts. Sam's death is a blow like no other. In two weeks my trial will begin. There will be a huge amount of press coverage.

'I'm sorry,' I tell you. 'I'm no company tonight.'

'What have you done today?'

'Nothing.'

'No drawing?'

'No.'

There is some news you want to give me, you say, that I might find heartening. But first I must promise to explain how I stole *The Flagellation*. Tomorrow. I nod. Okay.

'I'm meeting someone you once knew,' you say, satisfied. 'I'm hoping they will be giving evidence in your favour.'

Is that all?

'Who?' I ask, with an effort, for I see you are disappointed by my lack of enthusiasm.

'Charles Boyar,' you say. 'The man who first talked to you about painting.'

14

The transparency of other people's memory

'Elizabeth!'

Thank God. Yesterday you did not come and I grew weak with fear. The doctor does not know yet if my kidneys have been damaged. I try to tell you something without getting upset.

'Here,' you say, handing me the half-written letter that has fallen on the ground.

We both see my hands are shaking. A moment's hesitation and, briefly, your hand covers mine. Like the flutter of a bird's wing, a small animal brushing past; so too does your hand move. Startled, I wonder if I'm hallucinating.

'She stopped wanting my memories, long ago,' I say of Lola. 'But that was the only thing I could give her.'

You nod, gravely. There is no pity in your eyes, only understanding. Elizabeth! Elizabeth! Where have you been all these years?

'Other people's memories are too insubstantial,' is all you say.

I wonder how it is possible for a person to have such iridescent eyes. I want to weep. Everyone in the ward knows I have lost a brother and am waiting for a daughter who never comes. There is no privacy in this place. All punishment brings the death of privacy.

'We gave her a disjointed identity,' I say. 'Helen and I. We confused her.'

You look as if you want to speak, but then seem to change your mind.

'I can't blame her,' I say.

Sri Lanka isn't the only place where there is conflict, I tell you. Conflict and life are working partners. I should have accepted what happened to me as part of life. Not made such a fuss, not let it affect me. Why do you look so angrily at me?

'Your daughter is tougher than you think,' you say finally. I shake my head.

I don't want you to say such things.

'It was foolish,' you say, very quietly. 'What you did was extremely foolish.'

It is the first time you have passed judgement in all these weeks you have been visiting me. I bow my head, accepting. When I look at you again there is suppressed fury in your face. I know, I know, I want to say. I am worthless.

'But you are an idealist,' you burst out.

Startled, I see your eyes are full of angry tears. It is the second time. We sit, us two, washed by a sea of silent emotion. How strange is our companionship in these surroundings. A small, luminous happiness awakes in me. I do not resist it.

'Have you seen Charles Boyar yet?' I ask, and you shake your head.

'Not yet. I'm still talking to Alex Benson.'

A picture comes to mind, a garden, a grove of trees and a woman with a face like a fourteenth-century painting.

'His wife was very beautiful,' I murmur.

'So I'm given to understand.'

I glance at you, surprised by the tone of your voice. You are beautiful, too, I think. But of course I wouldn't dream of saying so.

'I think I showed her a photo of my Lola,' I say instead.

And it comes back to me; that evening, sitting on their terrazza. The fireflies rising up into the dark night like a string of fairy lights.

'Come back and see us,' she had said.

I saw then the way we are given a single moment in our lives. A brief flowering; for each one of us. We think there will be more, but there seldom is.

'She's in a bad way,' you say of Delia Boyar. 'According to Alex Benson.'

'She was a lovely woman,' I say again, pointlessly.

And then, boldly, I touch the back of your hand as it rests on your lap. Instantly you turn it over and clasp mine. We sit in petrified silence. Time stands still. Half-thoughts, like a flock of swallows, dart across my mind. The invisible sky, that which I can no longer see, is filled with them. Outside, in some other place, sunlight falls.

'Thank you,' I say.

'Wait till afterwards,' you say, a faint lightness in your voice.

'No,' I insist. 'Thank you. *Now*.'

'Don't worry about Lola, either,' you say. 'She'll come round. Let's get this trial over first.'

I have the distinct feeling we are talking about two sets of things.

After you are gone, I remember you never told me about Charles and Lola. I make a note to ask you on your next visit. The doctor arrives. He gives me more painkillers. Then the nurse removes the bandage and he examines my leg. I watch. He is young, Indian, perhaps; Sri Lankan, maybe. His fingers are long, dextrous. He is perfectly impersonal without being cruel.

For once, I hardly mind. I'm thinking of you, Elizabeth. I hardly know what my thoughts are about, only that the scent of lily of the valley is buried in them.

'How are you feeling?' the doctor asks.

Once long ago I remember swimming in a river, somewhere. The same scent had drifted towards me. Later I learned it was wild water hyacinths. How many lives have I lived, in total?

'It's healing, slowly,' the doctor says. 'And we'll have the results on your kidneys, tomorrow.'

I glance up at him. He doesn't mention the psychiatrist who visits everyone who tries suicide. His shirt is very white against his tanned skin. I wonder how old he is. Twenty-five? Thirty? I notice he has a Buddhist prayer thread tied around his wrist that he's doing his best to hide under his cuff.

'The trial isn't for another week, yes?'

I nod and he looks sharply at me. Assessing me. Do I remind him of some relative or other?

'I'm going to recommend you stay here until the trial,' he says.

I am grateful, but not for the reasons he assumes. I am grateful because you, Elizabeth, will be able to sit close to my bed. It's the furthest I am prepared to go in thinking of you, tonight.

'Good,' the doctor says, satisfied.

He sees the letter on my bed.

'Would you like that posted?'

Am I imagining it, or is there warmth in his voice?

'Thank you, but I haven't finished writing it.'

He nods. And then he leaves. A slight figure, walking determinedly away back into his life. These last two days have been filled with others leaving. But you, Elizabeth, you will return.

Lying in the hospital bed, listening to the sounds going on around, my thoughts return to Ma. Idleness keeps memory alive, I think. I remember, when she was killed, the cat that lived with us died also. Someone found its body later amongst the rubble.

It had hardly been important, but for many nights after, it had been the cat I had mourned, thinking of it lying purring on my legs as I fell asleep each night. Of these things was my child-hood made.

You return as promised the next day. For a moment we are both awkward. Your professionalism has been breached and I wonder what sort of night you have had. I know nothing of your life, Elizabeth.

'I went to the opera, last night,' you say, as though reading my mind.

I know nothing of opera, I tell you. Painting is my thing.

'It was brutal,' you say, and then you go on to tell me the story of *Salome*.

I listen, enthralled. Time moves sideways into an air pocket of stillness.

'It is very strange,' you say, 'but Richard Strauss saves his most lyrical music for the moment when Salome kisses the dead mouth of John the Baptist.'

I don't know how to respond. Your hair falls over your face.

'It's as if he wants us to see both sides of what love can deliver,' you say, and you shake your head like a little girl.

Why has no one loved you, properly, Elizabeth? It is clear to me that no one has. How is it that someone like you, living a secure life in the place where you were born, still should be so alone?

'Afterwards . . .' you say, and then you stop speaking.

'What?'

My leg is burning up. I can't believe that it is healing.

'I went out to supper with the friends who took me to the opera and . . .'

I move restlessly in the bed.

'I wondered what it would have been like . . . if you had been with us. I mean, I wondered what you might have thought of the opera.'

My heart rises at your words. I can no longer imagine being free, I tell you.

'You will,' you say. 'Your life will be very different when that happens.'

Once more I know we are talking of two different things. And then you remind me I have still not recounted how I came to steal the painting.

'If I am to help, you must not withhold anything. Do you understand, Ras?'

I cannot put it off any longer, however painful it is. So I tell you.

'I didn't set out to take it,' I say again.

This is the point at which I always stop talking because whoever is listening smiles cynically. Even the police laughed, before they handcuffed me. It's a good litmus test of other people's understanding of me. You do not smile and I am frightened by the grave gentleness of your look.

There was a song I heard, long ago, about just such a look. Sung by an old man in love.

'I simply needed to get away from the person I was,' I say.

I was trying to disappear. It was the next best thing to dying.

The flight to Bologna was uneventful, although something happened to me as we flew over the Alps.

'I felt some kind of release, the space to be a happier man.'

You say nothing, but I feel you know what I'm talking about.

'I no longer had anything to lose. There is some freedom in that.'

I think hard for a moment. What was it about Italy that had such a magical impact on me? Was it the melodious sound of the language? A smile plays on your lips.

'You should go back one day,' you say. 'When all this is over.'

In spite of the ridiculousness of the remark, I feel tears prick against the back of my eyes. Old fool, I think.

'I took a taxi to the hotel.'

The first thing I saw as we drove off was a huge hoarding with the image of a perfectly proportioned woman draped across a motorbike. The reflective chrome of the bike gleamed, the woman was covered in a sort of star-spangled oil. She was semi-naked and so thin that, had it not been for the gloss and G-string, it would have been possible to mistake the advertisement for a famine appeal. She was, in fact, a celebrity, someone who had discovered how to starve herself to fame. I stared at her. The white cab swung around the roundabout and headed towards the city. The driver said something.

'I'm sorry.' I shook my head.

The driver accelerated sharply and switched the radio on. Instantly the cab was plunged into a seismic confusion of Italian voices, high-pitched, hysterical and unintelligible.

'In spite of myself, even though the driver was clearly a maniac, my mood lightened.'

I found myself doing what people had done to me for years when I first arrived in Britain: talking loudly and slowly in English.

'Hotel Napoli,' I said clearly.

The driver had a disconcerting way of turning his head when he replied. Staring for far longer than was safe, nearly crashing into the cars ahead, but using the brake as a survival tool.

We hit a traffic jam. A motorcade of cars and police escorts streamed ahead. The Italian flag fluttered. Oboe sirens rose and fell. My face was wet with sweat. I had forgotten that sensation of Italian heat that I had loved the last time I was here. The driver was speaking on his mobile and swerving. My stomach lurched, nervously. Wasn't this illegal?

'Who is it?' I asked.

'Posh Spice!' the driver said. 'You. Americano! It's vonderful!'

He sounded as if he was being ironic. I laugh, remembering. All the rest of that day, resting on my hotel bed, walking out into the wall of heat in search of a pizza and a beer, falling asleep to the irritated buzz of motorinos, I *was* happy.

'Yes,' I tell you, nodding, certain of the memory. 'I *was* happy.'

The next morning it rained, light Mediterranean rain. Inoffensive and transient. Hours later, as I headed for Urbino on a combination of train and bus, the rain had cleared and the sun was shining again. I had booked myself into the hotel where I had stayed before.

It was late by the time I finally arrived in Urbino.

'I was disorientated and had to ask my way, but eventually I found the hotel.'

What struck me was how nothing had changed in the town, how the hotel and the restaurant nearby were all exactly as though I had left them only the day before. There were café tables out everywhere and students gathered in groups drinking and smoking.

'I thought about my last trip and how nothing much had changed for me either and how this was, by comparison, a dreary thing.'

And I wished again I had been born Italian.

I ate a solitary meal and walked around the town afterwards. Urbino shuts early, so I was mostly alone as I walked across the old part, along the castle. I planned to go to the palace in the morning and spend the day looking at *The Flagellation*.

'Then I would simply come home again.'

'And that was the only purpose of your trip?'

I nod. Yes.

'You had no desire to steal it?'

'Not the faintest inclination,' I say.

Our eyes lock. I don't know what you are thinking. Please, I think.

'When I look back on my life, I see my one abiding passion has always been for painting.'

218

People come and go, they love you and leave you, but art lingers on with its peculiar invincibility. Only art lifts you away from the awfulness of life. Only art is able to transform it.

'So, yes, when I tell you all I wanted was to see *The Flagellation* again, I mean it.'

I knew it would be the last time I would be able to afford to do so.

'But when I got to the Palazzo Ducale, I couldn't find it anywhere.'

I became frantic, rushing from room to room. Where had they moved it? Perhaps it was in a different building and I had forgotten where.

'Eventually I asked one of the attendants, but I didn't understand his reply. I repeated my question.'

A woman approached me.

'It is going,' she told me in English. 'To the UK.'

In despair, I shouted at her.

'They told me it wasn't coming! How can this be?'

'An exhibition,' the woman said, not understanding. 'Go to London. You'll see it there. Next month.'

I had come all this way, spent my savings for nothing. The woman shrugged. The loan had been organised years ago.

'Go to London,' she said again.

And then she left. I found the place where it should have been. Sure enough, there was a notice in both Italian and English, informing me of a temporary absence. I stood staring at the blank wall, feeling upset out of all proportion. It was the way everything was in my life, I thought bitterly. Always too late, always the last to arrive.

'What did you do?' you ask, your voice barely above a whisper.

'What could I do? I went back to my hotel and lay on my bed, staring up at the ceiling.'

I stayed there for the rest of the day. I was booked into the hotel for another day and a night before I could leave to go back to Bologna. I thought of what remained of my dwindling savings, the money I had put aside for Lola.

'I felt a rage so acute wash over me that I had to close my eyes.'

'Why rage? Why not disappointment?'

I shrug.

'Maybe it was the rage of disappointment,' I say.

Neither of us speak. I am unable to convey the rawness of my feelings that day.

'I don't know how long I stayed in my hotel room.'

The sun went down, church clocks kept striking the hour, doves cooed outside, but I did not move.

'I thought of Lola and Ma, and then I remembered Charles Boyar. I wished I could remember his address. At least I might have visited him while I was here.'

But Charles Boyar had, like everyone I had ever known, vanished.

'At last, towards nine o clock, hunger drove me out in search of food and I went back to the pizzeria.'

'And?'

I can see you are tense, waiting for me to finish my story. This is the first time I have spoken calmly about what happened, thought properly about what had been in my mind. This is the first space I have had to do so. Suddenly I understand what you've been telling me all this time; I mean *really* understand. It's simple. You want to help me, I think, amazed. Really, how extraordinary. A miracle.

'It was later,' I tell you. 'I was walking through the old part of the town, around the back of the museum, when I saw two men loading up a van. I recognised straight away, from the way we do it at the National, there were pictures in it.'

I stood for a moment, not really paying much attention, just thinking my own thoughts. The men were rearranging the boxed objects in the back. I heard one ask a question which I didn't understand.

'I heard the word, *"Flagellazione"*. It was clear. They repeated it several times.'

Then someone came out of the building. He was carrying a different box.

It was smaller than the others.

Small enough for me to know what it was.

'It was passed from hand to hand, then placed carefully in the van.'

I stood rooted to the spot, like an animal stalking its prey. The men were talking loudly. One of them was whistling. They said something to each other and laughed. Then they went back inside the building. You must believe me when I say that what happened next was totally unplanned. There was a dreamlike quality to it.

'I tried the door of the van. It wasn't locked. And there it was, leaning against all the others. So simple.'

To make it even easier for me, it was labelled. And that was it. I picked it up, closed the door of the van quietly and a second later I was walking briskly along the cobbled street, past the battlements, and down towards my hotel. On the way the van passed me, driving out of the town. I guessed they were on their way by road to London.

'And that was all there was to it,' I tell you.

At the hotel, the receptionist barely looked up as he handed me my key. I moved in a trance towards my room. No one saw me.

'Once there, I put the box down and stared at it. They must have taken the painting out of its frame, I thought. Obviously it wouldn't fit in my rucksack, but I decided I would simply put it in the hold as it was.'

I can hear you breathing hard and suddenly I want to laugh.

'Just like that?' you say, incredulously.

'In the fragile section.'

'What did you think you were doing? Were you planning to sell it?'

'No.'

'So?'

'I had stopped thinking, I suppose. Can you understand that? Can you understand how everything in me had come unstuck? And that anything was possible?'

'I suppose so,' you say faintly.

'I didn't sleep much. I was both excited and empty of emotion. Next morning I checked out of the hotel very early. I knew no one would be checking the van again until it reached the National Gallery. That wouldn't be for three days yet, and I would be home by then.'

You look incredulous, one eyebrow raised. I badly want to touch your hair. It's all right, I want to say. Don't look so worried. I'm still here to tell the tale. I'm paying the price. I don't mind, you shouldn't mind either.

'So what happened next?'

'Well, I was a bit nervous at the airport. What if they stopped me? What if they asked what was in the box?'

'And did they?'

I shake my head. 'No. I had to pay a small sum to have it put in "Fragile", fill in a form, get my passport checked. Then they just put a label on it and off it went. Couldn't have been easier.'

You are staring at me with your mouth open. I suppose it was a miracle I didn't get stopped. You clear your throat.

'When did you get the idea to use the theft to advertise what is happening in Sri Lanka?'

'Oh, when I was on the flight.'

I had stared out towards the Alps, thinking of the woman at

the Dispatch Club who had put her hand up and pleaded for the world to keep the tragedy of our country in the news.

'Why don't you give it more attention?' she had cried.

Well, I thought, staring at the dark snowless peaks, there was one way to get publicity for our cause.

'And that's when you thought of what you would do with it?'

I nod. I am very tired, now. I think you should go, but I don't want to say so. You are a lovely woman, Elizabeth. I would like to hold your hand again, perhaps touch your face; maybe kiss your lips. A better man than I might have this chance. A younger man. I smile at the thought and I see your face staring at me.

'What happened next? You told Sam?'

'No, I just went home.'

'Just went home?'

'Yes.'

I swallow. I remember I had been a little tense at the other end. But no one batted an eyelid, so I simply collected the box and left.

'I had decided to enjoy the painting for a bit. Have my own private viewing. Before I took it into work. Handed it in, I mean.'

'I see.'

You seem to have run out of steam, Elizabeth. Perhaps you, too, are tired?

'It wasn't a conscious decision,' I say, not liking the bleak look on your face. 'But when I thought of the children, the women . . . ' I'm not putting this very well ' . . . it became do-able.'

I made up my mind as we flew over those Alps into Switzerland, I tell you. I would use the painting to give us the publicity we needed. Perhaps then the world would do what it could to help us.

You are standing up, your hands briefly on mine, your bright eyes lowered, your moment of weakness hidden under your hair.

'Thank you,' you say softly. 'For being honest with me.'

And I watch as you walk the length of the ward, past the other beds and the curious stares of the nurses, the visitors. Heading towards the double doors and the pale light outside. And I imagine you walking out towards your car, your head held high, your thoughts held in perfect balance. Elizabeth. My friend.

IV

VI

15

A white bone of light marks the end of summer

'Life stopped and the world went on in the hands of others,' I say.

Yes, Elizabeth, I've shocked you, haven't I? What had you expected when you came here with your story of injustice going on somewhere foreign? No offence, Elizabeth, no offence.

'Delia didn't make a sound. That was the scariest thing ... her sudden, complete silence.'

I take a deep breath. I remember thinking: This is bad. What is happening to *her* will last longer than the event itself. I looked into her eyes; they were someone else's eyes. A cloudiness was beginning to gather in them. Pain advancing, I thought. Still she made no sound. She couldn't cry, she couldn't shout, she couldn't move.

'I stood, propping her up, staring ahead, disbelieving. This is Italy, I kept thinking. The war finished sixty years ago.'

I have silenced you, too, Elizabeth, haven't I? Maybe even offended you a little? The faintest sound of a car passing outside disturbs the skin of our thoughts. In the darkness the rain begins to fall.

'Someone's head should have rolled,' you say, at last.

I nod. Too damn right.

By now we were in a separate, private room. But still no sign of Giorgio. The police were outside, talking to some of the medics. I was worried about the fact that Dee was pregnant and evidently the thought had crossed the doctor's mind too, for she made her sit down and then sedated her.

We tried ringing Charles again. I mean, *I* tried.

Believe me, it wasn't a call I wanted to make.

After a while the medication began to work, but the doctor didn't want her to go home.

The police needed to talk to her. There were journalists all over the place and, well . . . there were things like the death certificate to organise. Oh God, it was a nightmare. And all the time, hanging over me like a sword, was the thought that Charles didn't know.

You look at me with shocked, enormous eyes and I am thrown. You are a striking woman, Elizabeth, I think again. Your client is lucky to have you.

'Then what happened?'

Delia looked as though a ton weight had fallen on her. She began making noises in her throat as if she were trying to say something, trying to push off the weights. Reminded me of the story of the king who sat in a room and tore at his clothes, saying, 'Oh my son, my son.' That was how it was; that was how she pulled at her neck with her nails.

She kept repeating his name, saying she wanted to see him, and the doctor was trying to dissuade her. Oh God! I don't think I will ever forget it.

'Matt, Matt,' she cried. 'Matt!'

I saw how it would be, then, until the day she died. They kept talking to her, over and over and over again; patiently. As though she was a sick child.

'What's the point?' they said. 'You've seen how it is, don't torment yourself, it's better this way, he could not have lived with such injuries ...' that sort of thing. And Dee went on saying they had no right to keep her away from her son. What son? I thought. That heap of scrap wasn't Matt. But I said nothing.

After what seemed ages there was a knock on the door and we were asked to pick up the phone. A call was being put through from the UK.

'Charles?'

I look at you grimly.

Yes. And guess who had to break the news?

I know I sound resentful. Had I been resentful at the time? Probably.

Well, of course he couldn't take it in. Even though I spoke very slowly.

Predictably enough, he thought she'd lost the baby. So I had to start all over again, reassuring him on the one hand and preparing him for the real news on the other. When it sank in, what I was saying, he asked me coldly to put Delia on the phone. But then, when he heard her muffled incoherence, I guess that was when he broke down. I left them to it. I mean, there was only so much I could do.

'You hated being involved, didn't you?'

Elizabeth, don't start. I'm doing you a big favour, remember. You dislike me, I know, but I too have been a casualty of this accident.

Anyway, Charles said he was taking the first flight out of Heathrow.

As there was nothing else left to do, I was encouraged by the hospital to take Delia home. They had work to get on with; the aftermath of bereavement wasn't their forte. So we went. I drove. It turned out her car was still up on the Prati somewhere. She had travelled down in a police car with her hope held tightly to her, hardly daring to breathe. She had held on, she now told me in a whisper, thinking he would be saved.

'Did you see him there?' I asked.

In the occasional light from a passing car she turned piteously towards me. It broke my heart, that shattered look.

'No,' she said, she hadn't seen him. Not then.

By the time she had got to the top of the Prati, frantic with fear, the ambulances were already there and he was being air-lifted. So no, she had not seen the extent of his injuries.

Later that night, when she had collapsed exhausted on her bed, I spoke to Charles. It was moments before he boarded his plane. He sounded drunk.

I had still not been able to get hold of Giorgio, but at about ten o'clock the phone rang again and I reached for it quickly.

I wanted Delia to get as much sleep as possible, for I knew that once consciousness broke through the painkillers she would be back at the beginning again.

It wasn't Giorgio on the phone but Mirella, his wife. Giorgio had not come home yet, she told me. He had spent most of the day with the families of the dead, and had assumed rightly that I was with Delia.

'What?' I asked, shocked. How many dead were there, for God's sake?

Mirella was crying. When she rang off, I poured myself a whisky. Delia would, I estimated, wake at any moment, and Charles wouldn't be with us until well after midnight; he was on the last flight to Pisa. I tried to imagine his sad moonlit journey, flying over the Alps, picking up the car, driving along the autostrada, following the course of the river towards our valley. Doing what he had always done, but differently, now. Not daring to think of what he was driving towards, or what his life would become from this moment onwards. I stood on the ter-razza, staring out at the fireflies. Thinking too, that last night seemed a million light years away. Then I heard a small sound inside so, picking up my glass of whisky, I hurried in.

'The moment Charles walked in the door, at . . . what was it? . . . almost two in the morning, I saw precisely what the underlying problem would be, Elizabeth,' I say. 'Over and above the obvious fact of Matt's death, I mean.'

I pour us both another drink and turn on the light. Then I close the curtains. I am finding the telling of this story extraordinarily difficult. It surprises me that there remains still so much anger in me when I think of how Matt's life was stolen from us.

'I'm talking about the subtext,' I say, checking you understand. 'I saw it clearer at that moment than I would see it afterwards.'

'Yes.'

The problem was perfectly clear. When Delia saw her husband, all she wanted him to do was make the pain go away, make it all right again. Somehow, the fact that Charles had been absent when it happened meant it was up to him to reverse things for her.

But Charles was struggling with his own pain. He'd been dealing with it all the way to the airport, all through the interminable flight. And he hadn't seen anything yet.

Every piece of information he had had was second-hand. Now he was faced, for the first time, with what it had done to Delia.

It must have been like having cold water thrown over him. He was exhausted with travelling, he was almost hallucinating, and now he was confronted with the reality of her *face*. He stared at it in terror.

He was on the brink of total shut-down. I must have realised this on some level in spite of my own confusion.

I pause, hesitating. Then I tell you:

If I were to be brutally honest, I would say I had been waiting for this moment for years. Not so dramatically. I hadn't wanted Matt to die, *obviously*, but the fault line that in my exhausted state I intuited was what I had always hoped for.

You move uneasily in your chair and I look sharply at you. Am I being judged?

'No,' you say. 'Go on.'

You make an impatient gesture with your left hand. I see it is a ringless hand.

'I was dog-tired,' I continue. 'But I couldn't leave them alone together.'

Watching them casting around for some sense when there was none to be had, I tried instead to make them eat something. They refused. Charles had clearly been drinking heavily and now he reached for the whisky, pouring us all some. His hands were shaking. I told them both what Mirella had said. I didn't tell them that she had believed Matt had survived.

'Giovanni, too?' Charles asked, wonderingly. 'All of them?'

I told them what I knew: that Giovanni had lagged behind, riding on his bicycle. This had saved him.

'Where is he?' Charles asked angrily. 'I want to talk to him.'

'Charles ... it isn't his fault. He didn't know there was a bomb. How could he?'

Delia was crying.

It was a hopeless night. A parody of all the nights we had spent together. Bewildered, I asked myself: were these children the last victims of a war fought long ago? A line from a poem, running through my mind: 'How sleep the brave'. In the room, under the deathly yellow of the electric light, Delia's hair shone. I was shocked by its beauty in the midst of such carnage. The armchairs, the furniture, all of it, looked terrifyingly normal, but emptiness was everywhere: in the framed photographs, the shoes lying carelessly around. I saw that nothing was true any more. Everything was lies, like the stories told to children to make their eyes glow. Upstairs, a door banged as it sometimes did when a breeze blew in from the hills. And I thought of the ways in which chance had ordered the fate of the mothers who had lost their sons during the war. But at least they had been prepared for that chance.

'Did that make their grief any better, Elizabeth?' I ask you.

You shake your head. You don't know either.

By four a.m. I was so tired and so drunk that I could have fallen down. I felt my head would burst. Charles and Delia sat huddled together on the sofa. They were both still in the clothes they had worn all day; the marks on Delia's dress a macabre reminder of all she had gone through.

Suddenly I realised they were both waiting for the moment when they could go back to the hospital. Back to Matt. I wondered which of us was in the best state to drive. I decided I would ring Mirella and ask her to take us.

Towards dawn, I tried again without success to urge them to get some rest.

'At least,' I begged, 'have a shower, get changed, get ready to leave.'

Reluctantly they went and I stepped back out onto the terrazza for a cigarette. The air had cooled; there was a slight mist. Something rustled in the bushes nearby. All across the valley a few houses had switched on their lights and I saw the darkness had become less intense. I smoked my cigarette and watched the faint change in the sky.

It was four thirty.

From the east, the light pierced through like a star, slowly lighting up the mountains. It was then I sensed rather than saw that both of them had come silently out too and were standing a little distance away from me. They had changed their clothes. We stood without speaking, staring up towards the sunrise, and I wondered if they might be thinking how, yesterday, on their last unknowing morning as a family, it had been this way too.

And as I stood there, smoking another cigarette and shuffling my aching feet against the cold, the east lightened and lightened and we saw that the dawn was about to arrive on this, their first complete day without Matt. And as we watched, the sun rose, pushing aside the scarves of mist, waking up the birds, ushering in the day.

'It's morning,' I heard one of them whisper.

And perhaps I imagined it, although I cannot be certain, that just for a moment there came upon them a stilling of their grief. Whatever lay ahead, whatever the day brought would have to be dealt with. But within this small pocket of time, as the bare, white bone of light gathered over the mountaintops, pausing at the spot where their son had lost his life, they were at peace.

Over in the next valley a sparrowhawk greeted the day with its uncompromising, harsh cry.

16

And now they were two

I finish speaking and close my eyes, engulfed by exhaustion. Everything was different after that, I tell you. I was different, they were different, the shadows were different, the streets, the houses, other people's news: they were all different. It was never going to be the same again for any of us. We had become children of another time, in some other place, pre-1945. We would be numbered amongst those who would never forget.

'It's over two years now since this all happened,' I tell you.

Your silence deepens like a fall of snow. I see there is nothing awkward or contrived about you, Elizabeth, and, in spite of myself, I am impressed.

'I am alone these days,' I tell you. 'Elena went long ago.'

She wrote to me afterwards; she had lived with a ghost for too long. The strain on her was more than she could take.

Again I am silent. The telling of this sad little story to another has made me realise that there are longings still present, still lurking in the background. It is getting late, Elizabeth. Forgive me, I am more upset than I thought.

'Would you like some bread and cheese?' I ask.

Hesitating only for a moment, you nod. I feel you, too, are weary.

'Perhaps they will never go away,' you say. 'Memory is nearly always impossible to wipe out.'

As we eat, you give me a glimpse of your real self. You are worried about your client's health, you tell me. He is frail. Only a thin hope sustains him. If that disappears, what then? You arouse in me a faint interest in this man who brought you to me.

'He's a very fine man,' you say, with pride in your voice.

He is lucky, I think. I don't know what else I might tell you. You are waiting to hear about Lola. I am aware of your patience.

'You must understand, their marriage was in trouble long before Lola appeared on the scene.'

I see you do. I see also you understand something else. You understand that whether or not their marriage was in trouble it would make no difference to me. I was part of that original triangle and therefore corrupted by it.

'But Delia had the other child?'

Oh, the pregnancy! I had forgotten about that.

'The following day, when we returned from the hospital, they had visitors.'

It was Giovanni and his family. They had come, as is the custom in those parts, to pay their respects to the family of the deceased.

Giovanni was completely unhurt. If you remember, he had been half a mile away, practising on his bike. When he heard the explosion he had at first thought the sound had come from the farm.

The farmer, too, presumably, had heard the explosion; Giovanni met him on the way. They had both hurried in the direction of the noise.

What Giovanni didn't tell the Boyars was that the crying came from only one person. From Matt, still alive – but only just.

The farmer had taken in the scene pretty quickly. Seeing the shattered bodies all around – a leg here, an arm in the bushes, a headless torso – he had moved Giovanni swiftly away while ringing the emergency services. But Giovanni had seen quite enough to last him the rest of his life.

What he had had was a swift and brutal history lesson on the Second World War, although he hadn't worked that out yet.

Anyway, after Matt had been airlifted, after the news of his death had filtered through to the villagers, the farmer took Giovanni home. His mother telephoned his father who came hurrying up with the priest.

The whole family was very religious. They wanted Matt's family to know they would be present at the funeral.

What they also wanted to know was whether Giovanni should say a few words about his friend. Of course they should have waited a bit.

Well, when Delia heard who had arrived, she went into the bedroom and refused to come out. Charles tried to persuade her, but she wasn't having any of it. In the end he had to talk to the family himself. They were very understanding.

But afterwards, Charles told me, Delia became hysterical again. An hour later she began to bleed and in panic Charles called first the doctor and then me.

'The doctor told us it was the shock that had brought on the miscarriage.'

There seems nothing else to say. I pour more wine. There is a bitter taste in my mouth.

'People thought it was the end of their marriage,' I say. 'That there was nothing left to salvage.'

Matt's remains were flown back to Britain and the funeral took place down in Suffolk, where his grandmother lived. Delia was adamant that it shouldn't be in Italy.

I think she inadvertently hurt a lot of people. I don't think they understood why she was rejecting their warmth and love for Matt. It was hard for them, especially when you take into account that there were other children who had died. Charles tried to get her to change her mind. The parish priest tried to see her too. She wouldn't see anyone.

I remembered the way they had left the house, in the slow, sad evening, heads bowed. People lined the road. I drove them to the airport in almost complete silence. Delia had stopped crying. She had retreated into what can only be described as a chilling absence.

A year later, she talked to me about that moment, the way in which they had left. How could tears, she asked me angrily, have expressed how she had felt?

When she got back to England, Charles persuaded her to see their family doctor, who told him that trauma affected people in different ways. She would come out of it in her own time, the doctor had said.

Delia never cried again.

Charles was marvellous with her. I don't know how he coped, but he did.

Many of their friends thought he would crack under the strain. Leave her, perhaps. Or have an affair.

'To put it brutally, by the time he met Lola, an affair was long overdue . . .' I pause. 'He had his work. I remember at the time he was in the middle of planning another big exhibition – for the National, of course – but that was all.'

Aware of the irony of my words, I stop speaking.

'The Pieros?'

I nod. It would have been the first time *The Flagellation* was allowed out of Italy.

'It was a stroke of diplomatic genius on Charles's part,' I say. 'To persuade them to give permission, I mean.'

'It must have taken years. I know these things do,' you say.

Again I nod.

'None of it counted for anything at home.'

At home he discovered a latent talent for nursing.

He decided to make it his life's work to nurse Delia back to some kind of health. And in a sense he'd achieved it, forcing her back to Cargalla, making her face the past. Perhaps only then was he able to face his own grief.

Reluctantly, I tell you something Lola said.

'It's all about *her*, isn't it?' she had said.

Lola hated Delia. She felt Charles indulged her far too much. 'Her grief, her beauty. God!' Lola had raged. 'What an ego!' I sigh.

'Lola . . . delved into things that weren't her concern,' I say.

'Don't you think,' she was always asking me, 'don't you think he deserves something himself?'

I didn't envy him, Lola. But wait, I don't want to talk about Lola, yet.

After the funeral I saw very little of Delia. She would not go back to Italy, and Charles wasn't prepared to leave her on her own, so it was I who shut the house up for them and brought back the key. By this time even I couldn't stomach living in Italy.

The winter came, the first winter without Matt. In the spring, Charles was meant to go to a conference in Paris. It had been planned a year before and suddenly Delia wanted him to go. I remember them arguing. Charles refused point-blank to leave her. He was like a devoted old dog, sending Dee to the verge of hysteria. She desperately wanted to be without him for a while, but still he refused. Finally, bitterly, she confronted him.

'Staying with me all the time won't bring them back,' she screamed.

I offered my services. I lived just around the corner, I was working at home, supposedly writing my next book. We could spend the three days that Charles was in Paris together, I told them both. Delia gave me a wry smile, but Charles accepted.

'Don't worry,' I told her when he had gone. 'I know you want to be by yourself. Just call me if you want me to come over.'

It was March now. The daffodils were out early in Kensington Gardens, the trees were sprouting a young green and the harsh winter snow from Siberia that had whitened London for so many months had begun to melt. Above us was a sky the colour of which we hadn't seen for months. Tentatively, I rang Dee, suggesting we walk in the park. It seemed to me what she needed were simple, small distractions that required not much effort on her part. I knew I was taking a risk, I knew that when he was small they had taken Matt to this park, but I needed to see if she could take this small step. To my surprise, she came. We walked slowly in silence. I kept glancing at her from the corner of my eye. She was painfully thin, skeletal. And still, to me, she was very beautiful. After a while she told me that she repeated Matt's name to herself all the time, talking to him about the past, seeing him in her dreams.

'If I eat an egg for supper,' she said, 'I always dream of him.'

She spoke calmly. I felt a jolt of fear. I didn't know what on earth to say.

'You think I'm going mad, don't you?' she asked, finally, into the silence.

And then she smiled for the first time in eight months. Taken aback, I smiled too.

'It's true, Alex,' she continued. 'I tried an experiment to test it.'

I remembered hearing Charles say she would only eat eggs.

'Charles made me a poached egg on the night of the funeral. I couldn't eat. I hadn't eaten for days and afterwards, when we came home, I sort of fainted. So he got scared and insisted I eat an egg. Well, it wasn't easy. I felt like gagging. I had just buried my child, how could I even think of food?'

I nodded, holding on to her arm. Food, she told me, was for the sustenance of the living. She was only half living. Dying was what she wanted.

'But then he sat with me and fed me! So what could I do but force myself to eat?'

She stopped walking and stood looking around her.

'Has the snow really gone?' she murmured.

It was as if she had been asleep for a decade. She had that look about her.

'Anyway, I began to feel very drowsy soon after,' she said. 'I wanted to sleep. Charles gave me my tablets, but I didn't want them that night. I didn't tell him this. Poor man had enough to deal with. I wanted him to stop worrying.'

I noticed she spoke of Charles remotely, as though she had no real concept of his feelings.

'And that night I dreamed of Matt. He was talking to me. Sitting on his bike and calling me. "Mum! Mum!" he was saying. "Come over here, quickly. Now!"'

She laughed quietly.

'I felt wonderful the next day. In fact . . .' she paused, looking guilty, 'I did not feel like a woman who had buried a child at all. I had to hide it from Charles. He would have thought I was going crazy.'

I said nothing.

'The next night,' she said, 'I didn't dream of him. I couldn't sleep at all the next night and it was terrible. In the end, towards dawn I had to take a tablet.'

She looked at me solemnly. When I still said nothing, she continued:

'I didn't eat any eggs for several days after that and the pain was terrible. It was so . . . physical . . . that I used the sleeping tablets like painkillers.'

Some days later, she told me, quite by chance, she ate a boiled egg late at night. That night she dreamed of Matt and also saw herself nearing the end of her second pregnancy.

In the dream she knew it was a girl child, and that it would be born perfectly healthy. She awoke happy. She had talked to Matt at length. He hadn't actually answered her, but she had called out to him and he had said her name twice. Had her dream gone on a bit longer, she was sure she would have seen his face. It occurred to her that the eggs might have had a connection with her dream. The very next night when Charles asked her what he could prepare for her, insisting that she must keep trying to eat, she asked for an omelette and this night too she dreamt of Matt. He was calling her again.

'Mum! Mum! Come here,' he said.

She told me all of this during that first walk in the park. I didn't have the heart to contradict her.

I must tell you, Elizabeth, that my obsession with Delia had changed somewhat.

'In what way?'

Her life, her suffering, her marriage to Charles, all of it, was something I could do nothing about. I had been living for so long through my eyes alone, feasting them on her, that my love had become almost abstract. Almost, but not quite.

It was simple enough to listen to her talk. Her voice had grown husky from so much grief. Now and then, the ghost that lived inside my head detached itself from me and went over to her and kissed her.

Luckily for me, Charles's trip was short. When he returned, I mumbled something about work and tried to distance myself from them both.

It was not easy. I felt I was drowning in their sorrow. The smell of grief clung to them even as they tried to cling to me. I threw myself into my work and shortly afterwards, as spring moved gently into summer, they decided to pack up the house in London and travel around the States. Matt had been dead a year.

Nearly another year passed after that. I travelled backwards and forwards to Italy. I met a girl from Genova. Her name was Beatrice; she had a similar colouring to Delia. She was older than any of my previous girlfriends and therefore had fewer expectations of me. Before long, I found myself telling her all about Delia and the accident. I intuited Beatrice understood something of how I felt. She asked no questions and this made me like her all the more.

So for a while, three or four months perhaps, I thought myself in love once more.

When the call came, as I knew one day it would, I was not surprised.

'It's time enough,' Charles told me. They had decided to come back.

His voice from New York sounded close by and familiar. The way he had of swallowing nervously before he asked me a favour, his gentle laugh, all of that came back to me. There was no awkwardness between us.

'How's Dee?' I asked.

'She's here, wanting to say hello!'

And he put her on the phone. Once again the accident was before me, in the timbre of her voice; the moment of bewilderment, the sun so fierce, the shock of realisation, the doctor's words. I stared at the window sill and saw the flies from some other summer darkening it. Listening to her voice, I noted that, although the fury of grief might have dampened, other things lurked there. Like the dead days of a finished time, they lingered. But, I suspected, dreams mattered less to her now. It's over, I thought thankfully, not knowing fully what I referred to. Her voice still had that breathy hoarseness that had once driven me wild, but it was calmer, steadier, older. I wondered how she looked. At the moment of Matt's death, pregnant and blooming, she had looked as beautiful as a young girl. But now? Listening to her speak, I too felt calmer. Most of all, Elizabeth, I felt glad the fever that had raged within me seemed somehow to have passed.

I was out of danger, I told myself, foolishly.

Of course, I agreed to supervise the opening up of the house. I would get Emma to air it and make the beds and get the grass cut. I would do all of this. And by late summer they would arrive, via London.

'We're both so looking forward to seeing you, Alex,' Charles said warmly. 'It's been too long.'

All would have been fine after that, had it not been for Lola. None of us had foreseen the problem of Lola.

I think for a moment.

'It was Elena who introduced her to me.'

A happier Elena, married now to a man who did not have a taste for sharing his bed with ghosts. That was what she told me. Had there been a touch of pity in her voice, I wondered afterwards.

Anyway, she rang up with some long involved story and told me, after the way I had treated her, I owed her a massive favour.

She had never asked me for anything, she reminded me. Never once reproached me about my behaviour.

Oh, it all came out, then. All the things she had bottled up, the resentment accumulated over many years.

A close woman friend of hers had had a rather tough time of it as a single mother. All the usual stuff: handsome, foreign husband, womaniser, deserter. It was clear whose side Elena was on, of course!

Anyway, what could I do, faced with this tirade of accusations?

The woman's daughter was, apparently, very talented. She wanted to break into politics, needed contacts.

'You've plenty of political contacts, Alex,' Elena said. And when I protested, she told me to ask around at the newspaper.

'Take her for a few weeks in the summer,' Elena demanded, adding that the girl would be my PA.

I needed no PA, I said crossly, but still Elena insisted.

'Cook, then? Cleaner?'

Elena had the knack of making me feel guilty. What could I do? I said yes.

'And that,' I tell you grimly, 'was how I met Lola.'

17

At noon there are no shadows

'Elizabeth, I told you, if it hadn't been Lola, it would have been someone else.'

You give me a sharp look and, in spite of everything, I smile at you. Yesterday you had bags under your eyes, but this morning you look rested. Yes, I will tell you about the lovely Lola.

Coffee? Before we begin?

Lola arrived that summer in a fury and turned the whole of their lives into a war zone.

I saw trouble from the very beginning.

'Why?' you ask, sharply.

I laugh. Where do I start? Sunlight falls on the ashtray where my cigarette sits smouldering.

'The first thing that really annoyed me was the way she used my house as if she had every right to be there.'

I hear my voice getting louder.

'She never contributed a damn thing in any way, except when it suited her. She was the laziest person I have ever met.'

'How old was she when she came to stay?'

'Twenty-three. Old enough to know better.'

I sigh. Possibly I'm being a little hard on her.

'In actual fact, there was something about her . . . a yarblockos, diabolicalness that I recognised!'

'Pardon?'

I laugh.

'I mean, there was a Clockwork Orangeness in her.'

'Oh,' you say, losing interest. '*That!*'

'Yes, that. It stirred the old Alex in me, I suppose. I didn't totally dislike her.'

'So, what was the problem?'

'Well, self-interest springs to mind.'

'In an adolescent way? But I thought you understood it?'

I sigh, again.

'I was an adolescent when I behaved as I did. But she was too old to be an adolescent. No, this was a young adult who had had her own way for much too long. Somebody had totally indulged her, maybe trying to compensate for things that had gone wrong in the past. I must say, I couldn't take too much of it.'

You look at me expectantly and I sigh again.

'Look, I had been told about a young, clever, ambitious girl who was looking for a way into politics via the arts.'

'And?'

Well, in a sense she was, yes, but . . . I had expected someone a bit more . . . *unsure*, shall we say? Lola was perfectly sure of herself. And what was more, she knew how to hide her confidence when it suited her. Oh, she was clever all right. Or should I say, cunning.

She saw my weaknesses, very quickly. As she did Charles's. And she knew how to work the system.

I shake my head.

'Really, she was all about hard ambition. I was never that.'

I pause. I had been all about denial, I think.

'She wanted to present herself as a kind of puzzle, a dazzling mystery, at once too difficult and too easy to solve. At least, that was how she presented herself. Maybe I am making her more sophisticated than she actually was.'

'Interesting. Give me an example.'

'Well . . .' I think for a moment. 'For instance, she made friends with several people her own age as soon as she arrived in the village. No hesitation there. She was out, from day one, on the back of some youth's motorino, swanning off to Pontremoli.'

I realise the resentment in my voice is showing.

'She wouldn't wake before midday and when she did it was simply to lounge around smoking. Even the cleaner started complaining about her mess. As for helping me, what a joke! She was a fake, acting as though she were a spoilt rich kid,' I tell you.

'Her parents were divorced.'

'I don't see how that made much of a difference.'

'Well, only that there would have been some turmoil in her life.' I laugh.

'Obviously, you haven't met Lola.'

'Just once and then she refused to talk to me, just snatched the letter I brought and slammed the door in my face. Although the description her father gives . . .'

'Oh, forget about the father.' I wave my hand. 'I can tell you what she was like.'

'Where did she meet Charles Boyar? At your place?'

'The first time? No. I can't be blamed for that!'

I feel myself getting annoyed.

'Does talking about Lola irritate you?'

I open my mouth to make an ironic comment, but then stop myself. You are right.

'She reminds you very much of yourself, doesn't she?'

Back off, I want to say. But instead I decide to tell you about the extraordinary way it happened.

She almost missed the trip with me to Parma that day. Having stayed up late drinking and phoning England (at my expense as

I discovered afterwards), she overslept and only woke when I banged on her door.

'You go, if you want,' she shouted. 'I don't mind staying in today.'

But then she changed her mind and decided to come with me. Eventually, she wandered out and poured herself a cold cup of coffee. I wanted to swat her. I had to get to the market before it shut and there she was, nibbling on the corner of a brioche.

'Can you hurry up? Or shall I just go?'

'I won't be long,' she said.

Apparently, I found out later, she wanted to force me to admit to being annoyed.

That was what she was like. Always this insatiable need to win in any battle of wills.

I pause. Immature little bitch.

'Lola, I must go soon,' I said. 'There won't be any decent fish left.'

She waved a fly away, took a last swig of the coffee before stubbing her cigarette out on the saucer.

'*Andiamo*,' she said. 'Let's go!'

I picked up the saucer and emptied its contents in the bin. Then I poured the rest of the coffee into the sink, pointedly, moved a damp towel outside to dry and picked up my car keys.

'Does your mother know how much you smoke?'

'She's not the one who cares! Dad left her because she smoked too.'

I sighed heavily. She folded her long legs into my car and adjusted her seat belt. Her hair was almost dry, its long tresses shone straight and chestnut in the summer light.

We parted company in Parma. She mumbled something about visiting the Baptistery. I told her I would meet her in a café nearby.

After I'd bought the fish and the artichoke, I went in search of melons. Then I bought some fresh pasta and remembered the wine. It was almost lunchtime. I passed one of the narrow streets that had tables spilling out onto the pavement. At midday there are no shadows. White tablecloths and green ferns blocked the path. A cat sat sunning itself, unblinking. A motorino buzzed past. My mobile phone rang. It was Lola.

'Where are you?'

She sounded cross.

'What's the matter?' I asked.

'I'm hungry.'

'I was just thinking the same thing,' I said pleasantly. Resisting sarcasm. 'Shall we have a bite to eat?'

I gave her directions to get to where I was. When she arrived, I could see she had cheered up a bit.

'I've had a text from home,' she told me. 'I've been shortlisted for that job I told you about.'

I remembered something about a graduate placement in Parliament. It was important, she told me, not so much for the money, but more for the contacts she would make. A great networker, is our Lola.

'I've got this theory,' she said, her face close to mine. 'The next big thing in Britain is going to be arts and ethnicity. There's a lot of people who've been playing the ethnic card. You know: let's get the foreigners into galleries. But they aren't going about it in the right way. That's all going to change, though!'

'Of course,' I said, unable to resist. 'Let me guess: you're going to change things?'

I'd no idea what she was talking about. She glanced suspiciously at me. Then she started some rigmarole about the numbers of Asians and blacks who visited the major galleries in London.

'What exactly did she say? Can you remember?'

'To be honest, I can't. Was it too many or too few? Anyway, she did tell me her father had been passionate about painting.'

'And you didn't make the connection, even then? With her father?'

250

'Why should I have? I had forgotten the man.'

'Even the fact that he had been Sri Lankan?'

'I don't know if I ever knew his nationality, and it was too long ago, Elizabeth, I'm afraid.'

You nod. I'm not in court, I think resentfully.

'What happened next?'

'Well, that was when we saw her.'

'Oh, look, there's that woman from last night,' Lola said.

I looked up from the menu.

'It's Delia! Must be out shopping. They're coming over tonight with the others.'

'Her husband is the art historian?'

'Charles? Yes, a writer. He did a television series on Giorgione last year.'

The waiter brought beers and I poured us both a drink.

'He hasn't done so much recently. Not since . . . not after what happened to him.'

She didn't know, of course.

'What happened to him? Did he lose his wallet or something?'

'He lost a child, actually.'

Four weeks with this lazy slut, I thought, closing my eyes against the blinding light.

'Oh.'

A car drove past at the same moment as Delia stepped out onto the street.

'Dee,' I shouted, but she didn't hear me.

She was searching in her bag for her mobile as she disappeared towards the centre of town. We could hear her shoes echoing on the cobbles. Lola made no comment. I was aware of her watching me curiously. Then she yawned without covering her mouth. Our food arrived and we ate in silence. Afterwards I asked her to amuse herself for a bit.

'Say for an hour? I've got to meet someone.'

'Can't I come?'

'No, it's a business meeting. Go on a sightseeing trip. I'll buy you an ice cream in the square, at two.'

'You going to shag someone?'

That was how she spoke. I resisted the urge to hit her.

'No, Lola, I'm not going to sleep with anyone. Although, if I were, I don't see how it would be any of your business.'

We regrouped at two. I was feeling a bit guilty for having abandoned her, but to my surprise she was in a good mood.

'I've seen the most beautiful man!' she cried.

'You didn't see me, did you?' I asked, laughing.

'No, not *you*. Someone much older than you.'

I raised my eyebrows, pretending to be shocked.

'Lolita! Did he ask you out?'

She grinned and shook her head. I thought with pleasant surprise that if she tried she could be quite attractive. It was hot; the dead end of the afternoon. I knew we should be getting back.

'What about that ice cream?'

I groaned.

'Are you serious? You can't still be hungry?'

But she was and I had promised, as she reminded me. We seemed to have reached a truce.

We found a gelateria that was still open and sat down at one of the outdoor tables behind a large pot of oleander. A boy on a push bike whizzed swiftly past, hardly disturbing the air. A church clock struck the hour, its tin sound echoing across the drowsy piazza. The pink buildings glowed in the soft light.

'So tell me about the beautiful man. Why didn't he ask you out? What's the matter with him!'

Pigeons cooed somewhere above us.

'Sshh!' Lola said fiercely. 'Look! That's him!'

I froze. Walking into the gelateria were Delia and Charles. They were less than five feet away from us, screened only by the

252

enormous oleander. They had not seen us. Afterwards I thought, had it been a different time of day, had the café been fuller, had there been music playing, we would not have heard them. Or we would have made ourselves known to them and then all that followed might not have happened. But as it was, both of us were struck dumb. At first their voices were just a blend of murmurs. Instantly we were straining our ears.

'. . . you look so nice.'

'I'm tired now.'

'We haven't had such a . . . last night . . . did you enjoy it too?'

'Mmm.'

My espresso tasted bitter. Lola, who had begun eating a huge *affogato*, put her spoon down quietly.

'Let's go back, let's not bother eating here,' Charles said. 'I'll make some pasta, you can have a shower . . . '

There was a silence followed by a rustling sound. One of them, I think it might have been Delia, sighed.

'I want you.'

There was the smallest of sounds. I swallowed. For a moment the words conveyed nothing at all. But the urgency of the tone, the breathlessness in it, vibrated in the air. A fly buzzed. I badly wanted to peer over the top of the oleander bush. I suspect Lola did too. We must have looked perfectly ridiculous. If we twisted our necks we could see the top of Delia's head, bent slightly towards Charles.

'I want you too. Let's go back.'

The words were barely above a whisper, but to us their meaning was clear as a bell and just as resonant. And then, with a scraping of chairs they were gone, their voices fading away into the hum of traffic moving on cobbled streets, while Lola and I sat on, speechlessly. To tell you the truth, I was hardly aware of Lola. A strong unidentifiable current of emotion was flowing through me and in spite of the heat I shivered. It was Lola who broke the silence.

'Let's get back,' she said roughly.

In the car we were both silent. The exchange between Charles and Delia could not have taken more than a few minutes. Why was I so shocked?

Back at the villa we avoided each other. I showered and then decided to rest in my room for half an hour before I started getting ready for the evening. The truth was, I couldn't face Lola. I wished I were alone. I cursed Elena for having lumbered me with this awkward, retarded adult.

Anyway, sleep was beyond me. The intimacy of the little scene I had inadvertently overheard needed sorting out in my mind.

Suddenly it was all back with full force.

'What?' you ask.

'My feelings for Delia.'

Every time I closed my eyes, I saw the two of them, heads bent towards each other. Lying naked on my bed the only recourse to relief was in the old way that I had employed before. Afterwards, loneliness descended and I slid into a sad, drifting sleep. When I woke it was past six. They would be here in two hours. Hastily I dressed and went out. Lola was waiting for me in the kitchen. She was smoking. And she had the look of someone who might have been crying.

'God! Look at the time!' I said, avoiding her eyes.

She stubbed out a cigarette.

'Look, could you not smoke in here?'

'Are *those* people coming to dinner?' she asked.

'Those people? I wonder who you mean.'

She laughed harshly. Your secret is safe with me, her laugh seemed to say.

'Was that your beautiful man?' I asked nastily, in return.

She looked at me and suddenly I felt sorry. She might be twenty-three but she had the mental age of a sixteen-year-old, I told myself.

'You like her, don't you?' she said.

I finished slicing onions and handed her the borlotti beans to pod. Then I put water on to boil and I poured us both a Campari. I sat down at the kitchen table and raised my glass.

'First,' I said, 'I would be grateful if you would do the washing up while I cook. We haven't got much time before they arrive. Okay?'

She nodded.

'Second. Since you've asked, yes, I like her, as you so charmingly put it. But it isn't what you think.'

'You mean you haven't had an affair with her because she doesn't want you? Or because of your high principles?'

'Neither. The subject hasn't arisen. Delia and Charles have suffered a terrible blow and . . .'

'You care?'

'Lola . . .'

I paused. Why was she deliberately trying to rile me? I looked at her steadily and she stared back. More than ever, I was convinced she was upset by something.

'Have you been crying?' I asked, and watched as her eyes filled up.

For the third time that day I felt sorry for her. It's hopeless, I wanted to say. Don't even go down that road. You saw how it was, need I say more? You're young, I wanted to tell her, don't waste your time on things that aren't for you.

'Look, Lola,' I sighed, 'let's have a good evening. You've got something to celebrate, being shortlisted for the job you want. Don't get yourself into their mess.'

She wouldn't look at me. It's just a crush, I wanted to shout. You don't want it to be anything else.

'Hmm,' she agreed, as if I had spoken.

There was a feeling of desperation between us.

She offered to help make the antipasto. She cleaned the

kitchen with surprising efficiency. Then she sliced tomatoes and mozzarella and unwrapped the fresh Parma ham. After that she took small citronella candles outside onto the terrace. In the middle of all this her mother rang and she spoke to her in her usual sulky, monosyllabic way. I wondered what had interfered with her growing up.

'That was my mum,' she said unnecessarily, after she had finished.

'Don't you get on with her?'

She shrugged. There were some issues, she said. On her mother's part, at least.

'How do you mean?'

Unusually loquacious, she told me her mother hated the fact she was still connected to Lola's father through Lola.

'I think she'd like to forget he existed, but she can't, because of me!'

'What do you feel? About your father, I mean?'

Again she shrugged, bored.

'He's okay. They're both okay. I don't feel anything, it's their problem.'

'Just okay?' I asked, curious. 'Was he a good father?'

'Good? Define "good". Do you mean, was he there all the time for me? The answer is no. Do you mean, did he forget me whenever he got a new inamorata? The answer is yes.'

I let out a breath. Tricky, I thought. And then:

'They're in the past. It's my generation who count, now. We're the future.'

She looked at me, pityingly.

'I see! How chilling. We're all of no account?'

She looked uncertain, not knowing if I was joking.

'I'm not being nasty,' she said finally.

I had invited some of the English ex-pats over along with two Italians. My friend Beatrice arrived first with the *dolci*. There were other people, friends of Elena who had heard about Lola's presence and wanted to talk to her. Everyone helped themselves to drinks and went outside, but by eight when the table was laid, there was still no sign of the Boyars.

'Let's start,' I said finally.

The pasta was ready and the fish would be overcooked. Everyone took their places at the long table facing the olive grove. And then, just as Lola was bringing in the salami and the calamari, there was the sound of a car and the Boyars walked in.

Lola sat next to Charles. Neither of us planned it this way, but as she had become the waitress for the evening she was the last to sit down and the space beside Charles was just enough for her to squeeze into. I raised my glass and toasted my waitress.

'Here's to our aspirant politician!' I said. 'I hope you get the job.'

There was a roar of mild disapproval.

'What, in Britain? You're joking! The place is in a good enough mess already. According to the Vatican, it's a Third World country!'

'Why d'you think we're all here?'

'It will ruin you, first!'

Lola was laughing. I believe she was enjoying herself, at last.

'Listen, m'dear, don't have any illusions. *Everyone* in politics is corrupt. It's the nature of the game. Power corrupts.'

I could see she was flattered by so much attention. Charles began teasing her gently. Across on the other side of the table, Delia was deep in conversation with one of our neighbours, her face partly in shadow. She looked frail. I saw her put her hand up to her hair and adjust one of the pins that held it. This was only her second trip out at night. Everyone was aware of it. She wore a sequined dress that caught the last of the sunlight as she moved. I watched her talking to a man she did not know, who did not know her either, but would surely have heard her story. The light on the hillside where her son had died was golden and mellow, untroubled. It made me dizzy. I had a momentary sense of my own life passing. I glanced at Lola, but she had moved and was talking to someone else and my melancholy passed. All that evening, Lola was super-sensitive to my needs and she caught my eye and obediently began clearing plates. I went in the kitchen and she followed with the dirty plates which she stacked in the dishwasher. She might have been a waitress all her life, I told her. We worked as a team, but both of us, I intuited, were working in a vacuum.

'I need a fag,' she muttered.

And she went to the kitchen door.

We went back in with the second course on large white plates: filleted bream, small delicious potatoes, hand-picked funghi, tiny tomatoes. Lola removed empty bottles of wine and I poured more into glasses. Water in cool jugs was handed around. Like conspirators, we worked to a rhythm of our own. I remember thinking we were united as voyeurs.

Charles stood up restlessly and went over to Delia. I saw his hand come down lightly on her shoulder while he talked to Beatrice. Then, with the smallest of pressures on her collarbone, he moved back to his seat. His expression had not changed. I watched Delia. Her face was clear, one could almost say radiant. I wondered what she was really thinking. How unlike anyone else she always was. She caught my eye and smiled, then continued to talk to the man opposite her. Always out of reach, I thought, friendly but remote. I turned away.

Lola was doing the best she could. I heard Charles ask her a question and I noticed her face close down with an air of curious shyness.

'You're far too alive for politics,' I heard him say.

He turned to me for support, smiling.

'Don't you agree, Alex?'

I saw Delia's ringed finger curl itself around the stem of the glass. Inside it, white wine sparkled.

'You're the first girl I've seen in a long time who is completely alive!' Charles told Lola, laughing. 'So I, personally, disapprove of a political career for you.'

In her bedroom that night I would hear Lola cry and cry. She would cry in a way I would never have believed her capable of. But at dinner all I saw was a faint tremor on her lips.

On the other side of the table, Delia smiled slowly at something Beatrice was saying.

'Alex said you were going to look at some paintings?' Lola asked.

Her voice was subdued. For a moment I saw her as she possibly thought of herself, uncertain and a little gauche.

'The Pieros. Yes, that's right. We were going, but . . . ' he hesitated a fraction. 'I think Delia doesn't want to move from the house at the moment. So probably I'll go on my own. Why, are you interested in them?'

'I . . . ' I heard her say.

'I'm only going to look at *The True Cross* on this trip. And perhaps the Madonna. You're welcome to come. I shall have to do some writing while I'm there, but I can certainly offer you a lift, if you want.'

Mesmerised, helplessly, I watched them both.

'Would she . . . your wife, mind? If I come, too?'

'Delia? No, of course not. As I say, she doesn't want to leave the villa for too long.

'We've been away for ages,' he said. 'And now we're back, she doesn't want to go off travelling for a bit.'

The last words were said softly. Later, Lola told me she wasn't sure if she had misheard him. The way he held himself as he spoke made her want to reach up and touch his hair.

'Yes, please,' she said. 'If you don't mind, that is. I've always wanted to see them,' she lied.

I saw Charles smile.

'Anything that will help turn you away from politics and towards art,' he said.

He leaned across towards his wife.

'Sweetheart, Lola here would like to see the Pieros. She's never seen any of them before.' He looked at Lola. 'Correct?'

Lola shook her head and Delia smiled at her. It was a smile of startling warmth, changing her face instantly. Charles must have thought so too, because he seemed to drift into a reverie.

'Why don't you take her, Charles?'

'Are you sure you won't come?' He had lowered his voice. 'Please?'

'No, Charles,' Delia said.

Later, Lola helped me make everyone coffee. My heart had the strangest of aches. It looked as though it might rain.

'There's a bottle of grappa in the cupboard,' I told her. 'Take it in. Some of them will want to add a drop to their coffee.'

She pulled a face of disgust.

'Tell me about the Boyars,' she asked.

'What do you want to know? They have the strongest marriage I've known anyone have.'

She looked at me shrewdly and I gave a laugh.

'I know he's taking you to see the Pieros, but take my advice and don't get any ideas.'

She frowned and made to leave the kitchen.

'Oh and, Lola . . .'

'What?'

'Take the honey in with you. You always drink grappa with black coffee and a spoonful of honey here.'

18

To return again is human

They were the last to leave that evening. I suspected that, having made the effort to come, they were reluctant to go home. I felt they had been surprised at the ease with which they slipped back into the community. No reference had been made to Matt. As I waved them off, I looked around for Lola. The light upstairs had gone off and I assumed she had gone to bed. Charles turned the car radio on and a burst of opera floated upwards, towards the trees. For an instant I caught the faint scent of Delia's perfume, a smile, a ghostly wave of the hand, and then they were gone. Leaving no sense of their presence behind.

Sleep was impossible. Delia was back, gripping onto my imagination. It was worse than ever. Lying awake, watching the slow glissade of the moon, listening to the sounds of the night, I felt profoundly disturbed in a way I hadn't been for years. I asked myself where on earth I was heading. I remembered that during dinner one of the guests had remarked in a quiet aside that Charles had changed beyond all recognition. How true it was, I thought. With his hair almost completely white, his body so much thinner, he looked as a man might who had reached a breaking point. While *she* was unchanged. Grief, in an act of kindness, had left her face untouched. Only in her gestures, the quick, restless movements of her hands, the sudden flutter of her eyelids, the brightness of her eyes, perhaps, was anything detectable.

'Come and see us tomorrow,' she had murmured, before they left, pressing her cheek against mine. And I had nodded, welcoming the old ache back.

Charles, coming into the kitchen where Lola was stacking dishes, her back turned away, had murmured his thanks, too.

'It was the best thing for her,' he said quietly. 'Thanks again, Alex.'

He had hesitated, looking at Lola's back. Wanting to speak, make a joke, not knowing if he should. Until at last, as she continued to clatter plates, he had simply repeated his invitation to go to Urbino, before he too left.

Lying in bed, I imagined them driving up the valley towards their dark house. Would they speak, would they be silent while the opera played itself out? And now I could admit the question that had been on my mind all day. Would they make love again?

Suddenly I could bear it no longer. Getting up, I dressed quickly and went outside. The light under Lola's door was switched off. It was almost two in the morning. I knew this way madness lay, but, picking up my car keys, I slipped out.

The moon was high in the sky, showing its damaged side, as I drove up the valley in the direction of the Boyars'. The air rushing past was wonderfully cool. Small animals scurried along the side of the road, caught fleetingly in the headlights. A large bird of prey flew silently past before vanishing through the trees. Driven by a terrible, sad desperation, I asked nothing of myself, just sped along the narrow road past Molinello and down into the hamlet where their house nestled in a crook of the hill. Parking the car, I walked the rest of the way until it loomed large in front of me. Then I stopped.

What did I see?

The house rested in darkness. Somewhere on its other side, facing the mountain, was the bedroom where they slept. Nothing stirred. I stood a moment longer and a small movement caught my eye. Petrified, I froze, not daring to breathe. A figure had appeared and was standing in the garden. I shrank back into the trees and as I did so I saw with fear that it was Charles. The sound of my car must have disturbed his sleep, perhaps. I waited for several minutes, not moving. He seemed to be staring ahead, stiffly, arms by his side, watching over nothing. I'm not sure how long we two stood in that darkness, each with the night in front of us. Then, with hardly a sound, he turned and walked back into the house.

The following morning I woke late. The day waited outside in silent reproach. There were signs of Lola: damp towels in a heap, sun cream, and breakfast, dirty coffee cup, halfeaten brioche. But she was nowhere in sight. I supposed she had taken my bicycle and gone into town. I showered and cleared up the mess. The morning sun had climbed over the house by now so I closed the shutters. I was due at the Boyars' for coffee in half an hour. Driving back up the valley, I shied away from last night's escapade.

I found them sitting on old cane chairs, on cushions unused for years, when I arrived.

'Hasn't the chestnut tree grown enormous,' Delia said.

Hearing her voice vibrate like a harp string being plucked too vigorously, I wanted to turn back. The tree now obscured the view. Charles brought the coffee out. I felt decoyed by love.

'I must start work on the garden,' Delia said.

From the smallest of branches, high, out of sight, came the sweet insistent sadness of a bird calling.

'Sweetheart,' Charles said, 'you shouldn't overdo it. The

doctor told Dee she should try to rest in the middle of the day,' he added, turning to me.

'A rest from thinking,' she said lightly. 'A siesta from my soul's sickness, a short space of oblivion, was what he meant.'

She sounded amused. No one said anything. Charles handed me a cup of coffee. I watched her through a dappled tenderness of light and shade falling across the pots of oleander that dotted the terrazza. The ageing fig tree was charcoal against the light.

'Why don't you talk to Alex while I make a phone call?' he suggested. 'I'll be back in a moment.'

Delia watched him walk off.

'He's so patient,' she said. 'Always the same. He never changes.'

Her voice sounded as though she was stifling. Why was Charles trying to keep up such a pretence? she burst out unhappily. Whatever she asked, he agreed to, and she could no longer bear it, she said. Whatever mood change the moment presented her with (sometimes it could be simply because of an absence of sunlight), he went along with it. I knew that it hadn't always been this way. That he had loved her more robustly, once, whereas now he was careful. Maybe it was progress of a sort, I suggested, but Delia frowned impatiently. I watched her from the corner of my eye. She seemed to have reached yet another breaking point.

They had aired the ground floor, opened the shutters, watered the plants, brought the rest of the luggage in. The house had opened its melancholy doors to them. It was like a cathedral, she told me, but one where, amidst the serenity, something is false. No amount of love could overcome it, no distraction make it fade.

Tonight they planned to go to their usual restaurant. For the last two nights, she had slept without her craving for eggs. Charles hoped she would eat a more varied diet, now, she told me, her voice becoming amused once more. Perhaps, though, it was the result of coming back, she admitted. It had been a risk, but he had told her that to return again was a human need. Her voice went on, softly. I listened drowsily.

'Charles doesn't know,' she said. But the fact was, mostly, she could not sleep. Nor could she bear the thoughts that ebbed and flowed of their own accord towards her. That she had not been here in this room, on the bed, for two years. Two years is enough to change the way a mind functions, but not long enough to change a place, she told me. I wanted to tell her I could not sleep either, now she was back. The house, she admitted, was different. Charles had seen to that.

'Or was it you, Alex?' she asked, suddenly seeing that possibility. 'Was it you who put the photos away in the drawers?'

I smiled, not disagreeing. The day overflowed with flat Italian light.

'Dear Alex,' she said. 'Who would have said our friendship would take such a turn? In any case, I have no need for images; my memory is vivid enough.'

This morning when she woke, somewhere outside the shutters, in a blur of green, a bird whistled. Obviously, it was a different bird, but still, how like its ancestors it sounded.

It was difficult to believe she was back, I told her.

'When we first talked about returning, it was in the depth of winter.'

Another pointless Christmas, watching the rain. She had expressed a desire, hastily suppressed, for the sun. But Charles, on the lookout for any small change, had heard her. That was when he had talked to her of the importance of returning. Persuaded her.

'Don't make me do something I can't,' she had pleaded after that.

Frightened.

'You'll have to face it one day,' he had said.

She had felt the air fill with cruelty. For wasn't she still living through those dead days of finished time?

'Please,' she had begged him. 'Not now.'

Closure, that was what he was asking for. And in the end, perhaps because she loved him, she gave in. As she had known all along she would. Love, she had thought bitterly, was like that, refusing to have its footprints erased even after it had fled.

Somewhere in the house there was music. Elgar. Before she could react, the door opened and Charles came back.

'Elgar?'

'Sorry, it was in the machine. I'll turn it off.'

'No!' she stopped him. 'No! If we're going to do this, let's do it properly.'

I saw that he was frightened. Closure was what he had desired. Not a breaking open of wounds.

'I've booked for San Giorgio,' he said, and hesitated, looking at me helplessly.

What did he want me to say?

'Mirella wants us to go.'

She froze.

'Look, we can't hide the fact we're back. Can we, Alex?'

Again the plea for help from me.

'By now, everyone will know we had dinner with you, last night,' she said.

So it was my fault now.

'No, of course not!' she said quickly, reading my expression. 'It's Charles. He keeps in touch with everyone in the village: Christmas cards, e-mails . . .'

She was no fool, she told me. She knew they asked after her.

'They simply wish us well . . .' Charles began, then seeing her face thought better of it. 'Look, you're right. I'll cancel the table, we'll eat in.'

'No!' she said quickly, her face suddenly unutterably weary.

I watched, saying nothing. And I saw more clearly how it was for them. In spite of the whispered words in the hot Parma air, they were close to the edge all right. Almost I felt a sense of vertigo. A car screeched around one of the many hairpin bends below and then faded away into an echo of itself.

'Last night was wonderful,' she added, belatedly.

A slight breeze lifted her hair, cicadas sounded everywhere. Almost like their former life, I thought; Matt could walk in at any moment.

We talked of other things and I watched her come alive to an audience. As if someone had poured water on powder. She was like a desert flower, with the same capacity to bloom falsely. The telephone rang. Charles went in to answer it and there was no more Elgar. The air was thick and languid and impossible to penetrate. I had waited for this moment and now it had come I could think of nothing to say.

'How long will you stay?' I asked, hearing my own voice, speaking to a stranger.

'I'm not sure. Charles wants to finish the first draft of this next book before we go back.'

We both paused. How remarkable that he had worked through the worst of it. A lesser man would have caved in. Yes, yes, they were a remarkable couple.

'What's this next book about?'

'I'm sorry, what did you say?'

She had been far away. Something dislodged within me.

'Is everything okay, Dee? You coping better?'

'It's the catalogue for the Pieros,' she said, smiling. 'He needs to look at the frescoes again. That was the reason we decided to come.'

'I'm very glad you did,' I told her solemnly. 'You've been missed.'

'That girl staying with you seems nice,' she said suddenly, brightening a little. 'Very pretty too.'

'Lola?'

'Yes. Lola. I wonder what it must be like to have a daughter.'

I looked sharply at her, but her voice betrayed nothing.

'Charles will enjoy taking her along with him to look at the Pieros, don't you think?'

Still, I could think of nothing to say.

'It will do him good. He loves teaching.'

Delia, I thought. You loved me, first. Do you remember?

'Have you noticed his hair? I was watching him as he slept, last night. His hair is white as moonlight.'

She knew, while all eyes had been focused on her, how the years had taken their toll on him unnoticed. She was aware of it and understanding, misplaced for so long, was beginning to stir within her. Was it possible they might recover in some way? Had she known he had been awake, walking in their garden, last night?

'Actually, I slept well last night. It was Charles who didn't.'

In his generous way, she told me, he had been glad for her. And lowering her voice, she confirmed what I had suspected: he had woken her towards dawn. It was something that still happened, had never stopped. Grief could not lessen his desire for her. The counsellor they were seeing at the time had said it was a good sign, showed they were still functioning as a couple. Neither of them had commented.

'It can only get better,' the counsellor had told them. Delia's mouth twisted in pain as she repeated the words.

They had stopped going to that particular woman and some months later Delia found another one whom she saw on her own. Charles had been glad. There were things she would talk about if he were absent. But things had not got better, not really, not deep down, and every time they made love after that, the counsellor's words had echoed in her ears. It could only get better.

'Desire was what we had left,' she said.

I saw that even as her beautiful face continued to arouse him, she knew she no longer cared one way or the other. The awfulness of it was this deadness.

'I want him to take that student to see the Pieros.'

If they were to live again, she felt very certain, it would be in a way more separate than before. The trick was, she confided to me, in disentangling themselves without causing more damage. That was what she said.

19

On the road to Urbino he was seduced by the painterly light

'So off she went. Hair not quite dry, rucksack hanging off one shoulder, slurping cold coffee, looking an almighty mess.'

With all the confidence of youth.

'I remember feeling angry as I watched her. From where did so much self-belief come?'

Charles rolled the soft top back. He had a look of indifference that I recognised.

'Good, I thought. Our little heroine will learn a lesson.'

Lola was eyeing the car suspiciously.

'What about my hair?'

I laughed, but Charles opened the glove compartment and handed her a thin scarf that I recognised as Delia's. The sight of it conjured her up instantly. It must have done the same for Charles, because he frowned and asked me to give her a ring later, check she was all right. As though I needed asking. Lola got into the car awkwardly and slammed the door. Something was irritating her too. I jumped back with an exaggerated movement of my hand.

'Hey!'

Only that morning I had warned her again: 'Don't get any ideas.'

She had glared at me. 'We're not all that different,' she said, somewhat nastily.

'I wouldn't bank on it,' I retorted. 'One: you've no idea what their relationship is like. I've known them for twenty years and they are still opaque to me. Two: people who have gone through what they have don't always fully understand themselves. There will be stuff going on between them that they haven't a clue about.'

'Thanks for the lecture!'

'All I'm saying is, don't underestimate the random nature of their behaviour. That's all.'

'Twat!'

'Don't be vulgar. I'm being helpful.'

'And Delia?'

'What about her?'

'Admit you've got the hots for her! Or should I say you *love* her!'

God, what a nasty little thing you are, I thought.

'What's there to admit? Everyone loves Dee. Don't you admire the way she's dealing with her life?'

Lola yawned. I took this to mean I had scored a hit. Why had we started this stupid conversation? I wasn't in any competition with her.

'And then there's her flawless beauty . . .'

Now I was deliberately trying to annoy her.

'Plenty of people have lost children. *And* had to deal with it. You just fancy her, that's all.'

'You're a pretty girl. Don't be jealous. It doesn't suit you!'

'Don't patronise me,' she snapped. 'You'll be telling me I have lovely olive skin next.'

Touchy! I thought.

I stop talking and I wonder again what on earth you are making of all this, Elizabeth. I watch as you write furiously in your notepad.

'It doesn't surprise me,' you say, at last. 'I knew Lola had another side to her. Ras simply idolises her.'

You don't like her, do you, Elizabeth?

'Well . . .' You pause, too clever to commit yourself.

Now understand, the rest of this sordid little story came to me via Charles, I warn you.

Afterwards, Lola avoided having too much contact with me.

'I bet she did!' you say.

It's the first really catty remark you've made and it makes me want to laugh. And hug you.

On the way to Arezzo they were both completely silent. Charles, perhaps feeling awkward, put some opera on.

'There's a map behind you,' he told her. 'Could you have a look at it for me? We're taking the main road towards Pisa and then we turn off towards the autostrada. Could you just check the turning?'

The book fell open on the local page. He glanced at it and saw the red circle drawn on one of the mountains. It was the one that faced their house. Keeping his eyes on the road he flicked the page over. For no reason at all he felt unbearably tired, drained of energy. What was he doing, driving along this mountain road to see frescoes he had seen many times before? Sighing, he glanced at his passenger, but she sat with her head bent, staring at the map. Obviously she hadn't a clue how to read it. Perhaps, he thought, they should simply have lunch and turn back.

'Here?' she asked, pointing at Urbino.

Her voice irritated him. Without taking his eyes off the road, he nodded. Her trainers resting on the floor of his car looked unsightly. They drove on. It became impossible to talk in any case once they were on the autostrada. So he turned the music up. Oleander bushes in full flower flashed past. The hills of Carrara appeared and then disappeared and the land flattened out into broad maize plains flanked by cypress trees.

'What time will we get there?' she shouted.

She looked a mess, hair all over her face in spite of the scarf that she had not wanted to wear. He turned the radio off.

'About three,' he said.

Once again he felt heavily oppressed.

'We'll stop somewhere in Bagno di Romagna for some lunch. There used to be a place that did wonderful Tuscan lamb.'

When she didn't answer, he glanced at her and saw she had closed her eyes. And this too irritated him. Exhausted, was she?

'Why don't you put the seat back and have a sleep?' he asked with heavy sarcasm, but she either didn't hear or didn't want to.

They drove for another hour, his resentment ebbing and flowing. Away from Delia, haunted by her still, he wondered if he would ever be able to put down the burden that was his life before it ended. When the opera came to an end he simply started it back at the beginning again.

By midday they reached the sleepy town of Acqualagna. He found the lane that led up to the restaurant. The last time he had come here had been with Delia and Matt. Another mistake, he thought grimly. The girl continued to sleep until the car slowed down. How exhausted could she be, he remembered thinking, almost amused. The sun sat harshly on her face.

'Aren't you very hot in all these clothes?' he asked as she opened her eyes. She shook her head, yawning.

'Well, you certainly were tired,' he said. 'This is the place I told you about. We're stopping for lunch.'

She told him she wasn't hungry and wanted only a beer. Then, climbing out of the car, she took her shoes off and walked barefoot behind him. A dog bounded towards them, wagging its tail and barking.

'*Buongiorno*,' Charles said walking in. '*Siamo in due.*'

They were led to a table in a corner and Lola went immediately to the washroom. He ordered drinks and waited, his annoyance ticking over. Why the hell had he agreed to take her with him? When she eventually got back, he was studying the menu.

'Don't you like wearing shoes?' he asked, without looking at her.

Instantly she tucked her feet out of sight and he felt sorry.

'My trainers were too hot. I want to buy some flip-flops, if there's a shop anywhere . . . '

He considered the matter gravely.

'We should be in Arezzo by the time the shops are opening again. I'm sure you can find some there.'

Suddenly she smiled, taking him by surprise. Abruptly he recommended a couple of dishes on the menu and, picking up a copy of the *Corriere della Sera*, hid behind it. When the waiter came to take their order she pointed to the cheapest thing on the menu.

'Is that all you're having?'

'It's all I can afford!'

He stared at her, disbelievingly.

'Oh, don't be ridiculous,' he said angrily. 'Of course I'm paying. Now have something proper, for goodness sake. Have the lamb . . . yes?'

And he turned to the waiter and ordered for her.

'Now,' he picked up his beer. '*Salute!*'

'Cheers!' she replied, scowling.

He burst out laughing and although the scowl did not leave her face the atmosphere seemed less oppressive.

'Sorry I fell asleep.'

He regarded her silently. Then he told her:

'I'm trying to pick up the threads of a book I was working on a couple of years ago . . . on the Pieros. I've also got a catalogue I'm working on for an exhibition at the National. It's proving to be hard work. I can't seem to get back into it.'

Neither of them knew what to say next. He folded the newspaper and sipped his beer, looking steadily at her.

'Tell me, what do you know about the Pieros?'

'Nothing.'

For a moment he was on the verge of laughing again. She seemed to be bracing herself, but all he said, very gently, was:

'I envy you. That's a perfect position to be in.'

They had lunch. Charles talked to her about the exhibition he had organised. He told her how sad and angry he was *The Flagellation* had been stolen. It was an act of supreme selfishness, he remembered saying.

'It's probably in the vault of some ghastly American collector,' he had said bitterly.

She had agreed. He talked about the use of blue in the painting. She listened intently, keeping her eyes on his face in a way that unnerved him considerably. Then he talked about the Piero frescoes that they would soon be seeing.

'Nothing is more susceptible to effacement than fresco,' he told her.

He didn't question his reasons for lecturing her. All he knew was that he felt safe talking about art.

'It is subject to any number of natural agencies,' he said. 'The fresco is no thicker than eggshell. So often it vanishes, leaving little more than documentary accounts of how, in a long-abandoned church, a Mary might have once floated between the cusps of a crescent moon.'

Lola was listening with flattering attention. She had almost finished her second beer.

'I'm told they've cleaned them beautifully in Arezzo. The last time I was there, years ago, they were under scaffolding and I couldn't see anything.'

She sighed. He felt a puzzling sense of well-being. The sunlight outside was sharp as a razor's edge. He ordered a strong coffee. Lola stifled another yawn. He wondered cynically if in fact she really wasn't interested in what he was talking about.

'Delia used to love that fresco,' he told her.

It was his first mention of Delia and it felt as if he had accidently splashed his face with cold water. Lola too looked startled. He saw beads of perspiration on her upper lip and he resisted the urge to touch them. The heat was thick and sour. He wondered what Delia was doing and his worry over her returned with force.

In the car, driving towards Arezzo, the top closed, in the intimacy of the space, he felt queasy with the heat. He turned on the air conditioning but not the radio. He went on talking to her, but what about, he could not later remember. Nor did he remember whatever she might have said. His eyes focused only on his own hands on the steering wheel. At one point he remembered the shop in Arezzo that sold paints.

'While you're on your footwear hunt, I want to buy some pigments.'

'Do you paint?'

She sounded wide awake, suddenly.

'Oh no! I just examine it. Delia's the painter.'

Again he felt a great weariness sweep over him, so he focused on the road ahead. They were passing through a sullen glare of light reflected off the maize fields. Large farm buildings flanked by trees appeared like exclamation marks against the sky and then vanished as swiftly from view. On the radio, which he switched on, jaunty music was playing. It covered the fact he had run out of things to say.

At the hotel they found they had rooms on the same corridor but not next to each other and by the time he had showered the shops were beginning to open. It was too early to ring Delia, she was probably out. He had the distinct feeling she would not stay in the house on her own for long.

'Ring me at six,' she had said. 'I'm going to Sarzana to the flea market.'

In all the years they'd been at the house in Italy, Delia never could sleep in the day. Siestas made her restless, she used to say in the old days.

Leaning out of his window now, he felt the heat hit him like a wall. It was his turn to be exhausted, but he knew the girl would be waiting to go shopping. Closing his eyes briefly, he thought what he needed was a smoke. Having given up years ago, he had not felt the need of one until now. There was a light knock on the door and he went to open it.

'Come in,' he said. 'I was about to call for you.'

She had got changed. Not that it made any difference, he thought. Again he was amused. She had appalling taste in clothes.

Almost as if she could read his thoughts, she looked at him challengingly. 'Ready?'

As he opened his mouth to answer, his phone went off. It was Delia, her voice far away and strained.

'I might be out at six,' she said. 'So I thought I'd ring now. Where are you?'

'Are you okay?' he asked, alarmed.

He turned his back to the girl hovering in the doorway and walked towards the window.

'I'll wait downstairs,' Lola said.

He barely heard her.

'I'm fine,' Delia said. 'I didn't want you to worry. Alex has asked me to go over at six, that's all.'

He felt his own tension ease a little at the sound of her voice.

'Good! What have you been doing?'

'Nothing much. I got up after you left and tried to paint. I mean . . . I laid out some colours. You won't forget to get my list?'

He shook his head.

277

'No. I'm going there now, actually. We've just arrived at the hotel. It's awfully hot here.'

'There are no mountains to cool you down, that's why. What's Lola like?'

'Oh . . .' he hesitated, looking over his shoulder, seeing the girl had gone. 'I feel a bit like a teacher taking out a reluctant schoolgirl. She's not very forthcoming, really.'

Delia laughed. The sound travelled through his ear and seemed to float out through the open window. It was slow and slightly girlish. Another knot of tension undid itself.

'I bet you made no effort,' Delia said. 'I bet you were completely silent and irritable. Preoccupied with your work!'

He smiled in spite of himself. They used to tease him about this, both she and Matt. Whenever they had gone on one of his painting trails.

'Dad's obsessing again,' Delia used to say and they had laughed.

He wondered if she was remembering too and then decided, perhaps not. And then he wondered if he was going slowly mad. He often felt he was simply living in one continuous bad dream.

'Talk to her, Charles.' Delia's voice was amused.

'Of course.'

He lowered his voice. 'Do you know what she did at lunch?'

'No, what?'

'She ordered the smallest antipasto, because the food was too expensive, she said.'

'What do you mean?'

'Well, she thought she'd have to pay for it!'

'Oh, Charles, were you teasing her?'

'No, of course not. It never occurred to me but that I was paying. Anyway, I sorted it all out. I'm going to pretend the hotel is being paid for by Alex. In case she's embarrassed.'

'Good idea. Hadn't you better go, if she's waiting?'

'Suppose so. Are you okay, though? I can come back at any point if you want. Don't ...' he paused, uncertain, the tension coming back, 'don't struggle on alone.'

'I won't. Now go. Love you.'

She was gone before he had finished answering her. He had the strangest feeling of them both walking very fast and slightly out of step with each other. There was nothing he could do about it. Closing the door, he went outside in search of the girl.

She was waiting for him in the hotel lobby, underneath a reproduction of a Piero della Francesca, her profile half in shadow. Charles hesitated. Her hair hung loosely and it made her suddenly look smaller and more delicate. He frowned as she turned and saw him and for a moment he held her eyes before lowering his.

'I'm sorry. That was Delia.'

She was holding a bottle of water and he thought she looked hot.

'Shall we go? Or are you too hot to brave the outside?'

She shook her head.

In the end, the rest of the afternoon was much better than he had expected. Almost, he could have said he enjoyed it. Maybe he too made more of an effort, but Lola turned out to be good company. They bought her sandals, they went together to the art shop and he bought all the paints on his list, and then they went to look at the *Legend of the True Cross* and Charles was electrified.

'My goodness! Just look at this!'

The restoration was indeed magnificent, and he talked Lola through the cycle of frescoes. In this way they stood in the cool, nearly empty chapel, the glare of the Tuscan sun in abeyance just outside the great door, talking about the Queen of Sheba and her story of eternity.

'Look,' he said, 'see how delicate her crimson robes are. Look at the faces, the delicacy of the drawing.'

'How on earth did he paint them so high up?' she asked.

'There was a study done recently that suggests he never saw the complete fresco because of the angle at which he painted it. So that makes the perspective all the more remarkable.'

'I like the trees,' Lola said. 'The leaves are the colours of the olive trees here, aren't they?'

Charles nodded. The frescoes were still capable of taking his breath away.

'Look at the Dream of Scipio,' he said. 'Look at the magical way he uses chiaroscuro.

'If you think how long ago it was all painted, how little in fact we know of Piero, it's all the more astonishing,' he told her. She was looking at him with unblinking enormous eyes. He had no idea what she was thinking, if she was bored even. He talked on, regardless:

'These frescoes are some of the finest examples of Renaissance painting,' he said, uncaring that once again he sounded as though he was lecturing her. 'That is why it is so awful that *The Flagellation* has been stolen. Western art, in all its glory, lost for ever.'

They were asked to leave when the church closed, going out into the dazzling light of Arezzo.

'What would you like to do?' he asked, as they both reached for their sunglasses.

'I'd like something cold to drink.'

To his surprise, he saw it was almost six. They found a bar and he ordered prosecco. He felt like someone who has been swimming in cold water for a long time and is surprised to find that dry land could be so warm. The girl beside him, the vibrancy of the images he had just seen, the restrained bustle of the passersby, all carried an air of unexpected pleasure for him.

'When was the last time you saw them?' Lola asked, and even this question, pressing on the wound that he always protected, did not make him flinch.

He glanced at her feet. She was swinging her legs slightly, her flip-flops dragging on the ground. Her toenails had chips of vanish on them. She had tiny feet. Once again he found himself feeling sorry for her. She's uncomfortable, he thought. And she has no money. Fleetingly, he was annoyed this trip had been forced on her. Delia was right, he should try to give her as enjoyable a time as possible. He poured them both some more wine and she suppressed a giggle.

'I haven't been back for over two years,' he told her slowly. 'We were meant to be doing another trip two years ago. I'd just got a contract for a book.'

He mentioned the name of his publishers.

'You might know them? They are the main publishers of high-quality art books. My last book had sold fairly well and I decided to write a more specialist book on pigments.'

He waved his hand towards the cigarette she was rolling.

'Can I have one?'

She handed him the one she had just made up and suddenly he felt reckless.

'Delia used to paint in her spare time,' he said. 'Well . . . whenever we came to Italy, or she wasn't working in the gallery.'

He thought about the way she used to grind her own pigments and bind them with linseed oil. Slowly, painstakingly, drop by drop, her face serious. Then he thought of how, long ago, before Matt was conceived, she used to sit beside the Ocean at Cape Cod and paint watercolours of the sea. Using seawater in a jar. And then he thought further back to when they first met. And her pen-and-ink sketches. He swallowed and took his sunglasses off. And stared into the light, squinting painfully. The smell of Delia's pigments had been in the art shop earlier, standing for past family holidays. The house used to reek of linseed oil and sunlight. Year upon year, he thought. All taken for granted.

'Thank you,' he said, as Lola lit their cigarettes.

'Did you write it?' she asked.

Charles shook his head, exhaling deeply. Then he looked at the cigarette.

'These are clove?' he said. 'Not funny cigarettes, I hope?'

He laughed. Not that he minded.

'No! They are from Sri Lanka.'

He remembered someone telling him she was half Sri Lankan. That would explain her wonderful skin, he supposed.

'Which of your parents is Sri Lankan?' he asked.

'My father.'

She frowned.

'I have nothing to do with Sri Lankans,' she said shortly. 'They have mangoes for brains.'

She waved her hand dismissively. He didn't know what to say. The light outside had changed again and it had become a little cooler. The colour of the Tuscan stone was rose-tinted and deeper now, and the girl's face was bathed in it. They decided to go back to the hotel before dinner.

20

Darkness brought its own problems

Are you sure you want me to go on, Elizabeth?

At dinner, Charles told me, later, he sat watching Lola devouring a mound of spaghetti and was surprised to find he too was hungry. Hollow legs, he remembered thinking, and the expression inevitably conjured up Matt's face. The past was wrapping itself around him like a vine, choking him.

'How long are you planning on staying in Italy?'

'Until the end of August, if I want.'

'But you don't want?'

'It depends,' she said.

She looked at him challengingly and Charles was plunged into confusion. He saw candlelight reflected in her violet-black eyes. He didn't think he had ever seen such eyes.

'Tell me about the Sri Lankan side of your family.'

'Why?'

He smiled, thinking: Goodness me, how edgy we are!

'No reason really, I'm just interested. We once had the chance to go there on holiday but didn't.'

Delia had been pregnant. The tropics had frightened her.

'What if I caught a bug?' she had fretted.

In the end they had decided to err on the side of caution.

'I have no idea what it's like there,' Lola said. 'I've never been.' Her voice was flat.

'Because of the war?'

He could see she had become uncomfortable, again.

'My dad has a big problem with the place.'

He nodded, not really knowing what to say. She paused and gulped down some wine. He was amused at the way she could knock it back.

'And you? What do you feel?'

'Me?'

She laughed. Then she broke off a piece of bread and wiped the remains of the pesto on her plate.

'I have no feelings either way.' She shrugged. 'I'm a Londoner. I belong in Britain. What I want most of all is to get into politics.'

'Yes, so you said.'

She was leaning towards him, her eyes very bright, her expression fierce. It wouldn't do to cross her, he imagined.

'You scare me,' he said lightly. 'I could just see you as Prime Minister!'

'British politics has lost its way,' she said seriously. 'I've been studying the conference speeches each party makes. They are all so unimaginative, so full of obvious lies. Politicians no longer even bother to hide their lies. We're simply fed a mish-mash of rubbish and then told that this is what the British people want.'

She drank some more wine.

'Let's deal with the problem of immigrants, they say. Let's talk about future generations, let's pretend we care!' she sneered. 'Actually, no one cares. Why should they? Memories are short-lived.'

'Well ...' Charles began, but she interrupted him, holding up her hand.

'The immigrants don't help. One minute they want to belong, the next they want the right to be separate. Everyone pulls in different directions and then they call it multiculturalism!'

Charles opened his mouth to comment, but then thought better of it.

'There's very little unity in Britain,' she said loudly. 'Everyone wants stuff.'

'Stuff!'

'Yes.' She glared at him and poured herself more wine. 'Haven't you noticed how, for example, the white middle classes hold on to the arts? And the migrants hang on to religion for safety?'

He didn't dare to speak.

'It isn't working, is it? Multiculturalism, I mean. The word is just an excuse for staying segregated. True multiculturalism comes only when races mix.'

She looked at him with an air of triumph. Charles suddenly wanted to laugh.

'Fresh blood is what's needed.'

She paused, looking confused.

'And here I am!'

He kept his face straight and she smiled, seriously, showing a set of beautiful teeth. She was more than a little drunk, he thought, not minding. It felt like a very long time since he had thought about anything other than his own affairs. To be sitting out in the balmy air, laughing, was something he was no longer familiar with.

'So you're going to sort out the problems in Britain all on your own?' he said, unaware at the way his voice had changed. 'A pretty girl like you! I'm impressed.'

'We're the fastest growing ethnic group in the country. Mixed race, that's us. The age of the mongrel, as Alex tells me, has arrived.'

'Did he say that? That was rude of him.'

She gave him a look.

'You don't really know him,' she said darkly.

Charles watched her put her empty glass down with a flourish. She shook her head so that the knot she had tied her hair in uncurled and cascaded down. It reminded him of a younger Delia. There drifted towards them the sweet sounds of an accordion.

'Listen,' he said, wanting to change the subject. 'There is a festa going on in the square. Shall we take a look?'

Lola looked startled. She seemed to shake off her crusading mood just as suddenly as it had possessed her. And Charles, who found he wasn't tired at all, followed her out onto the street with a new surge of energy.

The festa was in full swing. Long trestle tables had been laid out in lines and there were lights strung across the road. The whole town had turned out to eat in the square. Children ran amok while the adults helped themselves to food and wine.

'Oh!' Lola cried. 'We should have eaten here!'

At the far end of a makeshift stage in front of a series of spotlights a band was playing. An accordionist moved in time to the music while two older men sang into a microphone. The stage was crowded with dancers, with elderly couples, the bride and groom and the young, all chattering and laughing noisily.

'It's a private reception,' Charles said, and turned as if to go, but one of the players came over and took Lola by the hand.

'Dance with her,' he said, smiling at Charles, and he began another tune.

Everyone clapped, the bride and groom were smiling and nodding. There was nothing for it but to join in.

'Come on, then,' he said, and led her onto the floor.

A spotlight followed their halting progress. He was aware again of how small she was and also how young. He felt caught up in something remembered only dimly from years back and once again felt as if he was emerging from a long illness. The music came to a slow halt with a burst of applause, and began again almost immediately with a waltz as they continued around the floor. A glitter ball suspended from on high sent a never-ending stream of silver dots across the ground as they danced. He could hear Lola saying something to him excitedly and he bent down to hear her. She said it again, but still he couldn't catch what it was.

'Tell me in a minute,' he said, raising his voice. 'Let's go after this dance. I remember there used to be a nice little bar that stayed open late not far from here.'

This time when the music ended they slipped out through the crowds and headed towards their hotel.

'I don't want to go back,' Lola said. 'Let's find your bar.'

'It's a bit of a walk, you sure?'

'Yes, yes, c'mon.'

And she grabbed his hand and dragged him along. He said nothing. Her eyebrows looked like wings. he thought.

'Wasn't that just wonderful!' she said. 'You'd never get that sort of thing in London, not that sort of atmosphere.'

He could see she was very drunk and wondered if really they ought to get back to their hotel.

'I've an early start in the morning,' he said, uncertain. 'Look, perhaps we should get back.'

He thought uneasily that he couldn't remember if he had told Delia he would ring or not.

'I don't want you to get a hangover.'

'Oh, please. Just let's find your bar. It isn't late and I never get hangovers.'

'But I don't think you like getting up early,' he smiled.

She stopped walking and stared at him with a mock-horror look on her face. Then she burst out laughing.

'Who's been telling tales?' she said a little unsteadily.

In the end it was after midnight before he persuaded her back to the hotel. He tried ringing Delia from the bar, but the noise was too great and although the phone rang several times she was clearly out, so he gave up and left a message instead. He would ring her in the morning, he decided.

The day which had started out so stiffly had by some miracle turned into a very charming evening, he thought. He was aware they were both still laughing, but he could not say what about, only that everything seemed amusing and full of life. When they got to the hotel she did not want to go to her room, leaning against him with her eyes closed, smiling.

'Bed,' he said firmly, as though he was talking to a small child. 'And drink lots of water or you'll have a cracking great headache in the morning.'

She didn't move. Charles sighed. Then he took her key out of her bag and opened her door. Hesitating only a moment, he picked her up and walked towards her bed. Instantly, she put both arms around his neck. He was astonished by her lightness. Putting her down gently on the bed, he went to fill a glass of water. But when he returned she was already asleep and, after gazing a moment longer at her, perplexed by his own confusion, he left. It was some hours before he was able to find any sleep himself.

The next morning he was surprised to find her up and waiting for him at breakfast. She sat outside, at a table that sheltered under a vine. Sparrows darted about, picking up crumbs.

'Did you think I wouldn't get up?' she asked him.

'How's the head?'

'Fine. I slept like a log!'

'Yes, so did I,' he lied. 'Have you been waiting long? I was on the phone to Delia.'

He felt the heat press against him. Delia had been awake for hours already when he had rung. She hadn't been bothered that he had not been able to get hold of her last night. She had visited Alex.

'We had a very nice evening,' she told him.

'Good.'

They talked of other things. He told her he had bought her paints. She commiserated with him having to drag Lola around the Pieros. He thought she sounded different, but he could not put his finger on the difference.

'Lola's not really much of a problem,' he said at last. 'She followed me around the *True Cross* without a murmur. And when I told her the history of it, she listened patiently.'

Delia laughed softly. 'How kind of you, to take so much trouble over her. I hope she appreciates it!'

He had wanted to say that actually it was he who had got the better deal. That her company had been strangely cheering, but Delia had moved on to talk about something else. Afterwards, when they had said good-bye and he was on his way to breakfast, he tried and failed to remember what she had said she was doing today.

'So? Where next?' Lola asked.

'A day off,' he told her. 'The museums are closed today.'

She looked disappointed.

'But we're going through the mountains on the road to Urbino,' he said. 'So tomorrow morning we'll be the first to see the *Madonna del Parto*. You can navigate.'

In the car she was silent and it was Charles who broke the silence, finally.

'I've noticed,' he remarked, 'a silence from you means you are displeased about something.'

Her hair had blown all over her face in the wind and when he glanced at her she was frowning again. She looked as though she was about to throw a tantrum and he suppressed a laugh.

'I was wondering why you're so crazy about these paintings? To me they're just paintings, like all the others you see in galleries, all over the place. They don't have much relevance to everyday life, do they?'

He was silent, thinking, wanting to say how he really felt about them. Remembering Delia standing pregnant in front of the Madonna.

'They *are* relevant,' he said slowly. 'But you need to really look and look. Then slowly can you start to understand the ways in which they connect historically with all of Western history. And then finally you see how the story threads through the ages, connecting with all of antiquity. And the way in which painting itself developed. But in the subject matter,' he paused, forgetting for a second that she was with him, 'nothing has really changed since that first murder, committed in the name of God.'

'I don't think Western civilisation has much relevance for me,' Lola said.

Her voice was whipped by the breeze coming in through the open top of the car. All around them the Italian summer shimmered with ripeness. Charles smiled. Lola's certainty, or was it her youth, or both, filled him with a sweet optimism, as heady as perfume.

'My father,' she said, unexpectedly, following her own thoughts, 'when I think of him, the first thing I think of is his voice. Stories, stories,' she added dreamily. 'He was full of them, and I internalised them in a way I never did with real-life experiences.'

He hesitated, intuiting she was telling him something that mattered.

'You're a writer, perhaps?' he said.

She shook her head. And frowned. Then she said:

'My father broke my heart by leaving, and because I loved and trusted him as I loved and trusted no one else, I think I broke his heart deliberately. And now,' she hesitated, 'I'm simply not interested in him.'

An overwhelming sense of the moment made him almost unable to speak. He noticed the edges of his shirt cuffs were very slightly frayed. Soon, he thought, the thread would unravel altogether and the shirt would no longer be wearable.

'I'm not interested in Sri Lanka either,' she said firmly, as if he had asked her. 'It's just a place in the Indian Ocean. Quite pretty, I imagine. These places always are, but . . .' she made a face, 'who the hell cares? They're too full of emotion there. Asia is full of exaggerations, really. It's not to my taste!'

'So you turned your back on it,' he said.

'Yes,' she admitted. 'And, I don't think the government wants to really sort things out there. They just want to forget.'

Charles hoped he wasn't in for a lecture. He was thinking what beautiful hair she had. Neither dark nor fair but somewhere in between. Who was the painter, he thought, who had painted hair like hers? But the name evaded him.

'How old were you, when your father left?'

'Six. One minute they were arguing, and then he was gone.'

She remembered the glass of orange she had thrown to the ground, she told him. It had been a day of rain with a low sky.

'Did he contact you afterwards? After he had settled in his new life?'

Lola pulled a face. Charles searched it for signs of hurt and found none. She's brave, he thought.

'Oh yes. We had access days out with his bloody women.'

She paused.

'He was a weak man, I discovered. Sentimental, too. I hadn't realised how he tried to use emotion to bind me to him. Not until afterwards. I was just a symbol. His wonderful daughter! But he never tried to understand me. Not once.'

Suddenly she couldn't stick it any longer. 'Fake!' She had wanted to shout. Although later on, after university, she began to see that in fact he wasn't a fake. This was *him*, her father. In all his emotionally charged, whingeing way. Full of charm when he thought it was useful. Indifferent otherwise. It made her indifferent too, she said. So she began to see him just as he really was, she told Charles.

Charles said nothing, but it occurred to him that she was being a little hard on her father.

'And your mother?'

Her mother was another kind of fool, Lola told him scathingly. Having been dumped by her Asian husband, having given birth to a mongrel, all she did was extol the virtues of mixed marriages! Her mother was a left-wing junkie, Lola said.

'Full of impractical shit!'

Charles listened. He was good at listening. The perfect listener, Delia had always said. Other people's stories made a change from his own.

'I suppose I learnt quickly that there was an advantage in this mongrel thing! The best of both worlds, genetically, they say. Well, we are a fast-growing race, after all!'

'So you keep telling me. I'm a bit scared! You'll rule the world, soon, I'm certain.'

Once again he was only half-joking, but she started on another long tirade. He suppressed a yawn and stopped listening. This was obviously an obsession of hers. I'm an old-fashioned man, he thought. And she looks amazing when she's angry.

I stop speaking. I had forgotten about Lola's description of her mother, how like my own mother she had seemed. Yes, we did have certain things in common. Then I tell you:

You must understand the state Charles was in, Elizabeth. He had been struggling with his own life for so long that the real world felt lost to him.

Lola's voice was what he heard: young and full of the kind of resentful energy that had once belonged to Delia.

'They're very nice frescoes,' Lola agreed, later over dinner. 'But in the end Western art is white elitist art.'

He was finding it difficult to keep up with her ideas. All he knew was that seeing the painting again was a shock. Like knowing what would follow, like reading the future. It had been their last family holiday, only he hadn't known it at the time. The Queen of Sheba had had a premonition. Why hadn't he, he wondered. It was the last thing he remembered thinking that evening.

21

A rainfall of memory darkened the sky

He awoke to what he had done. The sunlight poured in through the skin of his eyelids. He had no idea what time it was, how long he had been asleep, even how he had got back to his room. Light raked across the bed. The curtains billowed once and his heart flexed. A rainfall of memory fell on him as he lay thinking. Her skin, he recalled, had a peculiar radiance as if phosphorus had been rubbed on it. The curtain billowed, filling the room with blueness, like a spoonful of water lifted out of the sea. They had been talking about her father. Snatches of conversation returned.

'I do love him,' she had said, pulling a face, a little embarrassed, he had thought. 'But in a sort of irregular graph way, with many downward swoops!'

They had both laughed and he had not seen it coming, even though their glance had become slower than an embrace. He had been dazzled as they had danced (where was it, which nightclub?) moving towards the last edge before stepping outside into the night.

'We must go back,' he had murmured.

There had been something about an early start, he remembered. But he was deep in it with her by now, no matter what the words. As if she had realised this, she had looked at him and for the barest moment he had thought she was frightened. Again his heart had missed a beat at this worn-away, eroded emotion.

'Yes, we should get back,' she had agreed.

And she dropped his arm, stopped dancing, looked at him with wantonness, confusing him further. It was he who was drunk, and now, cloaked by the erotic darkness, his mind exhausted the future and the possibilities that might lead from a kiss.

'I fell in love with you in Parma,' she said suddenly. 'I spent all night crying, thinking about you.'

The words stunned him. For a moment longer he lived in the dark intensity of her eyes.

'How?' he asked, when what he really wanted to ask was a different question entirely.

He understood the shortcomings of language. The girl stood waiting for him to decide what they must do. Matt used to look at him in this way when he wanted something. There was nothing else of any similarity; just this sense of youth from another time. Snaring him.

Daytime traffic moved past his window. He gathered from the sounds it must be late. He had no headache, no hangover, no tiredness. He remembered being struck last night by her underwear. Pink bows and hearts, straight from childhood. At odds with her fearlessness, her capacity for seduction. Lola! he had thought. Clearly, nakedness wasn't something new to her. She had looked at him boldly.

'Keep the light on,' she demanded.

What also surprised him, in the blur that followed, was the potency of her words. She had not repeated it again but still, they reverberated in his head. She had waited in his arms, moving her head a little from side to side, slowly, never taking her eyes from his. He had discovered he was trembling. He discovered it at the same time as she raised her arms and pulled his face down towards hers and spoke to him, coarsely and provocatively. He could not now remember what she had said, but he knew that whatever it was had excited him. And then he had stopped trembling as, holding him with one arm, she kicked off the bows and hearts. He had held her again as they knelt down together, sliding against the side of the bed.

There followed a gap, a locking down of all responsibility on their joint parts. He shook his head now, staring at the ceiling, watching light discs elongate and flicker overhead. What had he done? There had been so many undetected yearnings in him, fermenting for too long, that he had been unable to reveal himself in a single moment.

'I'm not breathing quite right,' she had said, afterwards.

Or perhaps she had said it moments before he entered her with the urgency of a man he no longer recognised as himself. Matt, he remembered his mind cried out once; acknowledging his betrayal in that single word. And he had seen his son through a film of blood; frame by frame, cut to blackness. He had not thought of Delia, once.

'Are you surprised?' Lola had asked, startling him.

'At *what?*'

'That we are two people again. Don't you always think . . . hope, that it will leave you as one person?'

'I feel very close to you.'

'Mmm.'

She nibbled his ear.

'I wonder when it was settled?' she had asked.

He looked at her helplessly. Most of the tension in him had left, but like an ache that had existed for too long he still had its scars.

'There's a moment, isn't there,' Lola was saying, 'when you

needn't? And then there's another moment when you know nothing in the world is going to stop it from happening.'

He smiled sadly. She's so young, he thought, so artless. And then he thought, but no, there was an experienced ring to her words too. To his surprise, this made him feel even more tender towards her.

'You have the most beautiful eyes I've ever seen,' he told her.

It was true. In certain light, he told her, they became violet underneath the brown. How was this?

'Stop it!' she had laughed. 'You'll have me looking in the mirror for weeks!'

'It's true, though.'

Her absurdly small knickers lay under the bed. He had held her so tightly that something tore as her dress crumpled under them. The small sound brought them to reality.

'I fell in love with you in Parma,' she said, once more.

Why did the words move him so much? And then he thought again that he had never seen anything so dazzling as the quality of her skin. There was a knock on the door; it was the cleaner waiting to do the room. He had not rung Delia last night. Had he been supposed to? His watch said it was nine. Hurriedly he reached for his mobile, but Delia's phone was switched off.

Feeling strangely detached, he showered and shaved. There were bluish marks around his eyes. He felt everything within him was coming out in bruises, now. Lola was waiting for him downstairs in the dining room. He walked towards her as if they were strangers. Last night was gone; the girl he had danced with was gone. He was someone else now.

'You should have woken me,' he said. 'I don't normally sleep like that.'

He couldn't remember the last time he had not woken up filled with anxiety about Delia. Making her tea with trembling hands, witnessing her pain, over and over.

'I thought if I left you, you might sleep forever!' Lola said.

When she smiled, her teeth were pearly white and small. Baby teeth, he thought, distracted. And he stretched out his hand and laid it over her arm.

'What now?' she asked.

He suspected a tilt of criticism in her voice but could not be sure.

'I want to show you something,' he said gently, taking her hand, spreading her fingers out under his.

And then he told her he was taking her to Monterchi this morning. To see the Madonna.

Delia did not answer the phone. Having tried once more before they set off from the hotel, Charles gave up. They were already late. He wanted to get to Monterchi before midday when the museum closed again until four. There would be one more night in a hotel nearby and then they would return home. They drove, first on the autostrada and then turned off onto the minor roads where the light was less harsh and the rolling hills were closer and more beautiful than they had appeared from behind the lorries. Once more he felt light-headed. Lola was sitting quietly beside him, looking at the map, biting her fingernails. It felt like years since they had left Pontremoli. He reached for her hand, preventing her chewing on her nails, unaware that the gesture was one he had done many times before, with his own child. He wanted her as close to him as possible in the car, but he was also aware they were not that close and this puzzled him too. Maybe, he thought, switching on the radio, time was what was needed. And then he told himself, hastily, it was best not to think too much.

'I must try to get hold of Dee,' he said.

Again he was aware that his reactions were not as they usually were. Why was he not more worried?

An hour later they were lost and had to get back onto the autostrada. They needed more petrol. At the service station Lola needed the toilet and he decided they would stop long enough for a coffee. He badly wanted to go to bed with her.

'Why don't you ring your wife?' she asked, coming back from the washroom.

Her fingernails, he noticed, had freshly applied nail varnish. He smiled. Was that why she had wanted the toilet? She stood drinking her coffee and frowning. He wanted to fold her in his arms but instead he went outside to ring Delia. He had no idea what he would say to her.

But Delia was still not answering the phone and now, only slightly more anxious, he wondered what he should do.

'Ring Alex,' Lola said, when he told her. 'Weren't they having dinner together? I bet he'll know her whereabouts!'

He hadn't liked the way she laughed.

'What do you mean?'

She gave him a look that said clearly, he was a fool. He felt that some slight but significant alteration had occurred, but did not fully understand what this might be.

'He obsesses over her, doesn't he!'

'What do you mean?' he asked again.

'He thinks she's wonderful,' Lola said, raising her voice slightly. 'Talented, beautiful, tragic. Like an old-fashioned hero-ine.'

Charles said nothing.

'She's no vampire-slayer, is she? And she isn't in your face. So Alex understands that.'

'You sound as if you don't like Delia,' he remarked, puzzled. 'But you don't know her.'

It was patently the wrong thing to say. She was looking angry now. They were on the brink of a row.

'Why should I dislike her? She's no threat to me.'

He hesitated, wanting to say the obvious, unhappiness clouding over, wanting to make it right again, and surprised too, by the intensity of this desire.

'I know, I know. That's not what I meant.'

He took a deep breath, his thoughts moving cautiously, wanting to get it right, wanting to show this slip of a girl that something had happened to *him*. Yes, he thought, that was it. Something momentous had happened and he was in disarray. He needed time to right himself. Time.

'What I mean is, Delia has nothing. She's lost everything that matters to her.'

He spoke softly. He didn't say they both had. He was no longer sure what he had lost or what he had gained. He was no longer sure of anything any more except that he wanted to take Lola back to bed. A beam of light fell directly on her hair. When she moved, it pierced her eyes with colours and he saw that he had been right and they were violet underneath the darkness. She was smiling at him, amused.

I stretch my arms above my head and stop speaking. We have been sitting still for too long, I think.

'No, Elizabeth, I don't remember when he told me this,' I say, breaking off to put the coffee back on the stove. 'I'm having more coffee. Would you like some?'

I can see you simply want me to continue. But I need a break, okay?

In fact he did not get hold of me until much later and by then many other things had happened. As you know, by the time they arrived at Monterchi the place was filled with reporters and television cameramen. There was a roadblock into the main street. People stood around in doorways watching as the press walked up the hill in the direction of the museum.

'What's happened?' Charles asked as they checked in at the hotel.

'They have found *The Flagellation*,' he was told. 'And a man has been charged. The television people want a photograph of the Madonna for tonight's news.'

'Golly,' Lola said, amused. 'They like a drama!'

The concierge stared at her but said nothing. Then he took two keys and pointed to the lift.

'Shall I knock on your door in a minute?' he asked Lola.

'In ten. I want to have a shower first.'

She yawned, then giggled.

'Your face!' she said.

'What about it?'

'You're trying to look respectable, and failing!'

He reached out to touch her head, but she had opened her door.

'Bye,' she waved. '*À bientôt!*'

'Wrong language,' he said, but she had already shut the door.

Half an hour later, when they had both showered, he made love to her once more. He had not attempted to phone Delia again and had, with surprisingly little effort, put her out of his thoughts. The idea of the girl had come alive in him. Like water poured on a small patch of dirt, he felt himself flourishing, becoming a lawn.

'Succulent,' he told her afterwards, sucking on each of her fingers, then moving on to her pierced nipple. For even that, even the ring through her belly button and the small tattoo of a crocodile (a crocodile, for God's sake!) entranced him.

'Does it hurt?' he asked, running his tongue through and around it.

In answer Lola bit him on the nape of the neck.

'Ouch! You have the teeth of a vixen. Stop it.'

'How many have you had?'

'What?'

'Vixens.'

'None. Only you.'

'*Women* then,' she asked in an exaggerated voice.

'I don't know. It isn't polite to ask.'

'Oh, bollocks. How many?'

'How many boyfriends have you had?'

'I'll tell you,' she agreed seriously, 'if you tell me first.'

'I could probably guess.'

She pushed him away with her foot.

'Don't be too sure. Tell me! Now!'

'Okay, okay,' he said peaceably.

He was silent for a moment, thinking.

'Two,' he said finally. 'Before Delia.'

'And after?'

'None. After Delia no one could match her.'

There was the smallest of pauses.

'Until now?'

'Yes.'

'Say it then.'

'Until now.'

They were both silent. There were sounds on the street below where filming was still in progress. Briefly he wondered how long it would be before *The Flagellation* would be back on view. Not that anything mattered at the moment.

'Did you know?' Lola asked.

'What?'

'I had earmarked you for myself from the first moment I saw you?'

She was laughing, nuzzling his neck. He didn't know what to say. But she was so young, he thought, once more.

'So now it's your turn,' he said.

There were other thoughts encroaching that he wanted to ward off.

'For what?'

'To tell me how many boyfriends you've had!'

She burst out laughing and rolled over to sit astride him. Then she began working on him with serious intent so that he groaned. He was going under again, he thought, closing his eyes, letting go, letting her do what she wanted. Astonished by her energy, frightened by it. Afterwards, when they were both soaked in sweat and she seemed only to want to sleep, he found he was fully alert.

'Come on,' he said teasingly, kissing her turned-away shoulder, 'you're not getting away so easily. Tell me how many boyfriends you've had.'

She was on the edge of sleep. Her voice, mumbled through the pillow, was faint and at first he could hardly hear her.

'How many?'

'Thirty,' she said.

They quarrelled after that.

'Did you think I was a virgin? Like the wonderful Delia?'

'I suppose I deserve that.'

'Is that what you're looking for?' she asked.

'I wasn't looking for anything. I'm so much older than you . . .'

He spread his hands out, helplessly. Panic clutched at him. Lola was speaking slowly. He tried to understand her.

'I'm not interested in your marriage,' she told him.

She sat up, defiant and naked, before him. Then she gathered up her hair and tied it into a knot at the top of her head. She looked so lovely, he thought, pained. But another part of his mind had detached itself and was in freefall.

'And I want you,' she said, deliberately.

Then she went into the bathroom and turned on the shower without looking at him. A moment later she was back, leaning against the doorway, laughing at him.

'And I always get what I want,' she said.

He was dreading going back to the villa and facing Delia.

22

But sometime later the light returned with greater force

Remembering happens before forgetting. Was it Delia who said that?

'Elizabeth . . .' I say, and I stop.

Do you realise our conversation has gone on for days? You know everything about me. I know next to nothing about you. Except, perhaps, that your client means more to you than you care to admit. Well, good luck to you. I shake my head. It is almost impossible to describe what happened next.

'Try,' you say.

Ah! Yes, I see, in spite of your own preoccupations, *my* story has affected you, too. You came here to solve the flaws of one person, and have been confronted by those of another. Well, it doesn't altogether surprise me.

Soon after Charles and Lola left, unable to do otherwise, I rang Delia.

'I'm enjoying the silence,' she told me.

I could hear her yawning. And then she gave a small sigh.

'It's good for Charles. We've been living in each other's pockets for too long.'

I badly wanted to invite myself over.

'Are you painting?' I asked instead.

'I am. It's a nice feeling.'

This was the calmest I had heard her in a long time.

'It's very strange but when I paint it's almost as though thoughts come rushing out of my fingers. I remember all sorts of things I'd forgotten about.'

'So paint,' I told her. 'And I'll cook dinner for you afterwards. Surely, once the light goes, there isn't anything you can do?'

But she would not be dissuaded. This time was hers, she insisted. I could see an invitation would not be forthcoming. I sensed this hard-won solitude, her first in two years at the house, was not something she would give up easily. She had told me that she carried all the guilt humanly possible for one person. Maybe being completely alone at last would ease things.

Naturally, Elizabeth, she felt it was all her fault. But perhaps what was less obvious was the effect Charles's constant presence had been having on her.

She carried two crosses, she once told me. So, knowing this, I left her alone.

I wasted most of that evening imagining Charles and Lola together. My thoughts oscillated between rage and envy.

Not that I would have wanted to take Lola on, you understand.

I kept thinking I should have warned Charles. It was obvious to me he was walking straight into a trap. Two days went by in this way until, unable to bear the silence any longer, I rang Delia again. There was no answer. I was working hard to reach a deadline and left it another day, but on the fourth morning I woke, worried. What if something was wrong? I had promised Charles I would keep an eye on her. Damn it, I thought, what was wrong with me? I tried ringing her after breakfast, and when there was still no answer I decided I would drive up and see her. Too bad if I ruined her moment of peace.

As things turned out, I wasn't able to visit until much later. A series of phone calls delayed me. I got some e-mails that needed urgent answers, so, all in all, it was close on six before I was able to leave.

There had been a small storm but then the clouds had rolled away and the air had become clear again. I drove along the ridge of the mountain from Molinello towards their villa. The sun had begun to set. Venus had already risen and church bells across the valley were ringing the hour in thin, metallic sound. I arrived at the top of the road that led down to their house and immediately saw Charles's car parked outside their gate. He was back early, I remember thinking, puzzled, but where was Lola? I parked on the edge of the road and started walking towards the gate, wondering vaguely why Charles had blocked the drive. Hearing their voices through the open windows I stopped walking. And then I realised it was Charles's voice, unusually raised, that I was hearing. I hesitated. They were having a row. Uncertain, I waited, knowing they would hear my car if I left. Their voices moved closer to me and I guessed they were now in the garden. Perhaps they were coming out to the car. Suddenly, panicking, I turned and hurried back to my own car and drove across the valley, home.

Two more days passed without my seeing anyone. Lola had vanished. On the second day, worried (she was, after all, in my care), I rang Elena, who told me, quite calmly, that Lola had left for England.

'What?' I asked, furious. 'Doesn't she go in for thank yous, any more? And what about all her things strewn about my house? What am I supposed to do with them?'

Elena seemed outrageously unmoved.

'Ah well!' she sighed. 'I expect she was upset.'

'Upset! Not as much as I am. Selfish little bitch. She came here, did nothing by way of helping me, just exploited my hospitality. I organised a trip for her with Charles Boyar so she could see the Piero paintings, she might have thanked me . . . '

'Well, well, so it *was* Charles!'

'How d'you mean?' I asked, although I was beginning to have a pretty good idea.

'She told me she's started an affair with someone,' Elena said calmly. 'Only she wouldn't say who, and anyway this other business has overshadowed everything else.'

I had no idea what she was talking about, although it wasn't long before I found out.

It was Charles who told me late that evening. A Charles I hardly recognised.

'Where's Delia?' were my first words.

In all the years we had been friends, through the worst of their tragedy, I had never seen him like this. Love, or possibly the desperation for it, had transformed him. Like a man who had glimpsed a different life through glass, he appeared transfixed. To tell you the truth, Elizabeth, I felt he was hardly aware of me. I was an irrelevancy. Pouring us both a drink I listened, mesmerised. He had planned to leave Delia, he told me. All the way back, holding Lola's hand, driving through the maize fields, he saw her as his last hope; his one chance to get over Matt.

'What?'

Oh yes, I nod. You've no idea, Elizabeth.

'Nobody knows,' he said, 'even I didn't realise until now, what I was feeling.'

I began to see the full extent of the damage.

'Have you told her?' I asked him quietly.

My heart was beating fast.

'She's gone,' Charles told me forlornly.

'*What?* Delia? Where?'

'No, not Delia. She's still at the villa. I mean Lola.'

I was confused.

'Doesn't Lola want you? I imagine she's been angling for this ever since . . .'

I stopped. Charles wasn't listening.

'Haven't you heard the news?'

'No. What news?'

'They've found *The Flagellation*. Haven't you heard?'

Again I shook my head.

'Do you know who stole it?'

I stared at him. He was shouting now.

'It was Lola's *father*! Can you believe it? That man . . . I've spoken to him, I *know* him . . . he came here. Alex, you *met* him! And now Lola blames me. Can you believe it?'

I thought: he's mad, he's finally disintegrated. It's happened.

'Can't you see? It's all over the newspapers. She doesn't want to have anything more to do with me.'

'Who? Why?'

'Lola,' Charles said.

He thrust a newspaper into my hands and helped himself to more grappa.

Theft of world's most enigmatic painting, ran the headline.

The curator and art historian Charles Boyar, who befriended terrorist Lynton Rasanagium, was unaware this would lead to the theft of a Piero della Francesca from the Ducal Palace in Urbino, Italy. The painting, found by an attendant in the stack in the National Gallery, led to the arrest of Rasanagium, an attendant at the museum.

Claims that the painting was stolen as a protest against the violence experienced by immigrants in parts of Northern Italy have been consistently denied by the Italian Government.

Piero della Francesca is an enigmatic artist of the fourteenth century who defies full interpretation but nevertheless enjoys cult status. Rasanagium stole The Flagellation *in order to fund the Tamil Tigers, who are demanding an independent state in Sri Lanka. The painting was due to go on show at the National Gallery early next month and was being prepared for road transportation at the time of the theft. Mr Rasanagium has been denied bail.*

I stared open-mouthed at Charles.

'You see,' he said, with a strange kind of triumph, as though he was enjoying his own downfall, 'it's in *every* newspaper around the world. All over the television. Even Delia knew about it when I got back.'

I tell you, Elizabeth, my first thought was: how very inconvenient for Lola. Her future career in politics spoilt . . . for the moment, at any rate. But equally I was certain, once everything died down, she would turn the notoriety to her own advantage.

'But why blame you?' I asked Charles.

He stared at me with bloodshot eyes. I saw he was exhausted, close to collapse.

'I'm going to have to give evidence in court. She doesn't want any more scandal attached to her. As it is, she probably won't get that job she was after.'

And then he began to weep. I looked at him without saying anything. He had still not said a single word about Delia.

After that we sat for some time in silence. I was grateful he did not subject me to a declaration of his love for Lola. I, who knew all about unrequited love, could not have stomached it. Besides, somewhere deep inside me, shamefully, a pulse of hope was beating.

'It's all over,' he said at last, as though he read my thoughts. 'I've told Dee. We're both really sorry . . . we've seen what it is that has happened, how it is, how it might be, in the time that's left to us.'

'You mean, you and Lola . . .'

'No, no. I don't think anything will come of that.'

I stared hard at him. Out of chaos came madness, I thought; out of madness, eventually, if you are lucky, comes understanding. For the first time I could say with total honesty I felt sorry for Charles Boyar, the man who had all the things I had wanted.

'Dee is going to have the house,' he said finally.

I swallowed.

'And you?'

'The stuff I was doing . . . in France,' he mumbled. 'I mean, that was what really interested me, d'you remember? I lost my way, when I left that work . . .' his voice trailed away.

What was he saying? That he regretted the whole business, his marriage to Delia . . . Did he regret Matt, too? He shook his head. He was a man, he told me, who had sifted sand all his life. He was used to looking at residue.

'When this whole business of the painting is over, when I have finished the exhibition, I want to return to those piles of stones, those small flints, the things that were used four hundred thousand years ago in the scooped-up hollows of the sand dunes.'

I had not heard him talk this way before.

'I was merely a windbreak in Delia's life,' he said. 'She'd be better off without me. Do you know she went up to the Prati?'

'No.'

It was many months before I heard the rest, Elizabeth, but when she told me about it, I understood that for Dee this had been an important step. A rite of passage that would lead her towards a kind of peace. Even the way in which she recounted her trip was different.

'Two years, three months, fifteen days and eighteen hours,' she told me. 'That's how long ago it was.'

Having made her mind up, when the summer sun was at its blistering peak, when all shadows had been reduced to their smallest point, she had driven along that road again. Possibly at the very moment Charles was driving on the road to Urbino Dee was on her own Via Dolorosa.

The sounds of goat bells carried on the breeze had sharpened her perspective and she saw now with perfect clarity how absence, felt for so many years, had at last become tangible. Still she did not stop the car but kept on driving, climbing higher and higher. She had forgotten the herds of brown and black-marked goats. She had forgotten how Matt had loved them, how he had persuaded them to buy one and lodge it with a nearby farmer. A picture of her son's face, not as he was in the end but earlier, in happier times, came to her. How could she have forgotten the goat? But she who remembered every last detail of that day in August could not even remember its name. Shocked, she realised that, while she had been focusing elsewhere, other things were disintegrating. The bells were louder now, their dull, burnished sound clearer. In the next moment the farmer appeared, leading his herd. A black-and-white dog ran along with them as the goats made a dash for the water trough, pushing and leaping over each other. The farmer waited as they drank, gazing at the distant horizon, his face turned towards the distant sea. Delia hesitated. Then she parked the car along the side of the dirt track, switched off the engine and got out. She was almost certain it was the same man she'd first talked to when they had decided to buy the goat whose name she still could not remember. Shading her eyes, she stared at the herd. Was it here? Was it still alive? Her heart lurched. Swallowing, she walked towards him.

'Scusi,' she said. 'Signor Romiti?'

When he turned, even before he answered in his deep baritone, she recognised him.

'You may not remember me,' she said in uncertain Italian, but before she could finish he strode towards her.

Of course he remembered her.

'You are the mother of Matteo,' he said, and as she stared, stricken, at him: 'And Blenheim is his goat . . .'

He pronounced it Blee-nam and she gazed at him for a fraction of a second longer before she understood. Of course! That was its name.

'*Ecco!* There he is!' the farmer said, beaming at her. 'A little older, but the very one.'

There was a pause.

'You come . . . first time,' he said.

She could not deny it.

'*Marito?*'

Delia shook her head.

'No. I'm on my own.'

The farmer nodded. Calmly he pointed towards the higher point of the Prati where a clump of trees screened his barns. Delia nodded. Yes, she knew.

'All together,' Signor Romiti said. '*Memoria.*'

He made a circular gesture with both his hands, cutting the air. A large black bird flew steadily above them and disappeared into the trees.

'Here?' she asked, uncertain. 'Or do you mean in the church?'

'No, here. Behind the trees. Giovanni's family, the other families, the bishop. Even the people from the commune came.'

They had driven to this very spot, the farmer told her. And then they had walked in a procession up to the trees.

'And think of you,' he said, nodding vigorously.

He pointed to himself.

'I organise it.'

She hadn't known. She was sorry she had not thanked him. He shook his head. He did not want thanks, he said. He was

312

simply sad that sorrow had come again to haunt this lovely valley after so long. He had hoped when the war was over that kind of thing had finished for ever. But clearly, it was not so. Delia listened, not quite following him. Then she pointed at the clump of trees, indicating she was going up there. He bowed and let her pass, not attempting to follow or intrude. On an impulse, she turned back, wanting to shake his hand, but he had his back to her and was still staring ahead and did not see her. The goats made a tinkling, restless murmur as she passed.

Someone had made a path up to the trees. She supposed Charles had been told when the stone had been placed. They had asked her to decide on the inscription. Even though there had been others, even though Matt had not been the only one to die that day, it had been Delia who had been asked to word the dedication. In her refusal she saw at last the full extent of her grief. For the first time she asked herself what the other families must have thought of her. Standing at the top of the mountain it was a moment longer before she saw the small white monument that she had wanted no part of. The marble, she guessed, would have come from up the road in Carrara, which Michelangelo had made famous. A well-known local sculptor, a friend of Giovanni's family, had carved it into the shape of a somewhat unrealistic tree, cut down before its prime; there were small branches covered with torn leaves. No matter, she thought, not minding. The names of the boys were carved beneath, in gold. *Alfredo, 16 anni; Attillio, 14 anni; Valentino, 13 anni; Matteo, 11 anni.* She had expected to cry at last, but she did not. The wind rustled slightly in the pines and a cone fell to the ground. The goat bells were fainter, now. The farmer must be moving them across the mountain, she thought.

O dio, she read, *buono e misericordioso. Concedi sempiterna requie alle fragili spoglie dei nostri figli qui tragicamente morti* . . .

Turning away, she thought: *nostri figli*, our sons. But she had only thought of one of them. And she saw the way in which the whole place had been tended. Someone had placed fresh flowers in a vase; there was a picture of the Virgin Mary. She herself had brought nothing, no flowers, no offerings. But what offerings was she meant to make to a God who had taken her children away? Relentlessly removing them from her grasp? Sadness, different from anything she had experienced in all this time, descended on her. It was thick and heavy, impenetrable, like the afternoon heat that pressed down upon her. No wound heals completely, she thought. In that moment she saw with the clarity afforded perhaps only once in a lifetime that she would somehow go on living. Her life was at its own apex and she would have to follow the path on which she had started out, whether she wanted it to be so or not.

Looking back at her son's life, she saw that it had been as complete a thing as was possible. It was her expectations that had been the problem. And she realised at last that, while understanding was beginning to come, it would take nothing away from the depth of her grief. But she was conscious, in this moment of release, that her life was a sacred thing, ready to change direction for the final time. She would have to move on. It was her duty to do so, at least for Matt's sake. He had gone on his own journey and, utterly determined not to be left behind, she had tried to go with him. And it was only then that she understood that it was not her, but Charles, who was alone; Charles had somehow lost more than she had. Below her in the next valley she could see the village of Cargalla and the church bathed in sunlight. And she noticed too, if she strained her eyes, she could see the corner of the veranda that belonged to them.

V

23

A narcotic yearning from deep within refuses to be driven out

So this is your surprise for me, Elizabeth; at the eleventh hour. The condemned man gets what he wants. You are being kind; you would like me to have some happiness before the trial. But I can see from her expression as she approaches that Lola is furious. And suddenly I am terribly afraid.

'I'll leave you to it,' you say and you go.

I recognise uncertainty in your voice as I turn to greet Lola. At last, I think. People are watching us in the ward. The cleaner pauses while emptying a bin. A nurse looks up from her clipboard. The young Asian doctor glances at us. There is a pot of hyacinths on the windowsill; blue, like your eyes, Elizabeth.

'Sweetheart?' I say.

She approaches swiftly, her arm raised. The guard sitting by the door stands up in alarm. He obviously thinks she's going to hit me. But all she does is stand over me, glaring. I can do no more than look pleadingly at her. Even as a child, long before I left, her temper had been there, simmering quietly. Waiting for release.

'Please,' I say, 'please, darling, sit.'

I have no idea what she will say, but I'm so glad to see her. She looks well: taller, lovelier. I haven't seen her for almost two years. She sits. I see that her hair has grown longer and also that she has tied it up in some complicated way. I remember the ludicrous story Elizabeth told me about an affair with Charles Boyar. It cannot be. Lola is too young.

'Let me explain,' I say feebly. 'You got my letter?'

How do you tell your only daughter that you are about to spend the rest of your days in jail?

'Have you any idea what you've done?' she says, through gritted teeth.

Her voice is surprisingly low.

'How could you do this to me?'

'I didn't,' I say, taken aback, shocked.

Is that what she thinks?

'Sweetheart, I didn't do it to *you*!'

'Who do you think you've damaged the most? Tell me!'

I can see her hands are shaking. I know her temper is running like a well-oiled engine. She is so effortlessly beautiful, I think.

'Have you thought of my career? Do you have any idea what you've done to me?'

She swallows; her eyes are burning with tears. I want to reach out and take her hand, but I know that I have forfeited my right to do so. She is so young, I think. And so angry. I see the terrible way in which I imposed my own disenchantment on her life. It is I who gave her this wildness. I alone am to blame.

'In the end, the only thing that always mattered to you is *yourself*,' she says. 'And that Third World hovel you originated from.'

I remain silent, looking at her, helpless. I'm old, I want to say, but I know this is the excuse of idiots. How stupid is my self-pity.

'Did you even give me a second thought, you selfish bastard? No of course not. That would have been the last thing on your mind.'

I open my mouth to speak, but she raises her hand threat-
eningly.

'Oh, no,' she mimics. 'Let me guess, your heart was broken.
Your lawyer told me you saw a film about some Tamil cretin.
And if it wasn't that one, then there was another. And another.
More and more, endlessly. Filling your heart with pity. While
your own family . . . '

She breaks off. I look at her. She is trying not to cry. As a
small child she had a way of flattening her eyebrows into a
straight line when she was about to cry. Now there is a hurt that
is unreachable.

'What are you smirking about, you old . . . you old scumbag!'
she screams.

Again the guard stands up. He begins to walk towards me and
I raise a hand, pleadingly. Realising there is someone else in the
room, Lola slumps back in her chair and closes her eyes.

'So,' she says and her voice has an adult weariness that breaks
what remains of my foolish heart. 'It's funny, is it?'

No, oh no! I want to say. There isn't anything funny in
remembering how much I loved you as a child. Or how much I
still do. I want to tell you that when you were small, when I saw
how you cried whenever your mother left the room, I vowed to
myself then that you must never be separated from her. But I say
nothing, simply bowing my head in shame.

'Have you *no* shame?' she asks. 'Is there nothing you bastards
feel except your own great sorrow?'

I raise my head at that, for I recognise where the phrase
comes from.

'How is your mother?' I ask.

'Hoping you rot in hell. Just as I am.'

Who is the man, I want to ask, who loves you? For I can see
love written all over your sweet face. Is it really Charles Boyar?

'Why are you looking at me like that? What more do you

want from me, you shit? Isn't it enough that you've ruined my life?'

'I was thinking . . . ' I begin.

She covers her ears.

'Shut up! Shut-up! Christ, I hope you die!'

Her eyebrows form a complete line, her eyes narrow and now she is crying in earnest. I watch helplessly, knowing that soon she will be gone and my longing will begin all over again. I have no one to blame except myself. I must say something quickly, I think. Something to stop me losing her altogether, before it is too late. But for the life of me I can't think how to begin.

'Lola,' I begin again, 'please try to understand how it has been for me. I didn't mean to harm you. I didn't think . . . The risk I took was a sort of debt I had to pay. It was not intended to cause any harm to you.'

'What do you mean? You are my father, you bloody Tamil terrorist.'

She takes a gasping breath.

'Yes, that's what you're being called in the papers! Do you know what it's like to be the daughter of a terrorist, awaiting trial?'

'No,' I say. 'No, no, no, I am no terrorist. I just wanted the papers to notice the genocide going on in Sri Lanka. I was fed up with reading how Sri Lanka was the number one holiday destination. Oh, darling, if only you knew . . . '

And then I stop speaking, because the mess I am in is inexcusable and I can no longer find the words to defend myself. She is right: I deserve to die. I am unable to face the enormity of what I have done. My heart is thumping, my leg throbbing. I cannot speak clearly any more. Please God, let it end, I think.

But she is speaking:

'You left that fucking place thirty years ago,' she is saying. 'Don't you have any loyalty for anyone or anything else? Don't you have a shred of compassion for your own family? Do you know how the journalists have been besieging Mum? We've had that watchdog lawyer of yours pestering us. Mum's come out in a nervous rash, she can't eat or sleep. She's had to take time off work. Do you care? Of course not! Why the hell should you care about us? We're English.'

She laughs without humour and tosses her hair; her eyes burn like a tigress's. Oh, that I might have the power to turn the clock back. The bell sounds, the hour has passed and she rises and turns away, walking out of my life.

And it is left to you, Elizabeth, coming in a couple of days later with some papers for me to sign, to pick up the pieces of my self-pity.

'It will be better when you know,' you say.

I don't want you to say anything bad of Lo, so I try to control myself.

'At least this wretched waiting will be over,' you tell me. 'And,' you pause, looking at me gravely, 'you'll go to a better place than this. There won't be the kind of bullying you've had to put up with. I'm certain of that, at least. The medical staff have written a report.'

The doctor will express his strong recommendations, you say. But I am no longer listening. Suddenly I am terrified and don't want you to leave. I don't want to learn about my fate in the morning. Despair overwhelms me. As if you understand this, you sit down again. You are no ordinary visitor and the guard does nothing because of this.

'Listen to me,' you say.

Your hands flutter slightly, I feel you hesitate. Then you lay your hands quietly on your lap.

'Whatever the sentence, it can always be appealed against. The main thing is to tell the truth, just as you've told it to me. Then we'll see.'

Again there is that slight hesitation.

'I shall see you, afterwards. And I shall continue to visit you even after you get sent elsewhere.'

I don't know what on earth to say to that. We both know that whatever the outcome tomorrow, there is little hope that I will recover any sort of life. My daughter will never speak to me, my ex-wife wants only to pretend I don't exist. I hear Lola's voice:

'I am the daughter of a convict.'

What can I do that will ever change that?

'We'll see,' you tell me, wanting to be kind, wanting to give me hope where there is none.

Again I think, as I have thought so many times before, why didn't the bomb fall on me instead?

'She is young,' you say of Lola. 'The young change faster than you can, believe me. I've seen so many of them! Life will change her point of view.'

I smile at you. A real smile, like the one I gave Ma long ago when I said good-bye.

'I'm just an old convict,' I tell you.

I notice when you smile there is a lightening within me. Like the dimple in your cheek, my heart pulsates. I have not seen you smile quite like this in all these weeks you have visited me. We both pause, awkward and not so awkward after all. What next? Your objective detachment wavers; I wonder with something akin to amazement what you might do next.

Elizabeth, I think. See how used I am to saying your name. Is the sound of it on my lips different? People have been saying your name for years, but I have only just begun. I wonder how many ways I could say it. Let me count the ways, Elizabeth, I think.

'Get some sleep,' you reply.

Your voice is soothing. And then you leave me.

'Elizabeth, my friend.'

24

Forest sunlight from long ago
returns to comfort him

And now morning sees me waiting to be handcuffed and taken out. I wear a suit. Lord, when was the last time I looked so formal? On my wedding day, I suppose. Ma, I think, where are you? You have been absent for so long, missing from most of my life, but I would like to think you are here, now, at this moment of my greatest need. I would like to think you are watching, sharing my fear, close by. Sam, I think. Elizabeth, where are you? Come soon. Soon. All night I have been thinking of you. Last night, before you left, I called you my friend. And, with only the smallest hesitation, you smiled, acknowledging intimacy.

You have warned me that there is a considerable amount of interest in this case.

'The Pieros were bound to get a lot of attention,' you said.

And then I remember something else.

'Ironically,' you had said, with a small twist of your mouth, 'Sri Lanka is also getting a lot of attention as a result of what you've done.'

I think of that and smile. You showed me yesterday's newspaper headlines. *Human rights issues in a forgotten tropical paradise brought to attention by a lost Piero della Francesca*, it read.

Ah, you see, Ma I have done some good, haven't I?

The door is being unlocked. The guard comes in.

'Come on then,' he says, indicating I should hold out my hands.

I see that I am lucky because he is the nice guard. He is the man who often made me wonder why he does such a job. I have been guarded on and off all my life, but here, perhaps because it is the end of some road, I've become more interested in these people. This one has a human face that cannot hide the life lurking within it.

'Why do you do this job?' I ask, before I can stop myself.

He laughs.

'Better than what you did, mate!' he says jovially.

True. I hang my head, chastised, silent. He handcuffs me to him.

'The money's good, that's why,' he says gruffly.

Ah, yes! Money!

'No need to be like that,' he says, good-naturedly enough. 'I've got kids, you see. They're all at private school because of me.'

I nod. I wouldn't dream of judging him.

'Yours came the other day, didn't she?'

Again I nod.

'Nice-looking lass.'

Yes, I say. The question he wants to ask hangs in the air, but he is a kindly man. He doesn't want to add to my despair with his questions. I thank him. It is all I have time for before I'm bundled into the van.

The courtroom looks as if it is a set for a television drama. Only, this is for real. Light falls harshly on the featureless furniture, on the grey comfortless carpet. Everywhere there are hard surfaces. I panic. Every breath is an effort. Lola isn't anywhere in sight. I hadn't expected her, but now I realise that hope had remained. So great is my disappointment that I can think of nothing else. I scan the room for a familiar face. When Lola was small, we had a cat. Once, when we took her to the vet, her paws made sweat marks on the examination table. Her fear came through her paws. Like my fear, now, coming through my hands.

As I stand, eyes slightly lowered, trying not to sway, I catch glimpses of faces I recognise yet cannot place. I understand the whole of these proceedings is designed to shame me. Everything inside my body curls up. My tie is a throat-cuff, threatening to suffocate me. What is my brother doing here? What has happened to his face, I wonder. I see my mother sitting quietly next to him. Then, Elizabeth, you enter and my heart rises. I haven't seen you for a couple of days as you have been preparing the evidence. You are dressed in an unfamiliar way. In one swift movement, with a swish of your gown, you are by my side and the room rights itself. Sharply defined black-and-white clothes, blue fighting eyes, ready to do battle. The faces become less elongated, the light sharper, Ma's expression less strained. I had not wanted to live any more, but you are pulling me back with a fury.

'All stand for the judge!'

The faces in the room are marked by the iridescent green light. How strange; after today, I will never encounter them again.

There is a scuffle at the back and a man is hustled out. He carries a flashgun. A journalist sits quite close to me, furiously taking notes. Another man, an artist, is drawing me! Am I going mad? Why is he drawing me? But of course, no Lola.

It is hot in the courtroom with its garish light. The furniture is designed for antipathy. Acid-green seats. They used to throw acid at the prisoners in the Batticlore jails, it is alleged. My thoughts are wandering and I make great efforts to tether them to me. I turn to study the judge; my fate is in his hands. At least, I think, I now am face to face with those who control my destiny. Never in my life has it been this clear-cut. The thought makes me shake my head. One of the last great realisations is that life will not be what you dreamed. People are moving about, passing bits of paper to the judge, whispering. Then the jury are dismissed because of course I am going to plead guilty.

I watch you approach me, Elizabeth, as from a long distance. I see your lips move, your eyes are anxiously on me. You point to the back of the courtroom. There is a man, someone I vaguely recognise but cannot place, looking at me. Slowly he nods. Charles Boyar. Is that who it is? Looking so much thinner, completely grey, a hollowed-out body encased in a linen suit, owlish eyes. We are the same, Charles, I think; both of us have lost a child. Both of us are in prison. I want to smile at the irony of this. But my face won't let me.

'There's Alex Benson,' you tell me. I nod without understanding.

'You okay, Ras? Can you hear me?'

I nod. Why is your voice so faint? Is it me or is it very hot in here? No Lola. No Sam, of course. My eyes are moist. I blink. One is never too old to cry. I feel as alone as the moment when I was born. Elizabeth, I want to say, your hands on your papers are slender and pale. But I can't speak.

'Take a deep breath,' you tell me in your low voice.

Then you turn to the clerk.

'Can my client have some water?' you ask coolly.

A glass is put into my hands, a paper hanky handed to me.

'Stay calm,' you say.

You are very calm, confident; there is a slight smile on your face as you turn and survey the room, nod to the other barrister, switch on your laptop. What an extraordinary woman you are, Elizabeth. I should have told you, but I lacked courage and now it is too late. I see, as from a long distance away, the dimple I saw yesterday, incongruous in this surreal place.

'Please be seated,' the clerk of the court says in a loud voice.

The judge looks briefly at me. He is a small man, made ridiculous by his costume. We are separated by only a few paces, yet there might as well be a universe between us. And in that moment I do something I had almost forgotten I could do. I turn a small space inside my head into a place of magic. Just as I did after Ma died.

We adjourn without any real understanding on my part of what has been going on. I am given another glass of water and return to my bed. Soon I shall swap this place for a cell, elsewhere. They give me food, expecting me to eat, but I cannot. I stare up at the patch of sky that I am allowed access to. It is as blue as another sky I stared at long ago. Spring has been a long time coming this year, I think. I have noticed an avocado plant sprouting in the warden's office and there was a faint smell of earthiness in the air when we took our exercise, yesterday. I take out my sketchbook while I wait. I have filled several black notebooks since I have been here. They are the visual diaries of the narrow confines of my life. You said they are beautiful objects in themselves, Elizabeth, but to me they are simply a searchlight on my world; a lifeline.

There is the sound of the door being opened and you walk in. Ah, I can see you are anxious.

'What is it?' I ask, instantly sensing something amiss.

'Ras . . .' you say.

You say my name in a way that penetrates the thick fog I am under. Your voice reaches me like the distant horns of summer. There is something wonderful in the brave effort you are making.

'Is it time to go?'

You stare at me, then you change your mind, and shake your head. You look at your watch.

'There's still half an hour. How are you feeling? Nervous?'

I want to tell you, nervous isn't what I am feeling. But I have no words to describe what it is that is lodged in my head.

'You will not be let off completely, you know that?'

I nod. Why are you telling me this now? We've discussed it endlessly. You know I'm prepared to spend the rest of my life in prison.

'You won't do that,' you say firmly, sounding angry.

Please don't be angry on my account, Elizabeth, I say. And you give me a ferocious stare. Is it me you are angry with? I've no fight left, Elizabeth. Please understand. I know you are doing your utmost, but, really, isn't it time to stop? Ah! I see I have really angered you now. I sigh. Is there anything I can do that doesn't anger someone?

'Stop it, stop it!' you say. 'Leave the self-pity until a bit later on.'

Your eyes shine very brightly, your chin is stubborn. I want to touch you. I have the feeling we are talking about different things, once more.

'Afterwards,' you say, 'Charles Boyar wants to talk to you.'

And then in no time at all we are back in Court Number Two and you are looking strangely beautiful in your wig. My feelings for you are distilled from somewhere near my heart.

'Your Honour,' you are saying in a voice I have never heard before. It has been a long session. I am tired. I want them to do what they must do.

'Listen,' the policeman interrupts my thoughts, pointing. 'Your barrister is beginning her summing up. Listen.'

'My client cannot dispute the fact he stole the painting. A theft such as this is punishable by law, he knows that. The law is clear on that count, but I put to you that we are not dealing with a simple criminal here.'

'Objection,' shouts the prosecution. 'We are dealing with a terrorist. National security could well be involved.'

'Objection overruled,' the judge says drily.

'Thank you, Your Honour. As I said, we are not dealing with a petty criminal, someone who wanted to make a quick fortune. The law must therefore take into account mitigating circumstances. All I ask is that you try to understand his motives when deciding sentence. I ask only that justice be tempered with mercy. Never shall I forget the day Lynton Rasanagium began to tell me his story. Your Honour, here is a man who, it might surprise you to hear, has a strong moral sense. A man able to distinguish right from wrong, who knows, furthermore, that what he did was wrong. A man who, had he even once been accorded justice, might have had a very different life.

'Your Honour, a child learns the rudiments of behaviour first from his parents and then from the society in which he lives. In Mr Rasanagium's case, his parents both died in horrific circumstances and the country into which he was born was engaged in a bloody and protracted civil war. Lawlessness is the norm there rather than the exception. So it would be entirely understandable if Lynton Rasanagium had become part of that violence in some way. But he did not. Instead he was interested in other, gentler things. Even as a small boy he used to draw pictures in the dirt of the birds that lived in the thicket behind his house. Later, using mud and paste and whatever colours he could acquire, he painted images of the natural world on a bombed and abandoned church near where he lived. Beneath a destroyed statue of the Virgin's feet, he painted frangipani and reeds. Whenever he had the chance, he would place shells found on the land-mined beaches in amongst the ruins. Lynton Rasanagium wanted to be an artist; his paintings were his way of making sense of his senseless world. But in a country where the language you spoke determined whether you lived or died, where guns and bombs were the currency, there was no place for such things.

'And so Lynton Rasanagium fled his home, determined to begin again. And begin again he did – or at least he tried to, even though his heart was not in beginnings. Sorrow dogged his footsteps and shadowed his vision. He wanted to forget all that had happened to him, knowing those who cannot forget are condemned. But, Your Honour, he is a survivor, and it is the survivors of atrocities who have enduring memories.

'When I first talked to him about his experiences, he told me that as a five-year-old boy he had witnessed a crime without a name. Later on, as an adult, he discovered a name for the thing that had been done to his people. Then, in prison for the first time in his life, he began to talk about those things that had shaped his life.

'Your Honour, I beg you to remember the evidence given by Professor Boyar. He does not think Lynton Rasanagium is a criminal but a man capable of a great understanding of art, a great love for a subject that, in different circumstances, might well have led to a career. A neglected intelligence, was what Professor Boyar called it.

'I do not pretend that what Lynton Rasanagium did was right. But I ask you to bear in mind, Your Honour, that this is his only criminal act, born of a misplaced love for his home.

'Here in Britain, we are all too ready to push people as far as we can, by our indifference, by our failure to see what is being done to them. And after we have stood by, ignoring their plight for decades, when at last they take their destiny to some foolish place, in whatever pathetic way they can, we are quick to brand them as terrorists. Therefore I would beg you to consider the mitigating circumstances of this case. For while my client fully understands that justice needs to be done, I nevertheless urge Your Honour not to overlook the need for mercy in determining the length of his sentence.'

You said other things; I can't remember all of them any more.

All I know is that my sentence was reduced from twelve to eight years. And then afterwards, long after Charles Boyar had visited and gone, promising to call again, you told me that Helen had been in the court all the time. Silently you handed me her letter.

I thought you might like to know about Lola, Helen had written. *She is going to stand as a candidate for the constituency of Brent. Our days will be spent campaigning, fund-raising, organising her publicity. Already she goes about amongst the people of Brent, appears regularly on the local news and is written about in the newspapers. Everyone is taken with the bold way in which she announces that the changing face of Britain is more to do with integration than with the separation of ethnic minorities. Minorities are a thing of the past. Intermarriage is where the future lies. I am so proud of her, as I hope you will be when you read this.*

Which brings me to the most important part of this letter. I'm sorry to put this so bluntly, but there isn't any other way. There is some urgency as you are about to be sentenced. The fact is, I don't want you to try to contact Lola any more. Not now, not at some later date, not ever. She is doing very well and your presence in her life will spoil the chance she has secured by her own hard work. Please don't be obstructive. Please, think of the child you abandoned so long ago. I ask this as her mother and also because Lola herself wants me to say it. We lived together once, you, me and Lo. Once I could not have dreamed of writing such a letter to you. But such is life.

I hope your time in that place will at least make you aware of other people. Our daughter has had a very difficult time since your crime became public knowledge. Please, Ras, don't ruin her life any more than you already have. I remember you as a stubborn man with a quick temper. I remember you as someone without compassion. Now I am asking you to show some compassion for our child.

The letter rambled on and on for a few more pages. I skipped some of it and read the last paragraph.

I hope my writing like this hasn't made things worse and angered you. I hope that your years inside will change you, make you happier, even. They say this sometimes happens. I hope so. I will sign off now.
Helen.
PS I am sending you a photograph. She doesn't know, but I thought you'd want to see it. She looks a lot like you.

I stare at the small photo cut out of a newspaper. It is my mother who smiles out at me.

Afterword

Lynton Rasanagium was released from prison on 24th September 2013. Elizabeth Saunders, his barrister and closest friend, had booked him on a flight to Bordeaux departing four days later. Charles Boyar, who had kept in touch with Ras throughout the five years served of his eight-year sentence, had invited him for a fortnight's walking holiday in the Languedoc, where he now lived. Ms Saunders planned to accompany him.

The couple spent Ras's first night as a free man quietly at Elizabeth's house. The weather in Oxfordshire had been balmy all day, and in the evening Elizabeth cooked a simple meal of an omelette and salad served with a chilled white wine from the Veneto. Ras, having visualised her small cottage for so long, was enchanted to be dining with her in it at last. Gillyflowers spilled out of window boxes, swallows lined up on telegraph wires preparing for their flight towards the sun, autumn light fell in gentle folds on Cotswold stone. The talk, as it had done so often during the difficult years of his captivity, returned to Lola.

'It's the English side of her that's made her so unnatural,' he told Elizabeth.

In the long pause that followed a bat moved across the wall as though it were a long black glove.

'The British have always been the cause of everything and Lola is a British woman. Like her mother.'

'Like me?' Elizabeth asked, gently, her face in shadows.

Ras shook his head, smiling at her lovingly.

'Shall we go outside, into your garden?'

His remark was not a question but a full stop and Elizabeth accepted it as such. A breeze brushed the tops of the trees. Ours was a civilisation which the West disturbed but could never acquire, Ras thought.

Elizabeth stood up and held out her hand. She knew that their future together would hold many problems, that there was always the danger that, in choosing to throw in her lot with his, she would leave one world for another. And that the leap she had taken so publicly and with such certainty might not be enough to sustain them both. She might easily get the worst of everything. The risk had always been present. But she was prepared to take it.

They went outside. The grass was moist underfoot.

'Write to her,' Elizabeth suggested. 'Show her the understanding she was unable to show you.'

She did not wish to push him. He had been pushed too hard for too long.

Ras raised her hand to his lips. He was good-tempered and affectionate, but she felt his resistance rising in the warm evening air.

'You want me to forgive her, don't you? You want me to pretend I am no longer hurt? But I can't, I am not an Englishman. I do not have your capacity to dismiss the pain she inflicted on me.'

'She was a child.'

'And I am not a machine.'

Elizabeth said no more.

After sun had set and the two of them were alone together in the soft, dark air, Ras was able to fulfil a dream and hold Elizabeth in his arms. At last he felt some release from all those emotions that had tormented his imagination. While Elizabeth slept, and the crescent moon freed itself from the tatters of a black cloud, and the night floated away to the sound of a nightjar, he was able to see the journey that had brought him to this point. Watching her sleeping face, seeing the scattering of grey hair at her temples, knowing she would not have wanted him to see them until now, he was moved beyond tears. Her face contained his world. No one could take this away from him, now, he vowed. He loved her; perhaps he had loved her from the moment he had set eyes on her.

Considering her tender desire to bring resolution to the one subject that still had the power to hurt him, he smiled, shaking his head. Lola and he would for ever remain apart. It was his choice, now. Dimly he understood that the imprisonment and all that had led up to it had narrowed the arteries of his temperament. He no longer had the inclination to reach out from the limited set of circumstances he had inherited to his larger yearning. From now on his capacity for loving would be kept to loving Elizabeth, alone. It occurred to him, with something close to triumph, that he could live in this way, contented.

Four days later, having closed up the house forever, they boarded a plane from London's Heathrow Airport. The plane taxied along the new, fourth, runway, built in spite of a barrage of protest. The sun was high in the sky; London from the air looked silvery in the early autumn light. The plane banked steeply and then followed the Thames estuary before speeding out to sea. The flight was short, fifteen minutes to reach the Channel, and then down towards France. And as they flew over the white cliffs of Dover, in a moment of dazzle and reflection an image he had not thought of for many years returned to Ras. He saw himself walking along that lighted lane from long ago. Neither his mother nor his brother were anywhere in sight. He was alone, only now he could see further into the trees to where the tobacco seller was lighting his lamp. And it seemed to him that his younger self walked before him. Leading the way forward to what was left of his life.

Delia went overland to Italy. She spent three days travelling; she was used to travelling alone, now. She stopped at Lake Garda before arriving at the village of Cargalla almost at the same moment as Charles was getting ready to go to the airport to meet Ras and Elizabeth.

A few years previously, Delia, who had been living in the US, had visited Perm in Russia where she had located the grave of her long-lost grandfather. Later, in the museum close by, she found to her amazement a photograph of some of the prisoners of war captured in early 1945 and set to work in the quarries around Perm. Of all the photographs, one young man in particular caught her eye. It was many days before she understood the sense of familiarity that she felt. By that time she was on the return flight to the US. Her grandfather's face, his curly hair, the serious expression of his mouth, the dimple on his right cheek, even the way he stood, with his head inclined to one side, was identical to her son Matthew. Delia was halfway across the Atlantic when she made this discovery, but the copy of the photograph was in her handbag. Taking it out, she stared at the man her son could never be. It was late evening in New York as they came into land; Italy was asleep. It would be many hours before she was able to phone Alex to tell him of her discovery.

This trip back to Italy was of special significance. For, on her return to Alex, she would drive to the Prati. Once there, she wanted to hang two framed photographs of Matt's great-grand-parents on the wall of the white memorial. She had brought nails and a hammer. She was prepared. The September air was sharp; soon autumn would be thrown down. But although winter came early in these parts, she knew it would leave early, too. Today there was no one in sight. The farmer who had called the emergency services on that day in July was down in a village, somewhere below. No goat bells sounded on the hillside.

Delia stood for a brief moment looking across the valley with its rustling, golden chestnut trees, its shafts of sunlight, its deep ravines. There were people all over the hillside, she knew, gathering mushrooms before nightfall. She saw that the small marble monument had begun to blend perfectly with the landscape. Time would not wither it, nor take from it the love it represented; time would simply make it part of the landscape. On the way up she had passed the house where once they had lived together: Charles and Matt and the child in her womb. There was a new family living in it now. Through the window she had caught a glimpse of unfamiliar faces, heard children's voices. The light was fading and soon it would be dark. Turning from the shrine she went back to where she had parked the car. Alex would have lit a fire in the house and would be anxiously looking out for her, hoping she would arrive before dark.

So, fastening her seatbelt, she turned her car around and headed back down the valley towards Cargalla.

At Gatwick airport a plane had just landed; one of the many hundreds that landed every five minutes of every single day. This one was from Colombo. Two of the passengers who had been in conversation for the last twelve hours looked at each other with a sigh.

'Long flight, huh!' the girl said.

'Not long enough!' said the man.

They had spent the entire journey deep in conversation and neither had bothered to sleep. The woman in the next seat wished they'd have shut up for a moment.

'Well, Lola,' the man said, 'here's my card. Shall we have dinner on Thursday?'

Lola Rasanagium grinned. She pushed her dark mane of hair away from her face in a gesture the young man had already grown to like. When she smiled, her eyebrows rose like wings.

'I've got work tomorrow, but yes, that would be great.'

'I'll ring you, shall I?' the man asked, as the flight attendant welcomed them to London.

'Sure. Do!'

The seatbelt sign had been switched off, the cabin lights flickered on again, passport control and the grudging September sky waited.

Tomorrow, decided Lola, as she waved good-bye and headed towards the Gatwick Express, she would contact her father and make her peace with him. He would have been out of prison for some weeks, she suspected. She hadn't seen him for five years, but the truth was, she no longer was all that angry. She felt like talking to the poor old bugger. He would be surprised to hear where she had been. It would be her turn to tell him about the country he had talked of for much of her life. Humming under her breath, flicking her hair over her shoulder, she boarded the train heading for London.

Acknowledgements

With grateful thanks to my agent Felicity Bryan and
my editor Clare Smith who nurtured this book.

Reading Group Guide

- 'Tearne brings her skills as a painter to her writing,' said the *Sunday Telegraph*. In what ways can you see the influence of Roma Tearne's painting on her novels?
- What does *The Road to Urbino* have to say about the power of art?
- The *TLS* described Tearne's earlier novel *Brixton Beach* as 'a lesson in the intricate consequences of violence'. To what extent might this description also apply to *The Road to Urbino*?
- Are Ras and Alex reliable narrators? What is the effect of their telling their stories to Elizabeth?
- What parallels are there in Ras and Alex's accounts? What consequences come of the connection between the two men?
- 'The British have always been the cause of everything,' says Ras. What does the novel have to say about colonialism and its legacy?
- 'Every act has a past. Events don't materialise from nowhere.' To what extent do the experiences Ras recounts justify his actions?